"I have a confession to make," Sam said. "About me."

"Are you…are you an outlaw? A wanted man?" Prissy held herself very still, as if she were afraid of the answer.

"No," he said.

"Are you…are you *married?*" Her voice was a shaky whisper. "Did you leave a wife behind somewhere?"

He couldn't stop the hoot of laughter that burst out of him and seemed to bounce off the twisted tree limbs hanging above them. "No, Prissy! No, I'm not married, or promised or anything like that."

"Then what could it be?" she asked, her blue eyes puzzled in the sun-dappled shade. "If you're not in trouble with the law, or married…"

"I'm sorry, I don't mean to make you play a guessing game," he said, contrite over the worry that furrowed the lovely brow framed by her strawberry-blond curls. "Here's my confession—I didn't come to Simpson Creek for the sheriff job."

"Y-you didn't? Then why—"

"I came to meet you."

Books by Laurie Kingery

Love Inspired Historical

Hill Country Christmas
The Outlaw's Lady
*Mail Order Cowboy
*The Doctor Takes a Wife
*The Sheriff's Sweetheart

*Brides of Simpson Creek

LAURIE KINGERY

makes her home in central Ohio, where she is a "Texan-in-exile." Formerly writing as Laurie Grant for the Harlequin Historical line and other publishers, she is the author of eighteen previous books and the 1994 winner of a Readers' Choice Award in the Short Historical category. She has also been nominated for Best First Medieval and Career Achievement in Western Historical Romance by *RT Book Reviews*. When not writing her historicals, she loves to travel, read, participate on Facebook and Shoutlife and write her blog on www.lauriekingery.com.

LAURIE KINGERY

THE
Sheriff's
Sweetheart

Love Inspired

™ LOVE INSPIRED BOOKS

ISBN-13: 978-0-373-82866-1

THE SHERIFF'S SWEETHEART

Copyright © 2011 by Laurie A. Kingery

www.LoveInspiredBooks.com

Printed in U.S.A.

Choose you this day whom ye will serve…but as for me and my house, we will serve the Lord.

—*Joshua* 24:15

To A.C.F.W., the American Christian Fiction Writers,
an amazing organization that inspires and informs me,
and as always, to Tom

Prologue

Houston, Texas, June 1866

"Hold him a moment, gentlemen," the silky voice purred, like a sleepy lion preparing to toy with some hapless creature his cubs had brought down.

Sagging between two burly men who each held an arm to keep him upright, Sam Bishop opened his eyes just enough to see Kendall Raney clenching his fist and drawing it back. The flickering lamplight winked from the pigeon's egg-size ruby on the man's ring finger. Sam closed his eyes, reluctant to watch the pain coming at him. Pinwheels of fiery light exploded in his head, and everything went black.

He awoke moments later when they dropped him unceremoniously on the filthy floor of another room. His arms were tied behind him, his legs bound together. He gave no sign he was once again aware, hoping the dust wouldn't make him sneeze. Unconscious men probably didn't sneeze, and the pain an innocent sneeze would send shooting from the ribs they had broken might make him groan aloud.

"You want us to finish him, Mr. Raney, and leave him in some alley?"

He heard an anxious whine and the scuffling of small paws on metal. Added to that was an acrid smell that suggested the beast hadn't been let outside lately. He opened one eye just a crack. His back was to the cage, so he couldn't see the dog; all he could see was Raney's booted feet and beyond him a square, squat safe on the floor against the wall.

"Wait till it's dark," Raney said. "Then we'll take him out to the bayou. I've seen half a dozen bull alligators out there sunning themselves on the banks. I imagine they'd relish a taste of this fellow."

The other two chuckled but their laughter was tinged with uneasiness. "Sounds like you've used those gators to solve your problems afore, boss," one of them said.

"Only when someone is foolish enough to accuse me of cheating," Raney answered in his silky voice.

Again, too-hearty chuckles. "Hope they don't mind if he's already dead by then," the other said. "He ain't hardly breathin'. I think I broke his skull when I hit him."

"I don't think they'll mind. Meat is meat, after all."

"You oughta take off that ring, boss. Looks like yer hand's swellin'. You might not be able t'git it off later."

"I believe you're right. Why don't you step outside a moment, fellows? Then we'll stroll down to Miss Betty's place for supper. It's on me, as payment for your services."

"Why, thanks, Mr. Raney," one of them said. "You want us to walk yer dog for ya?"

"No, we're going to take that cur along when we go to the bayou. He's nothing but a nuisance. He's too small for fighting and he chewed up my best gloves, blast his hide.

The gators can have him along with that senseless fool on the floor."

So Raney planned to feed him *and* the dog to the alligators? Now freeing himself meant even more than avoiding another beating.

Sam heard the sound of the door closing behind the other men and Raney's booted feet crossing to the window. There was a swish of fabric as he wrenched the curtains shut. Of course—he wouldn't take a chance that one of his henchmen would peek in and be able to read the numbers he turned on the safe's dial. Raney's crouched form hid the safe's dial from Sam, too, but it didn't matter. There wasn't a safe or a lock that could keep Sam Bishop out.

He heard clinking as Raney laid the money he'd "won" from Sam inside the safe, then the footsteps retreated and the door slammed.

Sam waited a full minute until the footsteps faded down the boardwalk, then cautiously opened his eyes and rolled onto his other side. In the corner sat a metal cage, and in it crouched a small black, brown and white canine—some sort of terrier mixed with who-knew-what. The dog cringed as Sam looked at him.

"Don't worry, fella, I'm not going to hurt you or leave you for gator food," he assured the dog, who cocked his head at the hoarse whisper. "When I leave here, you'll be free, too."

Once he broke free of the ropes and rubbed the circulation back into his wrists, he gazed at the safe. The dog watched him now, a down-on-his-luck cardsharp who'd been fool enough to stop in at The Painted Lady and think that he could beat the house with his skill at cards. And more foolish still to think he'd survive calling the proprietor a cheat when he'd detected the man's surreptitious palming of a card.

While Sam worked the lock, one ear pressed up against the metal to listen for the tumblers falling, he pondered his situation. It was time for a change of scenery. Houston's supply of gullible card players was played out, which was why he'd taken the chance of coming to this infamous waterfront establishment to begin with. He'd been a riverboat gambler before the war, and he could go back to that, but the large number of Federal troops and carpetbaggers coming south via the riverboats had made his southern drawl a professional liability.

And, if he was honest with himself, it was a lonely existence, always coming back to an empty rented room with a saggy, lumpy mattress. Maybe it was getting to be time to think about settling down. Maybe.

The last tumbler clicked and the door swung open. There it was, his pitiful pile of coins, Raney's enormous ruby ring—and more money than he had ever seen in his life, all neatly sorted into stacks of gold coins.

Staring at the money, he whistled. There had to be hundreds of dollars sitting there, right in front of him.

Take it. Why shouldn't you? You could be set up for life. Raney deserved to lose it.

But it wasn't Sam's money, and who knew if Raney had come by it honestly? It was tainted. Besides, such a sum would only weigh him down. He didn't know where he was heading, but he needed to get out of town fast.

But he was going to take that ring, he decided, gingerly touching his bruised, lacerated cheek. Never again would Raney wear it and inflict even more injury on someone he was punching. He stuffed it in a pocket, thinking perhaps he would sell it if he needed money down the line.

"C'mon, dog," he said, opening the cage door and walking out into the dusk. The dog scampered after him.

"Okay, boy, you're free," he told the dog. "Make the most of it. If you're smart, you won't come back here."

But the dog wouldn't leave his side. Sam chuckled at the mutt's determination. Ah, well, perhaps he could find the dog a better home on the way to some improved way of life he could find for himself.

Chapter One

Sam put two counties between him and Houston before
he remembered the newspaper he'd taken from the bar-
relhead next to the snoring liveryman and stuffed into
one saddlebag. The dog now rode in the other, perched
with his front paws hanging out and his ears cocked at a
jaunty angle.

"Let me know if you hear anyone coming up behind us,
boy," he told the dog, reaching for the paper. He gritted his
teeth when his broken ribs stabbed him, reminding him
of what Raney's henchmen had done.

The dog yipped in assent. Sam had gotten used to talking to his fellow traveler as they rode along, though he
hadn't bothered to name him. The dog didn't seem to mind,
answering him with a short bark or a wagged tail whenever
he spoke.

The *Houston Telegraph* crackled as he opened it. It was
a week old, but that didn't matter. Leaving Houston, Sam
had headed north with no particular destination in mind,
but now he needed to make a plan. Drifting like a tumble-
weed had gotten him nowhere previously—he hoped the
newspaper would give him an idea about where to go.

When he reached the back page, his gaze fell on an advertisement set apart by a fanciful scrollwork border.

Are you a marriage-minded bachelor of good moral character? Do you long to meet the right lady to wed?

Come to Simpson Creek in San Saba County, Texas, and meet the ladies of the society for the promotion of marriage.

If interested, please contact Miss Priscilla Gilmore, Post office box 17, Simpson Creek, Texas

Sam found himself grinning as he studied the ad. So the ladies of Simpson Creek were looking for husbands? He knew that a lot of single ladies had found the selection of men mighty slim pickings after the war. Simpson Creek's supply of eligible bachelors must have been harder hit than most.

If he remembered right, San Saba County lay northwest of his present location, plenty far away in case Raney came looking for him. He wouldn't write to the post office address, though. He wasn't about to hole up in some town, send an inquiry, and wait for an answer. He was still too close to Houston, where Raney was no doubt spoiling for revenge after finding his ring and his victims gone. It might be amusing to just take a ride up to San Saba County and see what the fair ladies of Simpson Creek had to offer a footloose bachelor.

He didn't want to become a dirt-poor rancher on some hardscrabble piece of land, though. It wasn't wrong, was it, to look forward to a *little* comfort after the rough, austere life he'd lived? And if it wasn't asking too much, he'd like her to be pretty, someone his eyes could take pleasure in looking at. But above all, she had to be honest, and she had to be a lady. As much as he appreciated down-to-earth working women like the saloon girls, he was tired of seeing his own jaded, experienced cynicism reflected in their eyes.

He wasn't partial. He admired a saucy redhead as much as a sunny blond beauty or a sloe-eyed brunette. He wasn't a bad-looking fellow himself, he knew—or at least he wasn't when he didn't have a cut on one cheek and bruises on his forehead, he thought ruefully. Women had complimented him on his bold dark eyes and thick black hair—though at the moment, Sam thought, he could use a shave and a long soak in a copper hip bath. Ah, well, there'd be plenty of time between here and San Saba to visit a barber and make himself as presentable as possible. He'd have to decide what to say about his visible injuries. He didn't want to look like a habitual brawler.

Sam arrived in the little town of Simpson Creek with the dog riding perched between the saddlehorn and his legs. He hadn't found anyone in any of the towns he passed who seemed interested in taking the beast off his hands, and by now he'd grown surprisingly fond of the little dog's company. And perhaps the dog's appeal would be just the entrée he needed with the young lady of his choice.

A trim little town, he thought, riding in from the south and pausing to look it over. It had everything a small town needed—a saloon at one end, a church at the other, and in between, a hotel, a post office, a mercantile, a bank, a jail and a barbershop-bathhouse. He'd availed himself of a bath and a shave in the last town and had changed into his black frock coat, trousers and a fresh white shirt. The bruises had faded into faint greenish blotches and the cut was healing—he hoped his neat appearance would help to mitigate the impression he'd been in a fight.

On his right sat a very imposing mansion of brick, surrounded by a tall black wrought-iron fence with an ornate front gate. He whistled under his breath. That must be the home of the richest man in town. Maybe he was the president of the bank. He'd have to make sure to become friends with that gentleman.

"I wonder how we're going to find our Miss Priscilla, dog?" he mused aloud, surveying the town from beneath the broad, wide brim of his black hat. He tried picturing "Miss Priscilla Gilmore," and couldn't decide if she was one of the available spinsters herself or some grandmotherly matchmaking type.

Should he try the post office? After all, the advertisement had listed a post office box address—surely the postmaster would be able to direct him to Miss Gilmore.

The post office, by unfortunate coincidence, sat right beyond the jail. Sam had always kept clear of local lawmen, finding they usually sized him up on sight as the gambler he was. But this time it couldn't be helped.

Just act as if you have a right to be here, he told himself. *You're just here to meet a lady. Nothing wrong with that.*

As he approached the jail, three people emerged from it—a well-dressed old man leaning on a silver-headed cane, a man about Sam's age who must be the sheriff, for his vest bore a silver star, and a young lady. Her face was hidden by the side of her fetching sky-blue bonnet, but strawberry-blond curls peeped from beneath it.

"Yes, I'm expecting the man today, Mayor," he heard the sheriff say to the older man.

Just then the dog erupted into a volley of barks from his saddle perch.

Sam tried to hush the beast, but it was already too late.

"Oh, what a darling dog!" the girl cried, and rushed forward. "What's his name?"

"I...I don't know, ma'am," he murmured idiotically, but he couldn't have made a more intelligent reply to save his life, for he was transfixed by the face looking up at him, framed by the bonnet. She had eyes the exact same sky-blue hue as the bonnet, sweeping, gold-flecked lashes, a sweetly curved mouth, all in a heart-shaped face.

She blinked in confusion and a faint color swept into her cheeks. "You don't know? Whyever not? Ooh, how sweet!" she cried, when the dog raised his paw and wagged his tail at her.

Out of the corner of his eye, Sam saw the lawman's face harden and his gaze narrow. He knew the man had caught sight of his lacerated cheek.

Wonderful. He was already under suspicion.

He touched the brim of his hat respectfully. "Well, not exactly, ma'am. He just adopted me, a ways down the road. I reckoned I might find him a home here," he said, aiming a brilliant smile at the girl. He saw her spot the healing cut on his cheek but he could still salvage the situation with the dog's distracting help. "My name's Sam Bishop."

"I'm Prissy—um, Priscilla Gilmore," the girl said, blushing a little more as she corrected herself.

Thunderation. He'd thought the good Lord had given up on him a long time ago, but surely this was a sign. He'd blundered right into the very lady he'd been looking for—and she was a far cry from grandmotherly. But did she have to be accompanied by a lawman who was already looking narrow-eyed at him?

"Miss Gilmore, I'm right pleased to meet you," he said.

"This is my father," she went on, nodding at the old man, "Mayor James Gilmore."

"Sir," he said, fingering the brim of his hat once more. Miss Priscilla was the daughter of the mayor? This just kept getting better and better.

"And Nicholas Brookfield, the acting sheriff."

"Sheriff Brookfield," Sam said, nodding at the man who was staring at him with that cold gaze that must come to lawmen as soon as they pinned on those tin stars. But what had she meant, "acting sheriff"?

"May I hold him?" Miss Priscilla inquired, reaching up for the dog, who wagged his tail again and positively wriggled with eagerness. Sam thanked his lucky stars he'd had enough sense to let that dog tag along with him. He handed down the dog into the girl's gloved hands and managed to conceal the grimace the movement caused.

"What's your business here, Mr. Bishop?" the sheriff inquired, surprising Sam with an English accent rather than the Texas twang he'd had been expecting.

But he was spared the necessity of a reply as the dog jumped up in Miss Priscilla's arms to lick her face enthusiastically.

"He likes me!" Priscilla said, and giggled—a sound that Sam Bishop felt down to his very toes.

"He surely does," Sam said with a smile, though he knew Brookfield was waiting for an answer. "I—"

"Say, you wouldn't be the man Nick was expecting, would you? The applicant for the sheriff's job we advertised for?" asked Priscilla's father.

"No, his name was something else," Brookfield said, his gaze no less distrustful than before.

Sam had to think fast. He'd have to have a reason for staying in town while he became acquainted with the enchanting creature who was now holding the dog, especially with the acting sheriff looking at him as if he suspected Sam were here to rob the bank.

"I may not be the man you're expecting," Sam said quickly. "But I did come about the job. I'd be proud to be Simpson Creek's sheriff."

Prissy watched, stroking the affectionate little dog, as shifting emotions played over Nick Brookfield's face— suspicion, skepticism and finally hope.

"Why don't you give him a chance, Nick?" she said, with the familiarity born of knowing Milly Brookfield's husband since the day he, too, had come to town a stranger. It was only fair that he give this stranger a chance, just as he had been given one.

"I'm voting with my daughter. After all, you did say the other fellow was several days overdue," her father put in. "Maybe he's changed his mind about the job."

Nick rubbed the back of his neck. "It's possible. I certainly thought Purvis would be here by now. Have you had any experience as a sheriff, Mr. Bishop?" he said, shifting his cool blue gaze back to the man on the horse.

Prissy wished Nick wouldn't sound so obviously suspicious. Why, Sam Bishop was apt to take offence and ride off before anyone had the chance to get to know him—and she did want to get to know this handsome stranger.

She tried to catch Nick's eye—it would have been too obvious if she'd reached around her father to nudge Nick into civility.

"Please, call me Sam," Bishop insisted, reaching out a friendly hand to Nick who, after a moment's hesitation, stepped forward and shook it. "And yes, I've had some experience—before the war, I served as a deputy to the sheriff back in Tennessee where I grew up. Lately I was a deputy sheriff in Metairie, just outside of New Orleans."

"And during the war?"

Prissy saw a shadow flash over Sam Bishop's eyes. The war didn't provide too many happy memories for any of those who had served in it.

"I was a blockade runner—I received the cotton that was brought down to Matamoros, just over the border, and took it out in my boat into the Gulf to a larger ship that transported it to England."

"What made you want to leave Louisiana?" Nick asked.

Bishop shrugged. "Tired of Spanish moss and alligators, I reckon. I wanted to see the wide-open spaces of Texas. And then I heard your town needed a sheriff. Mind if I ask what happened to the old one?"

"Sheriff Poteet died in the influenza epidemic we had here this past winter, Mr. Bishop," Prissy said. She felt a strange little tingle when he focused those dark eyes on her.

"Is that right?" he murmured. "I'm real sorry to hear that. It must have been a terrible time."

Prissy nodded, remembering when she and her friend Sarah had nursed Mr. and Mrs. Poteet. The sheriff had perished from the illness, and they'd nearly lost Sarah, too, for she'd caught the infection. Only Dr. Walker's medical skill and Heaven's intervention had saved her.

"Nick, it seems Mr. Bishop's arrival is a godsend," her

father said. "I know you need to get back to your ranch, spring being such a busy time and all."

"That's a fact," Nick admitted. "The hands are doing what they can, but what with all the chores, and the baby coming quite soon, I know Milly would feel better if I were at home…"

Yet he didn't look happy to be handing over the job, Prissy noticed. She knew him well enough to know it wasn't because Nick Brookfield had relished his role as sheriff. He could have had it permanently with the town's blessing. No, it wasn't that. Prissy sensed he still had some reservations about Bishop.

"I think we should give him the position," her father said. "Subject to council approval, of course, and a probationary period of a month, as we agreed upon when we met to discuss Poteet's replacement. The salary's seventy-five dollars a month, Mr. Bishop. I hope that's satisfactory—we're only a small town, you understand. But it includes your quarters, your meals at the hotel, and stabling and feed for your horse."

Sam nodded. "Sounds just fine, Mr. Mayor."

"Then the job's yours. Why don't you show him the jail and his quarters, Nick, then show him around town?"

"Thank you," Sam said, shaking Priscilla's father's hand. "I'll do my best to show I'm the right man for the job."

Nick unpinned the badge and handed it to Sam, his face inscrutable. Prissy watched as Sam pinned it on.

"I suppose I'd better give you your dog back, then," Prissy said, extending the wiggling mongrel. "Welcome to Simpson Creek, Sheriff Bishop. I'm sure we'll see you around town."

"You can count on that, Miss Gilmore," he said. "and

why don't you keep the dog? I was just holding onto the little fellow until I could find him a good home, and it seems like I've done that." His gaze made her feel like warm butter left out in the Texas sun at noon.

"Are you sure?" At his quick nod, she turned to her father. "Oh, Papa, may I?" she said. "It would be so nice to have a dog, now—" She stopped, not wanting to say, *Now that Mama is gone*. She'd never been able to have a dog before because they made her mother sneeze. Oh, what she wouldn't give to take back all the times she'd complained to her mother about not being able to have one.

Her father hesitated, glanced at Bishop, then said, "Only if he doesn't chase Flora's cat—Flora's our housekeeper and cook, Mr. Bishop. And his care—including any—" he cleared his throat "—*accidents* he might have, is entirely your responsibility, not hers. Understood, daughter?"

She nodded and ruffled the dog's ears, then turned back to Sam. "If I'm to keep him, he'll need a proper name. What town did you find him in, Mr. Bishop?"

"Sam," he insisted. "And I found him in Houston."

She blinked. Houston was considerably farther than "a few miles back down the road," as he had said. But surely it would be quibbling to point that out.

"Houston it is, then." She leaned over and spoke into the dog's ear. "Do you like your new name, Houston?"

The dog yipped and licked her face. Everyone—including Sam Bishop—laughed.

Prissy, flushed with pleasure, decided to try her luck still further. "Papa, perhaps we should invite Mr. Bishop to supper. Surely on his first night in Simpson Creek he shouldn't have to dine by himself at the hotel."

"That's very nice of you, Miss Gilmore, but I couldn't impose," Sam Bishop said quickly, darting an apologetic look at her father. "I'm sure the hotel's food will suit me fine."

Prissy realized she shouldn't have put her father on the spot as she had, but surprisingly, he came to her aid. "Nonsense. It's no imposition, Bishop," he said. "Flora usually cooks enough food for an army, as I know to my cost," he said, patting his paunch ruefully. "We seldom have company anymore, so this would be a nice opportunity to get to know you better. Come at six, and you can see how your little dog is settling in. It's the big house diagonally across from the hotel."

He took off his hat and bowed. "Mayor Gilmore, I'd be honored. Miss Gilmore, until later."

She inclined her head with what she hoped was regal dignity, trying to hide the unladylike excitement surging through her veins like Fourth of July fireworks over this new prospect for the ladies of Simpson Creek.

"Oh, Papa, you're the *best* father anyone could ever want!" she cried, after they walked out of earshot toward Gilmore House. "Thank you for letting me keep the dog, and for seconding my invitation as you did. I know I should have asked you privately first."

Her father patted her shoulder. "You don't demand much, daughter, and maybe the dog will be good company for us." But her father's worn, jowly face suddenly turned stern. "But as for Bishop, I'm letting him come to our table so I can look him over, Priscilla. We don't know him all that well, so don't you go flirting with him any more till I get a chance to see what he's made of. I won't have any man thinking you're forward."

"Papa! I was not flirting! I was merely welcoming him…" The denial that had sprung easily to her lips died away, and obedience took its place. "But don't worry. I won't do anything to make you worry. Sam—Mr. Bishop, that is—he was just so friendly, and so *handsome*."

Her father harrumphed. "Don't assume anything about a man you just met." He laughed as the dog yipped again, and his face softened. "See, your dog agrees with me."

Prissy smiled at her father, but she had a strange feeling that Sam Bishop was exactly what Simpson Creek—and she herself—needed.

"Papa, didn't you fall in love with Mama at first sight?" Prissy asked softly.

He sighed. "Aren't you an imp, to remind me of my own actions! Your mother should have never told you that. But remember, she was a preacher's daughter…"

Chapter Two

So Prissy lived in the very mansion he'd admired on his arrival. Thunderation, but fortune was smiling down on him now!

He straightened after he tied his mount's reins to the hitching post outside the jail, and found Brookfield studying him again. The Englishman's gaze was penetrating— *too* penetrating. It was as if he could see straight through Sam and into his not-so-admirable past.

"You watch yourself with Miss Prissy—Miss Priscilla, that is," he told Sam, and those eyes were as chill as the winds of a Texas blue norther. "Don't even think of trifling with her, or make no mistake, you'll wish you'd never ridden into Simpson Creek."

"You have nothing to worry about, Mr. Brookfield," Sam said, deliberately using "mister" instead of "sheriff" to subtly remind the other man he was no longer acting sheriff. "I find Miss Gilmore charming—who wouldn't? She seems to like me, too. But just what is it *you* don't like about me?" he said. It was best to get it out in the open, so he could counter it.

"I don't dislike you, Bishop, but I don't think you're being entirely honest about why you've come."

Uh-oh. He'd have to tread carefully here. "I came because of the advertisement," he said. That much was true, at least. He *had* come because of an advertisement—Priscilla's ad for the Society for the Promotion of Marriage.

"Where'd you see it?"

Sam said a quick prayer to the deity he hadn't paid much attention to in a long while. "In a Houston newspaper," he said, hoping vagueness would suffice.

Brookfield gave him a look he couldn't read. "Bring your saddlebags and come inside. I'll show you the jail and your quarters behind it. Then we'll take your horse down to the livery and we'll take a little walk around town so I can introduce you to folks."

The jail looked much as he'd expected; two cells and a desk, with a rack next to the door holding a pair of rifles and a couple of pistols, boxes of bullets beneath. A short hallway between the two cells led to a door that opened into his private quarters—as he'd expected, nothing palatial, just a room with a bed and another room with a table and two chairs and a cabinet, but no stove. Apparently even his morning coffee would have to be obtained at the hotel. He dropped his gear on the table.

Seventy-five dollars a month. He'd made that much and more in one night of card playing. Well, at least here he wouldn't be dealing with sore losers like Raney. And he'd have the chance to woo the lovely Prissy...

"So how does an Englishman come to be living in a small Texas town?" he asked as they walked back outside, down a side street to the livery, leading Sam's black gelding.

Brookfield gave him another of his inscrutable looks. "It's a long story," he said.

It seemed he was going to leave it at that, which made Sam curious. Did the Englishman have a past he wasn't proud of, too? Interesting. "Sorry. Didn't mean to pry," he said.

Brookfield gave him a sidelong glance. "It's I who should apologize," he said in his formal way. "I didn't intend to sound churlish."

Sam wasn't sure what "churlish" meant but he was relieved Brookfield seemed to be thawing a little.

"It's no secret, I suppose," Brookfield said. "I came to Texas to take a post at the embassy office in the capital, took a side trip to Simpson Creek, and met my wife, Milly. Now I'm a rancher instead of an embassy attaché. Life takes interesting turns, does it not?"

"That's a fact," Sam agreed. He wondered more about what Bishop had not said than what he had. Why would an Englishman take a side trip to a little backwater town like Simpson Creek? But Sam knew better than to probe further. He'd already irked the Englishman—perhaps it was best to douse his curiosity. After all, the code of the West dictated a man's past was his private business, if he wanted it to be.

"Here's the livery," Brookfield announced as they came to a large barn and corral, in which several horses stood, tails swishing. "Run by the Calhoun brothers, now that their father's died in the epidemic. Hello, Calvin," he said when a tow-headed youth came forward out of the shadows of the barn. "Meet Sam Bishop, the new sheriff. Calvin will take good care of your horse."

"I sure will. Pleased t'meet ya," the boy said, and took

the gelding's reins, leading him into the box stall nearest the door.

Before Sam could reply, shots rang out. He and Nick spun around to see a man sprinting toward them.

"Sheriff! Thank God I've found you! Ol' Delbert's liquored up again, an' shootin' out th' mirror and th' lights!" he shouted as he neared them.

Brookfield didn't take time to explain he was no longer the sheriff. "Is everyone all right?"

"Yup, George took cover behind the bar an' everyone else went out th' back door. Delbert ain't mad at anyone, he's just had too much rotgut is all," the man said, and surprised Sam by grinning. "Reckon you kin talk some sense inta him like always."

"Right. Come on, Bishop, it's time to make your first arrest. Delbert Perry isn't very dangerous," Brookfield told Sam as they ran toward the saloon, "once we take his pistol away, of course. He just needs some time to sleep it off."

There went his dinner with the lovely Prissy and her father, Sam thought, because once he had the man in custody, he'd have to remain at the jail. Perhaps Nick could make his excuses for him. He hoped Prissy wouldn't be too offended. It was not exactly the best way to start his campaign to woo her.

They stopped in front of the hotel that sat diagonally across the street from the saloon. "I'll go in from the back and cover you," Nick said, motioning in that direction. "Just be firm with him. He usually surrenders as soon as he sees the badge," he said, pointing to the tin star Sam now wore.

Sam wasn't so sure. He'd seen dozens of intoxicated men in saloons who were dangerously unpredictable, especially if they were armed as well as drunk. He wasn't about to sacrifice his life to keep such a man alive. If this Delbert fellow acted the least bit like he was going to shoot, Sam intended to drop him with the pistol he now held, a Colt he had purchased in the first town he arrived in after Dallas when he'd fled Houston.

They crossed the street cautiously at an oblique angle, heading for the near corner of the building. There they separated, Nick creeping around to the back to the exit, Sam hugging the front of the establishment, crouching low so his head didn't show in the dusty, fly-specked glass windows. When he reached the batwing doors, he straightened and peered over the nearer of the two.

Within the dim, smoky interior of the saloon he spotted a wild-haired man staggering unsteadily around, clutching a half-empty bottle with one hand, a pistol with the other. Silver shards of what had been a full-length mirror littered the mahogany bar. Delbert Perry's boots crunched the broken glass from the ruined chandeliers and a half-dozen bottles and glasses. The burnt smell of spent gunpowder filled Sam's nostrils and stung his eyes.

The drunken man faced away from Sam. Sam pushed one batwing door open and went in quietly, taking care not to step on noisy glass. His pulse throbbed in his throat. Who'd have thought he'd have to face a man with a gun in his first afternoon in this little one-horse town?

"Delbert Perry, it's the sheriff," he said, cocking his pistol. "Turn around slowly with your hands in the air, *now,* and you won't get hurt."

Perry turned, letting go of his bottle. It shattered on the floor with a splash of liquor and broken glass. The remaining whiskey gurgled out even as he raised both hands, including the one with the pistol, just as Sam had ordered.

He squinted at Sam through bleary, red-rimmed eyes. "Sheriff? You ain't Nick Brookfield. He's the sheriff. I don't know you." But he kept his hands raised nonetheless.

Sam kept his voice friendly. "But you see I'm wearing the badge, Delbert, don't you?" he said, nodding toward the tin star pinned on his vest. "We haven't had a chance to meet yet. I'm Sam Bishop, the new sheriff."

"N-new sheriff? B-bishop?" the man muttered, his words slurred and thick.

Behind Perry, Sam saw Nick inching forward from the back room, his pistol held ready.

"That's right. Now lay the gun down on that table by you." Nick was right; this man wasn't going to be difficult to take into custody.

Just then, Nick slipped on some spilled whiskey. He skated forward on the floor, glass crunching as he cartwheeled both arms, trying to regain his balance.

Perry whirled. "What in tarnation?" he screeched, and leveled his pistol straight at Brookfield's chest.

Sam fired before he even had time to think about it, neatly shooting the pistol from the drunkard's hands. Perry's bullet went wild, embedding itself in the wall beyond.

The man yelled, dropping his pistol and clutching his hand. Staring at Brookfield, who had now regained his balance, he cried in horror, "There's the real sheriff! Nick, did I shoot ya? Why'd ya have to creep up on me from behind like that? Are ya all right, partner?"

"I'm fine, Delbert," Nick assured him, though his face hadn't entirely regained its color yet. "Now turn around and raise your hands in the air, and tell Sheriff Bishop you're sorry for raising such a ruckus on his first day here."

Sam stared as Perry, meek as a lamb now, did exactly as Nick told him. "S-sorry, S-Sheriff. Reckon I j-jes' had too much t' drink."

Another man, wearing an apron and clutching a dingy dishcloth, crawled out from behind the bar. "Thanks," he said to both of them. "Nice t'meet you, Sheriff Bishop. Welcome." Then he stared glumly at the damage around him. "Guess I'm gonna have to cut him off after two drinks—not two bottles—from now on."

"Meet George Detwiler, proprietor of this fine establishment," Nick said, walking up behind Perry and pulling his wrists into the come-along he took out of his back pocket. "Where'd you learn to shoot like that, Bishop?"

"I used to shoot squirrels out of the trees growing up in Tennessee." Brookfield didn't need to know it was sometimes all he and his sisters had to eat.

"I'm much obliged. That could have ended much worse. Perry's fingertips are merely grazed. I'll take him by Doctor Walker's and have him bandaged up before taking him on to jail."

"No, he's my responsibility," Sam said. He may not have come here for the job, but he'd taken it on, and now he had to live up to the oath he'd sworn only hours ago.

"There's no need. I'm sure you'd probably like to tidy up a bit before you present yourself at the mayor's house. Go on back to your quarters, and I'll watch over Perry till you're finished with supper."

"But you must want to get back to the ranch and your wife," Sam protested, feeling guilty because he longed to take Nick up on his offer. "Go on home. It's my job now." He glanced at the drunken man, who stood with his hands shackled, gentle as a newborn colt and about as unsteady.

Nick Brookfield only smiled. "You just saved my life, Bishop. Believe me, my Milly won't mind if I show up a few hours later because I'm doing you a favor. Besides, I want to have a talk with Perry about the Lord."

Sam blinked, sure he'd misunderstood the Englishman. "You want to talk to *him* about God?"

"Indeed I do. We've had those talks before, haven't we, Delbert?"

Perry nodded and grinned as if he and the Englishman were the best of friends. "'Bout how th' good Lord loves me and has a better way for me to live, right, Sheriff Brookfield? Well, come on then, I'm ready."

Sam felt his jaw drop. Brookfield *wanted* to spend more time with this drunken fool and talk religion with him?

He shrugged. Far be it from him to tell Brookfield he was wasting his time trying to cure a drinking man of drink, by talking about God.

As far as Bishop was concerned, the Lord didn't have much to do with anything. Never did, never would. But he just thanked Brookfield and went on his way.

Chapter Three

Houston dozed in Prissy's room in a wide, flat basket lined with an old towel that Antonio had found for Prissy in the barn. To look at the sleeping dog now, it was hard to believe how fast he had scampered after Flora's orange tiger cat, which he'd encountered sunning herself by the stable door. The cat had sprung up, hissing, arching her back and puffing herself up to look twice as large as she was, but the little dog had refused to be intimidated and charged the cat, barking shrilly. The cat fled, and a merry chase ensued until the frantic feline finally took refuge up the massive live oak tree that shaded the front yard.

Flora had been miffed, and made it clear that until the canine learned better manners, he was not welcome in her kitchen, nor was Prissy needed to assist in the preparation of the supper, *muchas gracias,* which would now involve much more work, thanks to Prissy's short-notice invitation. Prissy knew she'd have to find a way to soothe Flora's ruffled feathers later.

If it hadn't been for Houston, the hours until she would see Simpson Creek's new sheriff again would have crawled by. But after the little dog explored each room and Prissy set up his bed and his food and water dishes, she had only an hour to get ready.

Prissy pulled dress after dress out of her wardrobe and held each one up to herself in the full-length cheval glass, then laid each one down on her bed with a sigh. Which one would Sam Bishop admire her most in, the blue-figured *broché* with puffed sleeves, the *crepe lisse* dress of the same green as spring leaves, or the pink silk with the white eyelet-lace trim?

Thank goodness Papa hadn't wanted her to continue wearing mourning for her mother. That black, and even the gray of half-mourning—such drab colors! Prissy still grieved for her mother, of course, but Papa said seeing his only daughter swathed in black only made him sadder. A month after his wife's passing he'd asked her to start wearing her pretty dresses again.

In the end, she chose the blue dress. She had just finished pinning up her hair in a becoming fashion that left tendrils loose around her forehead when Prissy heard Flora opening the front door in the hallway below. Houston erupted out of his basket in a flurry of barking.

Oh, heavens, she hadn't even heard Bishop knock. She had intended to be downstairs setting the table so she could be the one to open the door to Bishop herself. Now she would have to be content to make a grand entrance coming down the marble stairway, which was visible from the doorway.

Houston scampered out of the room, heedless of his mistress's attempt to grab him. Seconds later she heard the dog capering and yipping in the hall below, and Bishop's deep, murmuring voice.

Her heart started to pound. Would Sam Bishop find her

beautiful? Would his eyes light up as they had in front of the jail when he had first looked at her?

Prissy took one last look at her mirror and pinched her cheeks to bring the color into them. Perhaps a grand entrance would even be better, she decided, otherwise it would look as if she had been waiting at the window for the first glimpse of him coming in through the elaborate wrought-iron gates to the grounds.

Which she hadn't been. Had she?

Her father was already shaking Bishop's hand and welcoming him to the house when she set foot on the first step.

"Good evening, Mr. Bishop," she said, trying to descend with regal grace. "I hope you brought your appetite, because Flora's cooked something really special." In truth, since Flora had banished her from her kitchen, Prissy had no idea what was on the menu, but her nose had caught savory, spicy scents wafting from the kitchen. Whatever it was, it would be delicious.

Bishop scooped up the little dog and ruffled his fur. "Why, good evening to you, too, Miss Priscilla," he said. His lips curved into a smile of warm appreciation. "And yes, I have worked up quite an appetite, because I made my first arrest as Simpson Creek's new sheriff just minutes ago. I hope you weren't too disturbed by the gunfire from over at the saloon?"

Her father cleared his throat. "I heard it—unfortunately it's an all-too common occurrence. I assume no one was hurt?"

Bishop shook his head. "Delbert Perry's spending the night in the jail, Mayor Gilmore. Mr. Brookfield was kind enough to watch him so I could come to take supper with you."

Prissy clasped her hand to her neck in alarm. "Thank God you weren't hurt!"

"You're so kind to be concerned, Miss Prissy, but I assure you I was never in any danger. Mr. Brookfield and I disarmed him without too much trouble," he said, his eyes meeting hers, causing her pulse to race and a flush to heat her cheeks. What was going on here?

"Delbert Perry's a harmless ne'er-do-well, except when he's been drinking and takes his pistol to the saloon. I'll expect you to come up with a plan to combat that, Mr. Bishop," Mayor Gilmore said in a no-nonsense voice.

"I'll make that a priority, sir," Bishop assured him in a tone that matched her father's gravity.

Flora bustled into the hallway, an immaculate lace-trimmed apron tied around her waist. "Supper is served, *señores, señorita,*" she said, gesturing toward the dining room.

As they settled themselves in their chairs, Prissy found herself studying Sam Bishop. He spoke to her father with real authority—he seemed like such an honorable man. She'd have to invite him to the church. He'd make a fine addition to their community.

When Flora set down the meal, Houston sat up by Prissy's place at the table, waving his paws in the air and staring at her with liquid appeal in his dark shoe-button eyes.

"Prissy, I won't have a dog begging at the table," her father said sternly. "Make him go lie down."

"I'm sorry, sir. I'm afraid I allowed him to develop bad habits on the trail," Bishop said, coming to her rescue. "It was just him and me, and I'd toss him tidbits as I ate. He knew he could get more if he sat up like that, the rascal." He raised an arm and pointed to a spot on the floor away from the table. "Houston, *go lie down*." His voice was firm, and to Prissy's surprise, the dog immediately did as he was bid without a backward glance.

Her father resumed the tale he'd been telling. "So as I was saying, Nick Brookfield, Dr. Walker and the rest of the posse went after Holt and the Gray Boys Gang and brought back Miss Sarah safe and sound. That ended the rustling sprees in these parts," her father said.

"Sounds like I have tall boots to fill, sir," Sam Bishop said, laying down his fork on the empty plate that now held only the remains of Flora's chicken mole. "But I'll do my very best."

"I have every confidence you will," her father said, "if today is anything to go by."

I know *you will,* Prissy thought, sitting across from him at the long dining table, continuing to study Bishop while he spoke to her father. She wondered about his past, his childhood, where he'd grown up. And then she again wondered why she was wondering.

Her father put down his glass and rubbed his chin, a sure sign he was about to mention something that troubled him. "One recent development that's troubled me about this town has been the arrival of some undesirable types. You'll need to be aware of them."

"Go on."

"There've been a couple of gentlemen in these parts recently—real dandy types, fancy clothing, jeweled stickpins, brocaded waistcoats. They've brought with them a passel of drifters, hired guns. You know the type."

Sam nodded.

"The two fancy gents have bought a big ranch northeast of here, toward San Saba. From what I've heard, they're turning it into quite an impressive estate. Nothing wrong with that, but the rumor is, they're using these saddle tramps to pressure folks to sell their property to them, folks that've been hard-pressed to hold on to their properties what with the higher taxes the Federals have put on our backs—older folks, women who've been widowed by the war and so forth."

Sam's eyes were thoughtful. "I see."

"I want you to keep an eye on 'em—they call themselves the Ranchers' Alliance," her father said. "I won't have our townspeople being pushed out or harassed. If they're doing anything illegal, I want to know."

"Yes, sir. I'll look into it first thing."

Apparently satisfied by the answer, her father turned in his chair and said to Flora, who hovered at the doorway, "I believe we'll have our dessert now."

Bishop took advantage of her father's momentary inattention to favor Prissy with a smile across the table, a smile which sent heat flooding up her neck and into her cheeks. He grinned as he noticed her blushing, but he managed to wipe his amusement from his face as her father swung around in his seat again.

"What's wrong, Prissy?" her father asked, eyeing her.

"Oh, nothing," she said, feeling her face grow hot again. "I-I think Flora put a little more chili powder than usual in the *frijoles,* that's all. It made me a little warm…" She avoided Bishop's knowing eyes. What was wrong with her that a handsome man's smile could make her blush so?

Her father stared at her for a moment, then to her relief turned back to Bishop. "Our Flora makes the best pecan pie in San Saba County."

"*Mmm,* pecan pie's my favorite," Bishop murmured appreciatively. "Though it's hard to believe anything could be better than the main dish."

"Yes, we're very fortunate to have her to cook for us," Gilmore said. "Though Prissy's become quite the accomplished cook, too."

"With Sarah's help," Sarah admitted modestly as Flora bustled in with the pie, already sliced and laid on dessert plates, and began setting it at their places. "Sarah Matthews, that is—I mean Walker. She married Dr. Walker recently."

"I see. And what's your culinary specialty, Miss Prissy?" Bishop asked in his lazy drawl.

"Fried chicken," she said. "And biscuits." Thank goodness she didn't have to admit to Bishop just how hard it had been to learn the art of making light, fluffy biscuits. Her first attempts had been leaden disasters.

"Well, fried chicken and biscuits is just about the finest meal on this earth," Bishop declared.

"Then perhaps we could invite you back some time when I'm cooking it," she said, and quickly added, "I'm sure there are many people we'd like to introduce you to. A dinner party of sorts."

Bishop's smile broadened. "I'd like that, Miss Prissy," he said.

He made short work of his pie.

"Would you like to sit a spell out on the veranda with Prissy and me?" her father asked, when there was nothing but crumbs on his plate. "There's a nice breeze this evening."

"There's nothing I'd like better, sir, but I left Nick Brookfield guarding my prisoner, and I know he'd like to get home to his wife. I'd better return to the jail. I thank you both for your hospitality."

"Duty calls, eh?" her father said, clearly approving of his answer. "Well, welcome to Simpson Creek, Sheriff

Bishop. I hope you'll like it here and put down roots. Prissy, take that dog out, would you? He probably needs to go out," her father said.

As if he knew he was being referred to, Houston scampered up from where he'd been lying. Tail wagging, eyes shining, he came to Prissy's side.

"And don't linger too long, Prissy. I'm sure Flora could use some help with the dishes," he said with a meaningful look. "Good evening, Sheriff."

"Good evening, Mayor Gilmore."

Sam felt Prissy's father's gaze on them as they left the dining room and walked down the hall to the front door with Houston trotting alongside them. He opened the massive carved pecan-wood door and they stepped out into the soft, balmy twilight of the June night.

"I'm sorry," Prissy murmured, as they descended the limestone steps that led down to the lawn. "I'm afraid Papa's a little overprotective of me, especially since Mama died. He doesn't mean to sound so disapproving."

"Don't worry," he assured her, "I'm sure if I was the father of a daughter, I'd be overprotective too when a stranger was around—"

"But you're not a stranger," she protested.

"I'm barely more than a stranger," he said. He'd been just as fierce a guardian when young men had shown up to court his sisters, and had scared off a few shiftless ne'er-do-wells. But now his sisters were all well and safely married and each had two or three children, the last he'd heard. "We only met this afternoon, you know."

Her laugh was immediate and musical. "But that makes you an old friend, by Simpson Creek standards. We don't stand on ceremony here, Sam."

Was she always so open and unguarded, or only with him? There was an innocent artlessness about her that suggested no one had ever taken advantage of those qualities.

"That's good to know, because I wanted to ask you something," he said.

"Oh? And what's that?" She looked up at him with open curiosity as they strolled slowly toward the gate.

He'd been watching the little dog as he explored the lawn and dashed barking after a catbird that took hasty refuge in the boughs of the big live oak, but now he turned back to Prissy and smiled down at her.

"I know I really should ask your papa first," he began, smiling down at her with the smile that had melted the heart of many saloon girls, "and I *will* ask him, but I wanted to make sure it was agreeable with you first before I did."

"Go on," she said.

"I'd like to call on you again—if that's all right with you, that is. That's what I wanted to ask you, before I asked permission of your father. It doesn't do me much good to ask him if that isn't something you'd care for, now, is it?"

Her considering look wasn't quite the reaction he'd been expecting. Where had she suddenly found this womanly dignity? After a moment, she nodded.

"Was that a yes, Miss Prissy?"

She nodded again, flushing pink. Her blush was so charming, Sam nearly leaned over and kissed her, but he knew better than to do such a thing. Even if she did not object to his boldness, her father might very well be watching through a window.

He allowed his grin to widen. "That's settled, then. Give

me a couple of days to get settled into this sheriffing job, and then it will be my great pleasure."

"Sam, I hope you don't think I'm being very forward. But it'll be Sunday day after tomorrow…" Her voice trailed off, and she looked at him expectantly.

He went blank, wondering what she was hinting at. For years, Sunday mornings had been a time when he lay in some dingy hotel or boardinghouse room and groaned at the church bells that woke him up early to a headache.

"Would you—I mean, if you wouldn't mind, and if there are no desperate criminals in the jail at the time for you to guard—will you sit with Papa and me when you come to church?" she asked him, glancing up at him from under those thick lashes.

His heart sank. She assumed he was a churchgoing man, that he'd attend Sunday services as a matter of course. And suddenly he realized that in this little town, almost everyone *did* attend church as a matter of course, and if they didn't, it was noted. Mayor Gilmore probably wouldn't allow a man around his daughter who wasn't a churchgoing man, and he wouldn't keep the goodwill of the town for very long if he didn't go to church, either.

He'd just have to fake his way through it—for Prissy.

"Of course I will, Miss Prissy," he said with great heartiness, as if he'd always intended to. "What time do services begin?" There were worse things, he was sure, than spending an hour or so in a pew beside a beautiful girl dressed in her Sunday best. Though it was hard to imagine her any prettier than she was right at this instant.

"Ten o'clock," she said, looking very pleased.

"Until Sunday, then, Miss Prissy," he said. Houston ran up to them, as if knowing Sam was departing, and yipped.

Prissy picked him up, and Sam reached out a hand and ruffled the fur on the little dog's head.

"You be good for Miss Prissy, boy," he admonished the dog. "No more chasing the cat."

"Sam," she said, looking suddenly worried, "will you miss him very much? Perhaps I should give him back to you, for company."

He was touched that she'd make such an unselfish offer, for he could tell she already loved the little beast. "No, I've got Delbert Perry to keep me company, at least tonight. I'm sure the dog's better off with you. Besides, it gives me another excuse to come calling, doesn't it?"

Prissy smiled at him. "It does, at that. Good night, Sam."

As he left the grounds of Gilmore House, Sam could hardly believe how much he'd accomplished in a single day. New town, new job, new girl.

Yes, he could get used to Simpson Creek.

Chapter Four

"Thanks again," Sam said as he walked Nick Brookfield to the door of the jail.

"You're welcome. Flora's quite a cook, isn't she?" the Englishman said.

Sam grinned. "That she is."

Nick started to go out the door, then turned. "If you have any questions, please don't hesitate to ask. Dr. Walker's been a deputy—" he pointed at the doctor's office and home across the street "—and I come into town frequently. And you'll have to come out to the ranch for Sunday dinner after the baby comes."

Sam saw a softening in Brookfield's eyes as he spoke of his wife and coming child, and for a moment he envied the man his settled existence.

"—I know Milly'd love to have you," Brookfield was saying. "Ordinarily, I'd say you'd meet her in church on Sunday, but she's not finding that wagon ride into town very comfortable right now, so she's sticking close to home."

Again, that assumption that he'd be warming a pew in a

couple of mornings. "I'd like to come out, when she feels up to company."

The two men shook hands. Sam watched him stride out into the street, no doubt heading for the livery and his horse.

Brookfield had thawed quite a bit from his initial distrust, but there was still something in the cool blue eyes that warned Sam he'd be an implacable enemy if Sam played fast and loose with the mayor's daughter.

Don't worry, he thought as he rounded the corner and went down the side street that led to the livery. *I'm going to treat Prissy like a queen.* She was exactly what he'd hoped for—a beautiful girl who for some reason he could not fathom did not already have men from six counties lined up to court her. Were the men in this part of Texas blind? Once he convinced her to marry him, they could live happily ever after. He'd make sure she was never sorry he'd won her heart. It seemed he was not going to have to live a hardscrabble life as a dirt-poor farmer after all, and he couldn't find it in himself to feel guilty—only grateful.

He went back inside and locked the door, though he didn't think there was much chance of anyone trying to break Delbert Perry out during the night. The town drunk was now sleeping peacefully, the dishes and silverware from a supper brought from the hotel laid neatly on a tray on the floor. Brookfield had reported he was much closer to sober than he had been and would no doubt be fit to be set free in the morning, with an order to do some good deed like sweeping the saloon floors for a month in penance for his drunken spree.

Sam walked down the short hallway that led to his quarters and started putting away his things, stowing the clothes from his saddlebags in an old brassbound trunk that sat at the foot of his bed. It didn't take long, because he'd always believed in traveling light. Then he eyed the small bed, with its bare mattress of blue ticking, and the pillow and neatly folded sheets and blanket atop it. He was tired and ready to sleep, but he'd have to make the bed first.

As he bent over the mattress, something shifted in his pocket—the heavy gold ruby ring he'd taken from Kendall Raney's safe back in Houston. He couldn't explain, even to himself, why he didn't just put it at the bottom of the old trunk—no one was going to be searching through his possessions. Simpson Creek was the kind of small town where no one thought to lock their doors, and it wasn't as if Kendall Raney would ever trace him to this place. Maybe, if things worked out with Prissy Gilmore, he could make up some fanciful story of a rich uncle back East or the like, and have the ruby reset into a pendant for her. But for now he was going to hide it away.

Taking his boot knife, he cut a small slit in the underside of the mattress, then pushed the ring into the cotton stuffing. It'd be safe enough there.

A slight twinge pricked his conscience as he realized he'd just been planning to lie to Prissy, a woman who'd just invited him to church.

Perhaps he wasn't so guilt-free after all.

"You're up and about early," Sarah Walker commented as she opened the door for Prissy the next morning. "And who's this?" she said, spotting the little dog attached to Prissy by a braided leather leash.

"This is Houston," Prissy said, smiling as he yipped and wriggled on the Walkers' porch, clearly thrilled by the opportunity to meet yet another human. "I got him yesterday, and look, Antonio's already fashioned a collar and leash for him out of old bridle leather. Can he come in? I'll keep him on the leash so he won't get into anything he shouldn't."

"Of course. How are you, Houston?" Sarah said, laughing as the dog sat down and offered his paw. "It's nice to meet you."

"Oh, Sarah, I have so much to tell you!" Prissy exclaimed. "If you're not too busy baking, that is," she added, seeing that her friend wore an apron and had a dot of flour on one cheek. Tendrils of golden hair had escaped from her braid to curl around her forehead. "Mmm, it smells wonderful in here," she said, sniffing the air. "Molasses raisin cookies, unless I miss my guess?"

Sarah smiled back and gestured for Prissy to have a seat at her kitchen table. "Yes, and of course I'm not too busy to listen to your news. Might it have to do with the new sheriff of Simpson Creek?"

Prissy felt color flooding her cheeks. "Horsefeathers. I might have known I wouldn't get to be the one to tell you about him."

"George Detwiler told his mother about the incident in the saloon yesterday, and his mother told me when I went in the mercantile this morning. And Mr. Wallace was there, and he told me how he just happened to be peeking out of the post office window and saw y'all meet, and saw him give you the dog," Sarah explained with a grin.

"That's Simpson Creek for you," Prissy muttered. "No secrets here."

Sarah rolled her eyes in rueful agreement. "Why did he give you his dog?"

Prissy nodded. "Well, the dog apparently latched onto him in Houston—hence his name—and stayed with him all the way to Simpson Creek, but Sam says he was only keeping him till he could find him a good home, so when we met, he offered him to me."

"Sam? You're already on a first-name basis?" Sarah teased.

Prissy blushed again. "Well—only since I walked him to the gate last evening," she confessed. "I'm sure in public and in front of my father it must be 'Sheriff Bishop' for a while…" Prissy felt a little proprietary thrill as she said his name. "Sarah, he came to dinner last night! I was so surprised when Papa agreed he could come! Papa said he wanted to look him over, and he tried to act all stern and gruff, but I think he found him as charming as I did."

"Is that a fact?" Sarah said with a wry twist of her lips. Then she bent over and peered into the oven. "I think these are done," she said, snatching a potholder and pulling out a sheet of perfectly browned cookies. The savory aroma filled the small kitchen, making Prissy's mouth water. "Let's eat a few while they're still hot—that's when they're the best, don't you think?" She scooped a half dozen of them onto a small plate and laid it on the table between them.

Prissy broke off a piece of cookie, popped it into her mouth, then fanned herself. "Too hot! That's what I get for being impatient," she muttered, as Sarah rose and poured her a glass of cold lemonade from the pitcher on the windowsill.

"You still haven't told me what this paragon of charm looks like," she prodded.

"Oh! Well, let me remedy that," Prissy said. "We were just leaving the jail after paying Nick a visit, Papa and I, and he came riding up, and Papa figured out he was the man who'd come to apply for the sheriff's job. Just *wait* till you see him—dark hair, and he has the most *speaking* brown eyes! And he's tall, taller even than your Nolan—I should say six feet or so. And lean…"

"I can tell you're smitten already."

Prissy was thoughtful. "I'm trying not to make the same mistake I have in the past, Sarah—of throwing my heart in first and not thinking it through. And I know I *should* be merely delighted at Sam Bishop's arrival on behalf of the Spinsters' Club ladies, who will *adore* him…but I have to be honest, Sarah. I think he *could* be the one—the one for *me*."

Prissy's thoughtfulness sobered her friend. "I'm glad to hear you're thinking this through, Prissy," Sarah said. "I feel I must still point out you were this excited over Major McConley, too, though not so considering about it as you are now."

"Major McConley? Pooh, he can't hold a candle to Samuel Bishop," Prissy scoffed.

She frowned, remembering how she had thought she had found the man of her dreams in the dashing Major McConley of the Fourth Cavalry, whose regiment was stationed at Fort Mason. She'd held an engagement party for Sarah in the ballroom at Gilmore House and had assumed she could easily capture the Major's interest, but it had become painfully clear that the Major doled out flirtatious smiles to all the young ladies and made sure he danced with each one without appearing to favor any. Though she was his partner at dinner, it seemed he was being no more than courteous to her as his hostess, and by the end of the evening, he had made no effort to urge her out onto the veranda for a private tête-à-tête. She had been so sure the dress of hussar-blue silk that completely matched her eyes would dazzle him! And the rest of his regiment, perhaps aware that she had eyes only for him, had made no effort to single her out, either. That night had been a serious blow to her confidence, leading her to decide she wasn't as irresistible as she had grown up believing.

"I'm thankful he didn't respond to my flirting now. Why, if I'd married Major McConley and gone off to that lonely fort in the middle of nowhere…"

"This Mr. Bishop has already given you a gift," Sarah observed, as Houston leaped into Prissy's lap and made a lunge at the cookie that Prissy was bringing to her mouth.

Prissy restrained him. "No, no, bad boy! Down you go, until you learn your manners." She set the dog back on the floor. *"Sit!"*

Houston looked so immediately contrite that both girls laughed. Prissy broke off a small piece of cookie and gave it to him. "I hope you won't think I'm being foolish and impulsive, Sarah," Prissy continued, "but he's asked me if he can call on me again."

"And of course you agreed."

"I-I did," she admitted. "Oh, Sarah, he's quite handsome. I can't wait for you to meet him, to hear what *you* think," Prissy said.

"No time like the present," Sarah said. "As a matter of fact, I was baking these cookies to take over to the jail to welcome him to Simpson Creek. Just let me put another batch in the oven and as soon as they're ready, we'll have enough. Since you're here, you can introduce us, since I can guess you're just dying to have an excuse to see him again."

Prissy allowed herself a happy sigh. "Am I as transparent as that?"

"Transparent as glass—at least to me."

* * *

"You the acting sheriff? I'm Bob Purvis, here to apply for the job—I believe you're expecting me?" the man said as he entered in response to Sam's called-out invitation.

Sam, who'd been leaning back in his chair enjoying his second cup of coffee, set it down with a thump and stood up.

"Sam Bishop," he said, offering his hand. "And I'm afraid you're too late. They were expecting you, all right, but when you didn't show up, they hired me."

Purvis's shoulders sagged. "Too bad. Can't say I'm surprised, though. My horse went lame just outside a' San Antone and I had to hole up for a few days and rest him. Of all the rotten luck."

"I'm sorry," Sam said, meaning it. He felt a twinge of guilt at taking a job he hadn't even come here for, now that the man who'd really wanted it had appeared. But he had to have a way to support himself or Prissy's father would never let him approach his daughter. "Better luck next time," he said as the man reversed his steps and opened the door, just in time to hold it open for Prissy and another young lady.

The man touched the brim of his hat respectfully, and Prissy gave him a curious glance.

"Miss Prissy, the very one I was hoping to see," Sam said, relieved that Purvis had come before, not after, Prissy's arrival. "And there's my old trail buddy, Houston," he said, greeting the dog. "I see you've fancied him up some," he said, indicating the new leash the dog sported. "And who's this you've brought with you? And what's that delicious smell?"

"Mrs. Nolan Walker, may I present Simpson Creek's new sheriff, Mr. Sam Bishop? Mr. Bishop, this is Sarah

Walker, the doctor's wife, my best friend and Simpson
Creek's best baker. She wanted to welcome you to the
community."

Sam executed a gallant bow. "Mrs. Walker, I'm honored to meet Miss Prissy's best friend—and of course I'm
always happy to meet someone who can bake anything as
delicious-smelling as what you have there," he said, nodding toward the napkin covered dish.

Sarah grinned and presented the dish to him. "I'm
pleased to meet you, too, Sheriff Bishop."

The three of them spent a very pleasurable half hour
chatting until Sarah at last announced she had to leave
to fix dinner for her physician husband. "I hope you'll
come and have a meal with us sometime, Sam," Sarah
told him.

"I'd like that very much. It's nice meeting you, Mrs.
Walker. I look forward to meeting your husband. Miss
Prissy, I'll see you at church in the morning," Sam said.
He took her hands in his for a moment.

He wished he could look forward to going to church
for his own sake, instead of just an opportunity to be with
Prissy. He wished he hadn't lost his faith in the process of
struggling to keep food on the table for his sisters, when
the church near his home had done nothing to help but try
to split up his family.

The ladies walked back across the street to the Walkers' house in back of the doctor's office, Houston trotting
smartly alongside them.

"So, what did you think?" Prissy asked, after glancing
backward to make sure he wasn't watching them.

"Oh, I don't know, I suppose he's all right," Sarah said
airily, then laughed to show she was only teasing. "Yes,

Sam Bishop is very good-looking, and very nice, and I can see why you're so taken with him, Prissy."

Prissy waited for more, and finally said, "But what? I can hear a 'but' in your voice, Sarah."

By now they were at Sarah's doorstep. From the front, where Dr. Nolan Walker's office was located, came an ear-piercing wail.

"Oh, dear, Nolan must be examining the Harding boy again," Sarah said. "He's always sticking things in his ears or up his nose. I'm glad he's not my child…"

"But I sense you have reservations about Sam," Prissy persisted, not about to be distracted.

Sarah paused with her hand on the doorknob. "I don't know if I would call them reservations, Prissy dear, so much as I would ask you to be cautious, take your time."

"Cautious? Sarah, he's the *sheriff*."

"Yes, and two days ago you didn't know he existed, did you? I agree, he seems very charming. But go slowly, Prissy. There's no rush. *Pray* about it. Just because he wears a tin badge doesn't mean he's the man God has for you."

Prissy felt unexpected frustration at Sarah's words. Sure, she trusted God as her Savior, Prissy thought, but how was she to know His will? When she folded her hands and asked God to send her a good man, she couldn't hear an answer.

"Sarah, we can't all be like you, cautious and careful, taking months to decide what all of us in the Spinsters' Club knew right away, that Nolan Walker was perfect for you. I suppose it's understandable that you were wary, since your former fiancé turned out to be a murdering outlaw—"

Sarah's face lost color and her eyes filled with pain. Prissy knew she'd let her tongue go too far.

"I'm sorry, Sarah," she said, stretching a trembling hand to reach Sarah's shoulder. "That was inexcusable. I know you loved Jesse Holt once, before he changed so completely. Please, forgive me."

Sarah's gaze was steady and strong. "I have already. And I suppose you're right. I *was* very wary after I thought Jesse was dead in the war and that Yankee doctor showed up as my Spinsters' Club match. But I'm glad I didn't rush into courting with him. I'm glad that I got to know him first, and prayed about it, that we were both Christians when we married—what do you know of Sam Bishop's faith, by the way?"

"Nothing," Prissy admitted. "As you pointed out, we only met yesterday. But he's coming to church tomorrow— he must be a Christian."

Sarah said nothing, just raised an eyebrow, and finally Prissy sighed. "I know, I know, that doesn't prove anything. I suppose that's something I will have to discover, as we get to know each other. There's plenty of time for that."

Sarah regarded her steadily. "Yes, there is. I hope you will keep that in mind. Prissy, please don't be offended, but sometimes it seems that you're in love with love itself, rather than with discovering the right man to spend your life with."

"'In love with love?'" Prissy echoed. "I'm hardly picking out my trousseau yet," she said stiffly. "We have yet to go on so much as an outing together. It's quite possible that Sam Bishop is not for me, but for someone else!"

"There, now *I* have offended *you*," Sarah said, her face full of regret. "It was the last thing I wanted you to do,

Prissy. I only want you to be careful with your heart until you're sure, that's all."

"I will," Prissy promised, knowing Sarah was right. She extended a hand and placed it on Sarah's wrist. "I want you to be honest with me, Sarah—always. Now I'd better be going and make sure Papa's sitting down for dinner. Sometimes he says he's not hungry and just skips it, then he's famished by suppertime."

She was very lucky to have a friend like Sarah Walker, Prissy mused as she walked to her house, using the board-walks that ran past the stores rather than trusting her shoes to the dusty streets. She just wished she were as good a Christian as Sarah was. Sarah seemed to find great comfort in her prayers, and to be certain about the answers she sought with them, whereas Prissy's sometimes seemed to go no farther than the ceiling.

Envying Sarah's faith was better than envying her friend's success in marriage, Prissy supposed. But it was only natural to be a little wistful when three of the Spinsters had now found mates—Milly with Nick, Sarah with Nolan, and now Emily Thompson was to marry Ed Markison in a few weeks—while the contents of Prissy's hope chest remained unused. Perhaps she'd unconsciously assumed *she'd* be the first to wed. As the only child of a rich father, she'd usually gotten whatever she wanted it, as soon as she wanted it, whether it was a pony or a new hair ribbon.

Envy was the same as coveting, wasn't it? So she'd broken one of the Commandments, Prissy thought with a guilty sigh. She'd have to be sure to say her prayers tonight, and ask for forgiveness for that. *Help me to take Sarah's advice, Lord, and not be in love with love. Give me wisdom about Sam Bishop. Help me to see if he is for me—or if You have someone else in mind for both of us.*

She wanted to be in the center of the Lord's will, but couldn't help but wish the outcome would be the former.

Chapter Five

"Ah, Prissy, there you are," her father boomed as she made her way up the Gilmore House steps. "I was afraid I was going to have to leave a message with Flora."

"What do you mean, Papa? I was just coming home to have dinner with you." And then she saw the lady standing behind her father, a lady who looked to be about his age, in a stylish dress of lavender silk with black piping, smiling at her. "Oh! I didn't know you had company."

"I didn't know she was coming, either, until she appeared on our doorstep," her father said, his voice more jovial than she'd heard it in months. "Prissy, meet Mariah Fairchild. I grew up with her back in Victoria. We were in the same grade together at school—I used to dip her braids in the inkwell." He chuckled in remembrance. "That was long before I met your dear mama, of course. Her husband Hap was in our class, too."

"I'm so sorry to hear of your mother's passing," Mariah Fairchild said, coming forward. She was a statuesque woman with a wealth of silver hair done up on top of her head. "I saw her portrait in the parlor, dear child, and I see you are very like her—especially about the eyes. It's so nice to meet you, Priscilla. And what a sweet little dog," she added, glancing at Houston, who wagged his tail obligingly at her.

"You too, Mrs. Fairchild," Prissy said, wondering for whom the lady wore half-mourning.

"Yes," the lady went on. "I lost my Hap a year ago, and when I heard recently about your father's loss this winter, I just had to come pay a condolence call."

"Oh. Do you…live very far from here?" Prissy asked, hoping Mariah Fairchild would furnish her with a clue as to why she was here.

"I live in Austin, dear, but I…I'm thinking of relocating, now that Hap has passed on. There are too many memories in that old house I rattle around in," she said with a gusty sigh.

"I…I see," Prissy said politely.

"Your father and Hap kept up a correspondence, you know," Mariah Fairchild went on.

No, I didn't, Prissy wanted to say. As far as she could remember, her father had never mentioned Hap Fairchild— or his wife.

"And your father was always singing the praises of Simpson Creek. Why, we were so proud to hear that he was elected mayor, Hap and I." Mariah Fairchild sighed again and delicately wiped a tear from the corner of her eye with a lacy handkerchief. The scent of rosewater wafted toward Prissy. "I just had to come and see for myself if it was as good as he said it was, if this might be the town I would like to live in for the rest of my life." She smiled tearfully up at Prissy's father.

Prissy bristled. Papa had lost his wife only six months ago, and already this widow was swooping down on him, hoping for a new husband who was probably wealthier than her last one! She took a deep breath, trying hard to keep her voice civil as she said, "Oh, but if you're used to a big city like Austin, I'm sure Simpson Creek will seem very dull to you," she said. "If you blink while you're riding through, you'd miss the town entirely. There's no opera hall, and no library—"

"Prissy!" her father protested, "you're making our fair town sound like a backwater—"

"Oh, but I don't need those things," Mariah Fairchild assured her, with a glance at Prissy's father. "I'm content to lead a very quiet existence."

"Oh, it's quiet, all right," Prissy agreed. "So quiet you can hear a hummingbird's heartbeat."

Mariah Fairchild gave a trill of laughter. "It sounds perfect! Well, Prissy—may I call you Prissy?—your father was just about to walk me back to my hotel, and we were going to get a bite of dinner and talk about old times. Why don't you join us, dear?"

The woman was friendly, but Prissy had to smother the urge to respond like a sulky child. She knew rudeness would distress her father, and she had no real proof that this woman was doing anything more than what she said— paying a condolence call and merely considering moving here. What could be more logical than consulting an old friend who happened to be the town mayor?

"No, thank you, Mrs. Fairchild," she said with all the politeness she could muster. "Perhaps another time. I'm sure you and Papa have a lot of catching up to do."

Flora wasn't going to be pleased about this, either, Prissy thought, watching her father gallantly offer Mariah Fairchild his arm as they descended the steps. She had probably had dinner all ready to serve promptly at noon, when Prissy's father always wanted it, but now he was going to sashay down to the hotel and take his dinner there with this strange female. Prissy decided she would have to be extra appreciative of whatever Flora had prepared in order to make up for her father's thoughtlessness.

But she found Flora surprisingly philosophical about the situation.

"Ah, well, *chica,* it's not such a big thing. Your father is an important man—this is not the first time he has had to leave right before a meal. I can always give Antonio an extra share. That *hombre* is always hungry, you know."

"It's hardly part of the mayor's official duties to advise a lonely widow where to live in Simpson Creek," Prissy grumbled. "Did you see the way she looked at him?"

Flora raised a black eyebrow. "No, but I saw how *he* looked, Señorita Prissy," she said, her face stern. "Your papa is a lonely man. He misses your mother, no? He misses having a lady around to smile at, to make conversation with."

"Flora, he has *us* to make conversation with," Prissy protested.

"It's not the same," Flora said. "You are his daughter, and I am his employee, and a married woman."

"But it was only this winter Mama died!"

"Miss Prissy, he does your mother no dishonor by having dinner with an old friend," Flora said. "You must not be so possessive of your old papa. One day soon you will marry and move out, and then he will be even more lonely."

Sam Bishop flew into Prissy's mind before she could stop herself, but it would not do to think of Sam Bishop every time marriage was mentioned. What if he was *not* the man God had intended for her?

* * *

Sam thought Prissy, standing outside the church talking to a bevy of other ladies, was just about the prettiest sight he'd ever seen. She wore a pink dress—of silk, unless he missed his guess—with short puffed sleeves trimmed in white lace. There was matching braid around the bodice, and a pink ribbon belt with matching tassels that emphasized her slender waist, while the back was gathered into a small bustle. High button shoes of white kid adorned her feet. She wore a straw bonnet with a pink ribbon band that enchantingly framed her heart-shaped face. Her strawberry-blond curls streamed down her back.

There were a dozen or so ladies on the lawn, clad in pretty calico, gingham or muslin. Prissy outshone them all, in his opinion.

"Oh, Sam, there you are!" she said, turning to face him, her face brightening and her blue eyes shining.

"Good morning, Miss Priscilla," he said, tipping his hat.

"Ladies, I'd like to present our new sheriff to those of you who haven't made his acquaintance."

He guessed they were all members of the Spinsters' Club—or, in Sarah Walker's case, past members. He could practically feel them sizing him up.

"Prissy, have you told Sheriff Bishop about our Spinst— that is, our Society events?" one of the young ladies asked, fluttering her lashes at Sam.

The ladies of the Spinsters' Club were an interesting assortment—some short, some tall, some pretty, all friendly. It was on the tip of his tongue to mention that he'd seen their advertisement in that Houston newspaper, and that that was why he'd come to Simpson Creek, but just in time he remembered that he had supposedly come for the sheriff's job.

"No, I…um…haven't had a chance," Prissy murmured, suddenly seeming flustered by the other woman's behavior. "Goodness, Polly, he only came to town two days ago."

Polly chuckled. "I'm sure you haven't, bless your heart." She turned back to Sam. "Well, we are the Society for the Promotion of Marriage. You must come to our events. If you're a bachelor, that is. You *are* a bachelor, aren't you, Sheriff?" Polly asked, peering around him as if he had a wife hiding behind him.

"Yes, I am," he said, amused by the confusion on Prissy's face. Was it confusion—or jealousy?

"Well, good. We'll be happy to have you attend. We'd want our new sheriff to feel welcome, wouldn't we, ladies?"

"Reverend Chadwick," Prissy suddenly said as the white-haired gentleman appeared. "I'd like to introduce you to the new sheriff. Reverend, this is Samuel Bishop." Prissy seemed relieved to leave the topic of the Society, Sam noticed. Perhaps Polly's flirting simply embarrassed her. Or was it more than that?

"We met last evening. I'm afraid our new sheriff came upon me trying to sweet-talk my roses into blooming despite the heat. Again, welcome to Simpson Creek, Sheriff Bishop," said the old gentleman, whose gnarled hand gripped his with surprising strength. His gaze was direct, and Sam had the impression he saw deeply inside a person. Did he guess that Sam was not all he seemed?

"Thank you, sir. Please, call me Sam."

"I'll do that. I hope we'll get to talk more later, Sam, but now we'd better start the service. Sarah, are you ready?"

"Sarah plays the piano for the singing," Prissy explained.

The other ladies filed inside, but Prissy put a hand on his wrist. "I thought you weren't coming, that perhaps you had to capture some desperate outlaw," Prissy said, gazing up at him.

He shook his head. "No desperate outlaws passed through Simpson Creek this Sunday morning," he said, smiling down at her and placing her hand on his arm. "I was delayed by arranging something, which I'll tell you about later." He winked and enjoyed the blush that rose to her cheeks. The first piano notes of a hymn wafted out of the open door of the church.

They climbed the steps and entered, walking down the middle aisle to the front pew, with Prissy nodding at others who gazed at both of them with interest—and in the case of some of the ladies, with barely hidden envy. His amusement was almost enough to distract him from the fact that he was in a church for the first time in a very, very long time. If only his sisters, Etta, Lidy and Livy, could see him now!

He was amused to spot Delbert Perry, his face scrubbed, his threadbare clothing spotless, his hair slicked down, sitting midway toward the front. Delbert beamed at him as he passed.

So the town drunk was indeed trying to mend his ways. Perhaps there *was* something to church attendance, after all.

Sam also saw Nick Brookfield, the former sheriff, sitting a couple of rows back with some weathered-looking fellows who were probably his cowhands.

They reached the front pew, where Priscilla's father stood, holding a hymnbook with a lady Sam didn't recognize. Her father shot her a look of gentle disapproval because the congregation was already halfway through

"Onward Christian Soldiers," but then he turned back and resumed singing.

Prissy took a hymnbook from the rack in front of her, turning to the hymn being sung. Her soprano was clear and sweet in his ears. Sam knew very few hymns, so he just enjoyed listening to her voice and hoped that she would not read anything into his silence.

Reverend Chadwick, who'd been sitting to the left of the pulpit, rose and gestured for everyone to be seated.

"Good Sunday morning, ladies and gentlemen. Isn't it a pretty day?"

There were murmurs of agreement. "We are here to worship, but today we also have a special cause for thankfulness. As many of you may have heard, Simpson Creek has a new sheriff, Mr. Sam Bishop."

Sam was caught off guard. *He* was a cause for thankfulness? If that didn't beat all. After looking up at the preacher, he glanced around and saw everyone nodding and smiling at him.

Reverend Chadwick beckoned. "Sam, come on up front. You, too, Mayor. Sam, it's customary in Simpson Creek to swear you into your new office in front of the whole town, since you're promising to serve and protect them." He held a thick, black-leather-bound Bible in his hand.

Sam got to his feet and followed the mayor to the front. He hadn't thought about the fact that he hadn't been sworn in at the time he'd put on the badge. Now it was about to happen in front of everyone, in a house of worship. He did his best to keep his face expressionless and solemn, but he as took his place by the pulpit with Prissy's father, he was all too aware that he had come to town and taken this job under false pretenses. He had lied about his reason for coming to town as well as his previous experience. The only time he'd spent in a sheriff's office had been inside a cell, for petty crimes like disorderly conduct. And he'd turned away a man who probably did have experience.

He saw Prissy smiling proudly at him from the front pew. The very sight of her looking at him with such trust caused him to offer the first real prayer he'd offered up in many years.

Lord, please don't strike me dead for lying. It would upset Miss Prissy. I'm sorry, God, and I'll try to make up for it.

Mayor Gilmore stood facing him, with the preacher holding the Bible between them. "Place your right hand on the Good Book and hold up your left hand," he said, and waited until Sam did so. "Samuel Bishop, do you solemnly swear to serve and protect the town of Simpson Creek, to uphold the statutes of this town and the laws of Texas, as well as the Constitution of the United States of America?"

Sam nodded, relieved that no bolt of lightning had struck him—at least not yet. "I do."

A smile appeared on the jowly features of the mayor. "Then it is my distinct pleasure to announce that Samuel Bishop is officially our new sheriff. I'm sure the Reverend wouldn't find it out of place to give him a round of applause, folks."

Sam smiled as the congregation stood. They clapped their hands, and the knot of guilt in his stomach began to ease. He couldn't believe it. They were glad he was here. They were willing to take him at his word that he would wear that five-pointed tin star with honor. He suddenly felt humble, a feeling he hadn't experienced in a long time.

"You can take your seats, gentlemen," the preacher said.

"I know you'll all want to greet Sam after the service, but let's sing our next hymn before I start into my sermon."

Sarah began playing another tune as Sam left the pulpit and found his way back to Prissy. He hardly heard the Reverend's sermon. Instead, he thought about the trust that Prissy and all the people of Simpson Creek had just placed in him. He suddenly wanted nothing more than to live up to their expectations.

Beside him now, Prissy plied an ivory-handled fan with a delicate flower design as she concentrated on the sermon. Clearly coming to church was very important to her. Was he doing her a disservice by pretending to be a…what? God-fearing man? A believer?

Was he pretending?

Sam did notice, however, Prissy darting a look at her father—who seemed to be giving some sidelong glances of his own at the lady beside him. When Prissy returned her gaze to the pulpit after one of these glances, he caught an anxious look on her features. He wondered who this lady was that was causing Prissy concern.

The temperature in the little chapel climbed. Ladies wielded their fans faster and faster. Here and there gents pulled out handkerchiefs and mopped their foreheads. At last Reverend Chadwick stopped preaching, the congregation rose for a final hymn, and the service was over.

Before they even left the pew, the mayor stopped him. "I didn't want to interrupt the service when you came in, but I want to introduce you to an old friend from my childhood, Mrs. Hap Fairchild. She and her husband and I were friends back in school. He's passed on now, but Mariah—that is, Mrs. Fairchild—is thinking about settling down here."

Ah, Sam thought, understanding immediately why

Prissy looked so unhappy. Her father was a lonely widower, and Prissy didn't cotton to the idea of him putting another woman in her mother's place. Yet the woman's smile was genuine and warm, and there was no denying her effect on James Gilmore.

"Mrs. Fairchild," Sam said politely, taking the gloved hand she extended. "I've only been in Simpson Creek since Friday, but it already feels like home to me. I hope you'll be very happy here."

"I'm sure I will. It's nice to meet you, Sheriff Bishop. I'm sure the town's in good hands with you as sheriff and James as mayor."

He didn't miss the way Prissy's lips tightened, and was sorry that she felt threatened.

"I hope you'll be back," Reverend Chadwick said, as they came to the entrance. The preacher was shaking hands with each person as they left.

"Yessir, I'll be back," Sam said, warmed by the man's friendliness. He suspected he would be back—even if Prissy was the real reason he came. Before he could say any more, another man extended his hand.

"Sheriff Bishop, I'm Dr. Walker—Nolan Walker, that is." His accent was distinctly Yankee—from Maine, Sam thought. "You met my wife, Sarah, yesterday."

There seemed to be an interminable number of people who wanted to introduce themselves to Sam and shake his hand, from the homes and businesses around town as well as from outlying ranches. He was overwhelmed with names, friendliness and open interest.

So this is what it's like to belong somewhere...

When they were alone again, Prissy turned to him with avid curiosity. "Will you tell me what it is you were arranging before church?"

"I've arranged with the hotel to pack us a picnic bas-ket—but of course, I realize it's short notice, and you might have made other plans," he added. "If that's the case, perhaps I'll just give it to one of the other ladies." He glanced at the knot of Spinsters' Club females he'd met before church, who were gathered under the shade of a cottonwood, discussing the two of them, if their sidelong glances were anything to go by. "I wouldn't want it to go to waste."

She smiled at him, please by his gesture. "I have to ask my father, of course."

"Oh, but I already have," he told her. "Yesterday, as a matter of fact, after you visited me with Sarah. He seemed quite open to the idea. So now the only question remains, where are we to enjoy this picnic?"

Prissy was so astonished she could barely respond. "Sam Bishop, you are full of surprises."

He grinned, hoping against hope that the only surprises she would ever get from him would be pleasant ones.

Chapter Six

Prissy felt the warmth of joy bubbling up within her, warmer than the summer sun above her. He'd secured her father's permission to court her the very day after he'd asked her? And he'd gone to the trouble of planning an outing already? But wait—wasn't this all happening a bit too fast?

"Prissy, are you all right?"

"Yes! I was just thinking we *could* have our picnic over yonder, in the meadow," she said, pointing to the grassy, tree-lined field on the other side of the creek that had given the town its name.

He studied it. "Looks like a fine place for a picnic," he said.

"But that's where everyone goes to picnic—families… with little children running around…" She hesitated. "It's not exactly the most private location. There's always the possibility that we'll be talked about."

"And you know somewhere less crowded?"

"No! No, I mean…I…uh…" Suddenly Prissy was afraid she'd sounded too bold. She didn't want Sam Bishop to think she was not a lady. But she didn't want the entire town observing their picnic, either. "I just meant some-where where we could talk in peace, and not have to worry about a ball landing in the middle of the fried chicken all of a sudden—or whatever's in that picnic basket."

Sam chuckled. "No, we don't want that," he agreed. "Where did you have in mind?"

His smile was so warm she felt it like a physical touch. It was almost unnerving. "There's a place…" she began. "Oh, but we couldn't walk there, it's too far. Maybe we'd better go there another time."

"It just so happens I've checked with the Calhoun boy at the livery, and he's got a horse and shay we could borrow for the afternoon. He could hitch it up while we're picking up the basket at the hotel."

"My, you've thought of everything, haven't you? All right, then, there's this huge old live oak, just a little ways out of town. They say it's over a hundred years old."

"And there wouldn't be families and little boys throwing balls into the fried chicken there?"

"No. Chances are we'd have the place to ourselves today."

"Sounds perfect," he said.

Prissy felt her heart accelerate. She gazed up into those intense brown eyes and felt a niggle of doubt about the propriety of going off alone with this handsome man she'd so recently met. "But perhaps you shouldn't go so far from town, since you're the sheriff?" she said, twisting a fold of her pink skirt in her hand.

"I don't think there'll be a wave of lawlessness striking Simpson Creek on a Sunday afternoon," he said lightly but without ridicule. "Would you feel more at ease, though, if we asked Sarah and her husband to come along?"

"Sam, you wouldn't mind?" she said, relief washing over her.

"Of course not. They're talking to Nick Brookfield by his wagon. Let's go ask. I thought you might feel that way, so I told the cook to pack enough for four."

Impulsively, she seized his hand and squeezed it. "You are the most thoughtful man!" she exclaimed, and was rewarded with a lopsided grin—as well as some interesting looks from the ladies of the Society.

Sarah and Nolan were perfectly agreeable to falling in with their plan, but just as they started down the street toward the livery stable with them, a cowhand on a lathered horse galloped into the churchyard from beyond the creek and slid to a stop by Nick's wagon.

"Miz Milly says ya gotta hurry on home, boss! She commenced t' havin' pains 'bout the time you left, but she didn't wanna tell you. Figured you'd be back in plenty a' time. Now they comin' faster. She thinks the time's about here. She says you better come, too, Doc Walker, Miz Sarah! You take the horse, Mist' Nick—I'll drive the wagon."

Sarah turned back to Prissy. "I'm afraid we'll have to make it some other time," she said as Nick took off toward the ranch. "My sister needs me."

"Of course," Prissy said. "How exciting, Sarah—you'll soon be an aunt!"

After the excited Walkers and the wagon full of cowhands had departed along with the Walkers in the doctor's buggy, Sam turned to Prissy. "Perhaps you'd rather have our picnic over in the meadow after all?" he suggested.

She turned and gazed across the creek. Just as she had said, families were spreading out tablecloths on the grass, and children who'd been confined to the pews in their stiff

Sunday clothes were already wading in the creek, splashing and shrieking. She shook her head.

"We could always take the picnic basket and eat out on your lawn."

"And have Papa and Mariah Fairchild watching us through the window? No, thank you. He invited her to Sunday dinner, you know." Her voice sounded sulky in her own ears, so she took a deep breath. "No, let's stick to the original plan, and go out to the We—" She caught herself, not wanting to say "Wedding Tree"—the name the locals had given the venerable old live oak—it would make her sound like a desperate old maid. "To that old tree outside of town," she amended.

"All right, then." His brown eyes were serious, steady. "Prissy, I want you to know you have nothing to fear from me. We may not have known one another long, but I'd never do anything…anything that would make you not trust me."

"I know." She *did* know, she realized. "All right, let's go. I'm famished, aren't you?"

Long before they arrived under its gnarled boughs, he could see the ancient live oak with its limbs overspreading the narrow rutted road and the meadow on the other side.

"That's quite a tree," Sam said, genuinely awed by its massiveness.

"Isn't it wonderful?" she agreed, smiling at him. "It's called the Wedding Tree. Legend has it that the Indians used to come here to have…sacred ceremonies. Some of the early settlers, too—before there were churches, of course."

He guided the horse into the shade, set the brake, then

tied the reins to it before jumping down and reaching his hand up to Prissy. She descended with a graceful flurry of pink skirts and white petticoats, then stood by as he lifted the wicker picnic basket out of the shay, along with the broad canvas sheet the hotel had included.

Beyond the reach of the low-hanging branches, the summer sun beat down in all its fierce intensity and bees buzzed amid the flowers, but it was dim and cool beneath the wide, twisted boughs. It was as if they were enclosed in their own private world.

"You're right, Prissy, this is a perfect place for our picnic," he said, enjoying the way her bluebonnet-blue eyes lit with pleasure at his compliment.

"Here, help me with this," she said, taking one end of the canvas.

They spread it out just beyond where the roots of the huge tree stuck partway out of the ground, and Prissy began laying out plates and silverware, fried chicken, a napkin-wrapped basket of biscuits that were still warm, a covered dish of green beans, a jar of cold tea and mugs, and pecan pralines for dessert.

"The hotel cook made enough for an army," she murmured. "It really is too bad Sarah and Nolan couldn't come with us."

"Do you mind their absence?" he asked her.

"No," she admitted, laughing. "Although I'm sure we will now be the talk of Simpson Creek."

"To be honest, Prissy, I think we've been the talk of Simpson Creek since I shared your pew." Then, afraid he would spook her with his frankness, he added, "But I've got no issue with that. That is, if you don't."

She smiled her perfect smile and they sat down and began to eat.

"What is it?" she said, some time later, when she noticed him watching her while he lounged on his side, his head propped in his hand. Even in the shade, he could see the self-conscious flush blossom on her cheekbones.

He couldn't tell her he liked watching the delicate way she sat nibbling at the meat clinging to the chicken drumstick with pearl-like white teeth. She didn't have a man's hearty appetite, but she wasn't one of these belles who picked at her food, either.

"I have a confession to make," he said instead.

"Oh?" Her eyes widened and she laid down the bare drumstick on her plate. "What is it?"

"About me," he said, watching her. Would what he was about to tell her please her and make them closer, or would she become distrustful of him?

"Are you…are you an outlaw? A wanted man?" She held herself very still, he saw, as if she were afraid of the answer.

"No," he said, "no, of course not." He laughed as she let out the breath she had been holding. "Did you really think that's what I was going to tell you?"

She smiled a little nervously. "No, I certainly hoped it wasn't. I would have been shocked, of course! But when Sarah's fiancé—her former fiancé, that is—finally returned a few months ago—she hadn't seen Jesse Holt since he'd gone away to the war, you see—he'd become an outlaw, and he kidnapped Sarah, and Nick and Nolan and the posse had to track them down, and Jesse was killed. Poor Sarah—it was awful!"

"And you thought I might be a man on the run," he concluded. "I'm sorry, Prissy—I didn't mean to frighten you for a single second." He *was* a man on the run, though— from Kendall Raney and his henchmen.

"Are you…are you *married?*" Her voice was a shaky whisper. "Did you leave a wife behind somewhere?"

He couldn't stop the hoot of laughter that burst out of him and seemed to bounce off the twisted tree limbs hanging above them. "No, Prissy! No, I'm not married, or promised, or anything like that."

"Then what could it be?" she asked, her blue eyes puzzled in the sun-dappled shade. "If you're not in trouble with the law, or married…"

"I don't mean to make you play a guessing game," he said, contrite over the worry that furrowed the lovely brow framed by her strawberry-blond curls. "Here's my confession—I didn't come to Simpson Creek for the sheriff job."

"Y-you didn't? Then why—"

"I came to meet you."

Her jaw dropped.

All he could do now was hope for the best.

Prissy couldn't believe her ears. "You came to meet *me,*" she repeated. "Not to be the sheriff? Are you saying you saw the advertisement we ladies put in the newspapers?"

He grinned. "Yes, ma'am. But of course, I had no idea that 'Miss Priscilla Gilmore of Post Office Box 17' was going to be the loveliest lady in Simpson Creek. I'm just surprised that no one's snapped you up before, at least once the Spinsters' Club began—I meant, the Society for the Promotion of Marriage."

"That's all right, you can call it the Spinsters' Club—everyone does," Prissy said, unsure of exactly how to respond to his compliment.

"It's the truth. You're a very pretty girl, Prissy. And very sweet."

She suddenly remembered his words when he'd met her papa, Nick, and her. "But you told Papa you came to apply for the sheriff's job," she said.

He looked down. "Yes, and I'm ashamed of that fib," he told her quietly. "I'll confess it to him someday and ask his pardon." He raised his head again and, taking her hand, gazed at her. "But Prissy, I knew I had to have some sort of employment while we became acquainted. What kind of man would I be if I just took a room at the hotel and spent the livelong day courting you? Your papa wouldn't let a man like that within ten miles of his precious daughter," he told her. "Nor should he."

She thought about it a moment. It was true enough that all of the men who'd come to town to meet the spinsters had taken jobs of one sort or another—Nick had hired on as a cowhand on the Matthews ranch, Nolan became the town doctor, Ed Markison was a bank teller and Pete Collier, Caroline Wallace's late fiancé, had opened up a drugstore before his untimely death.

"I see," she said at last. "I guess that makes sense."

"The sheriff's job just seemed to fall into my lap. Besides, I think I'll make a good sheriff for Simpson Creek. Don't you?"

"If your first day on the job was anything to go by, you sure will," she said. "Why, Delbert Perry might have killed Nick if you hadn't been there."

"Oh, I don't know, it was just that Perry was startled, and—"

She interrupted his modest dismissal. "But, Sam, how can you be sure I'm the one you want to court? You haven't gotten to know the other ladies—some of the Spinsters you haven't even met yet."

He looked down again for a moment, and when he

looked up, his grin was broad. "Fishing for compliments, are you, Prissy? You want to hear that once I saw you, I didn't have eyes for anyone else?"

He expected her to laugh, but consternation filled her eyes.

"Sam, I, too, have a confession. I'm feeling somewhat guilty about you—"

He blinked. "Guilty? About me? How's that?" *What could she possibly mean? They hadn't so much as kissed. What could this innocent, beautiful girl have to feel guilty about?*

She nodded. "I'm president of the Spinsters' Club. By rights, I should be encouraging you to get to know all of the ladies and make your choice. But I haven't wanted to do that. I chose to…go on a picnic with you instead."

After a moment, he took her hand. "I'm glad you did, Prissy. Mighty glad you did."

All of a sudden there was no world beyond the sun-dappled shade of the ancient tree, no one but him and her.

"Once I saw you, I couldn't imagine that anyone could compare to you," he said.

Prissy felt she could hardly catch her breath.

She could smell his scent of bay rum and leather, and even the sweetness of the pralines they had eaten. She could have stayed in that moment the rest of her life.

They both heard the creak of an axle and the sound of laughing children at the same time. A moment later, a buckboard wagon lumbered into view, the bed loaded with wriggling children, a local rancher and his wife seated on the plank bench in front.

"Howdy, Miss Prissy, Sheriff," the man called, raising

a hand in greeting. "Thought I'd take our young'uns to the creek t'git cooled off. Are y'all havin' a nice picnic?"

"We sure are, Mr. Edwardson," she called, grateful she could remember the man's name in spite of the way her head was spinning, and hoping he and his wife couldn't see the way she was blushing in the shade of the old live oak.

"Have fun at the creek," Sam said.

The buckboard rumbled on, and she turned back to Sam, suddenly self-conscious.

The silence under the tree was broken only by the buzzing of a fly swooping low over the remains of the picnic feast. Sam waved the insect away.

She should start a new conversation. Her mother always said a lady should be able to make sparkling conversation about any interesting topic under any circumstance.

"Sam," Prissy began, "tell me about your home. You said you were from Tennessee originally? And your family—I don't believe you've ever mentioned them."

He was silent for a long minute.

"I'm sorry," she said, thinking she must have sounded nosy. "I didn't mean to pry—"

He held up a hand. "You weren't, Prissy. No reason to apologize. It's a natural enough question. Yes, I was born and raised in the hills of Tennessee."

"Did you live on a farm?"

He gave a short, mirthless bark of laughter. "To call those rocky acres a farm would be stretching the truth, but yes, I did."

"Are your parents still living? Do you have brothers and sisters?"

"No brothers, just three younger sisters, and our parents both died of a fever when I was about sixteen." His face had gone bleak, his eyes unfocused as he stared off into the distance.

She sighed and gazed at him, pity welling up in her. "How awful for you! Did you go to live with grandparents, or an aunt or uncle?"

His mouth tightened as he pretended great interest in a couple of ants marching determinedly across their picnic cloth. "No, our folks had come there from back East and burned their bridges behind them, I guess you could say."

"But there must have been someone," she said. "Some family to take you in."

"If we were willing to be split up, sure. One family was willing to take one of my sisters to mind their handful of young'uns, another wanted me to work on their farm that was about as hardscrabble as ours, another wanted one of my sisters to cook and clean for a family of twelve. And then there was the sixty-year-old widower who was willing to marry the oldest of my sisters—if our farm was included as part of the deal, and the rest of us found another place to live."

Prissy couldn't stifle a gasp of horror.

"But Bishops take care of their own," he went on, after a quick glance at her. "They don't take charity—if you could call what we were offered charity. I worked from sunup to sundown and kept food on the table and clothes on our backs until my sisters were older and made good marriages to good men. Then I left."

"You don't keep in touch with your sisters?"

He shrugged. "I've moved around a fair amount. If they tried, the letters probably got lost in the mail." He looked back at the ants, who'd been joined by a couple of their fellows. Prissy sensed there was more to the story than what he was telling.

"What about you?" she asked. "Didn't you try to write to them?"

He shrugged again. "I wrote a couple of times. Didn't hear anything back. There's no telling if they even received them."

"You might be an uncle several times over, for all you know."

His lips quirked upward. "They'd already had at least two young 'uns apiece last I heard. There's probably more now. Could be I'll try writing them again. I'll probably send it to Etta, the oldest—she'd be the one most apt to write back. I'll tell her I've met this wonderful girl in Simpson Creek with blue eyes and strawberry-blond hair, one Prissy Gilmore by name…"

Prissy couldn't help but smile.

Sam got to his feet, peering at the position of the sun through the gnarled branches of the live oak. "I suppose we'd better get back, before your papa sends out a search party for us," he said, extending a hand to help her up.

"Or before evildoers take over Simpson Creek," she responded wryly. She imagined it was likely her father was still enjoying the company of Mariah Fairchild and hadn't even missed her yet. She only hoped the fair widow hadn't been invited to supper, too.

Then she felt guilty for the selfish thought. She had spent a wonderful afternoon with Sam—should her father have to sit home alone, staring at the portrait of her mother that hung in his study?

But my mother only died a few months ago.

No. She wouldn't think of that now. She was too happy to let her worry about the widow spoil her joy. Sam had bared his very soul to her, daring to confess the real reason for his coming to Simpson Creek, risking her disapproval of the lie he had told her father, promising to confess it and apologize for it soon. And he'd confided in her about his arduous growing up, trusting that she wouldn't think less of him for his humble beginnings. He wouldn't do those things unless he cared deeply for her, would he?

"You're smiling," he said, as they neared Gilmore House in the shay. "Penny for your thoughts?"

She opened her mouth to speak as Sarah's words rang in her ears about being in love with love. She quickly tempered her response.

"Oh, I was just thinking what a pleasant afternoon I've had," she said lightly, as if she spent many afternoons so occupied with a variety of adoring swains. No matter what she thought she was feeling for Sam, it was necessary that she keep it to herself and use caution. A little self-protection never hurt anyone.

Chapter Seven

Sam stretched, feeling all his muscles tense and release, before settling into the chair he'd set outside against the jail. He tilted back in it till the front legs came off the ground and the back of it hit the wall. From here, he could keep an eye on most of the town to his right, as well as the church, doctor's office and adjoining house to his left.

He reckoned it was going on six o'clock, but after all that tasty picnic food, he wasn't hungry enough to amble down to the hotel for his supper yet. No, he'd just "set a spell," watching the town settle into early evening—and think about the afternoon.

He couldn't stop the corners of his mouth from turning up as he thought of Prissy. He hadn't imagined in his most optimistic daydreams that the picnic would go as well as it had. Not only had events conspired to allow them to go on the outing without the chaperoning presence of the Walkers, but he had confessed his lie to the lovely lady, and she still seemed to like him. He found her trust in him touching.

He only wished he felt like he'd earned it.

Before coming to Simpson Creek, he'd have thought

the best thing about Prissy's innocence was that she would be easier to woo and win, and thus secure a comfortable life for himself. But now he found himself valuing it for its own sake. He'd felt a certain protectiveness well up in him as they talked and shared their stories.

None of the females he'd spent any time with since leaving Tennessee had cared a lick about his hard upbringing—except that it meant luring him into marriage would not provide them with all the comforts wealth provided. And so his experience with all females besides his sisters had been unsatisfying at best.

But not only had Prissy not thought less of him because his folks had not been the social equals of hers, but she actually appeared to *ache* for the hardships he had endured. And though she'd been quick to realize that his confession meant he had lied to her father in front of her about his reason for coming to Simpson Creek, she hadn't gone all self-righteous on him about it. She'd taken at face value his pledge to make it right with her father.

Would she have been so sweet and understanding, though, if he'd told her the *whole* truth? That he wasn't quite sure he had a relationship with God? That he'd never been a sheriff, that he was nothing but a down-on-his-luck cardsharp, a gambler on the run from a man more unscrupulous than himself? That he had stolen an item of great value from that man? No, probably not. But Kendall Raney would never find him here, and he vowed he'd *become* the man Prissy thought Sam was—honorable, upright and law-abiding.

He was going to settle down in Simpson Creek and be the town's sheriff. He was going to marry Prissy Gilmore just as soon as he could make it happen, and raise up a passel of children with her—little girls with her sweet temperament and prettiness, and boys as wild and fun-loving as he had been, before his parents' death had brought all enjoyment in life to a halt. Yessir, life was going to be good.

The only thing that could make it sweeter was if the Walkers came back early with news of a baby and Sarah Walker allowed him to be the one to go tell Prissy. He wouldn't mind having an excuse to mosey down the street and knock on the Gilmore House door. Maybe he'd stroll by anyway, after he'd taken his dinner at the hotel and checked on the saloon, since the mayor's grand house was so close by. He might find her sitting on the lawn, playing with that rascally dog he'd given her. It would just appear that he was merely a dedicated lawman making his rounds, as the citizens of Simpson Creek had entrusted him to do—not some lovesick fellow who couldn't wait to see her again.

He wondered what his next move in the courtship should be. He could invite her to supper at the hotel. Or perhaps she would stop by the jailhouse with news of some social event that the Spinsters' Club was hosting—or the church.

"You look like a man with happy thoughts on his mind," a voice said, startling him so completely that he nearly lost his balance in the tilting chair. Once he'd righted it with a clatter, he saw that it was Reverend Chadwick who stood there.

"Good evening, Reverend," Sam said, wondering how undignified he'd appeared, nearly falling out of his chair. "Just enjoying the peaceful view of the town, and wondering what was on the menu at the hotel tonight. Anything I can do for you, sir?"

"As a matter of fact, there is. Mrs. Detwiler sent her

son over with some beef stew for my dinner, and there's way too much for me to eat. Might I invite you to share my supper? I'll admit it gets lonely in the parsonage from time to time, and I wouldn't mind some company."

"That's right kind of you, Reverend. I'd be pleased to accept." It would be nice to eat with the preacher rather than alone in the hotel dining room, and maybe he could learn more about the town's inhabitants—especially the mayor and his pretty daughter. There'd be plenty of time afterward to patrol the streets of the town, and maybe still a chance to "accidentally" encounter Prissy.

Supper with the preacher, however, took longer than he had anticipated. Sam discovered the old man was a fount of information and interesting tales about the first settlers of Simpson Creek. He didn't try to lure Sam into a discussion of religion, but he exuded a faith so natural it seemed just like breathing. Sam was surprised to feel a touch of envy at that.

Dark had fallen by the time he thought to look out a window. He thanked the preacher for supper and took his leave. So much for his plan to encounter Prissy. The only person he met was Delbert Perry.

"Evenin', Sheriff!" Delbert called.

"How are you, Delbert?" Sam responded, wondering if he'd already been backsliding and visited the saloon.

"Just fine, thank you. I'm out walkin' and talkin' to the Lord. Keeps me from drinkin'. Fine night, isn't it?"

"It is indeed," Sam said, ashamed at just how wrong his suspicion had been.

Well, if Delbert Perry could change his ways, surely Sam Bishop could become the man he saw reflected back at him in Prissy Gilmore's beautiful blue eyes. How hard could it be?

* * *

Prissy had just awakened the next morning when she heard a rapping at the door, which woke Houston from his slumber at the foot of the bed. He dashed to the door, yapping madly.

Who could that be at such an early hour? Throwing on her wrapper, she dashed to the window, peering discreetly out at first, then poking her head out all the way once she saw it was Sarah.

"Hello, Sarah! Is the baby born?" she called, just as Flora opened the door.

Sarah lifted her head, grinning. "Yes! Come on down, sleepyhead, and I'll tell you all about it in exchange for some coffee."

Prissy splashed some water on her face, then dashed down the stairs, barefoot, with the dog at her heels. She was glad that her rumpled appearance wouldn't matter to Sarah. She found her friend already ensconced in the dining room, with Flora filling her cup.

Sarah looked tired, and she smothered a yawn as Prissy and the dog entered.

"Antonio is at the back door, *señorita,*" Flora said. "He will watch the dog outside while you visit with your friend."

Prissy let the dog out the back door.

"Señora Sarah, you have some good news, eh?" Flora said as Prissy returned to the dining room.

"Is it a boy or a girl?" Prissy asked.

Sarah's grin was broad. "A boy, born at five this morning. They named him Richard Nicholas—Richard for both our papa and Nick's brother the vicar. Nolan guesses he's about seven pounds, maybe seven and a half, and does he ever have a good pair of lungs!"

"Does he have any hair?" Prissy asked, for Nick's hair was as light as his wife's was dark.

"Lots of brown hair."

"And Milly? Is she all right?"

"Fine, though she admits she feels 'a mite wilted.'" Sarah grinned. "She was sound asleep with the baby beside her before we left, and I just came home to sleep awhile. Then I'm going gather up some things and go back to help her for a few days. I just wanted to come and tell you first."

"How wonderful! The Spinsters' Club will have to give a party for her. We can get a wagon to take us all out there with the gifts and refreshments, so she and the baby won't have to go bouncing over the road," Prissy said.

"I'm sure Milly would be thrilled," Sarah said. "Thank goodness I finished crocheting that baby blanket in time. It came out quite nicely, if I do say so myself. I'm glad Mrs. Detwiler could teach me how, so Milly didn't know—" she tried unsuccessfully to smother the yawn that interrupted her sentence "—I was making it. Goodness, I'm a little wilted myself. I can't think when I last stayed up all night."

"You better get home and get some rest. And tell Milly I'll get right to planning the party," Prissy said.

"I will. Poor Nolan, it'll be a while before he can rest. Lulubelle Harding was already waiting in front of the office with all four of her youngsters when we arrived back at the house—says they've all got earaches. I don't doubt they've been putting beans in their ears again."

Prissy barely heard Sarah's last few words, for she was caught up with yearning. How wonderful that must be to share a new baby with a husband who so clearly adored his wife as Nick Brookfield did.

An image of herself holding a newborn, with Sam tenderly bent over her, admiring their child, filled her heart. *Lord, please, I want that—is that Your will for me? Please show me…*

Sarah's chuckle broke into her thoughts.

"You haven't heard a word I've been saying, have you? All right, we'll try a new subject. You haven't told me how the picnic went."

Prissy's grin was all the answer she needed.

Sam had seen the doctor's buggy arriving back in town and had been told the good news by Dr. Walker himself while Sam helped him unhitch the horse. Sam thought he'd go have some breakfast and coffee in the hotel before going to see if Prissy had heard about the birth, but just as he drew abreast of the hotel, the stage pulled up, dust welling in its wake.

"Forty-five-minute stop for those passengers continuing on to Richland Springs," the driver announced as the doors were flung open and the coach disgorged its passengers. Sam paused, honoring his duty as a sheriff to size up any newcomers arriving in town.

None of the half dozen people who descended stiffly into the dusty street, blinking sleepily, looked like desperadoes or cardsharps, however. There was a rumpled woman clutching the hand of a toddler boy who was intent on investigating a butterfly that had landed at the edge of a puddle; a middle-aged man and wife; a drummer with a big, black sample case; and a dapperly dressed man in a bowler that matched his light gray trousers and frock coat. He carried a silver-headed cane and looked as weary as the others, but Sam saw his eyes fasten on the tin star and his face brightened.

"Ah, the sheriff," he said, squinting in Sam's direction and indicating him with the end of his cane. "I wonder if I might have a word with you, sir?" The man's flat, nasal accent marked him as an easterner. There was a certain rankling imperiousness about his gesture, as if he were summoning a lackey, but perhaps, Sam considered, he was too tired from the long, jolting journey to remember his manners.

Sam straightened from the hitching rail he had been leaning against behind the coach. "Sure. What can I do for you, mister?" Sam asked, coming forward and extending his hand. "I'm Sam Bishop, sheriff of Simpson Creek."

The man shot a look at him as if surprised Sam thought his name was important. Then he feigned not to see Sam's extended hand and busied himself with brushing the dust of his travels off his coat.

"William Waters—William Waters the *Third,* to be exact. I'm here to claim my inheritance, and thought you might be able to direct me."

"Your inheritance?" Sam asked, wishing he'd been in town long enough to know what the man was talking about.

A huff of impatience erupted from Waters. "I'm speaking of the Waters Ranch, of course, just out of town. I'm the late William Waters's heir—his nephew, in point of fact. The bank president notified me of his death late last fall, and I'm finally able to come look over my property with an eye to moving here and enlarging the house. Naturally I must see it—and the town—before I consider living here."

"I see. Welcome to Simpson Creek, Mr. Waters," Sam said. He was glad he'd had supper with the preacher last night, for he'd told Sam about Milly and Nick Brookfield's erstwhile neighbor, the late Bill Waters. Waters had been an unpleasant, unscrupulous neighbor, and had caused Milly and Nick much trouble before being killed in the last Comanche raid. Since then his land had sat empty, and Nick Brookfield had been trying to scrape together enough money to buy it and join Waters's land to his.

It seemed Brookfield was to be disappointed, if William Waters the Third indeed stayed and made a go of the place. He couldn't quite picture the man before him as a rancher, but he supposed time would tell.

"Well, can you direct me to the property or not?" Waters snapped. "I would have thought a man in your position—" he narrowed his gaze on the tin star meaningfully "—knowledgeable about such things."

"Mr. Waters, as it happens, I'm new in town myself, this being only my fourth day to wear this badge," Sam said, keeping his tone matter-of-fact and nonapologetic, "but I'm told the Waters ranch lies about five miles outside of town out that road, yonder." He pointed. "You must be tired and hungry, though, after your long trip. Why don't you go in and have yourself some breakfast, as I mean to do, and then you can make arrangements to hire a mount to go out and see the place?"

The man glanced toward the hotel just as the door opened and the smell of frying bacon came wafting out from the restaurant like the olfactory equivalent of a beckoning siren.

"Perhaps that would be best," Waters agreed, his tone more conciliatory. "Would you care to join me, Sheriff? And perhaps you'd be good enough to accompany me on my tour of inspection? I fear I'm not an accomplished horseman, nor do I have a great sense of direction…"

Sam agreed to both. While he didn't have any real desire

to ride out of town with this easterner, it was probably his duty as a sheriff to make sure the man didn't get lost or come to any harm.

Looks like he'd have to postpone that visit to Prissy—again.

Prissy trudged back down Simpson Creek's main street toward Gilmore House, Houston at her heels. It was only noon, and she had already sent Antonio with a note to the Brookfield ranch to ask when Milly would like the Spinsters' Club to visit with gifts for the new baby, and she had just finished notifying the rest of the club's members about the birth and the proposed outing.

She felt at loose ends. Sarah was at the ranch helping her sister. Papa was at a council meeting. Sam Bishop wasn't at the jail, nor had she seen him in the street.

Where could he be? Off at one of the nearby ranches on some duty? Or at the hotel, having his dinner? She wouldn't be so brazen as to go into the restaurant to look, but if she were to happen past the restaurant window, surely if he were there he'd see her and come out to ask her to join him. She had to admit she'd worn a dress of yellow sprigged muslin with a pretty shawl collar and had taken special care with her appearance, hoping she'd encounter him. She wasn't quite sure if that was a good thing—or a bad thing.

She could see no one in the restaurant as she glanced in the window. She might as well go home and have her own midday meal. The day had become uncomfortably warm, anyway. She turned to step off the boardwalk.

"Oh, Priscilla! How nice to encounter you, dear," called a voice.

No one called her Priscilla. No one but the Widow

Fairchild. She stiffened as she turned and saw Mariah Fairchild coming out of the hotel. It wasn't fair that the woman had the perfect ivory complexion that made her look fragile and appealing in the dove-gray dress she wore, instead of washed out, nor that her elegantly dressed silver hair gleamed so that it complemented the gray dress rather than made her look old.

"Hello, Mrs. Fairchild," Prissy said, keeping her voice civil.

Houston, traitor that he was, had no such reservations. He went bounding toward the widow, practically wagging his tail off, lunging at the end of the leash as if he would perish if he could not get closer to this lady.

Mariah Fairchild stooped with grace, heedless of the dusty boardwalk, and stroked the little dog's head. She cooed, "Well, aren't you a handsome fellow? What a *good* boy! What a friendly doggie you are!"

Was that a way of covertly criticizing Prissy's own lack of warmth? "Yes, Houston doesn't know a stranger," Prissy murmured, wondering how quickly she could escape the woman without seeming openly rude.

Mariah Fairchild shaded her eyes and peered up at Prissy. "It's fortuitous that you happened by, dear. I was just hoping for a second opinion on some lace trim at the mercantile, as to whether it looks well with a particular dress fabric there or not. Mrs. Patterson is of the opinion it would be fine, but since she doesn't know me very well, I fear she's afraid to counter my opinion…"

And you think I know you well?

"Would you have a moment to accompany me to the mercantile to give your honest thoughts on the matter?"

You don't really want to know my honest thoughts, Prissy thought waspishly, but then was ashamed of herself.

It was very apparent the woman wanted Prissy to like her. Satisfying her request wouldn't take much time, and perhaps the shopkeeper would have an item Prissy could buy for Milly's baby gift, since she wasn't talented—as many of the other Spinsters were—in needlework.

"Certainly, I can do that," she said, watching as Mariah Fairchild gracefully straightened. They descended the boardwalk and crossed the side street that separated the hotel from the mercantile, and after Prissy scooped up the dog lest he get into mischief, they went inside.

"Hello, Mrs. Patterson," Mariah Fairchild called out breezily. "I'm back with Priscilla to give her opinion on that fabric and lace trim. I just cannot seem to make up my mind."

"Sure, Mrs. Fairchild, here it is," Mrs. Patterson said, turning around to reach on the shelf behind her for the bolt of cloth. "I kept them right up here, since you said you'd be back."

Now *that* was how a widow should dress, Prissy thought, eyeing the shopkeeper in her serviceable black skirt and waist. Mrs. Patterson had also lost her spouse in the flu epidemic this last winter. She spoke of him constantly. She certainly wasn't one who would put off her mourning clothes prematurely.

"Here's the lace I was speaking of, Priscilla dear," Mrs. Fairchild was saying, holding a card of ivory lace against the bolt of mauve. "What do you think? Please give me your honest opinion."

Prissy narrowed her gaze. There was nothing wrong with the combination, certainly, as far as its effect on the eye. But perhaps she might be able to discreetly hint about the proper behavior for a widow.

"You must do as you like, of course—this is just my

opinion—but perhaps the black lace, there—" she indicated another card standing upright on the shelf "—might be a more suitable choice," she said.

Mariah Fairchild blinked and gave Prissy a swift, sidelong glance. "Do you think so? Hmm," she said, as Mrs. Patterson held out the card of black lace to her. "Perhaps the black *is* more dignified, I suppose, for a woman of my years. I knew you could guide me, Priscilla! Thank you!" All of a sudden she reached out and enfolded Prissy in an impulsive hug. "Oh, I'm so glad I asked you! I'll take it, Mrs. Patterson. And I should have a look at your *Godey's* to see how I'd like to have this made up. Prissy, I don't suppose you would know a good seamstress, would you? I had a modiste back in Austin, but—" she shrugged with a smile —"I'm here now…"

And here she was determined to stay, the woman meant. Here in Simpson Creek, pursuing Prissy's father.

Prissy assumed a regretful expression. "Milly Brookfield is wonderfully talented as a seamstress, but she just had a baby, so I suppose it will be a while before she's taking on any sewing."

"Oh, but I've heard that Mrs. Menendez over by the fort is very good, too, and quite reasonable, Mrs. Fairchild," Mrs. Patterson put in. "It's the small white clapboard house right opposite the fort, just behind the bank."

"Perfect," Mariah Fairchild purred. "I'll go see her right after I pick out a style for her to copy. Prissy, since you have such good taste, would you like to look at *Godey's* with me, then accompany me to Mrs. Menendez's?"

Despite Mariah Fairchild's friendliness, the very last thing Prissy wanted to do this afternoon was dance attendance on this woman who was so blatantly setting her cap for her father. "Actually, Mrs. Fairchild—"

"Oh, please, call me Mariah, dear. No need to stand on ceremony."

"Mariah, then. I have some things to do at home this afternoon, and I need to purchase a baby present for Milly while I'm here, so perhaps I'd better get on with that," she said, and breathed a sigh of relief when the widow accepted her excuse and wandered over to a table where past issues of *Godey's,* full of patterns and dresses were displayed.

"What a nice lady," Mrs. Patterson declared in a whisper when Mariah was out of earshot. "So genteel! I believe she said she and her late husband grew up with your father, dear?"

"Mmm-hmm," Prissy murmured noncommittally. "May I see that silver cup and rattle on that upper shelf to your left? I believe that would make a lovely gift for Milly's baby, don't you?" The very last thing she wanted to do was fuel any gossip about her father and the widow.

She sighed as she realized how ungracious she was being. But she simply couldn't help herself. What if Mariah Fairchild's intentions were purely financial? She couldn't simply stand by and let her father be taken advantage of, could she?

She suddenly found herself thinking of Sam Bishop. Was it possible…that he had less than honorable intentions? Was she being a fool?

It wouldn't be the first time her trusting nature had gotten her in trouble, that was for sure.

Chapter Eight

William Waters III—or the Tenderfoot, as Sam had begun to call him in his mind—hadn't exaggerated about his inability as a horseman. As a result, it had been a long and tedious five miles out to his late uncle's ranch. Waters had fallen off his horse when the beast shied at a jackrabbit, forcing Sam to chase after his mount, and after that the man refused to go above a trot. Sam had hoped to give his horse Jackson some exercise during the outing, but it was plain that Waters was not up to enjoying a good gallop.

Finally they passed the arching gateway that read "Brookfield Ranch." He'd have much preferred to be paying a call on the Englishman, his wife and new baby with Prissy instead of riding alongside the fussy, nervous easterner, but there would be time for that another day.

Coming to Waters's inherited property, they trotted up the rutted drive to the ranch house. As they drew closer, Sam saw the man's jaw drop and his eyes widen. Panes of glass had been broken out of the windows, though jagged shards still remained in the bottom of the frames. The door hung loose on its hinges. Inside, scorch marks scored the floor and walls. An arrow was still lodged incongruously in a cushion on a horsehair sofa. A stain on the tile floor-ing looked suspiciously like blood. Waters stared fixedly at it. Had that been where the man's uncle had died?

It was evident that vermin had taken shelter in the house, and from the charred remains of a broken-up chair in the fireplace, Sam judged rodents were not the only creatures who had used the empty dwelling.

"This is appalling. It will never do," muttered Waters, his whiny, nasal accent grating against Sam's ears. "I had assumed I would be able to move right in, but obviously I shall have to put up in the hotel until this can be rectified. Would you happen to know some workmen who could start right away?"

Sam scratched the back of his head. "You could prob-ably ask at the lumber mill." Had the man really expected the house would be pristine, after a Comanche attack and months of neglect?

"I shall have to have funds transferred to the bank. I don't suppose this backwater boasts a telegraph?"

"It does," Sam countered, rankled at the man's dispar-agement of his town. Then he chuckled at his possessive-ness of the town he had come to so recently.

Waters bristled. "I wasn't aware I said anything amus-ing, Sheriff."

Sam rubbed a forefinger and thumb down his face as if to smooth away his smile. "You didn't, Mr. Waters, your question just made me think of something else. You'll find the telegraph office between the bank and the barbershop."

"Fine, fine." Once again, he pulled out his pocket watch and studied it. "We'd better start back. I don't suppose you could provide an introduction to the mayor, could you? It would be well to establish my credentials with him, I suppose. And perhaps *he* could expedite the renovation of this place," he added, wrinkling his lip as he took a last disgusted look at the disarray. Then he turned on his heel and stalked outside.

The pompous, little banty rooster. Did he think Mayor Gilmore was going to take charge of the project? He nearly lit into the man until he realized that escorting Waters to the house might afford him the opportunity to see Prissy.

"I'd be happy to make that introduction," Sam said. He glanced at the sun's position in the sky. By the time they returned and rode to the mayor's house at the dismally slow pace Waters insisted on, it would be late enough that Sam might be able to wrangle a supper invitation.

But it was not to be. They were passing the side of the saloon just as somebody was hurled out of the batwing doors in front, landing with a great splash in the horse trough. The fellow erupted from the trough with a bellow of rage, spraying water in a radius of several feet, and went charging back through the swinging doors, his clothes streaming water as he went.

"Would you look at that!" exclaimed the tenderfoot, as if Sam could have missed it. "Is such ruffianly behavior common in this town?"

Sam sighed and smothered a pithy reply. "The mayor's house is over yonder," he said, pointing. "I'm afraid you're going to have to go introduce yourself, Mr. Waters." He reined his mount toward the front of the saloon instead. It seemed his partner at supper was going to be some liquored-up rowdy cowboy, rather than Prissy.

Parting the doors of the saloon, Sam took a moment to allow his eyes to adjust to the smoke-filled light and to take stock of the situation in front of him. He dearly hoped he wouldn't have to do any shooting this time—or any fistfighting. His ribs still ached from Raney's beating, and the laceration on his cheek was finally almost healed.

Two men—or rather, one stocky man and a Mexican youth barely old enough to use a razor—rolled around on the floor, punching and clawing at each other. As he watched, the older man gained the ascendancy and, squatting on the boy, rained blow after blow on him, the blows landing with sickening thuds against the boy's face and trunk. Sam leaped forward to grab the back of the older man's shirt and drag him off the younger combatant.

The man turned on Sam, eyes wild, clearly intending to punish Sam in turn, but he found himself looking into the barrel of Sam's Colt.

"Stop right there, mister," Sam said, keeping his eyes trained on the panting, glaring man before him, who still looked as if he might do something foolhardy, in spite of Sam's cocked pistol and his clearly visible badge. Behind them, the boy scrambled up from the floor, his chest heaving, wiping his bloody nose on the ripped sleeve of his shirt. It had been the youth whom Sam had seen thrown into the horse trough.

"All right, you want to tell me why you were whaling the tar out of that boy?" Sam demanded. "You'd better have a mighty good reason, or you're going to jail."

The wild glare vanished from the man's eyes and a defiant smirk settled over his heavy features. He opened his mouth to speak, but before he could, the boy he'd been beating stepped forward.

"This man, he insulted my honor, Señor Sheriff," the boy claimed. "And the honor of my family. I could not call myself a man if I allowed that to go unanswered."

"What'd he say to you?" Sam asked the boy without

taking his eyes off the smirking man he still held his pistol on.

"He called me a dirty greaser," he said, his voice hoarse with rage. "He said he did not think he should have to drink with my 'kind' in the saloon. And when I told him I had a right to be in here as much as he did, he said filthy things about my sister—things that are not true!"

"That's a fact, Sheriff," George Detwiler confirmed from behind the bar. "I ain't never had a problem with Luis Menendez passin' time here—he pays for his drinks like anyone else. This stranger comes in and starts tellin' him he's gotta leave 'cause he's Mexican. I tried to point out it's my saloon and my rules, but this feller starts jawin' about Luis's sister, who he ain't even met."

The man sniggered. "I wouldn't be too sure about that. I think she left just before this Mex came in. She told me not to tell the kid she works upstairs here. What's her name, greaser? Rosita? Lucita?" Before he could even get the words out, Luis launched himself at the man again, managing to knock him down by dint of sheer surprise—aided, no doubt, by the whiskey the stranger had consumed.

Limbs flailing, the man lost his balance, then fell heavily on his side, and before Sam could intervene, the boy had grabbed a spittoon and brought it down on the back of the man's head. The man sagged and went limp.

Sam studied the prone figure, then raised his gaze to Luis. "You'd better hope he doesn't die."

The youth straightened, his dark eyes meeting Sam's without flinching. "I would go to the gallows proudly for killing this poor excuse for an *hombre,* Señor Sheriff."

Just then George stepped from behind the pecan-wood bar with a coiled length of rope in one hand and a glass pitcher full of water with the other. Before Sam could guess his intent, he upended the pitcher on the fallen man's head.

The stranger came instantly awake, raising up on his elbows, sputtering and wiping water out of his eyes and blowing it out of his nose.

"See? He ain't dead," George said. "Ya might wanta use that rope to tie him up, though, afore he collects hisself."

While Sam bent to do as the saloonkeeper suggested, George spoke again. "Like I said, he started the whole thing, insultin' Luis here, then talkin' nasty about his sister. There ain't a nicer young girl in Simpson Creek than Luis's sister Juana. She cain't be but what...fifteen, Miss Prissy?" he asked, looking over Sam's shoulder.

"Yes, that's right," she said.

Sam jerked his head around and saw her framed in the doorway. "What are you doing here?" he said, turning around again to keep an eye on the man still sputtering on the floor. "You shouldn't be in here."

He heard her chuckle. "I'm only standing in the doorway, but I've known George Detwiler and his mama for years, haven't I, George?"

"That's a fact, Miss Prissy," confirmed the barkeeper.

"And I just came in because I happened to be coming out of the house just as Luis was thrown in the horse trough, and then I saw you go in. Naturally, I was concerned."

"Naturally, she was concerned," mimicked the man on the floor. "That yer sweetheart, Sheriff?" he asked with a snigger.

"Shut up," Sam snapped, putting his boot squarely on the man's neck. "Miss Prissy, please, you'd better go," he said without looking at her. He was touched by her worry over both him and the boy but was too savvy to give the man on the floor less than his full attention. The stranger had enough fight left in him to take advantage of it.

He knew Prissy had done as he asked when he heard a swishing sound as the batwing doors swung closed and the light within the saloon dimmed again. Pulling on the rope that bound the man's wrists together, Sam hauled the man on the floor to his feet.

"Now, what's your name, stranger?"

"Tolliver," the man snarled. "Leroy Tolliver."

Now that he had the time to study him, Sam could see that Tolliver had taken some damage from the altercation as well as dished it out—a bruise here, a cut there, several scrapes. "You just passing through, Tolliver? 'Cause I suggest you get back on your horse and ride on. After you spend the night in jail, that is."

"Spend the night in jail?" the man demanded, his face incredulous. "What for? For teachin' a greaser where he don't belong?"

"For disturbing the peace and assault. Come along," he said, shoving the man ahead of him toward the door. "You, too, Luis."

"*Sì*, Señor Sheriff," the youth said. "You do not need to tie me."

Sam turned back in surprise. "You're not under arrest, Luis. I just want to talk to you."

Hampered by his bonds and the whiskey he had consumed, Tolliver stumbled and would have fallen if Sam hadn't rushed forward and steadied him. Keeping a hand on the rope between the man's wrists, Sam marched his charge down the street toward the jail.

"I ain't no drifter," Tolliver muttered as he trudged along. "I work for the Alliance bosses."

Sam stiffened. "'The Alliance?'" he echoed. That was the group the mayor had been concerned about, wasn't it?

"Yeah, the Ranchers' Alliance. The ones who're gonna be runnin' this county soon enough," Tolliver said with a sneer. "My bosses ain't gonna be happy 'bout you puttin' me in jail, Sheriff."

"Then you shouldn't have assaulted the young man."

"You'll be hearin' from my bosses," the man boasted. "You'll be regrettin' puttin' me behind bars, directly."

"Is that so," Sam said flatly. "Are you threatening me, Tolliver?"

"Me? Naw. But you don't wanna offend the men of the Alliance. I'm thinkin' you won't be wearin' that badge much longer, once they take over."

By this time, they had reached the jail. Leaving Luis outside, Sam lost no time pushing Tolliver into one of the cells and locking the door behind him. "Make yourself comfortable," he told him, then rejoined Luis.

"*Gracias* for not arresting me, Señor Sheriff," the boy said, as soon as the heavy door creaked shut behind Sam. "*Mi madre*—my mother—she would be so ashamed."

"My name's Sam Bishop," he said, extending a hand. "Defending yourself isn't wrong, Luis."

Luis shook his hand, still acting as if he couldn't believe his good fortune.

"You know anything about what Tolliver was babbling about? This Ranchers' Alliance?"

The young man hesitated, then said, "There have been many strangers in town in the last few days, Señor Sheriff. Wealthy-looking men, as well as *vagabundos*—how do you say it? Drifters, saddle tramps. They do not have the look of honest men, Señor Bishop. A couple of them have been swaggering around the saloon—Tolliver is one. His *compadre* bothered a woman who serves drinks there. Señor Detwiler sent her home early so the men could not bother her. The other man left before Tolliver started insulting me, *señor*. And I've heard wealthy men have been buying land from whoever they could frighten into selling it."

It jibed with what the mayor had told him. Sam wished once again he weren't so new to town that he couldn't differentiate between a stranger and a longtime resident. Sounds like he needed to keep his eyes and ears open.

"Thanks, Luis."

"It is my honor to assist you, Señor Bishop."

"Could I ask you for a couple of favors? I'd like you to wait while I write a note to Miss Gilmore, then take it to her home. And would you be willing to fetch supper from the hotel for me and that sidewinder in there?" he asked, nodding toward the jail behind him. "I want to keep an eye on him." He reached into his pocket and came out with four bits. "Here. For your trouble. And the information."

The boy shook his head. "I thank you, Sheriff, but it is not necessary. The old sheriff, he would have thrown *me* in the cell, not the other *hombre*. I will wait for your note, and then bring your meals. Though why that man deserves to eat, I do not know."

Sam went inside and quickly wrote a message to Prissy, explaining that he had a prisoner in his cell and would pay a call on her tomorrow if possible. He hoped she would read between the lines and not come to the jail to visit. He didn't want Tolliver laying his beady eyes on Prissy any more than he already had. The last thing Sam needed was for a man like Tolliver to think the sheriff had a weak spot.

He was going to have to make some inquiries about town

to see if anyone else had been harassed by this Ranchers' Alliance, as Luis said. If Tolliver's bragging was anything to go by, the Alliance certainly wouldn't benefit the good people of Simpson Creek.

When he returned outside with the note, Luis said, "Señor Sheriff, would you consider hiring me as your deputy? I would be honored to serve you."

He had to smile at the boy's earnestness. "Luis, I've just been hired myself. It doesn't seem like the sheriff of this town has enough to do to require a permanent deputy—at least right now," he added, when he saw disappointment in the youth's dark eyes.

"Sheriff Bishop, trouble is coming. You may change your mind," Luis said.

Sam considered his words. "You may be right," he admitted. "But I have to hope you're wrong."

Chapter Nine

"You want some coffee, Tolliver?" Sam asked the next morning, coming into the jail from his quarters. "I'm going down to the hotel for some."

The cowboy he'd arrested yesterday at the saloon clutched the bars of his cell and glared at him. "Naw, I just want outta here."

Sam paused. "You got the five dollars for the fine for disturbing the peace?"

"I told you I didn't yesterday. It ain't likely any money miraculously appeared in my pocket overnight."

Sam went past him toward the door. "Then you can wait till I've had my coffee." Surely he'd be able to tolerate the man's surliness once he'd had some coffee. If the man continued to insist he had no money, Sam would have to figure out some other way to penalize him for the incident yesterday. But either way, he was going to have to release him this morning.

Just as he reached the door, however, it was pulled open from the outside. A narrow-faced fellow stood there, medium height, his chin sporting a black goatee. He wore a rust-colored frock coat with a waistcoat of some sort of shiny black cloth with a gold watch chain draped conspicuously across it. His eyes were small and amber. The cumulative effect of his clothes and features put Sam in mind of a red fox.

He doffed his hat and entered with a sinuous grace.

"Good morning, Sheriff Bishop. I believe you have something of mine." His small amber eyes looked over Sam's shoulder at the man in the cell.

"I don't think we've met, sir," Sam said, and waited. This fellow wasn't one of the many people he had met at church on Sunday.

"Garth Pennington," the man said, bowing with a sardonic smile that was devoid of real friendliness. "And this ugly fellow behind you is one of my employees. What's he done?"

"The charge is disturbing the peace. Specifically, he assaulted a young man in the saloon who'd done nothing to provoke it. And he was additionally responsible for some broken glass."

"He weren't nothin' but a dirty greaser," Tolliver muttered.

Sam waited to see if Pennington would consider that a valid excuse, but if the man felt that way, he was too clever to admit it.

Pennington tsk-tsked in Tolliver's direction. "My apologies for my employee's actions, Sheriff. What's the fine? Naturally, I'll accept responsibility for what my employee did, and whatever it was won't happen again. Did you hear that, Tolliver?" His voice cracked like an expertly wielded whip.

"Yes, boss." The man's tone was docile enough to fool most people. Not Sam.

"Five dollars," Sam said, and was not surprised when

Pennington reached into his coat pocket, pulled out a gold half eagle, and handed it to him.

"Very well," he said, putting the coin into the center drawer of his desk until he could ask the mayor what was done with such fines. He pulled out the ring of keys from the drawer, then walked over and inserted the longest one into the cell door lock, turning clockwise until the door opened.

Tolliver walked out, smirking at Sam.

"How'd you know where to find him, Mr. Pennington?" Sam inquired.

Pennington's lips thinned. "A lucky guess. Leroy has a weakness for strong drink, don't you, Leroy?"

Tolliver's cocky grin vanished. "Yes, boss."

"So naturally, the saloon is the first place I looked when he didn't return last evening." Pennington turned back to Tolliver. "I trust your accommodations were…sufficiently *uncomfortable*—" Pennington glanced meaningfully into the cell, where the rumpled sheets on the cot and dirty plate, knife, fork and spoon on the floor were mute testimony of his recent occupation "—that you will not wish to repeat the experience anytime soon? If you wish to remain in my employ, that is." He laid a hand on Tolliver's shoulder, and Sam saw him push the man toward the door.

"You have a ranch around here, Mr. Pennington?" he asked, pretending the mayor hadn't already told him about it.

Pennington paused. "Yes, *La Alianza,* southwest of here, between Simpson Creek and Colorado Bend," He raised a brow as if surprised that Bishop had had to ask. "We're adding to our acreage every day—not just in that direction, but all around here. We enjoy a cordial relationship with the sheriff in Colorado Bend—I trust it will be the same with you, Sheriff Bishop."

Sam knew enough Spanish to know *La Alianza* meant "The Alliance." So "we" must refer to the bosses of this Ranchers' Alliance. He met the cold amber stare. "As long as you and your men are law-abiding, I don't see why we can't get along."

"You'll have to come out and pay us a visit sometime, Sheriff," Pennington said, gesturing broadly with his black-trimmed hat before he put it back over his oiled black hair. "I think you'll be very impressed."

"Perhaps I will." *If only to see what you're up to.*

The door closed behind him. For all of his genial cordiality, something about Pennington reminded Sam of Kendall Raney.

He sighed. No matter how far one rode, it seemed there were disagreeable men who wielded some sort of power. He had no proof as yet that Pennington used it to do more than buy up land—nothing except an apprehension that snaked around his spine and rattled in his brain like a diamondback.

He thought briefly of William Waters III, and wondered if he was part of the Alliance. If so, would he use his ownership of the land next to the Brookfields to pressure the Brookfields to sell out? Somehow, though, he doubted the easterner was one of the Alliance bosses. He was irritable and arrogant, but there'd been nothing sinister about him. Perhaps his disagreeableness had been nothing more than the fatigue of travel coupled with the disappointment of finding the ranch in such a deplorable condition.

Sam raked a hand through his hair. He still needed that cup of coffee, and once he'd had it and a bit of breakfast to go with it, perhaps he'd mosey down to Gilmore House and report his conversation with Pennington to the mayor. And he'd see Prissy, which would automatically make the world sunnier.

However, as soon as he stepped out of the hotel, he was stopped by Mrs. Detwiler, who was distraught because she'd found a stray goat eating her prized roses.

"Look at that beast. She's eaten the blooms off every one of them," the elderly lady moaned after Sam accompanied her home and caught the goat.

"Any idea who owns the critter?" he asked, hoping he wasn't going to have to ask from house to house, towing the pale-eyed brown and white nanny goat.

"Oh, it's the Menendezes' goat. They live down the road yonder. You tell Mrs. Menendez if I catch that goat in my garden again, I'll be serving *cabrito* for supper," she threatened.

"Yes, ma'am," Sam said, smothering a smile at the old woman's militant tone, and turned to lead the goat away.

"Thank you, Sheriff. Why don't you come back for supper tonight? Say, six o'clock."

"Oh, you don't have to do that, Mrs. Detwiler, I'm happy to help you." He didn't want the old lady to think she had to feed him just for doing his job. And he'd been hoping to spend the evening with Prissy.

"Horsefeathers. It's the least I can do to thank you. And bring Prissy, why don't you. You two make a handsome couple."

Ah, so word of their picnic had made its way around town after all. He wondered how Prissy would feel about that. "Why, thank you, ma'am, I'll accept," he said. "I'll go ask her as soon as I take this critter home."

He could only hope that she'd be pleased people thought of them as a "handsome couple," and not embarrassed.

There was only one way to find out.

Milly Brookfield sent a note back with Antonio telling Prissy that next Wednesday afternoon would be fine for the Spinsters' Club visit to meet the new baby, so Prissy went to spread the word to the members. She went first to the post office to see Caroline Wallace, hoping she could talk Milly's friend into making her famous peach punch to take to the party.

"I suppose I could," Caroline said in the lifeless monotone she'd used ever since her fiancé had passed away. She still wore the deep black mourning clothes she'd worn to his funeral service.

Prissy's heart twisted with pity for the girl. To have met the man you wanted to spend your life with, only to lose him to the same fever that had taken your mother, was a tragedy indeed.

"It'll be good for you to get out and visit, Caroline," Prissy told her, and hoped she didn't sound patronizing. "Milly especially hoped you'd come. How have you been?"

Caroline shrugged. "Fine." But her gaze strayed away from Prissy's as if she knew Prissy would see through the lie.

An uncomfortable silence fell between them like a heavy gray curtain. Prissy wondered what to say. If she could only remember the condolences others had spoken to her and her father right after her mother's death, she'd have the right words.

Should she prattle about the weather? There was nothing new to converse about there—it was hot and sunny as always. Should she even *try* to penetrate the melancholy that Caroline wore around her like an all-enveloping shield, and assure her from her own personal experience that time would heal her wound? But who had the right to say what would heal another's heart? Caroline might take offense.

Jesus, help her, she prayed, watching Caroline staring at her fingers as if she wished Prissy would go now that she'd accomplished her mission. *Please, Lord, bring joy into her life again. Show me how I can help her. Teach me what to say.*

"Well, I'd better be on my way to tell the other ladies," Prissy said, eager to return to the sunshine outside. "We'll meet at my house Saturday at one o'clock, all right? Antonio will drive the wagon—"

"Prissy, you mustn't worry about me," Caroline said suddenly, just as Prissy was turning to go. "I'll be all right. And I've got news—I'm to be the new schoolteacher this fall."

"New schoolteacher? But what about Miss Phelps?"

"She's going to India to be a missionary," Caroline announced. "She wanted to go before, but she didn't want to leave the Simpson Creek children teacherless. I…I decided I would be their teacher."

Prissy felt her jaw drop. "You, a teacher?"

Caroline lifted her chin. "Why not? I was valedictorian of my class, remember?"

Prissy smothered a smile. Caroline's class had consisted of six boys and girls, counting Caroline, but Caroline had been hands-down the smartest. "Why of course, Caroline. That's wonderful news."

"And since I'll never have children of my own now, I'll

have all the Simpson Creek children as mine this way, don't you see?"

"Never have children?" Prissy echoed. "But Caroline, it's too early for you to say something like that—"

Caroline's face turned to stone. She put up a hand as if it was a wall. "No. It's just not to be."

Prissy heard the door creak open behind them and was relieved—until Houston growled.

"Ah, can it be the fair Miss Gilmore? What a happy chance I find you here."

Prissy could barely smother a groan and smooth her features before she turned around to face William Waters—or "William Waters the Third," as he pretentiously referred to himself, as if he were one in a line of kings. He'd been a guest at supper last night. He'd stayed an interminable time, rambling on and on in an obvious attempt to impress them with his fancy house back East and his plans to make his late uncle's ranch the showplace of San Saba county. He'd pretended to admire her dog, until Houston's bared teeth made it clear the feeling wasn't mutual, then flirted clumsily with Prissy, oblivious to her father's glares, until she'd finally excused herself with a headache.

"Oh! Mr. Waters, good morning." A lady was always polite.

He made a great show of consulting his ornate gold pocket watch. "Why, it's a minute after noon, Miss Gilmore," he said. "If I may be so bold as to correct such a beauteous young lady—"

"Good afternoon, then. Heavens, I'm late for dinner. You obviously have a letter to mail," she said, nodding toward the envelope he held, "so I won't hold you up."

She turned back to Caroline just in time to see a smile quirking her lips upward. She was glad Caroline could smile at *something,* even if it was "William Waters the Third."

"Nonsense, I can mail this any time," he assured her. "You must allow me to escort you, Miss Gilmore. I had thought of another question for your father in any case." With an air of gallantry, he placed her hand over his arm.

"But—" For heaven's sake, how was she to escape this man? She threw a desperate look over her shoulder at Caroline, but the postmaster's daughter only flashed a sympathetic smile.

Waters led her out the door, still smiling down at her like a fond suitor.

And he would have walked straight into Sam Bishop, if the sheriff hadn't agilely stepped aside.

What was the annoying tenderfoot doing escorting Prissy anywhere? Clearly Sam should not have been so quick to point the man in the mayor's direction. Houston, walking at Prissy's side, looked none too happy, but wagged his tail when he saw Sam.

"Excuse me—" Waters began, then his eyes widened in recognition. "Oh, Sheriff Bishop! Good morning to you!" The man fairly beamed, obviously proud at being seen with the most beautiful girl in Simpson Creek on his arm.

He didn't have a clue about the anger that surged within Sam at the sight of them.

"Mr. Waters. Miss Prissy." He touched his hat brim respectfully at Prissy and saw the discomfort in those blue eyes. Not unease at being seen with a rival beau, but a plea for rescue. His jealousy subsided.

"I was just escorting Miss Gilmore back to her home,"

Waters announced importantly, and began to pull Prissy around Sam on the boardwalk. The little dog growled as Waters came near Sam.

Sam moved into Waters's path. "Actually, I'll be happy to take over that duty, as the mayor and I are dining together—town business to conduct, you understand." He kept his tone polite but firm, and stared down Waters until the man looked away.

"Actually, I needed to speak to him, too—"

"I'm sure he'll be happy to make time for you, sir. Later." He looked at Prissy, and was pleased to see the relief flooding her face as she let go of Waters's arm and took his. He was happy to be her rescuer.

"But—"

"Good day, Mr. Waters," she called over her shoulder as they set off down the boardwalk in the direction of Gilmore House, the dog trotting happily with them, his tail carried jauntily aloft.

"Oh, Sam, thank heaven you appeared just now!" she exclaimed when they were out of earshot. "I couldn't seem to get away from that tiresome man! He found me in the post office and just took over!"

He grinned down at her. "I was hoping you wouldn't mind if I cut in, so to speak."

"Mind?" Her laughter was music to his ears. "You were an answer to a prayer, Sam! Mr. Waters came to the house to speak to Papa last night, stayed until politeness dictated we invite him for supper, then stayed forever! Houston almost bit him once," she said, then smothered a giggle.

"They say dogs are good judges of character," Sam said. "Good boy."

The dog looked up, panting happily, and gave a yip as if he understood perfectly.

"I was afraid he was going to offer to take you to dinner at the hotel, since I would be busy with your father," Sam confessed with a laugh. "I'd have had to come up with another reason for you to be there, too, if he had."

"I want you to know, Sam, I gave him *no* reason to behave so familiarly with me," Prissy said, shuddering.

He patted her hand on his arm with his free hand. "I'm glad to hear that, sweetheart." The endearment came out naturally, as if he'd been calling her that for a long time. She blinked, then blushed. His sweet Texas rose—what a lucky chance that had brought him to this town!

"I actually *do* need to speak to your father, Prissy," he said.

"Consider yourself officially invited to eat with us, then."

He nodded. "And I have the pleasure of informing *you* we've been invited for supper by Mrs. Detwiler." He told her about having to capture the goat who'd eaten the old lady's roses.

"Oh, dear," murmured Prissy, amused. "Mrs. Menendez is lucky Mrs. Detwiler's mellowed so much. She used to guard those roses with a shotgun. But why has she invited us—together, I mean?"

Sam smiled. "Apparently she thinks we make quite a handsome couple."

To his great delight, Prissy blushed again. He was beginning to think he could spend his whole life making Priscilla Gilmore blush.

Prissy watched her father's brow furrow with concern when Sam told him about meeting Garth Pennington and the sullen mutterings of Tolliver about the Ranchers' Alliance.

"I've heard of several families leaving the area," her father said, "and I've met Pennington. Invited himself into one of our council meetings, just before you came, Sam. Full of hot air and importance he was, rattling on about his partnership with two powerful men of influence from Houston—"

A cloud passed over Sam's face and was gone so swiftly Prissy couldn't even be sure she had seen it. Was he remembering something unpleasant that had happened to him in Houston? Did it have anything to do with the cut that was still visible on his cheek, and the way he winced when he moved sometimes?

"—men who were going to 'transform San Saba county, maybe even all of Texas before they were through,' he claimed. He even tried to get himself a seat on council representing the ranchers of the area, but we soon disabused him of *that* notion," her father added with a snort. "Of all the sand! Comin' into this town and flashing money around, and thinking that gives you the right to speak for anyone. You keep me informed if you hear anything else, Bishop."

"I will, sir," Sam said, then took a sip of his tea. "And what shall I do with the money Pennington gave me for his man's fine?" He reached into his pocket and pulled out the gold half eagle.

Prissy's father eyed it as if it might turn into a snake. "Any monies the sheriff collects for fines and whatnot, we put into a fund for widows and orphans at the bank. Prissy can take it over there for you this afternoon, if you like."

Sam handed her the gold coin.

"Papa, we've been invited to Mrs. Detwiler's for supper, Sam and I. You don't mind, do you?"

"Not at all, not at all. You young people have a good

time. Perhaps I'll invite Mar—that is, Mrs. Fairchild, to come have supper with me instead."

Prissy kept her expression smooth. It wouldn't be fair to begrudge her father some company if she wasn't going to be there. "Th-that's a fine idea, Papa," she said, and was rewarded with a warm look of approval by Sam.

"Well, I'd better be about my duties," Sam said, rising. "You never know when another marauding goat might get loose. Miss Prissy, if you're going to the bank now, I'll walk you on my way to the livery. Think I'll take Jackson out for a little gallop, and see what I can see of this ranch of Pennington's."

Prissy rose, too. "Yes, I want to be sure to be gone when Mr. Waters comes to talk to you, Papa," she said. "I ran into him at the post office, and he said he had more questions for you. There, you have been warned," she said.

Her father groaned. "What a tiresome man he is. Don't they teach those Yankees any manners or sense? Dr. Walker isn't like that," he said, referring to Sarah's husband, who was from Maine.

Houston, who'd been content to lie at Prissy's feet during the meal, emerged from under the table and wagged his tail hopefully.

"Yes, you may come too, Houston."

Once they left the house, Prissy gave vent to the curiosity that had been plaguing her.

"Sam, what happened to you before you came to Simpson Creek? In Houston, I mean. You wince occasionally… and who gave you that cut?" she asked, indicating with a nod the now barely visible laceration.

She could only see his profile, but it was enough. The muscles in his jaw went rigid, and a vein jumped in his temple. He was silent for the time it took them to walk from the steps across the grounds, and Prissy was wondering whether she ought to apologize for the question, but then he finally turned to her again.

"Let's just say I ran into a man just like this Pennington fellow of the Ranchers' Alliance, Prissy—only worse. Power can make some men real ugly to deal with."

Prissy stared at him, but something about his shuttered gaze discouraged her from asking more questions.

She couldn't stop wondering, however, what Sam had been involved in to meet up with the person who had dealt him these injuries.

Chapter Ten

"Why, hello, Mr. and Mrs. Daugherty," Prissy said as she entered the bank, carrying her dog, and spotted the old couple waiting in front of the teller's counter. "I don't often see you in town except on Sundays."

The old rancher and his wife turned around to greet her. "Why hello, Miss Prissy," Mr. Daugherty said. "Yes, and I'm afraid this'll be the last time we see you. We're sellin' out and leavin'. We've jes' come t' pull our savin's out."

Prissy couldn't believe her ears. "Leaving? But why? You are one of the founding families of Simpson Creek, aren't you?"

Mrs. Daugherty tried to smile, but all she managed was a nervous twitch of her lips. "That's right. Mr. Daugherty an' I came here in a covered wagon back in fifty-one." She glanced over Prissy's shoulder, her eyes uneasy.

Following the woman's gaze, Prissy turned.

Two fellows slouched in chairs against the front wall of the bank. She didn't recognize them, but when they noticed her looking, leering grins spread over their unshaven faces.

One of them laid a finger on the brim of his hat, but it was a mockery of a courteous gesture.

Houston shifted in her arms and bared his teeth.

"Vicious little critter," one of them murmured, and the other guffawed.

Mr. Daugherty's mouth tightened, but he said nothing, just shifted his weight. "We've been offered a good price for the ranch, Miss Prissy, so we decided to take it."

"By why—" Prissy began, then decided her question would sound too nosy. She wondered if the presence of the rough-looking men lounging in the chairs had something to do with their decision. "But where will you go?" she asked instead.

Mr. Daugherty shrugged. "Maybe south, 'round San Antone. Alma's people live down there." He put his arm around his wife protectively.

"You be sure and tell yer papa we said good-bye," Mrs. Daugherty added. "He's a good man. We're gonna miss folks like him."

"And we'll miss you, too."

The teller finished counting out Mr. Daugherty's money and handed it to him. The old couple turned and left. And the cowboys rose and followed them out.

Chilled despite the overwarm day, Prissy watched them go.

"What can I do for you, Miss Gilmore?" Ed Markison, the teller, asked.

"I…I came to deposit this in the Widows and Orphans fund," she said, absently handing him the half-eagle coin. "What's going on, Mr. Markison? Who were those men?"

He shot a glance at the door as if to be sure they'd really

gone. "Pennington's men," he whispered. "He's one a' them fancy rich fellers who came up from Houston."

"Why are you whispering?" she asked, since they were the only two people in the bank office.

He jerked his head toward the bank president's office door. "'Cause he and another a' them fellers is in talkin' t' Mr. Avery. Miss Prissy, the Daughertys ain't the only ones whose ranches've been bought up by them Alliance folks. Th' widow Harrison was in here too, earlier this mornin', and she told me the Jacobsons are sellin' out t' them men as well."

Pennington and the Ranchers' Alliance—the very same people her father and Sam had been talking about over dinner.

"You be careful when you're out an' about, Miss Prissy," Ed Markison said. "I've told Emily th' same thing, told her to wait till I can go with her if she goes anywhere beyond the mercantile…" His voice trailed off as Mr. Avery came out and seized a pile of papers from a desk behind his teller.

"Will you be at th' weddin', Miss Prissy?" Markison asked in an overloud voice, as if apprehensive his boss could have heard them whispering.

"I sure will, Mr. Markison," Prissy said, watching the bank president rush back inside the office without even appearing to notice her before he closed the door again. "Your Emily's going to be the most beautiful bride." She spoke automatically, her mind racing at what Markison had told her. Sam and Papa would be interested to hear it.

Markison wrote out a deposit slip and she placed it in her pocket, wondering if the cowboys would follow the Daughertys back to their ranch to make sure they left.

She sighed and hoped this Pennington fellow really had given them a fair price for their land. Mrs. Pennington had appeared so frightened that they might have thought it safer to cut their losses and leave even if the money was less than it should have been.

She opened the door and walked back out onto the dusty boardwalk, shielding her eyes against the glare of the sun. Her mind had barely registered the creak of leather and the snort of a horse behind her when a voice drawled, "Well, hey, Miss Prissy, we was wonderin', are you really...uh, prissy?" She whirled to see the cowboys sitting on horses behind her. Immediately each took a position flanking her, riding so close she could have extended an arm and touched a stirrup on either side. She felt a frisson of fear mixed with irritation.

Houston bristled, and would have snapped at one of the cowboy's booted feet if Prissy hadn't tightened her hold on the dog. "Excuse me, sir," she said, and kept moving.

"*Excuse me, sir,*'" the one on her right echoed in a high falsetto to the one on her left. "Jace, I reckon she *is* prissy, all right. Prissy an' proper."

Houston growled and barked at each of them in turn, and Prissy had to struggle to hold on to the little dog in her arms.

"Mind yerself, Joe, she's liable to sic that killer dawg on you," the other cowboy said, then both guffawed. "It'll prob'ly rip yer throat out."

The street was deserted. She had only to cross the street diagonally to reach the safety of the post office, she told herself. Neither of the horses appeared anything but placid, and each cowboy rode with negligent ease, one hand on the reins, the other on his upper leg. Yet there was something so intimidating about being so closely surrounded by the tall beasts ridden by men who only had to knee their mounts closer to stop her in her tracks—or reach out and grab her.

If only she'd carried a parasol against the sun as Mama had always taught her to do to protect her ladylike complexion. Then she'd at least have some sort of a weapon. She could take its metal-tipped end and jab one of her tormentors' legs. But it was hard to manage a parasol when she had to pick Houston up to enter a business, so she had only worn a bonnet.

If she kept her eyes straight ahead of her, the bonnet's sides kept her from seeing the men, only the horses they rode. Houston continued to bristle and growl alternately at each cowboy.

And then she spotted the pile of horse droppings directly in her path. They were steering her straight toward it. If she kept moving forward, she would have no choice but to walk through it, and with Houston struggling to be free of her grasp, she would have trouble even picking up her skirts.

Tightening her grasp on the dog with one hand, she slowed just enough that she was even with one of the horses' hips, then reached out and smacked it with the flat of her hand, yelling, *"Hyaaa!"*

It worked. The startled horse lunged forward into a crow-hopping buck, allowing her to sprint behind it on unsullied ground and reach the sanctuary of the post office while the other cowboy was still reacting to what she had done. Once inside, Prissy slammed the door behind her. The men's hoots of laughter came through the open windows on each side of the building.

As soon as she freed Houston, the dog threw himself against the door, barking and bristling with fury.

"Miss Prissy! What's wrong? You're as white as a full moon in December!" Mr. Wallace asked as he dashed from behind the counter to reach her side.

Beyond the door, she could hear the sound of thudding hoofs galloping down the road.

"Those men—they...they were..."

The postmaster left her side and dashed to the door, peered out for a moment, then returned inside and fetched Prissy a chair.

"Nothin' left of 'em but a cloud of dust, but I reckon I know who you mean. I've seen those fellers in town lately, hootin' and hollerin', bullyraggin' people who were mindin' their own business. Ranchers' Alliance men, I heard they were, though I don't know any Simpson Creek ranchers who'd join that thing—not voluntarily, anyway," he added, glaring in the direction they had gone.

"Prissy, I thought I heard you come in—" Caroline began, coming from the living quarters behind the counter. "What's wrong?"

Prissy told her what had happened, shuddering as she did so. Now, of course, with Mr. Wallace bringing her a glass of water and Caroline kneeling by her side peering worriedly up at her, it seemed ridiculous that she'd been so frightened. She was Priscilla Gilmore, daughter of the mayor. She wasn't about to let some filthy cowboys bother her! She'd dealt with their harassment and escaped them, after all.

"I-I'm all right," she assured them, getting to her feet. "I came back, Caroline, because I forgot to ask you this morning if there was any correspondence for the Spinsters' Club?"

A smile reminiscent of the old Caroline curved the other woman's lips and she straightened also. "I can well imagine why you forgot, what with that tiresome Mr. Waters bothering you and the sheriff showing up in the nick of time. As a matter of fact, Madame President, there are three letters I've saved for your perusal. Come on back to the kitchen—I'll give you some cold lemonade while you take a look at them."

Prissy rose on legs which still felt unsteady and followed her.

"It was very wise of your uncle to suggest advertising in the newspapers of closer towns, as well as Houston," Caroline remarked as she handed Prissy the letters, "and kind of him to write the editors and urge them to run our notices. As you see, it's borne fruit—these letters come from Austin, Mason and Fredericksburg."

Prissy was pleased to hear some enthusiasm creeping into Caroline's voice. "So if we were to invite these gentlemen to a party, we wouldn't have to wait weeks for them to receive the invitations, reply, then travel to Simpson Creek," she said. "Hmm, this fellow from Fredericksburg sounds German—'Frederick von Hesse.' I hope he isn't one of those dour, ever-so-serious Prussians," she said, making a face. Caroline giggled.

Before an hour was up, Prissy had decided to hold a barbecue, complete with dancing in the evening, at Gilmore House. The whole town would be invited, of course, along with the Spinsters' Club and the bachelors.

"We can discuss the menu with the other ladies on the way out to the Brookfield ranch next week," Prissy said.

"I'll write the letters and send them out this very afternoon," Caroline said, after a glance at the grandfather clock which stood in the hallway. "I've just time before the stage comes through."

"Then I'd better get going and leave you in peace,"

Prissy said. "Caroline, thanks for your help. It's great that you're working on this with me." Did she dare utter her thoughts? "Maybe—"

Caroline held up a hand. "I know what you're about to say, but don't. This is just something for me to do, that's all. I like a party as well as anyone, but don't plan on throwing me at any of those men. I'm quite content with my decision to become the schoolteacher this fall."

Prissy shut her mouth, but she couldn't help hoping. *Please, Lord, let one of those bachelors be just the right man to bring Caroline out of her mourning.*

But first, she needed to straighten a few things out with Sam. It was time for her to get the full story on Mr. Bishop so she could put her fears and questions to rest. After their dinner with Mrs. Detwiler, she was going to demand some answers. Right after she ruined the mood by telling him about the Alliance cowboys.

"What an enjoyable time," Prissy remarked as they watched lamplight flare near the window after Nolan Walker entered his darkened home.

She'd been pleased to discover Mrs. Detwiler had also invited Nolan Walker to supper, since Sarah, his wife, was still out at the Brookfield ranch helping her sister. It was good for Sam to get to know Nolan better, Prissy thought, because while the doctor had come to faith only recently, he spoke of the Lord and spiritual matters as easily as one would talk about the weather. She still didn't know exactly where Sam stood in his faith journey, but he didn't talk about it.

The food had been delicious, the conversation on the porch afterward even better. Sam had obviously enjoyed conversing with their elderly hostess and the town doctor.

As Mrs. Detwiler had put it, the four of them had "gotten along like a house afire."

Now they had walked Nolan home, and they were alone again. Dusk was fast edging into dark.

"Yes, it was. Shall we stroll a little?" Sam asked. "Or do you have to go right home?"

"I don't think Papa would mind if we strolled a little," Prissy murmured. She felt slightly nervous, though she couldn't say exactly why.

His face was shadowy in the growing dark. "I believe we could get the best view of that big full moon from over there in the meadow," he said, pointing past the church and across the creek. "There's no little boys shrieking like wild Comanches over there tonight," he added with a wink.

"I believe you're right. There's a bench on the far bank of the creek that would be just perfect for moon watching."

Their footsteps echoed as they stepped onto the wooden bridge that spanned Simpson Creek, forming a counterpoint to the chirping of crickets and the burble of the creek beneath. Somewhere below, a splash of water announced a fish's leap at an insect. An owl flew past them on silent wings, startling Prissy into grabbing Sam's arm with a squeak of surprise. He chuckled, putting an arm around her with exaggerated protectiveness.

They crossed the bridge and stepped onto the soft earth of the meadow. Grass brushed her skirts shin-high. She could just make out the moonlight-dappled bench under a big cottonwood tree.

Prissy didn't want to spoil the mood, but she knew she had to tell Sam what had happened this afternoon before she said anything else. She hadn't wanted to bring it up while at Mrs. Detwiler's, lest it alarm the old lady. But since Sam was the sheriff, he needed to know about it.

"How was your trip out to the Pennington ranch?" she asked as they reached the bench and sat down. "You didn't say anything about it, so I thought perhaps you might not want to discuss it in front of the others."

"I never made it," he admitted with a rueful smile. "I was only a little way beyond town when Jackson cast a shoe. I took him to the blacksmith, but by the time we were done it was too late to ride out that far because of our supper plans. I'll go tomorrow." Her expression must have given him a hint that something was on her mind, though, for he studied her face more closely. "Why? Did something happen?"

She told him about the rough-looking men loitering in the bank, and the Daughertys telling her they'd been bought out and were leaving. "Mr. Markison told me Mr. Pennington was back in the bank president's private office right then. And, Sam, it looked like those rough men were watching the old couple to make sure they were actually getting ready to leave."

Prissy had delivered her account matter-of-factly to this point, but when she started telling him the rest, about the cowboys suddenly appearing on horseback when she came out of the bank, and the panic she'd felt when they'd surrounded her by their horses, it all became terrifyingly real to her again. She could almost smell the overpowering scents of saddle leather, tobacco and stale whiskey. Prissy couldn't suppress a shudder, and before she could squeeze her eyes shut, big wet tears escaped down her cheeks.

And then he was holding her, one hand stroking her hair. "Prissy, sweet Prissy, don't be afraid. I'm not going to let anything or anybody hurt you." His voice was raspy but soothing, right next to her ear. "Aw, Prissy, don't cry…"

"But they were *so close,* Sam. I didn't know if they

were going to make their horses step on my feet, or if they were going to snatch me up onto one of their saddles." She wanted to stop crying, to show him that she wasn't a frightened little rabbit, but he felt so solid, so *safe*. It felt so good to be held by this man.

"I'll ride out there bright and early to put Pennington on notice that there's to be no repeat of this kind of behavior," Sam told her. "Don't you give it another moment's thought, Prissy."

"Oh, Sam—" she began, but she couldn't go on because she was overwhelmed by his kindness, by the feel of his hand on her hair.

"I want to protect you, Prissy. You bring that out in me."

"Do I, Sam?"

He drew back and rested his forehead against hers. "You do. I hope you feel like that's a good thing."

She was about to say that she did when the moonlight fell across his face, illuminating his cut and fading bruises. But before she could say anything, he stood, and stretched out a hand to help her to her feet.

"There's something I want you to see on the way home," Sam said.

"What?"

He laid a finger on her lips. "You'll just have to wait, Miss Inquisitive. It's over on Travis Street."

Just as they left the bridge, Delbert Perry walked by and tipped his ragged cap to Prissy. "Pretty evenin', ain't it, Miss Prissy, Sheriff?"

"It is," Prissy agreed, and watched, bemused, as the man walked on, mumbling under his breath.

"Delbert's out walking and talking with the Lord," Sam explained. "He told me it keeps him from drinking."

It would have been the perfect moment to ask Sam about his faith, but she couldn't do it. She couldn't ask any of the questions she'd planned to ask. Why? Perhaps a part of her didn't actually want the answers.

"You know where this is leading, don't you?" he asked as they stepped onto Travis. Travis Street ran behind the hotel, the mercantile, the post office and the jail, and ended at the side yard of the church. It was dotted on both sides with dwellings of various sizes.

She didn't know what he meant. "You said there was something you wanted me to see…?" She saw the dim shapes of the backs of the post office and the jail.

"No, I meant my courting you. I'm not going to rush you, Priscilla Gilmore, because a girl like you deserves a proper, thorough courtship, but you must know I want to marry you someday. Someday *soon,* Prissy."

She stopped stock-still.

"Is that a proposal?" she asked. She felt a tingling all over at the hoarse, earnest way he'd said it he wanted it to be *soon.* "But—but I—"

She could see his grin by the light of the moon. "Call it a preliminary to a proposal, if you like. When I do the real thing, Prissy, you'll have it with all the trimmings— me down on my knees and all the rest of it."

"Preliminary?" was all she could stammer.

"Then I'll give you a *preliminary* acceptance," she said with mock-haughtiness, and then laughed up at him. "Oh, Sam, I want to marry you, too! If it was just up to me, we could ask Reverend Chadwick to marry us tomorrow. But—"

"Now your papa wouldn't stand for it if we married too soon, and your papa is right. You need to know me better, to make sure I'm the right man for you."

There was something so uncertain, so vulnerable in his gaze. She opened her mouth to agree, to say that yes, she did need to know him better and that in fact she had questions, but no sound would come out.

"But if you do decide to marry me, have you thought about where we'd live, Prissy? What would you think of living here?"

He was nodding toward a white frame two-story house on his left, a house that obviously stood empty. The moonlight illuminated upstairs windows that were cracked and a shutter that hung precariously from one remaining hinge. The flowerbeds were choked with weeds and the paint was chipped and faded.

"The old Galloway place?" It had been deteriorating since Mr. Galloway was killed in the war, and empty since his poor widow had died in the influenza epidemic this last winter.

"It's available," he told her, excitement and moonlight gleaming in his dark eyes as he looked down at her. "Mr. Avery told me the estate's been settled and the bank would like to sell it. Wouldn't it make a great home for us, Prissy? It's close to the jail, but not too close, and I could pay for it over time out of my sheriff's salary."

Prissy blinked up at him in confusion, then stared at the old derelict house. "Sam, this is—I hardly know what to say…"

"I've walked through it. It just needs a family, and a little loving care. I could fix what's broken easy enough. And it's roomy—we could fill it up with children, Prissy."

He smiled, and she felt her heart jolt with joy at the picture he was painting with his words, of a big house noisy with the sounds of laughing children—*their children*.

She shook her head to clear her thoughts, but it didn't

work. Marry Sam Bishop? Should she even consider it, before she knew all about him?

And…did he actually…love her? Is that what he was trying to say?

"It's not as fancy as Gilmore House, and I'm sure your father would offer to set us up somewhere else. But I want to stand on my own two feet, sweetheart, not lean on your father because he's wealthy. He earned his money, didn't he? I want to do the same."

He gently turned her around so she could see the house. "Think about it, Prissy—think about this place with a fresh coat of paint and new glass, and all the weeds pulled from the flowerbeds and flowers growing there. Look at those fine shade trees on both sides of the house, and picture our boys climbing up into them, and one of our girls swinging from a swing hanging from one of those stout boughs."

It was more than Prissy could take in. She could hardly speak.

"Prissy, are you all right?" he asked softly.

She nodded slowly. "I need to think. Maybe you'd better take me home now, Sam."

Despite the obvious disappointment on his face, they were the only words she could muster. And Sam, to his credit, did as he was told.

Chapter Eleven

Sam tossed and turned on his narrow bed that night, full of conflicting emotions. Prissy had seemed stunned, which was not a good sign. But she hadn't been angry or insulted, which *was* a good sign. Had he misread her?

Perhaps he'd just moved too fast. The house might have been too much.

He smiled in the darkness as he pictured himself painting the house and repairing the dangling shutter, with Prissy in the kitchen baking bread. He'd stop his labors at dinnertime and come in the kitchen and she'd give him a sweet kiss.

With a little patience, maybe he could make that a reality.

He'd enjoyed supper at Mrs. Detwiler's immensely. The elderly woman was full of hospitality and wry, unexpected humor, and her welcome acceptance of him both as the sheriff and as a suitor for Prissy encouraged him. He'd enjoyed his conversation with Nolan Walker, too. The physician had obviously been through much heartbreak, both before and during the War Between the States, yet he spoke of the Lord as if He were an ever-present friend—just as

Reverend Chadwick did. Could there actually be something to this faith they shared with Prissy?

Prissy's recital of her treatment by Pennington's two men was the thing truly keeping him awake. If it had been daytime when she'd told him about the incident, he would have felt compelled to take her straight home and ride to La Alianza immediately. Perhaps she'd known that and wanted to give him time to cool down.

But he'd make up for the lapse in time, sure enough. As soon as the sun was up, he'd ride out to pay Mr. Pennington a call, and if he disturbed the man at breakfast, so much the better. He'd make it clear that there was to be no repetition of such behavior, or more Alliance men would be occupying his jail cells—after he'd pounded the sand out of them.

It was time to do everything possible to prove to Prissy that he had what it took to be her husband. To be hers.

It was just eight o'clock when Sam reached the impressive wrought-iron arch at the entrance of La Alianza. From there he was escorted by two Alliance men all the way down the winding, pecan-tree-lined lane to the sprawling limestone house. The door was opened by a stocky, impassive Chinese butler flanked by two other men whose vests also bore the Alliance insignia. The butler showed Sam into the marble-floored dining room; they were followed by the two Ranchers' Alliance men.

"Welcome to La Alianza, Sheriff Bishop," Garth Pennington said, looking up from a plate of bacon, eggs, toast and fresh fruit at one end of an immense, elaborately carved mahogany table. He was dressed in a luxurious brocade dressing gown, but if he was embarrassed to be found not fully dressed yet, or angry at this surprise early visit, nothing marred his genial expression. "I wish you had let me know you were coming, for I would have waited and breakfasted with you. You couldn't possibly have eaten before you came. But that can be easily remedied—Wong Tiao, bring Sheriff Bishop the same as I had."

Even as the servant bowed, Sam held up a hand. "That won't be necessary. I've come to discuss something with you."

"Sit down then, and make yourself comfortable," Pennington purred, pointing to a chair next to him. "Some coffee, at least?"

"No, thank you." He remained standing.

Pennington studied him blandly for a moment, then nodded to the Chinaman and the two men behind Sam. "Leave us, gentlemen. I'm sure I have nothing to fear from the sheriff."

Just as the other men were leaving, another man entered the room. He was sepulchrally thin, with hollow eyes, but his clothes spoke of wealth.

"Ah, there you are, Francis. Sheriff Bishop, this is Francis Byrd, one of my two partners in the Alliance. Mr. Byrd is in charge of the ranches we hold east of here. Francis, Mr. Bishop has something to talk over with us, and based on his demeanor, I fear it won't be pleasant."

"Is that right?" Byrd's voice was raspy as dried reeds rubbing together in the wind. "Do inform us, Mr. Bishop."

Sam didn't care for the faintly supercilious tinge to the man's voice, but he guessed Byrd was hoping to get a rise out of him. Ignoring him, he plunged ahead with a terse recital of yesterday's incident. Pennington and Byrd listened attentively, Pennington rubbing his goatee, Byrd staring, unblinking, into Sam's eyes.

"This Miss Gilmore, the mayor's daughter—I'm told she is your sweetheart, Sheriff?" Pennington asked, his pale amber eyes holding a hint of…mischief? Amusement?

Sam felt anger sparking in him, mixed with surprise that Pennington knew anything about his relationship with Prissy. How did he know?

"What does that have to do with anything I spoke about?" he ground out, his gaze boring into Pennington's. "As sheriff, I won't stand for disrespect to *any* of Simpson Creek's citizens—man, woman or child."

Pennington rose, his movement smooth and unhurried. "Calm down, Sheriff. What you've told us is deplorable, of course. The men involved will be disciplined. It will not happen again."

The same thing he'd promised about Tolliver's drunken brawling. "I'll hold you to that," Sam said. "And as long as I'm here, I'll ask why you're buying up ranches right and left. What's your game, gentlemen?"

Byrd raised a pale brow. "Game? Land acquisition is hardly a *game,* Sheriff. And it's perfectly legal. We find folks who want to sell—the elderly and distressed widows and the like—and we have money to buy. It's as simple as that."

Sam remembered the way Prissy had described the old Daugherty couple—fearful, skittish, unwilling to look at the cowboys who sat like vultures as they withdrew their savings—and felt his ire deepen. "You'd better make sure every 'i' is dotted and every 't' is crossed in your land dealings, Mr. Byrd."

"We seem to have unintentionally ruffled your feathers, Sheriff," Byrd observed. He seemed pleased.

Sam recognized he was being baited and kept his voice

level. "I'll be watching, and I won't have anyone bullied into selling. Do I make myself plain?"

"Abundantly," Pennington said, his voice conciliatory as Sam continued to meet Byrd's basilisk stare. "Sheriff Bishop, I regret we've gotten off on the wrong foot, so to speak. As I said, there will be no repeat of any sort of disrespectful behavior from my men. We're here to benefit the citizens of this part of Texas, not persecute them. Now, let me show you around La Alianza, as I promised I would."

Sam would have liked to refuse point-blank and stalk out, but he realized he might have more to gain if he let himself appear to be placated and was able to take a look around. Knowledge of this place might prove useful.

He shrugged. "Why not?"

Without a word, Byrd got to his feet and left the room. Sam was relieved to see him go. He didn't like or trust Pennington any more than Byrd, but Pennington at least put on a pretense of affability.

"Splendid. Allow me to go dress—I won't be long. Why not reconsider about that cup of coffee, while you're waiting?" As if he'd been reading his employer's mind—or hovering outside the door—Wong Tiao reentered the room bearing a fresh pot of hot coffee, and Sam accepted a cup.

Pennington was as good as his word, and soon Sam was following him around as Pennington showed him a large guesthouse, servant cottages, a greenhouse full of flowers, a magnificently appointed stable with its prized stock of thoroughbreds and Arabians, a separate barn housing a fine selection of horses for working cattle, a smithy and a poultry barn. Then another employee wearing a Ranchers' Alliance vest brought Jackson and a mount for Pennington, and they rode past pastures containing cattle, more horses, fields of cotton with a gin at one end, rows of corn, beans and other vegetables, and peach and apple orchards. Everywhere there were workers bearing the "RA" emblem, tending the cattle and the crops. It was like a feudal fiefdom.

"Quite an operation you have here," Sam murmured.

Pennington smiled from atop the sixteen-hand thoroughbred he rode, a horse that had tried more than once to take a nip at Jackson, much to Sam's gelding's annoyance.

"We have other such holdings between here and the coast, as well—smaller, most of them, but very self-sufficient."

"Where does the 'alliance' part of the Ranchers' Alliance come in?"

Pennington blinked. "What do you mean?"

Sam shrugged. "Inside the house, you said you were here to benefit the citizens of the area. How's that, other than buying them out so you can take over their land? That benefits you and your partners."

Pennington's smile was urbane. "That's precisely what many of them are most benefited by, of course—the chance to start over elsewhere with cash in hand. But if they *choose* to stay on their land, they may ally themselves with us as Alliance employees, and receive the benefits of Alliance protection and the ability to purchase needed goods at a bargain price. We buy in bulk, so we're able to do this for our members."

"And what's in it for you, if they choose to do this?"

"We merely require service from them from time to time," Pennington said vaguely. "Most of the workers you see in the fields are satisfying the terms of their contract.

Others, such as the ones you saw guarding the gates, are permanent employees."

As were the ones who'd come to town and harassed Prissy.

"I'll ask you again, like I did inside—what do y'all hope to gain with this 'Ranchers' Alliance,' Mr. Pennington?"

Pennington met his gaze. "Power," Pennington said simply. "Control of a region, like Richard King has south of here. He controls a huge chunk of Texas, Sheriff. But why should he be the only one?"

They'd come full circle and were now back at the entrance gate. It struck Sam then that he'd seen no ladies in the big house and only a few Mexican women tending the gardens.

"Are you married, Mr. Pennington? Is Mr. Byrd?"

Pennington raised an eyebrow, as if he found the question intrusive, but Sam didn't care.

"Yes, I am. Mrs. Pennington still lives in Houston, but I hope to bring her up here soon, now that we have things under way."

It was an ironic understatement, Sam thought, gazing about him at the carefully organized splendor.

"What about Byrd?"

"His wife has passed on. And you, Sheriff Bishop? Do you hope to tie the knot sometime soon with the beautiful mayor's daughter?"

It was a fair question after Sam's inquiry, but Sam was reluctant to speak of Prissy with this man and only nodded.

"Splendid, splendid. She is a prize, by all reports."

He spoke of her as if she were the spoils of war. Fury clenched Sam's free hand into a fist at his side.

"Where did you get the money to start all this?" Sam asked, willing to counter rudeness with rudeness.

Pennington stared at him, and for a long moment there was no sound but the buzzing of insects and the stomp of Jackson's hoof as he sought to dislodge a pesky fly.

"Ah, that'd be telling," Pennington murmured. "But if you'd care to throw in with us, Sheriff, you can be privy to all our secrets."

Sam blinked. "Thanks, but I have a job."

Pennington waved a hand. "Oh, you could continue as sheriff, if you wished. Collect both salaries. It would be good to have the law in our corner, so to speak. Or you could leave the job and throw in with us completely. Miss Gilmore could live in the lap of luxury here as your wife, in an even more opulent house than her father's, rather than some humble abode you could afford in town on your own. She could be my hostess until my wife joins me. Think of it, Sheriff—isn't that the sort of home you'd like to provide for her?"

Unbidden, his mind flashed an image of Prissy dining at the long mahogany dining table, dressed in the finest gowns, never wanting for anything, rather than in the ramshackle old house he wanted to fix up for the two of them.

For a moment, Sam could only stare at him, dumbfounded—not only because of the man's audacity in saying it, but because he knew he once would have jumped at the chance.

But now the idea of accepting filled him with disgust. His father used to quote the old saying, "He who sups with the devil should bring a long spoon." The offer sounded like just that sort of situation.

"Thanks, but I've always been my own man. Reckon I'll continue doing that."

Pennington shrugged, untroubled at the refusal. "Very well, but if you decide to leave genteel poverty behind, the position will be open—at least for a time, Bishop. The sheriff of Richardson is considering it, but I'd rather have you, I believe."

Sam ignored his last words. "Thanks for the tour, Mr. Pennington. I'd best be getting back to town."

He started to rein Jackson around and head him out through the gate, but Pennington put up a hand. "Oh, say, Sheriff, you'll have to come pay us another visit soon when our other partner comes up to visit from Houston. We'll be having a reception, and I know he'd like to meet the sheriff. Perhaps he could make joining us seem more attractive to you."

"I doubt it."

"Oh, don't be so sure," Pennington said with a smirk. "Kendall Raney could charm the birds out of the trees, if he had a mind to."

It took all of Sam's ability to keep his features blank. The day had become hot enough to wither a fence post, but he suddenly felt cold all over.

Kendall Raney was coming to San Saba County. Kendall Raney, who had overseen Sam's being beaten to a pulp, and who had planned to feed him to the gators. Kendall Raney, whose safe Sam had cracked, whose valuable ring he had stolen.

"Are y'all having a big braggin' party to see which of you has gobbled up the most land from down-on-their-luck ranchers?" He asked the question lightly, while all the while his mind raced. Raney had only seen him the one time, at night, and his features had been covered in blood by the end of it. Sam's injuries had mostly healed, and if they met at all, Raney wasn't likely to remember the hapless gambler he'd once decided to dump into a bayou for the gators when he saw the sheriff of Simpson Creek. He might not even come into town, but be content to stay in the sumptuous luxury of La Alianza.

"Among other things," Pennington said. "But he mainly wants to set up a gambling palace in Simpson Creek, such as the ones he runs in Houston. Profitable places."

Profitable for the house, Sam knew. Not for the gambler. "We already have a saloon, if anyone wants to play poker or monte," Sam said dismissively. "Simpson Creek isn't a rowdy town. He ought to try his luck in San Francisco or New Orleans."

"Oh, but he sees the possibilities, Sheriff. If Simpson Creek's saloon owner doesn't want to sell, he can always erect his gambling palace elsewhere in the town. Gamblers would flock to such a place, the only one of its kind in the hill country. You might find yourself sheriff of a booming city, Bishop."

"We'll see about that," Sam said as he headed through the gate, ignoring the fear that had taken hold in his stomach.

Chapter Twelve

Sam unlocked the sheriff's office, taking down the "Sheriff Is Out" sign, eager to do some quiet work at his desk after his return from La Alianza. He'd stopped at Gilmore House to tell the mayor about his visit, and Prissy's father had decided to call a council meeting to discuss the matter.

Sam wanted to get his thoughts and recommendations down on paper while his impressions were still fresh. He planned to urge the council to call a town meeting to warn against the Ranchers' Alliance, to urge the townspeople to neither sell their property to them nor join. He wondered if they could pass an ordinance against new saloons or gambling halls. Was such a thing legal, and would it be enough to discourage the scheming Raney? He outlined his thoughts on a sheet of paper, point by point.

The idea of encountering his tormentor again had rankled his nerves at first, but during the ride back to town, Sam's resolve had stiffened. Even in the unlikely event Raney recognized him, he had no power over the sheriff of Simpson Creek. If he harmed a lawman, it would bring the federals down on him and his cabal. He wouldn't want that, for they'd poke their noses into the land-buying scheme.

And he couldn't prove Sam had taken the ring. He might not have even realized that Sam was the one who had taken it, for Sam had left the safe locked up again, and he might not have missed the ring right away. Sam only hoped some unlucky employee of Raney's gambling emporium hadn't taken the blame for the theft instead.

He'd known the so-called Ranchers' Alliance was a bad thing, but now that he knew Raney was part of it, it was even worse. He had to defeat Raney and his coconspirators, not only to achieve his own revenge, but for the sake of the town and San Saba County.

And for the sake of the life he was trying to build here. With Prissy.

Sam began writing with such force that the lead broke in the pencil he'd so painstakingly sharpened to a point. Thunderation. Now he'd have to whittle it down again.

He'd just pulled his knife out of his pocket when the door was wrenched open. William Waters III burst in, slamming the door behind him.

"Sheriff, it's about time you put in an appearance!" he cried. "I've been looking for you all morning."

Sam had heard the term "purple with rage" before, and he judged the easterner's complexion was only a couple of shades away from that. His eyes bulged as if someone had a chokehold around his neck. He was practically hopping from foot to foot in his fury.

"The very least you could do if you're out is to have a deputy here to take your place," Waters went on. "But no doubt you were lollygagging at the mayor's mansion, mooning over his daughter."

Sam smothered his irritation at the accusation. So the

little banty rooster was jealous, was he? It wouldn't do him any good. He'd never have had a chance with a woman like Prissy Gilmore, even if Sam and she had never met. Sam said in a mild tone, "Happens I was out investigating a citizen's complaint, Mr. Waters." The man didn't need to know the citizen was Prissy. "Sorry I wasn't here. What can I do for you, now that I am?"

"You can order those Ranchers' Alliance fellows not to push me around, that's what!"

Sam straightened. "Simmer down, take a seat, and tell me what you're talking about," he said, pointing to the chair on the other side of the scarred old desk. "What did they do to you?"

Waters sat down with a huff of breath. "I hadn't been here twenty-four hours before that Pennington fellow paid me a call at my hotel room offering to buy my ranch. Said he'd do me the favor of taking it off of my hands, if you can believe the effrontery!"

"You told him you didn't want to sell, didn't you?" Sam wasn't sure the man wouldn't be wiser to sell to someone, as ill-suited as he was to be a rancher in this rough country, but Waters's land abutted the Brookfields' and Sam certainly didn't want Nick and his wife to have the Ranchers' Alliance as a neighbor.

"He offered me a pittance compared to what it's worth, and I said no and thought no more of it," Waters said. "Then he sent some of his men out yesterday—dangerous-looking fellows, 'hired guns,' I believe you'd call them. They repeated the offer to buy me out, though for less money than the day before, with their hands on their pistol butts the whole time. Today all the men I'd hired to do the work have either disappeared or are dead drunk in the saloon—and when I went to claim the lumber I'd ordered at the mill, the mill owner told me the order had been cancelled—but not by *me,* you may be sure I told him!"

"Sounds like someone's trying to discourage you from settling down out there," Sam murmured. "Mr. Waters, I'll be attending a council meeting called to discuss this very subject tonight, and—"

"Fine, I'll be there. At Gilmore House?"

"Hold your horses a second," Sam advised. "I wasn't asking you to attend. I can bring your report to the council, along with those of others who've been pressured to sell their land. Then we'll be calling a meeting of concerned citizens, and you're welcome to attend that—"

"And in the meantime, I'm to cool my heels?" Waters yelped, jumping to his feet and pounding on Sam's desk. "Allow these ruffians to threaten me?" He was fairly jumping up and down in his agitation.

Sam stood, extending his hand palm down. "Now, I didn't say that. I was just out to Pennington's ranch this morning, and I was about to say I would pay another call there and officially order them to leave you in peace because you don't want to sell."

Waters stared at him, his beady eyes narrowed into mere slits. "How do I know I can trust you?" he demanded. "How do I know you're not in league with them to defraud me of my land?"

Sam took a deep breath, knowing he towered over Waters. As sheriff, he'd taken an oath to defend obnoxious people like William Waters just as much as kind, pleasant folks like Mrs. Detwiler. "You don't," he said shortly, "except that I'm wearing this—" He jabbed his thumb into the five-pointed star he wore on his shirt. "And out here, if a man says he's going to do something, we trust he will. As an easterner, you might not have been aware of that."

Waters took a step back. "I...I apologize, Sheriff," he said. "I suppose I spoke too hastily. I-I'd be grateful if you'd speak to Mr. Pennington."

"I'll do that. Now, in the meantime, who did you hire to bring the lumber out to your property? I'll mosey down to the saloon and have a word with them about starting the work they promised."

"Thank you, Sheriff," Waters said, all the fight gone out of him.

Sam took down the names, realizing they were going to need more than a council meeting to rein in the Alliance.

Prissy smiled in triumph as she took two apple pies out of the oven and saw that both were evenly browned.

"Ah, *señorita*," Flora said, coming back into the kitchen. "They smell so good!"

"Even Sarah wouldn't be ashamed to claim these as her own," Prissy said, pride at her accomplishment welling up in her. She had definitely come a long way in her cooking ability.

At Prissy's feet, Houston gave a yip, his liquid eyes pleading for a sample. But she'd already given him scraps of dough left over from the piecrust she'd rolled out. "Sorry, boy, no more for you. I'm leaving one here for Papa, Flora and Antonio." She would cover the other with a napkin and take it down to the jail as a treat for Sam.

She smiled at the thought of the handsome sheriff, though she surely had been confused by his "preliminary proposal." Last night she had served as secretary at the council meeting and taken down the minutes, so she had gotten to watch Sam from under lowered lashes as he and the others discussed strategies to deal with the actions of the Ranchers' Alliance. She had felt a rush of pride as it became clear that the other men respected his opinion. Only once had he stolen a glance at her and smiled, all while the others at the meeting were listening to something Dr. Walker was saying. She'd looked down, feeling the heat spread up her neck and face clear to the roots of her hair.

Her father had appeared troubled at Sam's mention of the harassment William Waters had experienced. As soon as Sam finished up by saying he was going to speak to Pennington about it, her father turned to Prissy.

"Don't you and the Spinsters have an outing planned for next week out that way? To visit Miss Milly and the new baby out at the Brookfields' ranch?"

"Yes, Papa. But I'm sure we'll be fine," Prissy had said, afraid her father meant to forbid the outing. "They have no reason to bother a wagonful of ladies."

"Still, I don't like it," her father said, steepling his fingers. "Perhaps—"

"Excuse me, Mr. Gilmore, but I'd be happy to escort the ladies to and from the Brookfield ranch," Sam said.

Her father had looked at Sam, grateful. "Very well, then. Thanks, Sam. I surely would feel better about that."

So Sam would be escorting the wagon that carried the Spinsters out to the Brookfield Ranch. Sam had seen the need for their protection, and he would be riding with them to protect them. How impressed the ladies would be! Her heart nearly burst with pride. Of course, she hadn't accepted Sam's offer. She'd had so many questions she hadn't known where to start.

But she could be proud of him anyway, couldn't she?

At the end of the meeting, the council decided to call a town meeting after church, since most of the ranchers would already be in town for the church service. It would be quite interesting to see how that meeting went. She was looking forward to seeing what Sam had to say about it all.

Actually, to be honest, she was just looking forward to seeing Sam, regardless of what he had to say about it.

Perhaps she didn't have so many questions about him that needed answering after all.

She had just donned her bonnet, attached Houston's leash to his collar and scooped up the napkin-covered pie when a knock sounded at the front door. Houston charged toward the sound, nearly yanking Prissy off her feet. Prissy lost hold of the leash, and it was all she could do to keep her balance and hold on to the pie so it wouldn't fall face-down on the floor.

Oh, bother—her fingers had gone right through the crust, marring its perfection. Who could it be at the door? She didn't want to be delayed taking the pie to Sam— she needed to see him, to make sure that he…that he… Well, she wasn't sure, but she just knew she needed to see him.

Mariah Fairchild stood at the door, holding a parasol of lavender silk that exactly matched her dress. "Why, good morning, Priscilla dear! Is your papa home? I wonder if he's forgotten about the walk we were going to take this morning? Mmm, whatever you're carrying smells delicious!"

Prissy reminded herself it wasn't Mrs. Fairchild's fault that the dog had nearly made her drop the pie. Still, her very presence was a reminder that the friendship between her papa and the widow was progressing.

"Good morning, Mrs. Fairchild. I…I believe Papa's in his study." *Papa has a right to happiness,* she reminded herself sternly, and added, "There's another pie cooling in the kitchen. You're more than welcome to sample it."

"How sweet of you, dear. Now, don't let me keep you—"

But Prissy had already grabbed Houston's leash and was sailing out the door, satisfied she'd done her duty of being courteous to the widow. She had not passed the gate when she heard the sound of carriage wheels slowing in the street.

Houston was lunging in that direction, barking.

She stopped and turned, for her bonnet impeded her sideward vision. The driver of the carriage wore livery; he tipped his hat to her even as a gentleman alighted from the victoria and did likewise.

"Miss Gilmore, I believe?" The unknown gentleman possessed pale amber eyes that seemed to pierce right through her, and not in a pleasant way.

"Yes," she began uncertainly, controlling Houston with difficulty. "Quiet! No, I'm sorry, sir, I meant the dog. Y-you have the advantage of me…"

"Garth Pennington, ma'am. I'm sorry to interrupt you— you're obviously on the way to somewhere, but I'm happy to have found you before you left."

"Why? What can I do for you?" she asked bluntly, recognizing his name as that of one of the leaders of the Alliance whom Sam had visited yesterday.

Antonio had emerged from the barn and came to Prissy's side. Grateful for his presence, she handed him the pie, which left her hands free to pick up her agitated pet.

"My, what a fierce little protector you have there," Pennington said with a chuckle, but Prissy was not amused. Pennington apparently saw that, for he sobered. "Miss Gilmore, my intent is not to delay you on your errand, but to apologize for the distress my men reportedly caused you a couple of days ago." He reached into the coach and brought forth a lush bouquet of blood-red roses, which he held out to her. "I pray you will accept these as a token of my humble and abject regret that you were subjected to such treatment—no doubt in an excess of high spirits on their part rather than any real malice, I assure you, Miss Gilmore."

Prissy stiffened. There was something too glib in the way the words of apology slid off the man's lips for her to believe any real regret on his part.

"That's not necessary, Mr. Pennington, but I thank you." She made no move to accept the flowers.

"The men involved have been disciplined, Miss Pennington. You need not fear a repeat of such behavior." Bending forward with a flourish, he added, "Please accept these lovely roses from the hothouse of La Alianza. They cannot be as lovely as you, if I may say so, but—"

"Leave the lady alone."

Prissy had been so absorbed in what Pennington had been saying and in fending off the roses he offered that she hadn't heard Sam approaching on his black gelding. Neither had Pennington, for he startled at the voice and straightened abruptly from his bow, gaping at Sam.

"Sheriff, you mistake me. I was not offering any disrespect to Miss Gilmore, I assure you, but merely apologizing for my men's behavior—the behavior you reported to me."

"Miss Prissy, please, go back inside the house," Sam said, keeping his narrowed eyes on Pennington. The sun glinted off the tin star on his shirt.

Prissy had never been so glad to see anyone in her life as she was to see Sam Bishop at that moment. But she took only a couple of steps backward, curious as to what he intended to say to Pennington.

Sam half turned, his gaze locking with hers. "Please. I said go back inside the house. I'll join you in a moment." His tone was steely.

She hesitated no more, lowering Houston to the ground and taking the pie back from Antonio. The dog dragged at the leash, clearly torn between wagging his tail at Sam and growling again at Pennington, but after she gave it a firm yank, he heeled at her side, carrying his tail stiff and straight.

"Really, Sheriff, was that necessary?" Prissy heard Pennington protest. "I told you I meant no harm, only—"

Sam interrupted, "Mr. Pennington, you've saved me another ride out to La Alianza. I have a bone to pick with you."

By then she was out of earshot, and knew she would have to wait until Sam finished with Pennington to hear what he'd said. She'd been planning to stand just inside the door and listen but she found her father and Mariah Fairchild there. Her father, cane in hand, was just taking his hat from the hook by the door.

"Prissy, what's wrong?" her father said. "You look upset. What's going on out there?"

"It's Pennington," she said, and explained what had happened.

"I'm going to give that sidewinder Pennington a piece of my mind," her father growled, putting a hand on the doorknob. "You stay here, Mariah. I'll just be a moment."

Prissy dashed forward and put a hand on her father's arm. "Wait, Papa, please. I think Sam would prefer it if we all stayed here right now."

Her father raised an eyebrow and then turned to the window. Prissy followed, and she did not like what she saw.

"That was churlish of you, Sheriff. Surely there can be nothing wrong with a heartfelt apology for my men's actions, accompanied by a bouquet of La Alianza roses from the hothouse."

Sam was standing very close to Pennington with his hand resting on his holster. He very much doubted Pennington's heart felt anything but self-interest. "The lady didn't want your flowers. And she heard your apology, so there's no further need for you to speak to her."

Pennington's cold amber gaze locked with his for a moment, as if trying to find a chink in his armor, but when Sam did not look away he said, "Very well. You said you had something to speak to me about?"

Sam nodded. "William Waters informed me your men have been trying to intimidate him into selling his land. He doesn't want to, so leave him alone."

Pennington blinked, then gave a little chuckle. "My, my, you don't beat around the bush, do you, Sheriff? Aren't you the protective sort? First your lady, now the whiny little Yankee. We've done nothing illegal. We're just businessmen, trying to conduct lawful business in a free country."

"If Waters doesn't want to sell, he doesn't want to sell— especially at a lower price than what you first offered him. That's his choice. My job is to make sure he has that choice."

Pennington tsk-tsked. "Pity he feels that way. It's a prime piece of land with good water, even with the derelict house. I figured he'd be happy to hightail it back East, now that he's had a bitter taste of life in Texas. And I'm sorry you don't want to work with us, instead of against us, Sheriff. You seem like a stalwart fellow to have on one's side. But if we can't work through you, I suppose we'll just have to work around you." He waited for a moment, but when Sam remained still and silent, he turned to his driver and said, "Tackett, my business is done here. We'll be going back to La Alianza."

Sam waited until the carriage had rolled out of sight down the road before he turned and walked through the wrought-iron gate. He wasn't surprised when Prissy opened the door before he could even knock, or that her father was waiting in the hallway, along with Mrs. Fairchild.

Briefly, he told them the gist of his conversation with Pennington about the harassment of William Waters. "I've warned him, and now I don't intend to tolerate any further shenanigans from him or any of the Alliance men."

"Quite right, Sheriff Bishop," Mayor Gilmore said, extending his hand. "You have the full support of myself and the town council. I knew I was right to give you that badge."

Sam took his hand. "Thank you, sir." The mayor's approval of the way he was doing his job meant more to him than he could say. He hoped his approval of Sam wouldn't diminish if and when Sam told him he wanted to marry his daughter, too, but there he was, getting ahead of himself again.

"My daughter was just about to bring you something, Sheriff," Mayor Gilmore said, nodding to a napkin-covered dish on the side table, the same one Sam had seen Prissy holding when she'd been accosted by Pennington. "Mrs. Fairchild, why don't we adjourn to the kitchen and sample the one she left us?"

"Pie before noon," Mrs. Fairchild murmured, her voice amused. "Scandalous."

Mayor Gilmore chuckled, and the two left Sam alone with Prissy in the hallway.

Prissy walked over to the table, lifted the dish and held it out to Sam.

Even though the dish was covered by a napkin, he could smell the delicious odor of fresh-baked apples and brown sugar. He lifted a corner of the cloth and inhaled deeply, while his mind wondered what the present meant after her indecision the other night.

He looked into her eyes, getting lost in the clear, blue, untroubled depths of them. At the very least, he thought he could read that she wasn't angry at him for his "preliminary proposal." But did that mean she was considering it favorably? If only he didn't need to return to the jail, and could have a longer time alone with her.

"Sam," she said, "how did you know Pennington was coming to see me?"

He shrugged, sure he shouldn't admit he'd been lingering on the boardwalk outside the hotel, staring across the street at Gilmore House and thinking about Prissy. "I just had a feeling," he said.

"Well, I'm mighty glad you listened to that feeling," she said, her eyes shining. "It was so wonderful that you were right there when I needed you."

I want to be right there when you need me always, Prissy, he wanted to say, but he'd learned his lesson the other night, and kept his thoughts to himself. He hoped he would recognize when she was ready to hear all that was in his heart.

Chapter Thirteen

Wednesday, the day of the Spinsters' Club outing to visit Milly and her new baby, dawned bright and clear after a heavy rain during the night which did much to alleviate the summer heat. At the appointed hour, all eight of the other active Spinsters' Club members assembled by the Gilmore stable. Laden with gifts and covered dishes, they climbed into the mayor's victoria and an additional shay driven by Maude Harkey.

"You ladies all ready to go?" inquired Sam, smiling down at Prissy sitting in the victoria. Prissy hadn't seen Sam since the town meeting on Sunday when his suggested ordinance against more saloons or gambling halls had passed. Waters had aired his complaints about the pressure from the Alliance to sell, and Prissy had seen nods of confirmation from other ranchers who'd also been pressured. Her father exhorted everyone to resist, even pledging to loan money if anyone needed it to keep their property.

The meeting had gone well, but they'd had no chance to talk.

Now, she enjoyed the sight of him sitting tall in the

saddle on his black horse. If there'd ever been a more handsome man than Sam Bishop, she'd never met him. She was aware of the admiring looks of her friends, but she realized she wasn't feeling jealous or possessive as she had at church that day.

Because they were looking at her like she was already his.

The party had been a great success, Prissy judged, gazing around the parlor of the Brookfield ranch house. Milly beamed at each of them as they passed around her new son and made much of him, just as she had *oohed* and *aahed* at each gift, now piled high on the small table beside her—crocheted blankets, embroidered bibs, hand-sewn baby clothes, and the silver cup and rattle Prissy had bought at the mercantile. She could hear Sarah content-edly humming a hymn in the kitchen as she cleaned up the dishes from their potluck feast. Her husband would be coming to fetch her in his buggy soon, and she was no doubt looking forward to their reunion after the ten days she had spent helping her sister after the birth.

Sam had gone off with Nick to see a newborn colt, which was really just an excuse, Prissy guessed, for the two men to escape the feminine chatter and squeals of delight at the opening of each gift. He'd smiled at her before he'd left, and after he'd gone, the ladies made almost as much of that as they were making of the baby. Prissy simply smiled and said nothing.

Little Nicholas had made the rounds of the Spinsters and was once again cradled in his mother's arms. How happy Milly Brookfield looked, how fulfilled, Prissy thought. Would it be that way someday when she had their first child? A sudden yearning struck Prissy. Looking around the circle of women, she saw that emotion mirrored in each face. A new baby had that effect on women.

"What else is going on around town?" Milly asked. "Goodness, I've been cooped up for weeks on this ranch—maybe next Sunday I can return to church."

The Spinsters were happy to fill her in. "Mavis Hotchkiss is expecting again, she said in church last week," Bess Lassiter said. "Didn't she just have a baby a few months ago, right before the influenza hit?"

"Goodness, she's going to be a busy lady," Faith Bennett said.

"And you remember Emily's getting married very soon," Caroline said. The bride-to-be smiled radiantly.

"But the most interesting news is that romance is blooming at Gilmore House," Faith Bennet said, winking at Prissy. "Sheriff Bishop sure is smitten with you, Prissy."

"Yes, that was certainly nice of him to ride out here with us," Maude Harkey said. "Seems he can't bear to be parted from our Prissy."

Prissy blushed with pleasure. "I—"

"Tell us," asked Polly Shackleford, with a knowing look. "Is it official? Is our handsome sheriff courting you, Prissy?"

"He *is* quite handsome, Prissy," said Milly, smiling.

"Prissy assured me that she's considering her feelings about Sam very carefully. She's not rushing into anything this time," Sarah said, coming from the kitchen.

"Is that so?" Milly said, raising an eyebrow. "Good for you, Prissy. I think that's wise—"

There was a sudden report of a gunshot off to the northeast. Everyone froze.

"What was that?"

Milly remained calm, for the shot had not been close enough to disturb her sleeping baby. "Probably just one of the hands shooting a snake," she said. "I've learned not to worry about the occasional gunshot here or there, now that the Comanches have been leaving us alone for a—"

Several other shots in rapid succession interrupted her words, and they all jumped up.

"Oh dear heavens," Milly said.

Prissy saw the color drain from Milly's face like water flowing out of a tap. The baby began to wail and she clutched him tightly to her.

Everyone except Milly ran to the back door and saw the ranch hands running from the bunkhouse toward the barn.

"What is it, Bobby?" Sarah called to the youngest of them, who was the last one out of the bunkhouse.

He stopped. "Dunno, Miz Sarah, we were just fixin' t'go back out to the creek pasture t' mend fences when we heard the shots!"

Prissy ran after him to the barn. Sam and Nick were each saddling their horses with haste. The ranch hands began to do likewise.

Prissy dashed to the stall where Sam was cinching up Jackson's girth. "What is it? Who's shooting out there?" she cried.

His face was grim. "We don't know, but we're going to go find out. Nick says it's coming from the direction of the Waters ranch house."

"Listen up, men!" Nick shouted from the next stall. "Elijah, Isaiah, Caleb, saddle up and follow us as soon as you can. Micah, Josh, Bobby, you stay here and guard the house—"

"Go in the house, Prissy, and stay there," Sam ordered.

"Please," he added more gently, when she stayed rooted where she was. "The cowboys staying here will keep you safe. Now *go!*"

She wanted to ask him not to go, to be one of the ones who remained to guard the house, but she knew that a sheriff couldn't choose to avoid danger. She was overwhelmed with the desire to kiss him, to beg him to be careful, to throw her arms around him and keep him rooted to the spot.

But of course she couldn't do any of those things.

So Prissy took one last look at him before trudging back out into the sunlight. Her heart pounded, her eyes stung with unshed tears. She felt helpless and terrified, and all the more so when she saw a black plume of smoke rising from the direction of Waters's ranch house.

But she and the other ladies weren't helpless, she reminded herself as she ran the rest of the way to the kitchen door. At least they could pray.

And they did so, flinching as they heard several more reports echo from the direction of the Waters ranch, then a terrifying silence.

More than an hour later, they heard a horse and wagon approaching the house. Prissy ran to the back door. "One of your men is driving, Milly," she reported.

"But what about the rest of the men?" Milly asked from the parlor.

"I'm not sure," Prissy answered, her heart in her throat. "Let's find out."

Sarah stayed in the house with the baby while all the other women ran outside, joining the cowhands who'd remained behind to guard them as the wagon drew up in the yard.

"What happened, Isaiah? Where's Nick and the rest?" Milly demanded.

Prissy's eyes were drawn to a blanket-covered form in the wagon bed and she began to shake.

"That's not—that's not—"

The cowhand mercifully addressed Prissy first. "It's that Waters fella, that easterner. This is his wagon we found there."

The Spinsters gasped. Isaiah turned back to Milly. "The rest of the men went after the men that killed 'im, Miz Milly," he said, nodding towards the body. "We got there just as they was ridin' off. Soon's they caught sight a' us, they scattered in all different d'rections, so I don' know if they gonna be able to ketch any of 'em. But they're sure 'nough gonna try."

"Could you see who attacked the ranch?" Prissy asked, able to breathe again now that she knew it wasn't Sam lying in the wagon. "Was it Pennington's men?"

Isaiah said, "We couldn't tell. They all had on masks. And that Waters ranch house, Miz Milly, it's burnin' to the ground."

Prissy sighed, certain Pennington was behind this. No one else had a reason to harm Waters. The easterner had come to Texas with such big plans and high hopes—now he had lost his life and his efforts had come to nothing. She only hoped he hadn't suffered.

"Mr. Sam, he says for you ladies to wait till Dr. Walker comes for Miz Sarah, then Caleb and I are t' ride along with y'all back to Gilmore House. He doesn't know when he'll be back."

Prissy hadn't even thought about the journey home, with Pennington's murderous henchmen on the loose. She wanted to stay right where she was until she saw Sam return, safe and sound. It was all she could do not to drop to her knees. *Lord, please protect him while he's off in pursuit of these evil men.*

A volley of barks from Houston announced Sam's arrival just as Prissy lit the lamp in the hallway. She dashed past Flora to the door.

"Oh, Sam, I'm so glad you're finally here!" Only Flora's presence stopped her from launching herself into his arms. "Come in, come in." Even in the gathering dusk, she could see his clothes were stained and dusty, and his face was etched with weariness. Beyond him in front of the steps Jackson stood, head down, where Sam had dropped his reins.

"No, thanks, I'm all dirty," he said, "and Señora Flora wouldn't appreciate it if I tracked dirt into the house." He attempted a wink in the housekeeper's direction, but he was clearly exhausted, a dark expression on his face. "I just wanted to make sure you were all right."

"Yes, I'm okay," she assured him, though she was practically shaking again, reliving the terror she'd experienced when she thought it had been Sam in that wagon.

Dr. Walker had examined the body while the ladies were inside preparing to leave. Though he had assured them Waters had died quickly, there was something in his troubled gaze that told Prissy he was only trying to comfort them.

"Sam, is that you?" her father said, coming into the hall from his study. "Prissy told me what happened. A terrible business, terrible. Were you able to catch up with any of the murdering scoundrels?"

Sam's gaze fell and his shoulders slumped. Prissy's heart twisted with compassion for him.

"No, sir. They had too much of a lead. Nick and I followed one that ran north, then west. We thought he might turn southwest and circle back to La Alianza, but we lost his trail. We stopped there anyway and demanded to look around, but no man or horse looked like he'd just come in from a hard ride."

Her father whistled. "You've covered a lot of ground today. Did you tell Pennington you suspect his men did the killing?"

Sam shook his head. "He wasn't there. But I spoke to Francis Byrd. Of course he pretended complete ignorance of the raid and acted shocked that we would blame Alliance men. We'd have a hard time proving it, seeing as they were masked, but I made the accusation anyway."

"Was Waters alone out there? I thought he'd hired men to help with the rebuilding of the ranch house," her father said.

Sam narrowed his eyes. "He'd had trouble with them not showing up. We found him lying among the piles of lumber and stone he'd bought, but I don't think he could do that sort of work, not by himself."

"Did they rob him?"

Sam shrugged. "There wasn't any money in his pockets, but I don't know if he was carrying any."

He blinked suddenly, as if he'd thought of something, but before Prissy could ask him about it, her father spoke again. "Maybe that'll be the end of it, now that they know we're onto them." But he said it without any real conviction in his voice.

Sam didn't look convinced, either. "I'll stop by the hotel now, see if I can find any next of kin's address among Waters's effects, so I can notify them of his passing."

His eyes looked like two burned holes in a blanket,

Prissy thought. "That can wait until tomorrow, Sam. Come in and have something to eat. I'm sure you haven't had a bite since noontime, and the hotel restaurant's closed down now."

He tried to smile and failed. "Thanks, but I need to take Jackson back to the livery and rub him down, see him fed. Then I'm turning in myself. I'll see you at church tomorrow, Prissy. Good night, Mayor."

"You will wait at least until I make a sandwich for you, Señor Sheriff," Flora commanded. "I will wrap it up and you can take it with you." She bustled off to the kitchen without waiting for an answer.

"You're a good man, Sam Bishop," her father said, coming forward and extending his hand to Sam. "I'm proud to know you. Go and get some rest. I have full confidence in you, confidence you'll bring Waters's murderers to justice and find a way to get Pennington and his kind run out of San Saba County."

Prissy's heart felt full to bursting as she watched her father's words sink into Sam. How humble he was, in spite of her father's praise. She beamed at her father.

"Thank you, Mayor Gilmore. I'll do my best to be worthy of your confidence in me," he said hoarsely. "Good night, sir. Good night, Prissy."

It was all she could do not to follow him, fling her arms around him and tell him that yes, she would indeed marry him. Happily.

The mayor's undeserved praise and Prissy's radiant smile seared through Sam's soul like flaming swords as he trudged down the darkened street, leading his horse. He wasn't worthy of Prissy's father's high regard or his confidence, and if he knew that Sam had come to Simpson

Creek with a stolen piece of jewelry, in search of an easier life—and a beautiful wife—he'd slam the door in his face.

So he thought all Sam needed was a good night's sleep, and then he'd awaken refreshed, knowing how to discover the identity of the murderers and the way to rid the town of the Alliance?

He uttered a bark of ironic laughter that startled a sleepy bird roosting in the rafters above the livery doorway. He doubted the workmen would be able to shed any light on the attack, so he didn't have a clue how to prove an Alliance man had killed Waters any more than he had a plan to defeat the triumvirate bent on taking over San Saba County. Maybe he'd know how to proceed if he'd ever been a sheriff or even a deputy, but he was nothing more than a liar and a thief himself.

Any day now, Kendall Raney could arrive at La Alianza, and then it was only a matter of time before he and Sheriff Sam Bishop would meet. And if Raney recognized the hapless gambler in the present sheriff, Sam Bishop would be exposed as a fraud.

What on earth had he gotten himself into? How on earth was he to avenge the murder of William Waters?

He could run, he knew. He could leave his tired horse here and take one of the livery's other mounts, ride out of town in the dead of night and start over elsewhere. He'd always hankered to see the Rocky Mountains, or even California. He'd heard San Francisco possessed marvelous gambling halls.

But that was the easy way out, and it no longer seemed desirable since it meant giving up his chance with Prissy and causing her sorrow and pain.

Maybe he should leave, though. Maybe a woman like

Prissy would be better off without a liar pursuing her. Prissy deserved a man of integrity, a man of his word, a man whose life wasn't built on lies. He'd cause her just as much sorrow and pain if he stayed as he would if he left.

He didn't have any answers. All he knew was that he was in deep—and there was no good way out.

Chapter Fourteen

Sam's first priority the next morning was tracking down
the men who'd been hired to help Waters rebuild his house
at the ranch. Following a hunch, he found them sitting
down in the shade of a cottonwood below the lumber mill
by the creek, sharing a bottle.

No, they didn't know anything about the attack, though
they were sure sorry to hear about it, if only because it
meant now they couldn't count on earning the wages the
fool tenderfoot had promised them. One of them said he'd
received a message purportedly written by Waters telling
them they didn't have to work the rest of the week.

Sam found no reason to think they were complicit in
the murder.

He asked George Detwiler to keep his ears open if any
Alliance men grew boastful under the influence of his
whiskey. If only he had a man who could infiltrate the
Alliance ranks, but who? He didn't want to risk anyone
else's life. And he didn't dare pretend he'd decided to ally
himself with the Alliance—if Raney ever did come to the
area, that would be too close for comfort.

An uneasy quiet descended on Simpson Creek during

the week that followed. Sam saw half a dozen more wagons driven by longtime residents, piled high with household goods, leaving town—and an increasing number of strangers riding into town, some with families and goods of their own in heavily laden wagons. Some of them, he discovered, were moving onto the very ranches just vacated by Simpson Creek settlers, but when he asked Mr. Avery, the bank president, about it, he admitted the ranches had been bought up by the Alliance. And Pennington was pressuring him to let him buy the Waters place, now that its heir had met with an "unfortunate accident." But Avery had insisted he had not received instructions from the man's heirs in New York as yet, so there could be no sale.

"He smiled at me like I'd said they could buy it tomorrow," Avery reported. "Thinks it's as good as theirs. I wouldn't be surprised if he's already sent a telegram to those New York folks, offerin' them a 'bargain,' but of course the telegraph operator can't ethically divulge the contents of any messages he sends."

"A bargain like he offered Waters?" Sam had asked.

Avery's mouth had twisted. "I can't give details, either, of course, but I can tell you that no one who's left got anything remotely resembling a bargain. I think they got motivated to sell by something else entirely, if you catch my meaning."

Nick Brookfield told him that he'd turned Pennington and Byrd away on Monday when they'd come calling to offer to buy the Brookfield ranch, "now that the Waters ranch would soon belong to the Alliance." His men reported potshots taken at them while they were out in the fields so that they'd had to resort to standing watch from the small fortification they'd built atop the hill next to their ranch.

"It's like last summer all over again," Nick said, having told Sam about last year's raids by the Comanches and the harassment by a group called the Circle who had tried to run off the ranch's cowhands simply because of the color of their skin.

Sam took a morning and rode west to Colorado Bend. He wanted to assess the sheriff there, a man named Hantz, since Pennington had already boasted of the "cordial relationship" they had with him. Hantz merely shrugged his shoulders at Sam's concern and said he couldn't find anything illegal about a group of fellows buying land from individuals, and even when Sam had confided his suspicion that the triumvirate was behind the murder of a legal heir to a property, he seemed unmoved.

"Coulda been done by anyone," he said with a shrug. "You said yourself you didn't have no proof a' who it was. Don't look like you have no case against the Ranchers' Alliance, Bishop," he added with faintly veiled derision.

When he rode east to San Saba, however, it was a different story. Sheriff Wade Teague seemed as troubled as Sam was about the encroachment of the three-man partnership, but had no idea what action to take.

"I heard that last partner's comin' up from Houston. You don't want to ruffle this Kendall Raney's feathers, from what I hear tell. Real ruthless character, he is. You watch your back, Bishop. Don't rile him less'n you have no choice."

You don't know the half of it, Sam thought.

"Time was, we could sic the Texas Rangers on a bunch like that," the San Saba lawman went on. "But it don't look like they'll be reorganized any time soon. Them Texas State police—" he spat to show what he thought of that organization "—didn't do nothin' Throckmorton didn't want 'em to do, and they ain't apt t'be any different with Pease now he's governor. Shoot, I dunno if you could even count on the Army unless those fellows came in with their hired guns at their back and tried to take your job and the mayor's."

So he was alone.

On Sunday, Reverend Chadwick preached on the topic of fear, as if he could sense what was on Sam's mind and the minds of so many other Simpson Creek residents.

"The words of Romans 8:31 ring true for us now just as they did when the Apostle Paul wrote them—'If God be for us, who can be against us?'" The pastor's voice quavered with age but nevertheless rang with authority and assurance.

But Sam wondered if he had the right to think of himself as part of "us." Though he'd always made sure he and his sisters attended Sunday services back in Tennessee when they were growing up because it was the proper thing to do, he'd never quite felt that they had God on their side. He'd taken His name in vain when the hand of cards he'd been dealt had gone against him, had cheated when he could get by with it.

And he'd stolen that ring.

By thunder, he was going to have to find a way to do some good with that ring, to get it off his hands—and off his soul. Then he wouldn't imagine he felt it burning a hole through his shoulder at night when he lay on his mattress trying to sleep. Maybe then he'd feel worthy to become part of the "us" of the Simpson Creek Church.

Beside him, Prissy sat listening attentively, unaware of the turmoil of his thoughts.

"Dearly beloved, we are gathered together today to bless the union of Emily Thompson and Edward Markison,"

Reverend Chadwick intoned the following Saturday afternoon.

Prissy glanced at Sam, sitting on the pew beside her, sitting ramrod-straight in his freshly brushed black frock coat. He'd promised to put the town's problems aside while attending the wedding and the festivities afterward, but clearly he was having trouble doing it despite his best intentions.

He's so dedicated. Simpson Creek is fortunate to have him.

As if sensing her thoughts, he smiled down at her and took her hand for a brief moment, squeezing it gently. Although they had still not spoken of his preliminary proposal, something had shifted between them after the incident at the ranch—after she'd thought she'd lost him.

"Emily looks so happy, doesn't she?" she whispered, returning his smile.

"So does Ed," he whispered back, nodding toward the groom, who stood facing his bride at the altar, grinning from ear to ear. "He told me she's the most beautiful woman he's ever seen." He held her gaze for a moment longer, studying her face.

Prissy felt her face flush with color as he stared at her. She suddenly found herself imagining walking down the aisle toward Sam.

In the row ahead of them, Sarah Walker, who was sitting with her husband, Milly and Nick turned around, and winked, as if she knew exactly what was happening. Prissy smiled at her, then cast a hasty glance on her other side, where her father was sitting. He was staring toward the bridal pair, completely focused on them, unaware of his daughter's blushing at the possibility of marrying the handsome man next to her.

Beyond her father sat Mariah Fairchild, resplendent in another dress of the dove-gray she looked so dignified in. The widow seemed forever at Prissy's father's side these days. He was going to marry her, Prissy knew that now. He hadn't said as much, and Prissy would never dare to ask him, but she now saw it was inevitable. It was just as well—her father deserved happiness, even if it was with the widow.

"'Charity suffereth long, and is kind, charity envieth not'—now, we know Paul meant love when he wrote about charity, didn't he?" Reverend Chadwick was saying.

Prissy winced inwardly. It served her right that she should begin listening again in time to feel convicted by the Scriptures. She hadn't been kind in her thoughts just now. Her father wasn't the only one who deserved happiness—Mariah Fairchild did, too. It was time she started being a bit more charitable, more welcoming.

She felt Sam would approve. And she realized she quite enjoyed his approval.

After the service, the bride, groom and guests feasted on food contributed by the Spinsters' Club and the magnificent four-tiered wedding cake Sarah had baked. The bouquet was tossed and caught by Polly Shackleford, who giggled about the suggestion that one of the bachelors coming to Prissy's barbecue next Saturday might turn out to be her match.

"Pooh, anyone with eyes in their head can see that you'll be the next one married, no matter who caught the bouquet," Sarah whispered, while Polly paraded around the social hall with her prize.

Prissy laughed. "Time will tell," she said.

"Tell what?" asked Sam, who had just rejoined them.

"Who will ask me to dance first," she told him, fluttering her lashes at him. "Listen, the fiddler's tuning up outside."

"You don't have to wait for time to tell you, sweetheart, I'll be the one to ask you first," he said, sweeping her along with the guests thronging for the door. "And I hope you'll save most of your dances for me," he whispered in her ear.

The worst of the heat had faded with the sun's setting. Prissy and Sam and the rest of the wedding guests spilled out of the church social hall and onto the lawn, where lanterns had been strung and lit, and a temporary platform for the fiddler erected. The bride and groom were already dancing, soon joined by Emily's parents and the best man and his wife, who had come for the wedding from Buffalo Bayou, where Ed Markison was from.

Later, when they were breathless and thirsty from dancing, Prissy sat on one of the benches around the dance area while Sam went to fetch them some punch.

"Sure miss some of the old faces that used to come in from the ranches to attend doin's like a wedding these days," Mrs. Detwiler, sitting nearby, was saying to Prissy's father, the widow and old Zeke Carter, who usually sat outside the mercantile whittling. "You didn't get to meet them, Mrs. Fairchild, but there are so many long-time settlers who've just packed up and moved away. Don't know what things are coming to in Simpson Creek."

"It's worse than that," the old man said. "Some folks are actually joinin' that Alliance, can you believe it? I heard tell Clyde Knight's joinin' so's he kin keep his ranch, he says. Huh! I gave him a piece a' my mind, let me tell you."

Prissy sighed. Even at a wedding, the threat of the Alliance and the changes it was bringing to Simpson Creek was a topic that couldn't be forgotten.

"And I've seen them strangers on the street with that emblem on their shirts," Zeke went on. "I passed right by 'em without so much as a nod. The very idea! Sheriff, you got to do something!" he said, as Sam returned with two cups of punch.

"Pardon me, sir?" Sam listened politely, head bent, as the old man told him what they had been talking about. How patient Sam was being with the old man, she thought.

"It's a wedding, Zeke. Let the sheriff have a little time away from the troubles," Mrs. Detwiler said, with an apologetic look at Prissy.

But the graybeard was not to be deterred. "And what about that murdered easterner, Sheriff Bishop?" he demanded. "He wasn't exactly one a' us, but it ain't right that a man inherits a piece a'land and he ends up dyin' afore he ever gits t'live on it."

"I'm doing everything I can to discover the identity of the murderers," Sam began.

"Pshaw, you know sure as God made lil' apples them Ranchers' Alliance fellas did it," Zeke retorted. "If you was to go arrest a couple of 'em and string 'em up, I reckon that would put them scoundrels on notice."

"Zeke, Sheriff Bishop can hardly arrest men at random and hang them just to teach the Alliance or anyone else a lesson," her father put in hastily. "Simpson Creek has always been run by laws and principles of justice. And maybe we ought to save this discussion for a more suitable time," he said heavily, with a meaningful glance at the ladies present.

The old man snorted. "I ain't forgot you're up for election soon, James Gilmore."

It was a retort Prissy was all too used to hearing aimed at her father.

"Feel free to run against me, Zeke," her father said, unperturbed. "Ah, the fiddler's striking up a waltz. Mariah, would you do me the honor?"

Sam turned to Prissy, about to speak, but he paused at the sound of hoofbeats approaching.

A moment later she saw them—Ranchers' Alliance men approaching on horseback, with Tolliver riding in the center of the pack.

Tolliver raised a hand and they all reined in their horses. "Well, lookee what we got here, fellas," he said. "An' here we was sayin' the saloon didn't have no pretty girls t'dance with. That was 'cause they were all down here dancin'. And here they got fancy food an' even fiddlin'. We're lucky we found the party afore it was over. Reckon we'll join y'all," he said, dismounting from his horse. All around him, his cronies were doing the same, eyeing the Spinsters and the punchbowl.

Sam felt Prissy bristle beside him and saw Reverend Chadwick leave the folks he was sitting with and begin to make his way toward the interlopers.

"Stay here, Prissy," Sam murmured. He then moved to intercept the elderly preacher. "Let me handle this, Reverend."

Striding rapidly over to where the saddle tramps were tying up their horses, he called out, "Sorry, fellows, but this is a private party, a wedding. You'll have to ride on."

Tolliver faced him, hands on his hips. "Ride on? But we want t' dance with th' bride, offer her our very best wishes, drink a toast. Ain't that right, boys?"

The others chorused their agreement.

"Not this time. Ride on," Sam repeated, pushing his frock coat back to display the gun belt he wore, glad he'd listened to Nick's advice to wear it everywhere he went, even at social events. Out of the corner of his eye, he saw Nick and Dr. Walker and other men of the town move, some of them behind him, others forming a solid barrier between the Ranchers' Alliance men and the ladies.

"Now that ain't very hospitable of ya," Tolliver complained. "We was just tryin' t'be neighborly, t'be a part of the town. I have a notion I'd like t'dance with your sweetheart," he said, throwing a leering look toward Prissy.

Sam ignored the personal gibe. "I said ride on, Tolliver."

"Or what?" jeered Tolliver, the others echoing him with catcalls.

Sam hated the fact that this happy event was about to be marred by an ugly scene, at best. He wished he could to turn around and indicate to Prissy that he wanted her to herd the women into the safety of the church social hall. But he dared not shift his eyes away the cold-eyed saddle tramp.

"Or spend a night in my jail again, Tolliver. Your boss won't like that."

"Shoot, I don't reckon he wants me to take any more guff from no law dog like you," Tolliver sneered, stale fumes of whiskey drifting toward Sam. "We're fixin' t' run this town, an' it's time you learned what that means. Fellas, make sure this fight's just between th' sheriff and me, would ya?"

As one, the rest of the Alliance men drew their guns and aimed them at the men who'd come to back Sam up. Then he clenched his fists and began circling Sam.

Sam watched Tolliver's eyes, waiting for the sign that presaged his lunge.

"I'm gonna mess up that purty face a' yours, Sheriff," Tolliver taunted. "I don't reckon you kin fight worth beans."

All at once Reverend Chadwick threw himself between them. "Please reconsider, son," he entreated. "You don't want to spoil a happy event. Come back tomorrow morning, come to church. We'll welcome you with open arms, I promise."

"Get outta my way, preacher!" snarled Tolliver, shoving the preacher so roughly that he fell backward, cartwheeling his arms in a vain attempt to regain his balance before he landed heavily on the ground.

Somewhere in the crowd, a woman screamed. Sam darted a glance over his shoulder to see that Nolan was tending the fallen preacher, then launched himself with a roar of rage at the sneering Tolliver.

The man was waiting for him. Tolliver threw a fist that took Sam on the chin and rocked him back for a costly moment, then punched him in the abdomen, sending nausea—and fury—surging through Sam. A red mist drenched his brain, a hatred of these vermin who'd had the gall to intrude on a happy, innocent event and soil it with their presence.

He threw himself at Tolliver, landing a staggering right hook that snapped the other man's head back. They went down on the lawn with a crash, arms flailing, legs thrashing.

Tolliver gained the uppermost position on top of him

as the heavier man, but Sam was wiry-lean and had the strength to throw him off. Tolliver rolled and crouched, spitting, then threw himself at Sam again, grabbing at Sam's pistol. Sam knew he must not let Tolliver gain control of his firearm or all could be lost. It gave him a desperate energy that propelled him on top of Tolliver, and he rained blow after blow down on the struggling man, bloodying his nose, splitting his lip, punching his abdomen and knocking the wind out of his assailant.

He leaped off of Tolliver, his chest heaving. "Give up, Tolliver," he ordered. "The rest of you men take off, and he's the only one who'll be behind bars."

But Tolliver still had plenty of fight left in him, and wasn't ready to admit defeat in front of his cronies. He used the second Sam had taken to address them to whip a Bowie knife out of his boot.

Sam yanked his gun out of his holster and shot the knife from Tolliver's grasp. Tolliver clutched his bloody hand, howling in pain. Half a dozen guns were cocked behind Sam as Nick, Nolan and the rest drew on the saddle tramps to cover Sam.

"Come along, Tolliver, the doctor can treat you in jail—" Sam began.

And then he saw something, lying in the grass where they had been struggling only a moment ago. It gleamed dully in the light from the lanterns—a pocket watch. Keeping the pistol trained on Tolliver, who stood hunched over, his bloody hand clutched against his belly, Sam picked it up.

"Where'd you get this?" he demanded of Tolliver.

Tolliver said nothing.

Sam turned it over and saw the engraving—W.W.III.

He walked over to Tolliver and grabbed his arm, forcing him to stand upright.

"Leroy Tolliver, I'm arresting you for the murder of William Waters III."

Chapter Fifteen

"I found that watch," Tolliver whined. "You cain't prove I killed that tenderfoot, just 'cause I have his watch." Prissy could tell by the sound of his voice that he was lying.

"Yeah, you don't have no proof," insisted another of the Alliance men. "You can't hang a man for findin' a watch and pickin' it up."

Sam ignored them for a moment, his eyes searching until he found Reverend Chadwick, who had been helped to his feet. "Reverend, you all right?" Sam called.

The old man nodded. "Don't worry about me, I'm fine."

He turned back to Tolliver and his cronies. "He'll have a fair trial. Any of you other Alliance men want to share a cell with Tolliver? We could let the judge decide which one to hang."

The others eyed each other uneasily, then stalked off toward their horses.

Sam turned Tolliver roughly around, and using a length of rope someone had brought from their wagon, tied the man's wrists behind him.

No one suggested resuming the celebration—the festive

mood had been ruined. Now all the townspeople clumped together, including the new bride, who huddled tearfully against her groom. Prissy was still astonished by the fact that Sam had been able to shoot that knife right out of Tolliver's hand. She couldn't take her eyes off him.

"I'll come with you to the jail and treat his injuries," Nolan Walker said to Sam. "Sarah, you go on home. I'll be along when I can."

"You fellows tell Pennington an' Byrd what happened!" Tolliver called after the men who were already mounted and heading for the road. Then he wrenched around to glare at Sam, though one of his eyes was rapidly swelling shut. "I reckon this'll bring Raney up from Houston, right enough. You done poked a hornet's nest, Sheriff. This town won't survive to hang me."

Sam ignored his bravado. "That's enough out of you," he said calmly.

Prissy was overwhelmed with pride over Sam's bravery, even though she knew it would mean she wouldn't get to see him for quite a while. Now that he'd have a murderer in his jail, worse yet a murderer with powerful allies, he couldn't just leave it unguarded.

Luis Menendez materialized out of the crowd. "Reckon you need a deputy now, Sheriff," he said.

"I reckon he's right, Sam," her father agreed. "At least for the time being. Deputize him. And I'm calling a town council meeting. We'll have to set up a rotation of guard duty, so there's always two men guarding the jail till the circuit judge can arrive to convene a trial. Mr. Jewett," he said, addressing the telegraph operator, "I'd appreciate it if you'd notify the circuit judge. We're going to need him and a prosecuting attorney soon as he can get here."

She watched as Sam began to lead his prisoner away while the townspeople thanked him over and over.

"Much obliged, Sheriff!" Ed Markison called after him, his arm still protectively draped around his bride. "Reckon you saved us from much worse."

"You must be very proud of your beau," Mariah Fairchild said, smiling at Prissy. "Such a courageous, handsome man. And he loves you—I can tell."

Prissy felt herself thawing toward the woman who had a hand over her father's arm. "Yes, I am. Very proud. And I love him, too," she said, shifting her gaze toward her father, to see what he would say.

James Gilmore cleared his throat, his eyes glistening as he looked back at her. "I couldn't approve more, Prissy. Come on, let's walk Mrs. Fairchild back to the hotel, and then we'll go on home."

"But we—the Spinsters' Club—were going to clean up the social hall—"

"Time enough for that after church tomorrow," he insisted.

Houston's shrill barking woke her in the early dawn. He jumped from his cozy place at her feet and threw himself against her bedroom door. Someone was pounding at the front door below.

Struggling to orient herself, she threw on her wrapper and padded barefoot into the hallway. Her father was just emerging from his bedroom and pulling on his dressing gown, his thin hair askew, his face wrinkled from sleep.

Antonio was already at the door.

"You got t' wake the mayor!" someone at the front door shouted to Antonio. "The church is on fire!"

Prissy gasped. With the front door open, she could smell it now—smoke.

"Organize a bucket brigade with water from the creek!" her father shouted down the stairs.

"Already done!" the voice called back up the stairs. "But it had a good start afore th' smell woke the reverend and the sheriff."

"Antonio, bring every bucket you can find from the stable," her father called over his shoulder, already heading back to his room to dress. "Prissy, bring some old bedsheets to tear into bandages in case anyone gets burned."

They dressed as fast as they could. Prissy secured Houston in the kitchen, and then they joined the throng running toward the church in the pale light of dawn, their ears filled with the roar of the blaze and the shouts of the townspeople, their eyes on the ominous black cloud that stained the purity of the morning sky.

Prissy's heart sank as she neared the end of the street. It was true—Simpson Creek's only church was engulfed in flame. As they drew to a horrified stop in front of it, a shower of sparks flew upward and the roof caved in. The bell in the steeple fell into the midst of the inferno with one last, desperate clang.

Her eyes sought and found Sam, already at the head of the bucket brigade, throwing water onto the conflagration. She wanted to tell him it was useless, to step back and just watch the building die lest flying sparks singe him and the others, but she knew that in the tinder-dry conditions of a Texas August, nearby buildings such as the parsonage and the undertaker's were still in danger.

Luis Menendez stood at the door of the jail, a rifle held at the ready in case someone tried to take advantage of the emergency to break Tolliver out. She saw Reverend

Chadwick, too, standing next to Mrs. Detwiler, unashamed tears streaking down his pale cheeks.

"Prissy, there you are," Sarah said. "Good, you brought bandage material. Take this bucket of water and dipper and see if any of the men need a drink. They're working so hard they won't even notice being thirsty. And send anyone who's burned to me."

By the time the sun had fully risen, the church and social hall were nothing but a smoking, blackened ruin. A total loss. No one would ever worship again in the building that the first settlers had erected when they founded the community in the decade before. The townspeople stood in disbelieving clumps in the churchyard, some hollow-eyed, some weeping.

Sam, his shirt sweat-drenched and gray with soot, found her in the throng. He reached out a hand and she went into his embrace, sobbing against his shoulder.

"It'll be all right, sweetheart," he said, his hand smoothing her hair.

He couldn't understand, she thought. He hadn't lived here all his life, hadn't grown up worshipping in that church. He probably hadn't imagined her walking down that aisle to meet him at the altar, as she had just hours ago at Ed and Emily's wedding.

Or maybe he had, she thought as he gazed at her with such concern it nearly made her heart break.

Sam turned to Reverend Chadwick. "Could there have been a candle left burning in the social hall?"

The old pastor's eyes were red-rimmed. He shook his head. "I made sure they were all out before I went to the parsonage, just as I always do every time there's an event at church. Everything was in order."

Sam cast an eye at the sky, which was clear and cloud-free. "There wasn't a storm, so lightning couldn't have caused this."

"Wasn't no lightning. Those Alliance fellers did this, for revenge," Zeke Carter muttered, voicing the suspicion that had been in everyone's mind.

"Did you see them? Did anyone see them?"

No one had, though Reverend Chadwick had thought he might have heard horses galloping off.

Sam heaved a sigh. "It probably *was* Tolliver's men, but proving it is another thing."

Reverend Chadwick cleared his throat. "In the meantime, we must get ready for our worship service today."

Prissy gaped at him, along with everyone else, thinking perhaps the tragic event had addled his mind. Their church was a smoking ruin.

"We have much to be thankful for," Reverend Chadwick said. "No one was hurt, neither fighting the fire or last night, and the outcome could well have been much different. And don't you see, if we don't have our worship service, and we sit around today mourning over the loss of a mere building, these men win in a way. We cannot allow that to happen. We must find a place to worship together."

Everyone was silent, digesting his words.

Prissy's father rubbed his chin. "I suppose everyone could come to the ballroom at Gilmore House," he began.

"Why don't we just assemble in the meadow across the creek?" Reverend Chadwick suggested. "That will do in good weather, and we can use the ballroom when it rains. An open-air worship, in the midst of God's creation. What could be better?"

There was a murmur of assent, even approval.

"Very well then. Let's all go home and clean up, change into our Sunday best, and assemble back in the meadow, say, in an hour."

"Go on over to the worship service. Luis and I'll watch him," Nick Brookfield said, laying his hat on Sam's desk.

"Yeah, go on over and pray with them pious people," Tolliver jeered from inside his cell. "You kin both go," he said to Nick. "Me 'n' the greaser'll pass the time a' day together till Pennington comes fer me."

"Silence, *malvado!*" snapped Luis, who sat in the jail office's only other chair, facing the prisoner, a rifle across his knees.

Sam and Nick both ignored Tolliver. "I'm the sheriff. I should stay," Sam said. "Thanks anyway."

"Nonsense," Nick said in his clipped British accent, but his blue eyes were warm. "You'll be right across the creek in the meadow," he said, pointing out the cell window. "We could shout for you, if need be—and it's only for an hour. Then you'll return here and we'll meet with the town council. Go ahead. I'll bet Prissy's waiting for you. They're already singing the first hymn."

Was Nick too polite to say Sam needed to attend church more than he did? Still, he supposed he should go. As sheriff, perhaps his presence would be encouraging to them. "All right," Sam said at last. "Much obliged."

He could hear them singing as he stepped out the door.

"Lord of all to Thee we raise, this our hymn of grateful praise."

He could see them now, too, as he stepped onto the wooden bridge, facing the creek where the choirmaster led them in their piano-less singing. He could see Prissy in the midst of them, singing along with the rest. They looked happy. They sang of being grateful, of praising— after their church building had been burned to ashes by hateful men.

And then he realized *his* presence wouldn't be their encouragement. They didn't need the support represented by a man with a tin star on his vest. They already had a relationship with the source of all encouragement.

He felt suddenly humbled. *He* was the one who needed encouraging, not only because they knew he was a lawman facing a challenging time, but because of what they *didn't* know—that he was unqualified for the job, that he was nothing but a scapegrace gambler and a thief.

It was all he could do not to break into a run the last few yards so as to be with them that much faster. It seemed he was finding his way back to God, something he didn't quite believe would ever happen.

"We're glad you could join us, Sheriff," Reverend Chadwick said, beckoning him with a smile. "Come here, we'd like to pray for you."

Sam knelt in the sun-warmed grass. Chadwick hadn't asked him to kneel, but as undeserving as he was, it seemed like the right thing to do. Then the preacher laid his hand on Sam's head and prayed for the Lord to protect and guide him as he dealt with the accused murderer in his jail and the powerful band of men bent on taking over their town. Prissy stood by him on one side and the mayor on the other, and folks had come forward to lay their hands on his back and shoulders, murmuring their own prayers for him.

He was so unworthy. He kept his eyes shut tight, afraid

the tears would escape down his cheeks and he would have to confess everything.

I'm sorry for the man I've been, Lord. Please change me and make me clean, so they don't find out what I really am. I don't want to be that man anymore. Please show me what to do. He felt Prissy's hand in his, and he squeezed it. *From here on in, Prissy, with God's help, I'll be a new man. I'll be a man deserving of your love.*

Everyone sat in the grass on blankets and sheets, some with traces of soot still streaking their faces, as Reverend Chadwick gave his sermon about laying up treasures in Heaven rather than on earth.

"Our church wasn't fancy, and the new one we build on this site isn't likely to be, either, for we've always believed worship doesn't rely on how many stained-glass windows we have or gold offering plates," he said. "The church building we had is gone, but the church is not, for we, the townspeople of Simpson Creek, *are* the church, and we're still right here."

When the service was over, people milled about, exchanging opinions about how the new church should look and wondering how soon it could be built. Many wanted to speak with Sam, but he needed a moment with Prissy.

"I'm not sure when I'll see you, Prissy," Sam said. "We're having the town council meeting now, and after that, I have a prisoner to guard. But I do need to speak to you—soon."

She just nodded as if she'd already assumed as much. "I understand," she said. "And yes, I need to speak to you, too. We have much to discuss. The Spinsters are meeting now to decide if the barbecue should still take place next Saturday, otherwise I'd steal you away for just a minute."

"What do you think the group will decide?" he asked. It would be too bad to call off the party they'd been looking forward to so enthusiastically, especially since he'd decided after recent events that it would be the perfect occasion to officially propose to her. He'd already taken Mrs. Patterson at the mercantile into his confidence, and had purchased a sapphire ring from her. He couldn't wait any longer to declare his love for her. But he needed to come clean with Prissy and tell her everything, and hope that she would still have him.

"I'll suggest we go ahead," she said, "but change it a bit—use it to raise money for the new church. Papa and I will still provide the barbecue, of course, but we ladies will all make pies and cakes, and auction them off to the highest bidder. And I'll see if Mrs. Detwiler will auction off one of her quilts—did you know she was an accomplished quilter?"

He shook his head, charmed by the undefeated enthusiasm of this girl he loved.

"You know, Papa could just pay for the new church materials, and he has already pledged a substantial contribution, including a new stained glass window in memory of Mama. But Reverend Chadwick says that it's important for the town to feel that the church belongs to all of them—do you see what I mean? It won't mean as much if Papa just hands over the money. Does that make sense?"

Sam nodded. Dread filled him as he looked at the wonderful woman in front of him and imagined telling her about his past, and his lies.

It was almost more than he could bear.

Chapter Sixteen

Much to Sam's surprise, neither Pennington nor Byrd came to protest Tolliver's being accused of murder. As far as anyone knew, they remained holed up at La Alianza.

"Looks like they abandoned you, *hombre*," Luis taunted Tolliver, after a second day passed without a word from either man, or even a visit from one of his cronies. "They won't even come to see you hang."

"They'll come, and it won't be t'see me swing, neither," Tolliver snarled back. "They're jes' waitin' fer the right time, greaser."

That's what Sam thought, too. He maintained constant vigilance with the rotating two-man guard shifts that had been set up on Sunday. He insisted on being one of the men of each two-man shift, and Luis Menendez, who'd proved himself utterly reliable and dedicated, served as the other at least half of every day or night. Brookfield and Walker also took stints, as did other men of the town.

Every time a new man came on guard duty, one of the men whose time was up fetched food from the hotel, so there would never be a moment without two fully armed men on guard. Even at night they took turns, one man sitting up guarding the sleeping prisoner while Sam or the other man caught a few winks. Sam never slept soundly when it came his turn, fearing the attack would begin while he slumbered.

The circuit judge had sent word he and the prosecutor couldn't be there until next week because they were in the middle of a trial in Harkeyville. That meant an even longer time to guard Tolliver than Sam had anticipated, a longer time for everyone's nerves to be stretched thin.

Prissy had come down to the jail on Monday to bring him fried chicken and biscuits she'd made herself, and they had sat in front of the jail while they ate, away from Tolliver's leering gaze. He'd drunk in the sight of her in her pretty gingham dress, listening as she recited all the details of the upcoming party. It wasn't that he longed to know that Milly was bringing fried chicken and Faith Bennett shoo-fly pie, but he loved the sound of her voice.

Just as he'd begun to wonder if it was the right time to talk to her, two Alliance men rode by and gave them a long look. Fearing it presaged an attack, Sam hustled her across the street to have Dr. Walker see her home. Letting her see his regret, he'd asked her not to come again for the time being, fearing the Alliance men would make some move specifically because she was there and his attention was divided. He figured he couldn't be too careful about her safety, even if it meant seeing her hardly at all.

The next day, via Antonio, she sent him a small, brown-wrapped bundle. He unwrapped it to find an oval-framed daguerreotype of her. In an accompanying note, she confessed it belonged to her father, but he'd agreed to loan it to Sam until they could see each other again. He placed it in his desk where only he could look at it, so Tolliver couldn't feast his eyes on it, too. Sam believed Prissy loved him, too. Would it be enough to get them through everything he had to tell her?

She started writing him a daily note, which she sent to the jail with Antonio or her father. Redolent of the lilac scent she usually wore, the notes were light and newsy, telling him what amusing thing Houston had done, or how she had changed the menu for the barbecue yet again. Then she told him, simply and honestly, how proud she was of the dedicated way he did his job. And she'd copy some verse from the Bible to encourage him, and asked him to read a chapter a day from the book of John, saying she was doing that, too, and that it was nice to think of both of them reading the same thing.

He read her notes over and over again and he started writing her back from his desk, telling her how he missed her, how much he longed for the trial to be over and the Alliance banished from Simpson Creek forever so they could once again go on carefree picnics under the Wedding Tree. He imagined her smiling as she read those words.

"Bet he's writin' that purty yaller-haired girl agin, th' one I saw him with at the weddin' we busted up, ain't he, greaser?" Tolliver gibed from behind his bars. "I heard tell it was the mayor's daughter. Ain't you the smart one, Bishop, sparkin' a rich girl? Soon as you marry her, you kin stop bein' a law dog chasin' desperadoes like me and become a man of leisure, cain't ya?"

"Shut up or I'll tie your noose so you slowly strangle to death on the gallows," Luis threatened. Sam held up a hand to quiet his deputy. Tolliver thrived on baiting them, but Sam thought it was better to pretend not to hear the snake hissing behind the bars.

Simpson Creek was a law-abiding town, but inevitably, there were still times when Sam had to see to other problems not related to the Alliance. Two days before the barbecue, Nolan took over guard duty while Sam walked down Travis Street to the boardinghouse to resolve a dispute between a boarder and the proprietress. After he'd enforced the latter's right to make the rules in her own establishment, he walked back to Main Street just in time to see Pennington driving past in his carriage, with another man sitting beside him—a man Sam recognized the instant he met his hooded, intense gaze.

Kendall Raney.

At the sight of his nemesis, Sam felt a chill of icy sweat trickle down his spine. It was all he could do to stand still on the boardwalk and force himself not to pull his hat down a bit in an attempt to escape notice.

He knew any such effort was in vain, for Pennington had spotted him and ordered the driver to halt.

"Why, Sheriff Bishop, we meet again," Pennington crowed. "And what a fortunate encounter, for I have the pleasure of presenting our third partner, Mr. Kendall Raney."

Sam straightened, his throat gone dry as a mud puddle in August. His heart thudded dully in a chest suddenly too small for it. He cleared his throat to make sure his response came out level and not croaking.

"Mr. Raney. Welcome to Simpson Creek."

Did Raney look at everyone that way, the way a snake stared at a mouse that it had cornered, or was he recognizing the bruised, bloodied, half-unconscious gambler in the lawman who stood before him? Sam's ribs ached as if in remembrance of this man hitting him until a couple of them cracked. His face stung as if Raney had just laid his cheek open with that ring.

"Sheriff Bishop," said Raney, looking him up and down. "Thank you. Happy to be here."

Sam wanted to say he needed to get back to the jail but he dared not be the one to cut the encounter short. It would cause Raney to think about him too much.

Pennington was also watching him. Sam wanted to taunt the man with the fact that he had Tolliver in a cell, accused of murder, that he knew that his men had burned the church down, that he would find a way to prove it and make them pay. But that would extend this encounter, and in any case, Pennington would probably claim he'd fired Tolliver prior to Waters's murder.

So Sam forced himself to relax, to appear politely interested in Raney's arrival.

"Are you here for a visit, or are you relocating?" he asked, his tone casual. "Mr. Pennington tells me you hail from Houston."

Raney gazed at him a moment too long before replying. "Wonderful city, Houston—completely unlike this part of Texas. Ever been there?"

Sam needed. "I've been there. A little too humid for my taste. I like it better here."

That hooded gaze missed nothing, Sam thought, seeing the black eyes narrow as they dueled with his.

"As to whether I'm staying," Raney said, "it remains to be seen. A pleasure to meet you, Sheriff. I'm sure we'll—"

At that moment, Prissy came out of the mercantile, her arms laden with packages. She smiled at Sam and started toward him.

Then she caught sight of Pennington and halted uncertainly.

"Oh, I'm sorry, I didn't realize you were speaking to someone," she said, and looked to Sam in a clear plea for direction.

Pennington touched his hat brim. "Miss Gilmore, no apologies necessary, your interruption is a happy accident and our pleasure." He turned to Raney. "Miss Priscilla Gilmore, the mayor's daughter," he explained, almost as if presenting a commoner to royalty, Sam thought, feeling his jaw tighten in anger. "You'll remember I spoke of her father, Mayor Gilmore."

"Yes." Raney tipped his black derby with a flourish to her. "Miss Gilmore, enchanted. I pray we will meet again." His eyes slid back to Sam after he said this, as if daring him to object.

Sam remained immobile, fighting the urge to leap into the carriage, yank Raney out, and beat him senseless. Now Raney's gaze returned to Prissy and crawled over her. Sam felt his hands clenching into fists.

"Miss Priscilla," he began, hoping she'd take her cue from Sam's formality, "I'll walk you home. I need to speak to your father." He wasn't going to allow Raney to breathe the same air as his beloved a moment longer.

Tentatively, she came forward, putting a hand on his arm.

"Miss Gilmore, nice to make your acquaintance. Good day," called Raney, but she merely nodded with a chilly hauteur Sam would have found humorous if not for the circumstances.

He stifled the urge to take a huge, relieved gulp of air. Raney hadn't appeared to recognize him—yet. *Thank You, Lord.*

But What if Prissy had had Houston with her, the very dog Raney had planned to feed to the alligators along with him? The dog might well have been enough to trigger Raney's memory. Perhaps he should tell her to keep the dog at home from now on. But what excuse could he have for saying that?

"'Miss Priscilla?'" she teased, as soon as the men in the carriage were out of earshot. Then, when he did not respond with a smile, her own faded and she murmured, "Did you really need to speak to my father?" Her voice trailed off and she peered up at him.

He nodded. It was probably a good idea to notify the mayor that the third member of the triumvirate had arrived in Simpson Creek. "Sweetheart, let me carry your packages," he said, forcing his voice into a normal tone.

"Thanks," she said, handing them to him. "Mrs. Patterson got in some lovely tablecloths that will be just perfect for the party. And she had the prettiest ear bobs that will set off my dress perfectly," she continued, clearly trying to distract him.

Why had Raney come just now? Did the fact that he had finally arrived have anything to do with Tolliver being accused of murder, or was it merely coincidental? Were they going to intervene to set him free, or leave him to his fate?

You are not alone. I'm fighting alongside you.

He was so astonished at the reassuring voice within him that he almost stopped stock-still in the middle of the street.

"Sam? Are you all right?" Prissy asked him, her pretty brow furrowed with concern.

He smiled now, and felt a surge of hope in spite of the dangers he faced. He gazed down at the woman he loved. "It's a beautiful day, and I'm walking with you and the Lord. I couldn't be better."

The following day the Spinsters came to Gilmore House to help prepare for the party. Prissy had already helped

Flora make sure everything sparkled within the mansion, of course, and Antonio had groomed the grounds to perfection. But they couldn't leave everything to the two servants, and so Gilmore House was a beehive of activity on Friday. With Houston yipping with excitement and following everyone around, begging for tidbits, the ladies prepared the food that could be cooked ahead, set up tables, and decorated them with gaily colored streamers and centerpieces they'd made.

"But what if it rains?" Polly Shackleford wondered aloud, staring at the crepe paper that festooned the tables, the verandah, the fiddlers' stand, and even the big live oak that shaded the tables.

"It won't," Caroline Wallace said with calm assurance. "I consulted Papa. His big toe would be aching if it was going to rain. It's not, so quit fretting."

"Caroline showed the bachelors to the hotel today," Hannah Kennedy said. "*After* serving them all dinner, the clever girl! The rest of us haven't caught so much as a glimpse, and she's already on speaking terms with them."

Caroline reddened as if she'd been caught stealing cookies. "Well, goodness, they all showed up at the post office about the same time, right at noon, and they were hungry from traveling. It wouldn't have been hospitable not to."

"You said they're all nice and quite handsome, right, Caroline?" Hannah prodded.

Caroline nodded with a half smile. "I think you'll all be pleased, ladies," she said.

"But what about *you,* Caroline? Weren't you just the least bit interested in any of them?" asked Jane Jeffries curiously.

"You deserve happiness, too, Caroline," Maude Harkey chimed in.

Caroline held up a warning hand. "Now, let's not start *that* all over again, ladies. I'm enjoying helping with the party, but this is just something to get out of the house for a while, so I don't constantly have to be hearing about the state of Papa's big toe."

Everyone chuckled.

"Listen, ladies, I learned one of them has a partiality for green dresses—didn't you say your dress for the barbecue is green, Polly?"

Polly nodded excitedly.

"And another has a penchant for pecan pie. Wasn't that your contribution, Hannah? Half a dozen pecan pies?" Caroline asked.

It was, Hannah confirmed.

"And the third man says he's crazy for girls with freckles," Caroline said, looking right at Bess Lassiter, who clapped her hands over her freckled cheekbones.

"And to think I've been trying to get rid of these for years!"

Maude Harkey gave Caroline an admiring look. "And you learned all this with skillful questioning while they ate? You could have been a spy in the war!"

Caroline shook her head. "I didn't ask any questions, ladies. It's all a matter of listening."

"But which man had which preference?" Polly Shackleford asked. "Tell us, so we'll each know which man to concentrate our wiles upon."

"Ah, but where would be the fun in that?" Caroline asked coyly. "Those things are for you ladies to discover!"

"Caroline, how dare you tease us so!" Polly cried, exasperated.

They stayed till dusk, and finally only Sarah Walker, whose husband would be coming down to walk her home, remained.

"You're worried about him, aren't you?" Sarah asked.

"Papa? No, I'm sure he'll be home any minute now. He and Mrs. Fairchild are dining at the hotel tonight, so as to stay out of our way, and—"

"No, I mean Sam," Sarah said seriously. Prissy had told her earlier about their encounter with Pennington and his newly arrived partner, Kendall Raney.

"No, I'm sure it'll all—" Prissy began, then dropped her gaze. "Yes, I am," she admitted with a sigh. "He's just got so much on his shoulders right now, what with holding that accused murderer in his jail and wondering if the Alliance men are going to try and break him out."

"Is he going to be able to come to the barbecue, at least for a little while?" Sarah asked, her eyes warm with sympathy and understanding. "From what you and Nolan have been telling me, he could use a little time away to relax and enjoy himself."

Prissy sighed again. "I don't think so. He has so much he has to look out for right now. I'll enjoy watching the other ladies meet the bachelors, and I hope we raise some money for the church rebuilding, but it'd be so much more fun if I could do it…with Sam."

Sarah gave her a thoughtful look. "You've come a long way, Miss Prissy Gilmore," she said.

Prissy blinked. "What?"

"Only a few weeks ago, you would have stomped your foot and pouted that your beau couldn't make it. That man loves you. I'll bet he going to ask for your hand."

Prissy smiled at her friend. "I can't hide anything from you, Sarah, can I?"

"No, you can't," Sarah agreed with a grin.

"I know that these troubles won't last forever. I just wish that old judge could have come this week, and the trial could be over. But I know Sam and the rest of the men will find a way to bring peace back to Simpson Creek."

"We just have to be patient, and pray for wisdom for the sheriff and the other men," Sarah said.

"Like your Nolan."

Sarah smiled again. "I take back what I said about you being in love with love, Prissy. Sam Bishop's been good for you."

Prissy threw her arms around her friend and hugged her, tears springing to her eyes. "Thank you, Sarah. Your approval means the world to me."

Flora came in just then, carrying Houston, who had a length of crepe streamer tangled in his collar.

"That dog just treed my cat again, after chasing her all across the tables," Flora scolded. "You'd better keep him in your room tomorrow, Señorita Prissy, or he'll undo all your hard work—if he doesn't get trampled underfoot by someone's horse as the carriages arrive."

"I'll keep him locked in my room, I promise, Flora," she said penitently. "Thanks for bringing him in."

Just then Dr. Walker arrived to collect his wife. "I'll see you tomorrow, Prissy. The party starts at one, doesn't it? I'll be there at noon to help you. And perhaps Sam will get away for a moment, even if just to say hello to you." Sarah winked at her.

Prissy could only hope so. She wasn't sure she could go on much longer without seeing Sam Bishop—and telling him exactly how she felt.

Chapter Seventeen

That night, when it came time to get some sleep, Sam tossed and turned, then fell into a restless sleep, only to dream he was once more tied up in Raney's back room in the Houston gambling den. In this dream, however, he wasn't working to free himself. Raney and his henchmen stood over him, gloating at his misery, preparing to carry him and the dog out to a waiting wagon for their trip to the bayou and the alligators. Once more, he'd felt compelled to feel the underside of his mattress, to reassure himself that the ruby ring was still there. He *had* to find a way to rid himself of that thing, especially now that Raney was here.

In the morning, his deputy dozed in his chair, facing the cell that held Tolliver, who also slept, snoring with buzzing gusto. No troubled conscience there, apparently. Sam stood in front of the window that looked out on Main Street, drinking coffee and awaiting the arrival of whomever was to relieve Luis—his sleepy brain couldn't remember who it was supposed to be. There was a list somewhere.

The weather looked fine for Prissy's barbecue. Sunny, but with a pleasant breeze. If only he could be there. He could tell himself till he was blue in the face that there would be a lifetime of other celebrations with Prissy, but he wanted to ask her to marry him—today. Before the party started. He could picture her, radiant with joy, telling everyone, showing off the sapphire ring he now fingered in his pocket.

If she accepted him, that is. After he'd told her everything. He supposed a man shouldn't be *too* confident.

He sighed and dipped his head toward his coffee again, only to raise it when a wagon trundled past with Milly Brookfield on the driver's seat next to one of their cowhands. Her husband and another man rode beside it. Then Brookfield and the other horseman peeled off and stopped at the hitching post in front of the jail.

So it was the Englishman who would keep him company guarding Tolliver today. He was glad of it, but it seemed a shame Nick would miss the barbecue, too. Nick took down a basket that had been tied onto his saddle horn.

The other man tying up his horse looked vaguely familiar. When he turned to follow Nick to the door, Sam recognized the sheriff of San Saba, Wade Teague.

Sam opened the door before the men could knock, wondering if Teague was here because there had been trouble at the county seat. But Brookfield's cheerful countenance belied that notion.

"Good morning," Nick Brookfield said. "My good wife's sent breakfast, and then perhaps you ought to go down to the barbershop and spruce up. You're looking a little the worse for wear, Bishop."

Sam rubbed his beard-roughened cheek. It had been days since he'd allowed himself the luxury of the barber's attention, and he'd done a poor, hurried job of shaving himself. "Yeah, I know, but—"

"And that won't do, Bishop," Nick went on, interrupting without apology, "for you've a party to go to. Teague here, good fellow that he is, has come to help me mind your prisoner for the day while you go Miss Prissy's barbecue."

Sam's jaw dropped. "But I can't leave like that. It wouldn't be right."

"You not only can, you will," Nick told him with a smiling firmness. "I've secured the mayor's approval, and Teague's ridden all the way from San Saba to do a good turn, so we mustn't waste that, must we? Of course not. Sit down and eat, then hie yourself down to the barber. Have a bath while you're there. You'd frighten the ladies, looking like you do now."

Sam couldn't believe his ears. "But surely you'd like to attend with your wife. I should stay here with Teague— thanks for coming, by the way, Wade—"

"Nonsense." Nick interrupted him. "Milly will be so busy showing off the baby she won't know if I'm there or not. I'll wager you and Miss Prissy haven't had a proper moment together since that blackguard took up residence, have you?" he said, jerking his head toward the snoring Tolliver. "Think how happy and surprised she'll be to see you."

"You don't know the half of it," Sam said, grinning in spite of his misgivings. He told the two men how he'd been wishing he could ask Prissy to marry him before the barbecue began.

"And now you can," Teague said, grinning.

"Ah, that is good news, Señor Sam," Luis added, yawning and stretching his lanky frame.

"Congratulations, old fellow," Brookfield said, clapping him on the back.

Sam dug into his pocket and brought out the ring.

"That certainly ought to persuade her, if she weren't already willing," Nick said approvingly. "Right, then. A man about to propose marriage needs sustenance," he said, taking the basket and spreading the breakfast his wife had sent out on the desk. The four men tucked into the bacon and freshly baked biscuits and jelly Milly had sent. For a moment, Sam almost believed everything would turn out just as he hoped.

"You bring any grub for me, limey?" demanded Tolliver, who had woken up at clatter of forks and crockery. "I'm hungry, too, ya know."

Brookfield eyed him narrowly. "Mind your manners, fellow, and I might give you a share. But only if we don't have to listen to your prattling."

Sam ignored their byplay, caught up in a wave of hope. Thanks to the selfless kindness of these two men and the mayor, he would be at Prissy's side during the barbecue, hopefully with his ring on her finger.

He pulled open the drawer and glanced at William Water's pocket watch, which he was keeping as evidence. Nine o'clock—he'd have plenty of time for a bath and a shave before the party started. He dashed back into his room and grabbed up his good trousers and shirt, making sure he transferred the ring into the new trouser pocket.

"I can't thank you enough," he told Nick and Teague. "Whatever I can do for you, Nick, and anytime your jail needs minding, Wade—"

"Bring me back some barbecue, Sheriff," Tolliver demanded. "Must be nice, hobnobbing with the mayor's daughter."

All four of the men ignored him.

Nick made shooing motions. "Run along now, my good

man, and don't come back until you can tell us you've won the fair Prissy."

He felt as if his boots had sprouted wings as he headed down to the barbershop-bathhouse.

Prissy bent to pull a tablecloth even, hearing footsteps behind her.

"You can put those last chairs at that table over there, Mr. von Hesse." The German carpenter from Fredericksburg had come from the hotel early—to get a jump on the competition, Prissy suspected with amusement—and had been agreeable to being put to work with the last-minute touches. "Goodness, I'm glad the hotel was willing to loan us some chairs. Ordinarily, we'd have borrowed them from the church social hall, but as you've no doubt heard or seen, our church burned down—"

"Who's Mr. von Hesse?" asked a familiar voice. "The name's Bishop."

She whirled, hardly able to believe her eyes. "Sam! You came!" she said. "But how—who's at the jail?"

He told her how Nick had shown up with Teague in tow and taken over his duty during the barbecue.

"Oh, that's wonderful!" she exclaimed. "I could cry, I'm so happy! I so wanted you here, but I thought there was no way you'd be able—"

He looked at her with a seriousness she'd never seen before in his eyes. "Well, I need to ask you something before any more guests arrive," he told her.

All at once she thought there was something wrong after all, and reached out to him with a shaky hand. "What is it?"

Something sparked in those dark brown eyes, and then

suddenly he was kneeling before her, taking hold of her hand. His other hand held a sapphire ring.

"Priscilla Gilmore, would you do me the honor of becoming my wife?"

And then before she knew what she was doing, she was kneeling in the grass with him, heedless of her new pink marquisette dress, laughing—yes, and crying—all at once.

Around them, the Spinsters, Flora and Antonio stopped what they were doing and applauded. Then they were crowding around them, too, congratulating and embracing each of them in turn. Someone must have run and told her father, for suddenly he was there too, smiling proudly and embracing both of them.

"But what is happening?" Prissy heard Mr. von Hesse ask Polly.

"That," Polly said, "is how a Spinster graduates from the Spinsters' Club."

Prissy looked back to Sam, full of joy. He looked happier than she'd him look before, but there was something in his eyes, something off. She could only hope he was still worried about the Alliance, but a little voice inside her told her something else was amiss.

Prissy had to admit that their sudden, unexpected engagement had been just the thing to get the party off to a good start. As the townspeople arrived and learned the happy news, the intense focus was taken off the Spinsters and their bachelor counterparts, and they were able to meet one another without being the cynosure of all eyes.

Later, full of barbecue and all the trimmings, as well as Hannah's pecan pie, she sat on the wooden swinging bench on the verandah with Sam's arm around her and they lazily watched the ladies flirt with the new candidates.

"Looks like the Spinsters made a lot of money for the new church," he said, nodding toward the basket near the refreshment table that was full of coins of various denominations.

"Yes, isn't it wonderful? Hmm, I see Bob Henshaw's partial to a lady dressed in green, just as Caroline reported," she murmured, watching the way Polly Shackleford flirted outrageously with the hardware store owner from Austin, and he just as obviously relished it. "And that rancher from Mason must have been the one who liked freckles," she added, seeing Bess Lassiter dimpling and blushing as a tall, rangy fellow with the weathered face of a man who spent his life outdoors teasingly reached out and touched one of Bess's freckles.

"Who's that handing that German fellow another huge piece of pie?" Sam asked. "I've kept track, and it's his third."

She chuckled. "Hannah Kennedy," she told him. "It's her specialty. Caroline was able to gather some preliminary intelligence on these bachelors, and the Spinsters are putting it to good use."

Love was in the air. She sat on the gently swinging bench with Sam and saw the beginnings of courtships. Faith Bennett, Jane Jeffries and Maude Harkey were chatting animatedly to a group of cowboys who had caught wind of the festivities and ridden in from a ranch between Simpson Creek and Sloan. Emily and Ed Markison, the newlywed couple, were arm-in-arm, talking to Reverend Chadwick. And of course, Mariah Fairchild had come to the party and never left her father's side.

Caroline Wallace, however, had gathered up the

townspeople's children and was supervising a game of "Duck, Duck, Goose" over by the barn—as if she were already their teacher. Laughter rang from the circle of children and Caroline looked content, Prissy thought. But she wished Caroline could find her special someone, too. Silently, she said a little prayer for Caroline's happiness.

Prissy turned to Sam, about to inquire as to the hint of sadness she saw in his eyes today when the clinking of a spoon against the punch bowl startled her. She straightened on the swinging chair.

"Looks like that rancher from Mason—what was his name?—is going to make a toast," Sam said.

The rancher clinked against the glass again, and conversation subsided.

"Thank you. I'm no speechifier, but the other bachelors elected me to thank Miss Priscilla Gilmore and her papa the mayor, before th' fiddlin' starts, for havin' this party so we fellas who'd like t' git hitched could meet a passel a' nice like-minded young ladies. We appreciate yer hospitality, Miss Prissy, Mayor Gilmore. But not only that—we're happy for your news that you're about t' git hitched soon, too, to th' sheriff. To Miss Prissy and Sheriff Bishop—long life and much happiness."

Glasses clinked, and those who weren't holding them applauded as a blushing Prissy and Sam stood, his arm about her waist, and took a bow.

"Well, now, isn't this a pretty picture."

The townspeople turned as one to see Kendall Raney, the man she'd been introduced to when he was riding in Pennington's carriage. Pennington had accompanied him again today, as well as another man, wraithlike in his thinness and paleness—could this be Francis Byrd, whom Sam had told her about meeting?

Beside her, Sam went rigid, his face a mask. She saw Raney's gaze focus on Sam, as if trying to place him, just as it had the other day. Her father bustled forward, bristling.

"Mr. Pennington, this is a private party, and I don't believe you were invited."

Pennington affected great surprise. "Is that so? My apologies, Mayor Gilmore. From the way the town was buzzing about it as the social event of the summer, I was under the impression it was 'come one, come all.' I believe my feelings have been hurt."

"Come one, come all" was indeed the message she and her father had given out, Prissy knew, but they had never imagined Pennington and his partners would even hear about the event, much less put in an appearance.

Sam stepped forward, the sun glinting off the five-pointed star on his shirt. He took a wide stance. "You heard the mayor, gentlemen," he said, tight-lipped. "You aren't welcome here. I'm asking you to leave."

"But surely the townspeople would like to meet their future mayor?" Pennington countered, his pale amber eyes gleaming with vulpine slyness. "Everyone, may I present Mr. Kendall Raney, your next mayor."

"What are you talking about?" Mr. Avery demanded. "I'm the head of the Simpson Creek Elections board, and I've had no applications for anyone to run against Mayor Gilmore, with the exception of myself." Avery ran against her father every election, "just to make it fair," and every election, he lost. He was so good-natured about it, it had become something of a joke between the two men.

But Pennington didn't look as if he was joking.

"But you aren't eligible to run," Avery told Raney. "You haven't been living here long enough."

"According to your bylaws, which you were so kind to let me see last week," Pennington said to Avery, "he's eligible to file after he's been here a month. And as the election is not until November, that'll be plenty of time to convince the populace of the benefits to having Kendall Raney as your mayor."

"Not that he'll have to convince as many as there used to be," Byrd added in a raspy voice. "According to my calculations, more and more residences are becoming Alliance properties in and around Simpson Creek every day. By fall we ought to have an easy majority."

Prissy gasped, watching her father's face turn a dangerous purple. "Who do you plan to have live at the Waters ranch, you murderous scoundrels?" he demanded. "Don't think we're unaware you had that poor easterner killed, and I don't doubt we'll be able to prove it. The judge will soon be here to try your man Tolliver, and he'll say who paid him."

Raney shrugged, looking untroubled. "I don't have the least idea what you're talking about, Mr. Gilmore, but I was brought up to be polite to my elders. And to ladies. Good day, ladies." He doffed his cap and bowed deeply to Prissy and the silent, watching Spinsters before turning on his heel.

Just then, Prissy saw the side door open. Antonio backed out of it, carrying two fresh pitchers of punch. As he did so, a black and gray and white blur streaked past his legs and headed straight for Prissy, yipping his joy at finally achieving freedom and rejoining his beloved mistress.

"You come back here, you naughty dog!" scolded Flora, dashing after him. She reached down to grab the little canine but came up with empty air. "Oh, I am sorry, Señor Gilmore, I don't know how the dog escaped. We had him tied to a chair leg in the kitchen, for he whined and carried on so in Señorita Prissy's room, we were afraid he would damage the door trying to claw a hole through it—"

By now, Houston had reached Prissy, and he leaped up into her waiting arms.

"It's all right, Flora, no harm done," Prissy said. "I'll just take him back inside, and give him a bone to chew on."

At that moment, Prissy looked at Sam and was startled to see that all the color had drained from his face.

Sam saw Raney's eyes narrow at the sight of the dog, and then fill with recognition. Raney looked from the dog to Sam, back to the dog, and finally at Sam again. His lips curled in a terrible smile.

"Folks, we'll take our leave," Kendall Raney said, bowing again. "But you'll be seeing a lot of us around your fair town. I look forward to getting to know you all better."

His gaze caressed Prissy, standing at Sam's side. Then the small black eyes once more found Sam. "I'll be seeing you in particular...Sheriff," he said.

The crowd turned to watch the three men go as the carriage took them away. A buzz rose from the townspeople like the hum of an insect swarm.

"Why, I never..."

"The nerve a' them fellows! Why, I would never vote for the likes a' that man."

"Mayor Gilmore's the man for me. Always has been."

"Yeah, I didn't like the look a' that man. Somethin' about him makes me think he an' the devil are on a first-name basis."

Prissy, still clutching Houston, went to the trio of

bachelors and apologized for the unpleasant confrontation they had been forced to witness, reassuring them that the party would continue. Then she signaled to the fiddler to commence playing before disappearing into the house with the dog.

If only he hadn't given in to the impulse to bring that dog along with him or had left him near some town or ranch house. If he'd done so, Raney might never have made the connection between the hapless, beaten gambler and the sheriff of Simpson Creek. Raney's gaze promised that now that he'd recognized Sam, he would do something about it.

But what? And when?

He also cursed himself for giving in to impulse and proposing to Prissy without telling her about Raney, without telling her the truth about who he was.

There was nothing he could do about it now, except wait it out or explain the situation to her right away.

Neither was an option leading to a good outcome.

Chapter Eighteen

Raney waited only an hour after Sam returned to the jail before appearing at the window, beckoning.

Sam stepped out into the darkness. A half moon and the glowing red tip of Raney's cheroot were the only sources of light. He let his hand linger near the pistol riding in its holster at his hips, wondering if Raney's men lurked in the alley across the street, ready to cut him down in a hail of bullets. His heart hammered in his throat.

Lord, please protect me.

"You've done well for yourself, Bishop—sheriff of the town, soon to marry the prettiest, richest girl in it…very well indeed."

Sam waited, seeing the black eyes glitter in the moonlight. Raney blew a smoke ring, and Sam could smell the acrid stench of the cheroot. He felt a trickle of cold sweat trace its way down his backbone.

"What do you want?" he asked at last.

"What do I want? I want what you took from me," Raney said, feigning surprise.

"You can have your ring," Sam said. "I just can't get at it right now." Luis was sleeping over it, unaware of what lay hidden in the mattress. "Other than that, I only took what was mine—the money you won by cheating."

"You took my dog," Raney pointed out, amused. "And gave it to your sweetheart."

"As if you miss him. You were going to feed him to the gators—along with me."

"No, I don't care about the cur," Raney admitted, his voice still light, convivial. "What I do care about is the deal we could make."

"Deal?" Nothing Raney could have said would have surprised him more—or made him warier.

"You left a considerable sum of money in my safe, after you took that pitiful amount I won from you."

Sam shrugged. "It wasn't mine."

Raney rolled his eyes at him. "Don't be a self-righteous prig, Bishop. It could be."

Sam shook his head, amazed—and thankful—that it was so easy to refuse it. "I don't need it."

The black eyes glittered again. "But you're marrying the daughter of the richest man in a one-horse town. I can offer you much, much more, Bishop."

"Is that right?" Sam was careful to keep his tone bored, even disdainful, while his eyes searched the darkness. "Not interested."

"A wise man would be interested enough to hear me out."

"A wise man wouldn't have walked into your gambling hall."

Raney's smile was sardonic. "True enough. But you did, didn't you? And I'll wager you don't want sweet Priscilla Gilmore to know that, do you? She has no idea the kind of man you were."

Sam shrugged again. "Gambling's not illegal, only a

fool's way to earn a living. It's not as if I murdered some-one, like your fellow in the cell in there," he said.

Raney's jaw clenched and his mouth tightened to a thin line, then relaxed again. "All right, here's the deal, Bishop. I have the money you left in the safe with me. It's yours if you want it—"

"I already said I didn't. Who'd you steal that money from, anyway?" Sam asked, allowing his contempt to show.

But Raney wasn't insulted. "I swindled it from a bank in Houston. As I said, the money can be yours, along with a position in the Alliance. Power. Property. Women. It's richly rewarding, working with us, Bishop."

Sam had only recently read about the time Jesus had been tempted by the devil in the wilderness. The devil had offered Him all the same sort of things. Now Sam could guess how Jesus may have felt.

"In return for what?" There was always a cost, Sam had learned from that Bible story. And from life.

"For testifying on behalf of Tolliver in there."

"I'm surprised you care about him," Sam said, making his voice callous instead of curious. "Let him hang, Raney. What's it to you? Hired guns are a dime a dozen, aren't they?"

"Oh, I don't care about him, not really. He was an idiot to get caught with stolen goods—but then you know all about that, don't you, *Sheriff?* I *do* care about the Alli-ance's reputation, and I've found it's very nice indeed to have a sheriff or two in my pocket. Comes in handy at times."

Sam thought of the sheriff of Colorado Bend, who hadn't been willing to discuss opposing the Alliance. "Like

I said, I'm not interested. Now, if that's all you have to say, I'll bid you good night."

The black eyes flashed. "Don't be a fool, Bishop. Take the money and join us. Or I'll see to it that the town learns you're nothing but a thieving gambler. How do you think your precious Priscilla will feel about her gallant sheriff then, Bishop? Especially when you're hauled off to prison."

Prissy hardly slept that night. Her mind whirled with the plans she and Sam would have to make for the wedding. They'd have to discuss a date, of course. It was now late August—could they pull everything together by October? That was a lovely time in the hill country of Texas, with the worst of the summer heat gone and plenty of clear days with only a hint of chill in the early morning…

Some decisions about the wedding, of course, would be hers alone. She had already asked Milly after the party if she would be able to make her dress. To Prissy's delight, Milly said she'd love to do it. Prissy would need to go out to the ranch as soon as possible for a fitting and to discuss the design. And who should be her bridesmaids? Sarah would be her matron of honor, and Milly…but who else? She'd always imagined having four. She would ask Caroline, but Caroline would decline, Prissy was sure, for it would mean donning something other than the mourning black she seemed determined to wear the rest of her life. Perhaps Hannah and Bess? She could not have all the Spinsters stand up with her, of course, and they would understand that, but it was hard to choose just four ladies when she liked all of them so much.

Who would Sam choose as his best man? As a newcomer to town, he wouldn't have many choices—she supposed it would be Nick or Nolan, but both men would stand up with him. He might want to invite Luis Menendez, the youth who had proved such an invaluable help of late, to be a third. But they would still need one more man, if she had four bridesmaids. She made a mental note to consult Sam on that issue.

They'd return to Gilmore House for the wedding dinner, of course. What should be on the menu? She'd have to consult Sarah about that, and commission her to bake the wedding cake. But—white cake or yellow? Or even strawberry?

She and Sam would have to meet with Reverend Chadwick about the wedding service. She hoped he'd pick his text from First Corinthians, Chapter Thirteen—she thought one could not hear the beloved words describing the qualities of true love too much.

Prissy realized with a pang that she was still picturing the wedding taking place in the old church as it had been. The idea of everyone having to travel to San Saba to use a church there for the ceremony didn't appeal to her. It involved too many arrangements, and inevitably, someone wouldn't be able to make the trip. They would have to use the ballroom below, she supposed. While it would be easy and comforting to be married in the house she had grown up in, she'd always pictured being married in a church. By the time October arrived the townspeople would probably be hard at work on a new church, but it wouldn't be finished by then.

And she didn't want to wait till it was finished to be Sam's wife. *Mrs. Samuel Bishop….Sam and Prissy Bishop…* She smiled in the dark as she whispered the names, trying them out.

Both Sam and Papa would need new suits. Would they

be willing to make a trip to Austin to have them expertly tailored?

Prissy sighed, realizing that as much as she loved the idea of a trip to Austin, it was impractical. Unless matters improved in Simpson Creek rapidly, neither Sam nor her father could leave town right now. Even after the trial was over, there was still the threat of the Alliance to deal with.

Suddenly Prissy remembered the unease she'd seen in Sam's face earlier when Raney had showed up. She'd been reminded in that moment of all things she still didn't know about Sam.

But there was plenty of time to find out—the rest of her life, in fact.

Prissy had already asked Flora to make up a basket of leftovers from the barbecue for her to take to the jail after church. She knew Sam would not feel free to leave his duty to attend the church service in the meadow—even as close as it was to the jail—as he had last week, not after Nick had substituted for him there most of the day yesterday. And especially not after the way Kendall Raney and his cronies had so rudely invaded the barbecue, with Pennington obnoxiously boasting about his partner beating her papa in the next election. Sam didn't trust the Alliance not to try to break their man out of jail, and so he would feel bound to stay on guard.

Raney and his two partners cast the only cloud over their happiness, Prissy thought with resentment. Why did they have to choose San Saba County, and particularly Simpson Creek, as their center of power, and use ruthless, murderous toughs like Tolliver to carry out their will? Not only had their choice cost poor William Waters his life, but it cast a pall over the entire town.

She only hoped discussing the wedding over delicious food would distract Sam, at least for a little while, from all the trouble that faced the town. It seemed to weigh so heavily on him, especially after Raney had shown up. The enmity appeared especially strong between the two men, even more so than between Sam and Pennington or Byrd.

Which was surprising, since he had only met Raney the other day in front of the mercantile. Had they had a confrontation after that meeting, and he had not wanted to worry her by telling her about it? That would be just like him, she thought, as she began to fall asleep, drifting toward dreams of her life with Sam Bishop.

Sam appeared to do his best, hours later when they sat together in front of the jail and devoured barbecued chicken sandwiches washed down with lemonade, to join in her excitement over the wedding plans, agreeing with every suggestion she brought up.

He agreed early October would be a fine time for their wedding. With any luck the trial would be past them by then, and with God's help and the town standing together, they might have also persuaded the Alliance to pack up and move on. Yes, he thought First Corinthians Thirteen would make a fine wedding text, once she started reciting the verses of it. She had to remember Sam hadn't grown up reading the Scriptures as she had.

He chose Nick to be his best man, though he was happy to have Nolan Walker stand up with him, too. Prissy guessed the two men would have been sufficient for him, but when she said she wanted four bridesmaids, he mentioned Luis, as she'd thought he might. She offered to compromise by having only three bridesmaids.

Yes, he supposed he needed a new frock coat and

trousers made for the wedding, and promised to go see Señora Menendez without delay. But even though they were in complete harmony with the choices she suggested, she sensed there was something else on his mind—the upcoming trial?

After all, if Sam was able to prove that Tolliver's possession of the gold pocket watch meant Tolliver had murdered William Waters, the man would be executed. A sobering thought. Her father would push for any execution to take place outside Simpson Creek town limits, for he'd never held with the common practice of making a hanging into a social event in the middle of a town, with everyone turning out as if it were a picnic. She shuddered at the thought and deliberately introduced a new subject.

"Sam, I realize what with all that's happening, you probably won't be able to finish fixing up the house down the street before the wedding," she began. "Realistically, we might have to start our marriage in that little cottage on my father's grounds, much as I know you wanted us to start out in our own place." She reached out a hand and touched his beard-roughened cheek, wishing she could smooth away the furrows in his brow. Poor Sam, he looked as if he hadn't slept much last night.

He gave her a rueful smile before kissing her forehead. "Once the murder took place, I didn't even had time to go talk to Mr. Avery about buying the house, let alone working on it. After all my fine talk about providing for you." He sighed. "I appreciate your understanding, Prissy. I'm a lucky man."

"Wherever we are, darling," she added, "if I'm with you, I'll be happy."

He smiled at her again, but his attention was captured a moment later by something beyond Prissy. She looked around to see a man walking toward the jail. As the man drew closer, she recognized Mr. Jewett, the telegraph operator. He waved a paper.

"Afternoon, Miss Prissy, Sheriff," he murmured, reaching them. "Good news. The judge will be arrivin' a little early, Tuesday 'bout noon. He says to notify the prisoner that the trial will begin on Wednesday, so his lawyer better be ready. Oh, and he asks that you secure him and the prosecutor hotel rooms for the duration of the trial."

"Oh, but that won't be necessary," Prissy said. "Papa wouldn't hear of him staying at the hotel. We'll put him up at Gilmore House." She'd met Edwin Everson, the circuit judge, once before, and remembered him as a dry, austere man.

The news of the judge's arrival seemed to relieve some of the heaviness which had weighed down Sam's smile. Prissy was glad, though she knew proving Tolliver's guilt would be no easy task. The prosecuting attorney would have to prove his case without a shadow of a doubt.

"Any lawyer show up for Tolliver yet?" Jewett asked. "Th' law says even a man like Tolliver's entitled to legal representation."

Sam shook his head. "Not yet, but the Alliance might send someone now that the judge is coming."

"Probably some no-account carpetbagger that Raney b—uh, scoundrel—" Jewett corrected himself hastily, with a glance at Prissy "—will haul out of a Houston swamp, the ink still wet on his forged lawyer papers."

"We'll just have to wait and see, won't we," Sam said with a tight smile that didn't quite reach his eyes.

I won't let the sun go down today without telling Prissy the whole truth about what happened in Houston, Sam resolved that morning. *Everything Raney had done—and what he had done, as well. Before things go any further.*

Judge Everson and the prosecutor, Gabriel Bryant, arrived promptly at noon, as promised, but the judge announced they would be staying at the hotel rather than Gilmore House—to avoid any appearance of bias, as he put it, though he and Bryant accepted an invitation to supper with the mayor, Sam and Prissy. And he stated they would begin the trial the next day, whether the defense was ready or not.

"No use in dillydallying," he announced in his dry, no-nonsense way over supper at Gilmore House. "I have trials waiting to start in Chappel and Sloan, then back in Harkeyville again. And I understand you two have an upcoming wedding to plan, as well, so there's no use wasting time," he said to Prissy and Sam across the table. He had a way of smiling without the smile ever reaching his hound-dog-sorrowful eyes.

"The accused man's lawyer visited him this morning," Sam informed the judge, picturing Lamar Hammond, the attorney who had shown up without warning to speak with Tolliver. If Pennington reminded Sam of a fox, this fellow was a javelina, with his small, mean eyes and coarse, bristly hair. All he needed was a pair of protruding tusks. "He's got a room at the hotel. I can stop by on my way back to the jail and tell him to be ready to start tomorrow morning."

He hoped Everson would offer to inform Hammond himself, since he was going to the hotel, too, but the judge apparently wanted to keep a sense of separation between himself and the defense attorney, for he said, "Good, good. Tell him nine o'clock sharp. I won't abide lateness. A delicious dinner, Miss Gilmore. I'll bid you good night now."

"I'll tell our cook," Prissy said, smiling as she rose also.

"Prissy, may I speak to you for a few minutes before I leave?" Sam asked, knowing that the conversation he'd put off for so long couldn't be postponed any longer.

"Of course, I'll walk you out." Her smile was so innocent. She was unaware he was about to shatter her belief in him. When he was done talking, she would know him as a liar and a thief. Would she still love him after that? Would he still be the sheriff, after she had told her father?

The judge put up a hand. "Sheriff Bishop, I think you and Mr. Bryant should discuss the case, since you're the chief witness."

"You gentlemen can use my office," James Gilmore said, rising.

Sam stifled a groan. He wished he could refuse. He didn't want to wait another minute to get his confession to Prissy over and done with. But hopefully he could steal a few moments alone with her when the attorney was done with him.

He had to tell Prissy what Raney knew about him before Raney exposed his character flaws in front of everyone. He'd heard nothing further from Raney, and he hoped his own silence had served as his answer to the man. But he had little hope that Raney wouldn't carry out his threat to expose Sam, and he couldn't risk embarrassing Prissy by not confessing to her first.

He saw Prissy looking at him, and when their gazes met, she gave him an encouraging smile. *This will all turn out all right,* her eyes seemed to say. *You can do this.*

Sweet Prissy, you don't know what "this" is.

Chapter Nineteen

Darkness had fallen by the time Gabe Bryant was done going over the facts of the case and let Sam go. He agreed Tolliver's possession of the watch might not be enough to convict him, but he hoped by skillful questioning to trip Tolliver up while he was on the witness stand and get the man to convict himself with his own words.

Flora came out of the kitchen when Sam left the study. "Señorita Prissy has gone to bed, Sheriff. She knew you had a lot to do and needed to get back to the jail, so she said she'd see you at the trial."

Sam sighed in frustration as he bid the servant good night. Prissy couldn't have guessed how deep his need was to speak to her. As he stepped out into the night, he looked back up at Prissy's window, but no light shone through the curtains there.

He went on to the hotel and found Tolliver's lawyer in his room, curled around a bottle and holding a losing poker hand. At the table sat Pennington, Byrd and the last man Sam wanted to encounter, Kendall Raney.

"Just the man I wanted to see," Raney said, rising. "Deal me out, fellows."

Sam shook his head. "I have to get back to the jail. I only came to tell Mr. Hammond the trial begins at nine tomorrow. The judge said not to be late."

Hammond nodded, his eyes bleary. "I'll be there."

"I'll walk with you, Sheriff. I know you're a busy man," Raney said smoothly, and gestured Sam out of the room. There was no way he could gracefully refuse.

They walked down the shadowy boardwalk, their way illuminated only by the half-full moon.

"Is this what you were after?" Sam asked without preamble, reaching into his shirt pocket and holding out the ruby ring he'd retrieved from his mattress.

"Among other things," Raney murmured, reaching out for it, his teeth gleaming in the dimness like a wolf's. "Tell me this, Bishop. Why did you take my ring, of all things? You don't seem a man of expensive tastes," he said, with a meaningful look at Sam's simple trousers, shirt and vest.

"I'm not," Sam agreed. "But at the time it seemed important to make sure you couldn't ever lay open some poor fellow's cheek with it again."

Raney's lips curved upward. "I did leave a bit of a scar, didn't I?" Then his face hardened. "But I didn't come along with you to discuss your looks, Bishop. You know I want an answer."

"I would have thought you'd have guessed, a clever fellow like you," Sam said. "The answer is no."

Raney blinked. "*No?* Have you found some loco weed to chew on, Bishop? Do you know what you're giving up?"

"I'm not giving up anything I want," Sam said. "My good name's become more important to me than what you're offering, Raney."

Raney shook his head and smiled as if he was trying to explain philosophy to a lunatic. "I don't think you understand, Sheriff. When I get done with you, you won't have that, either. Think the mayor's daughter's going to stand by you when you're a disgraced *ex*-sheriff? Not on your tintype! Want to change your answer? This is your final chance," he warned.

Sam shook his head.

Raney stared at him. "You're a fool, Sheriff. You're going to wish you'd given me a different answer."

The trial would take place in the Simpson Creek Saloon, since the town lacked a courthouse and the church had been burned. Prissy's father had offered the ballroom of Gilmore House, but the judge deemed the saloon a better choice as it was neutral ground. The saloon was the only other building with enough space to seat everyone who would want to attend, and as it was, George Detwiler had had to borrow every chair and bench Gilmore House and the hotel could spare.

Since she had only to walk down the street to reach the saloon, Prissy had taken her time with her toilette, wanting to look suitably dignified and a credit to her father and to Sam. As a result, it was five minutes to nine o'clock when she left the house in her sedate but pretty skirt and waist of navy trimmed with white piping and its short matching jacket. She suspected the day's heat would soon cause her to shed the jacket and rue the long sleeves of the blouse, but for now she felt her ensemble would strike just the right note.

The chairs had been set into two sections with a narrow aisle in between, with the bar serving as the judge's bench. Her father's big chair from his study had been pressed into service, and was raised slightly above the level of the bar on a hastily built platform.

It appeared half of Texas sat in that room. Every chair was occupied and people were crammed together on the benches. Prissy knew that if she hadn't been the mayor's daughter, she might have had to stand in the back, but her father had motioned her to an open seat in the second row. She saw Pennington, Byrd and Raney sitting in the first row on the other side. The room buzzed with speculation about Tolliver and the murder.

As she started to make her way toward the front, Sam appeared at her side. Apparently she'd missed him standing at the back.

"Oh, there you are, Sam," she began with a smile. She peered at him more closely. His gaze was tense, his eyes haunted. "What's wrong?"

He bent and spoke in a low tone into her ear, "Prissy, I only have a minute before the judge will come down from upstairs, so please listen."

"I'm listening—"

"Prissy, I—"

"All rise." Her father's voice rose above the hum of the crowd, and Prissy and Sam turned to see Judge Everson making his way down the steps from the upper floor.

Next to her, Sam closed his eyes for a second. Under the rustle of clothing and the creaking of chairs, he whispered into her ear, "Prissy, no matter what you might hear, I love you. Believe that, will you?"

"Sheriff Bishop, is the prisoner present and ready to stand trial?" the judge called out as he reached the bottom.

Sam turned away from her and faced the judge. "He is, Judge Everson. I'll escort him from the back room now."

Prissy was left to make her way quickly to her seat, aware of the judge's eyes on her, wondering what was troubling Sam. As she settled herself in her seat, murmuring a greeting to Nick and Nolan in the front row, Sam brought the prisoner, followed by his lawyer, out of the back room.

Tolliver wore come-alongs on his wrists, which Sam now bent and unfastened before taking his own seat in the front row across from the three men of the Alliance. If he realized he was on trial for his life, it didn't seem to bother Tolliver. He smirked at the crowd as her father directed him to place his right hand on the Bible and swear to tell the truth. He winked at Pennington, Byrd and Raney as he sat down, and Prissy saw them grin back at him.

The judge pounded his gavel. "The prisoner will remember he is in a court of law," Everson snapped, evidently irritated by Tolliver's cocky expression. "Mr. Bryant, you may call your first witness."

"Sheriff Samuel Bishop."

Prissy watched, her heart full of pride as Sam raised his hand and took the oath. But something was wrong—very wrong. She could see it in his eyes. She'd heard it in the words that still rang in her ears. What could it be?

Sam's voice was strong and sure as the lawyer led him into a recital of the facts—how William Waters III, the nephew of the late William Waters, who had owned a ranch southeast of Simpson Creek, had come to town to take possession of his inheritance, how Sam had ridden out with him to inspect the property and had first seen him consult the big gold pocket watch that would later be the critical piece of evidence.

"Is this the watch in question, Sheriff?" Bryant asked, dangling the object in front of Sam so that he and the crowd could see it.

"It is."

"And when did you become aware that Mr. Waters felt threatened?"

Sam told how Waters had come to him and said he was being pressured to sell the property to the men who headed the Ranchers' Alliance, who had lately been buying up property in San Saba and neighboring counties, and how he had ridden out to their large ranch, La Alianza, and told Pennington and Byrd to order their men to cease harassing the easterner.

"And are these men present in the court today, Sheriff?"

"They are."

"Will you indicate them to the court, Sheriff Bishop?"

Sam pointed. "That's Garth Pennington there, and Francis Byrd, next to him."

"And is it your understanding that there is a third man who also heads the Ranchers' Alliance?" Bryant inquired.

"Mr. Kendall Raney, sitting next to Mr. Pennington, is also part of the Ranchers' Alliance, but he had not come to town as yet," Sam answered.

Prissy saw Raney smile as Sam pointed at him. She thought the devil himself could have no more sinister a smile.

"Please tell the court about the day William Waters III was found murdered."

Sam recounted how he and the ladies of the Society for the Promotion of Marriage had gone to the neighboring ranch of Nick and Milly Brookfield to celebrate the birth of their new son, and how he and Nick had heard shots, seen smoke, and had ridden over to investigate, finding Waters dead in front of his burning ranch house.

"And did you suspect the employees of this so-called Ranchers' Alliance of being guilty of his murder?"

Sam said he did. "But I had no proof—until Leroy Tolliver was witnessed by several people to have the watch in his possession."

"Tell us about that event, Sheriff."

Prissy listened as Sam painted a picture of the intrusion of Tolliver and the other hired guns at the wedding reception, of the struggle that had ensued and the pocket watch that had fallen out of the accused man's pants.

"And how did you know the watch did not belong to Leroy Tolliver, Sheriff Bishop?" Bryant asked.

"Apart from the fact that I didn't believe a hired gun like Tolliver could have afforded to buy such a valuable object," Sam said, glancing at Tolliver, who glared sullenly back at him, "the watch had the initials 'W.W.III' engraved on the back."

Prissy expected Tolliver's lawyer to object to Sam's disparagement of his client, but he remained still and untroubled, a bland expression on his face, seemingly content to be bide his time and wait for his turn.

"Your honor, I have nothing further," Bryant said.

Apprehension gripped Prissy's mind like an icy glove. What was the lawyer up to?

Judge Everson had listened intently throughout Sam's testimony, and now he turned to Tolliver's lawyer. "Mr. Hammond, do you wish to cross-examine Sheriff Bishop?"

"No, Your Honor."

"*No?*" Judge Everson repeated, eyebrows beetling. "You don't wish to question the state's witness against your client, sir? Why ever not, may the court inquire?"

Prissy, staring at the lawyer along with the rest of the courtroom, saw Hammond's lips curve into a slick smile.

"Because, Your Honor, we accuse Sheriff Samuel Bishop of being an unreliable witness, and unfit for the office he holds."

Prissy's jaw dropped. She stared, first at Hammond, then at the man she loved sitting in the chair to the left of the judge. The color had drained from Sam's face, leaving it white as bleached bones. The haunted look which Sam's eyes had held earlier had transformed itself into a hunted look, as if he was now cornered prey.

What on earth was Hammond saying?

The saloon-turned-courtroom had gone utterly silent. Not a bench creaked, not a petticoat rustled. Women who had been fanning themselves laid down their fans. Even the half-dozen flies which had been bedeviling those in attendance seemed to cease their infernal buzzing. Prissy could feel her heart thudding in her chest.

"Explain yourself, Mr. Hammond." The judge ground out the words, leaning forward, his chin jutting pugnaciously out. "And I warn you, I won't allow my courtroom to be turned into a circus."

Prissy shifted her gaze to Pennington, Byrd and Raney. Even from the side, she could see that they were grinning from ear to ear.

"Yes, Your Honor," Hammond said with obsequious deference. "We do not make these charges lightly. Samuel Bishop is unfit to be the sheriff, upholder of the law in Simpson Creek, because he himself is a thief, having swindled the sum of two thousand dollars from the First Bank of Houston, Texas, as well as a ruby ring from Mr. Kendall Raney, here present."

Sam jumped to his feet. "It's a lie! Your Honor—Judge Everson—he's lying!"

Prissy froze in her chair as everyone started talking at

once. The judge pounded his gavel repeatedly until the room was once more quiet. She saw everyone staring at Sam, and then some turned and fixed their gazes on *her*.

Furious at their avid curiosity, she trained her eyes on Sam, but his eyes were fixed on the judge the way a drowning man's eyes would be fixed upon a man who might or might not throw him a rope.

Judge Everson cleared his throat, which had the effect of hushing those who had begun to whisper and point.

"Mr. Hammond, I warn you that I will not tolerate mischief, even from a so-called lawyer. Do you have any proof of these outrageous charges you're making?"

The lawyer's face was the epitome of smugness as he nodded. "Yes, Your Honor, you have but to send someone to search Sheriff Bishop's quarters. You'll find the money and the ring there, I'm sure."

Everson stared at him for a long moment. "And just who do you suggest I send to do that, Mr. Hammond? I'm certain you had someone in mind."

"I did, Your Honor," Hammond answered. "I took the liberty of asking Sheriff Hantz of Colorado Bend to be present today as an impartial party capable of making such a search. Sheriff Hantz, will you stand, sir?"

Prissy turned in time to see a stocky man rise from a bench at the back of the room, a man wearing a tin star similar to the one on Sam's shirt. She gasped, remembering how Sam had told her how the sheriff of Colorado Bend had been unwilling to listen to his concerns about the Alliance.

"He shouldn't go alone," her father said, standing too. "I'll go, to verify anything he finds—if he finds anything, which I doubt he will."

"And I, too," Reverend Chadwick said, getting to his feet.

"Very well, gentlemen," Everson said. "This court will be in recess until you return."

He raised his hand to bang the gavel once again, but Hammond stepped forward. "Your Honor, surely you don't mean for Bishop to be at liberty while they search," the lawyer suggested in his oily voice. "Why, he could do anything—flee, or even follow Sheriff Hantz and attack him."

Judge Everson glared at Hammond, but the man merely smiled with a meekness Prissy knew was false.

"Mr. Hammond, you're treading on thin ice," Everson said. "Please don't presume to advise me again."

"No, Your Honor."

Everson ignored him and looked at the man sitting next to Prissy. "Nicholas Brookfield, it's my understanding you have served as a deputy in times past. Would you be willing to stand guard over both Mr. Bishop and Leroy Tolliver in the back room of this saloon while these three men leave to search Mr. Bishop's quarters, until such time as they return and report to this court?"

Nick Brookfield stood. "Yes, Your Honor."

Everson banged his gavel again. "Very well. Mr. Brookfield, I'm holding you responsible. Sheriff Bishop and Mr. Tolliver are not to speak to one another, much less— ahem!—come to blows."

"Yes, Your Honor, I understand."

Sam threw Prissy a look desperate with entreaty before he allowed Nick to march him and Tolliver toward the back room.

Her father looked at her, too, a look she couldn't interpret, before he followed Reverend Chadwick and the Colorado Bend sheriff out of the courtroom.

So that's what Sam had been trying to tell her, she thought, sick with horror. He'd been trying to confess that he was a thief and a swindler. Was the love he'd professed for her nothing but a lie, as well?

Sarah reached her side before anyone else and laid a comforting hand on her shoulder. "Prissy, I'm sure they won't find anything. It's all trumped-up nonsense."

"Yes, Tolliver's lawyer is only making trouble, trying to obscure the facts that clearly point to his client's guilt," her husband agreed.

"Prissy, dear, everything will be all right," Mariah Fairchild, who'd been sitting down the row, chimed in.

But Prissy couldn't answer them, couldn't even thank them as they kept the gawkers and the nosy gossips at bay during the painful hour that followed. She kept her face buried in her hands, heedless of the tears that soaked through and trickled onto her skirt as she replayed each moment she'd shared with Sam over the past weeks, looking for a sign.

How could she have been so wrong about a man?

Chapter Twenty

Sam walked back into the improvised courtroom on legs that felt like wooden stilts and listened as Sheriff Hantz was sworn in. He tried to catch Prissy's gaze, but she only stared with tear-swollen eyes at some point on the saloon wall closest to her.

She believed he was guilty, he realized. Well, of course she did. Why wouldn't she?

Hammond stepped forward to question the other sheriff. "Sheriff Hantz, tell the judge what you found in Sheriff Bishop's quarters."

"I found the money, all two thousand of it, hidden within the mattress on the sheriff's bed. I sent the mayor to the bank to fetch this sack that now holds the money, Your Honor—" he raised a sack, grunting slightly as if it was very heavy "—but I kept the Reverend with me to guard the money. Oh, and we also found this, Your Honor."

Sam saw the Colorado Bend sheriff shove a meaty hand into his vest pocket and come forth with the ruby ring he'd returned to Kendall Raney only last night. He closed his eyes in misery.

"Count out the coins, Sheriff Hantz, right here on

the bar—ahem!—*bench*—in front of me," the judge ordered.

Sam opened his eyes but kept his gaze lowered as the coins spilled out of the sack, clinking together on the wooden bar. He listened as the Colorado Bend sheriff counted the twenty-dollar gold coins into stacks, each one thudding like a death knell, until the sheriff had counted one hundred coins.

Sam knew with a sick certainty that Raney had had the money and the ring planted there as soon as he and Luis had marched their prisoner down to the saloon-courtroom. The jail was empty then, and no one would have been watching it—everyone for miles around Simpson Creek had gone to the saloon to attend the trial.

"That must have made for a pretty lumpy mattress, Mr. Bishop," the judge commented. "How did you ever sleep on it?"

"I—" Sam began. What was the use? He could tell by the fact that the judge had called him "Mister" instead of "Sheriff" that he doubted him already. How could he possibly fix this?

"Your Honor," Gabe Bryant said, rising to his feet. "With all due respect, any questions you have for *Sheriff* Bishop should be held until the sheriff is once more on the witness stand."

"I'm considering Samuel Bishop still under oath from his earlier testimony," Judge Everson snapped.

Out of the corner of his eye, Sam saw Lamar Hammond ooze forward.

"Your Honor, as Mr. Tolliver's lawyer, I'd like to suggest Mr. Tolliver be freed, since the state's key witness has been revealed to be a criminal. His testimony is clearly unreliable, and so Mr. Tolliver should be let go, as there is no convincing evidence to hold him."

Judge Everson gaped at him, then snapped his jaws shut and fixed Hammond with a furious glare. *"Silence!"* he roared, leaning on the bar with both hands. "The court will entertain no such outrageous suggestions from you, Mr. Hammond. You make any more and I'll cite you for contempt!"

"Sorry, Your Honor." Hammond said, but his lips twitched as he attempted to smooth out his satisfied smile. He darted a glance at the three men in front, who had received no such orders from the judge and were grinning broadly.

Sam wished he could shove a fist into each of their faces in turn—Raney's first, of course.

"The Simpson Creek jail has two cells, doesn't it?" the judge demanded, his question aimed at Nick.

Brookfield looked uncomfortable. "Yes, Your Honor."

The judge turned to Tolliver's lawyer. "Mr. Hammond, I assume you can prove your outrageous allegation with testimony by this Houston banker?"

Hammond inclined his head. "Yes, Your Honor. Mr. Gregory Timkin, president of the First National Bank of Houston, is due to arrive in Simpson Creek tomorrow, if the weather holds."

"Very well. Mr. Brookfield, I understand you were acting sheriff until Mr. Bishop came to town, and I'm giving you that job back until further arrangements can be made. Are you able to carry out that job impartially, even though you and Bishop have been friends?"

Nick Brookfield's face was stony. "I am, Your Honor."

"Samuel Bishop," the judge said, "you're under arrest

on suspicion of stealing two thousand dollars from the First National Bank of Houston and a ruby ring belonging to Kendall Raney." He turned to Nick. "Acting Sheriff Brookfield, you and Deputy Menendez are to take this man—" he pointed straight at Sam "—and Mr. Tolliver back to the jail and install them in their cells."

"Yes, Your Honor."

"Sheriff Hantz, do you have a set of come-alongs he could borrow?"

"I do, Your Honor," Hantz said, and handed them to Nick.

"Stand and stick out your hands." There was no hint of warmth in Nick's tone, and no hint of regret in his eyes.

Sam complied, nausea churning in his stomach, and held out his wrists, feeling Hantz's come-alongs snap with cold, metallic finality over his wrists.

Prissy jumped to her feet and opened her mouth to protest as Sam was being led away, but no sound would come. Once the batwing doors swung shut again after the men had left, her father turned to her.

"We're going home, Prissy."

"But—but you have to do something, Papa!" she cried. "You can't just let them put Sam in jail! He didn't do anything—I know he didn't! You can't let them put Sam into a cell next to that murderer as if Sam was a criminal, too!"

Everyone was staring, whispering. Her father's face seemed to have transformed itself into stone, just like Nick's. "We will talk *at home,* Priscilla." He put a heavy hand on her shoulder. "Come."

Mariah Fairchild fluttered behind them, clearly at a

loss as to what to do. Her father seemed to remember her at last.

"Mariah, perhaps it would be best if I called upon you later. Priscilla and I need to discuss what has happened. Will you be all right, my dear?"

"O-of course, James…"

Sarah said, "I'll come see you later, Prissy. It'll be all right, you'll see. There will be an explanation."

And then her father put Prissy's hand upon his arm and guided her out of the makeshift court.

Flora met them at the door of Gilmore House, her eyes full of questions, but her father just shook his head, and the servant let them by.

"Prissy—" her father began, but she waved her hand helplessly at him and ran up the stairs.

She made it to the sanctuary of her room before she collapsed into tears and threw herself on the bed in a paroxysm of weeping. Houston leaped onto the bed and tried to console her, but she pushed him gently away. At last he contented himself with huddling close to her on the quilt, and she drew what comfort she could from the dog Sam had given her.

Her father came to her room some time later, after she had cried herself out. She'd been staring at the sapphire ring on her finger when he entered, but she shoved her hand under her skirt so as not to remind him that she wore it. She wasn't going to give it up, any more than she was going to give up on Sam—at least not without hearing what he had to say.

"Priscilla, sometimes we make mistakes," her father began, "in trusting—loving—certain people, and I know it hurts when events prove us wrong."

"I'm not wrong," she said. "I love Sam, and he loves

me, and I *know* there is more to this story than what we've heard so far. We have to go to him, to listen to what he has to say. There has to be an explanation!"

"I went to see Bishop after I brought you home," her father said. "I made sure he was comfortable. But he wouldn't talk to me. Evidently he has nothing to say, now that he's been found out as a thief and a swindler."

"Papa, we have no one's word for it but that snake of a lawyer's!" Prissy retorted indignantly. She could hardly believe her ears. Was this her father, who had always been open-minded, never believing the worst of a man until he'd given him every chance to prove otherwise? Evidently his open-mindedness stopped when it came to her.

A muscle jumped in her father's right temple and his jaw set. "Priscilla, that stolen money and that fancy ring didn't stuff themselves into Bishop's mattress. He's been caught red-handed with stolen goods, daughter."

"I don't believe he took those things. I'll never believe it. Why should he take such a big sum of money and then apply for a job that pays as little as being sheriff does? He could have bought property, set himself up as a gentleman of leisure," she argued. "I think the money and the ring were planted."

Her father sat down heavily on a chair by her bedside, looking suddenly twenty years older. "I spoke to Nick Brookfield, Priscilla. It seems he had his doubts about the man from the start. He suspected Bishop had never been a lawman before he came to Simpson Creek. He admits he'd thought he was wrong about Bishop, but he put the question to him when he put him in the cell. Bishop admitted it, right before I came to the jail."

Prissy stared at her father as the words thudded dully

against her aching heart. "He admitted to Nick that he lied about being a sheriff in Tennessee and Louisiana?" she repeated.

Her father nodded, his face downcast. "Prissy, honey, I know it's hard for you to hear, but you're a young lady of means, and some men…well, they're willing to take advantage of a trusting heart. They don't want to work for their fortune. They merely want to marry it."

"But…but Sam didn't want us to live off of you, when we're married. He said so," she protested. "He wanted to buy that old house on Travis Street and fix it up for us, and live on his sheriff's salary. He told me that, and I believe it! Why are you so quick to think the worst of him?"

"Prissy, did he ever actually *buy* the house, or was it all just fine talk to convince you he loved you for yourself?" her father asked, his red-rimmed eyes sad.

"He-he didn't get a chance to!" she cried. "Before he could speak to Mr. Avery, Tolliver was arrested, and Sam was spending every spare moment at the jail guarding him!"

Her father cleared his throat. "Be that as it may, the engagement is over now. My daughter will not be marrying a convicted thief. We should just thank God we found out before you married him and he dragged your good name into the mire along with his own."

Who was this cold man who got heavily to his feet now? It couldn't be her papa, for her papa would never have been so unfeeling. Beside her, Houston growled, and her father glared at the dog.

Prissy rose from the bed with as much dignity as she could muster and placed herself between the dog and her father, eyeing the latter through eyes swollen with shed tears. When she spoke, her voice croaked. "I think I have something to say about whether or not my engagement to Sam is over, and I say it isn't. I won't believe anything you're saying about Sam, not unless I hear it from Sam himself. I'm going down to the jail right now."

Her father stood before her. "No, you're not. I forbid it. You'll hear all his sordid lies soon enough when that bank president from Houston arrives and Sam's trial begins, if you insist on going. If I were you, though, I'd stay home and spare yourself the embarrassment."

She was silent for a moment, wondering what the best tactic was to use with her suddenly obdurate parent. "He's going to be proved innocent, Papa, you'll see."

"And what if he isn't, Priscilla?" her father countered. "What if he's convicted of stealing two thousand dollars from that banker? And the ring?"

"Then I'll wait for him, Papa. I love him, and he won't be in prison forever."

Her father's eyes bulged and his face flushed a dangerous purple. "I'd hoped it wouldn't come to this. I love you, daughter, more than I love my own life, but the day you marry a convicted felon is the day you will be disinherited, Priscilla. Imagine what it would be like, marrying him years from now, your youth gone, with nothing but the clothes on your back, daughter, and nowhere to live except shabby rented lodgings he *might* be able to provide for you. And what will he do to earn a living then? I'm sorry, but I don't think he's worth it, and after you have time to reflect, neither will you."

All she could do was look at her father. Astonishment had robbed her of speech for the second time today.

"You are not to go to the jail, Prissy, do you hear me?"

Slowly, she nodded. "Yes, Papa, I hear you."

* * *

"Reckon yer not so high an' mighty now, are you, Bishop, now you don't have that star on yer chest no more," Tolliver sneered from his cell. "Soon as that bank president gets here from Houston t'confirm Mr. Raney's story, I reckon I'll be a free man, yessiree. They ain't gonna put no rope around my neck on the word of a thief. Maybe Raney can even find a way to pin that tenderfoot's killin' on *you,* and you'll be the one on the gallows."

Sam didn't show by so much as a twitching muscle that he'd heard this latest taunt from Tolliver, who'd been at it ever since they'd returned from the saloon—when he wasn't griping that Sam had gotten the cell with the window. He didn't bother telling Tolliver Waters's murder was the one thing they couldn't pin on him, since he'd been with a group of ladies on the day of the murder, and had been standing with Nick Brookfield in his barn when the shots were fired. And Waters's body was still warm when he'd been found, so it was not as if he could have killed him earlier in the morning and then ridden back to Simpson Creek in time to escort Prissy and her friends out to the ranch.

Not that it mattered. The only thing he feared had come to pass. His past had been exposed, and all of Simpson Creek now knew he was not the upright man they'd thought him, but a fraud. A thief and a liar. And the loss of their good opinion, as much as the idea hurt, paled in significance next to the stricken look he'd seen in Prissy's eyes, the look that told him she didn't believe in him anymore, either.

Because he'd lied, his testimony was no longer believable, and the murderer in the cell next to him would probably walk free. There was nothing he could do to change that now, and after realizing he'd lost Prissy forever, he could hardly bring himself to care. Even if Tolliver could be convicted of Waters's killing, Waters would still be dead.

He'd listened silently when Prissy's father had come to tell him that he would forbid Prissy ever to see him again. Gilmore didn't have to do that, he'd thought. He'd seen the hurt in her eyes when Hantz had announced what he'd found in the mattress, and he knew she'd never want to see him again anyway.

He'd thought loving Prissy, taking on an honorable job, and learning to believe in and trust the Lord Prissy served was the answer to putting his past behind him. But it wasn't true. His past had risen up and defeated him, all because of one good thing he'd done—saving the dog Raney would have killed—and one wrong thing—taking Raney's ring. God didn't care about him, just as he'd always thought.

I am with you always, a voice whispered inside him. *I have forgiven your sins, and I will save you.*

He uttered a short, mirthless bark of laughter. What a time to be hearing voices again. No doubt he'd be good and loco by the time he was sentenced to prison.

"What are you laughin' about, Bishop? Seems t'me you ain't got nothing t' laugh about," Tolliver jeered. "You're in a cell, same as me, an' that purty lil' girl you been sparkin' don't want nothin' t' do with you no more. Even if she did, her rich papa told you she can't see you agin. Soon as that fellow gets here from Houston, you're goin' t' prison for swindlin', so I figger you ain't got nothin' t' laugh about."

Luis Menendez still believed in him, wonder of wonders. Sam couldn't imagine why. Or perhaps it was just that

Sam had been decent to him, so he wouldn't let Tolliver torment him.

It went some ways to make up for the cold contempt Nick Brookfield had favored him with ever since he'd led him away from the saloon. Brookfield now thought his first instincts about Sam had been correct, and he wasn't a man who liked being made a fool of.

Sam heard the door, but he didn't bother to open his eyes and see who'd come to gawk at him or tell him off for trying to pretend he was what he wasn't. Then he heard a voice he never thought he'd hear again, and it took all his self-control to keep his eyes closed and pretend to go on sleeping.

"Nick, I need to see Sam," Prissy said, her voice anxious and strained. He knew she had spotted him in his cell. "Sam, wake up," she called. "I'm here. I have to talk to you!"

He heard the scrape of Nick's chair—which had been *his* chair only this morning, Sam thought bitterly—as it was scooted back. "Sorry, Miss Prissy, but your father left strict instructions that you were not to see Bishop. I need you to leave."

"But you can't do that! I have to see him, Nick! I have to tell him—to find out—"

"I'm sorry, but I really must insist, Miss Prissy."

Sam heard her start to cry and it broke his heart. He rolled over on the narrow cot and stood.

"Go home, Prissy. I don't want to see you," he said, keeping his eyes on the worn wooden floor so he wouldn't see her eyes shining like flooded blue jewels in the heart-shaped face he loved. "There's no point. It's over. Forget about me." Then he turned back to his cot and lay down, his face to the wall.

Chapter Twenty-One

Prissy heard voices in her father's study when she returned to the house. "But, James, if you forbid her to see Sam now, you'll break her heart," said Mariah Fairchild. "If that nice young man is convicted, he'll go to prison for years. She may never see him again."

"Mariah, no daughter of mine is going to be allowed to breathe the same air as a liar and a thief," her father snapped. "She's upset, and I'm sorry about that, but I have to be thankful we found out now and not after she married him. Sam Bishop saw her as an easy way off the outlaw trail, nothing more."

"James, surely that's too harsh," Mariah protested.

"Mariah, he was caught with the money and that big, gaudy ring right in his mattress!" her father thundered. "The guilt was written all over his face—didn't you see it?"

"But we haven't heard his side of it," Mariah argued. "Isn't a man innocent until proven guilty in this country? He hasn't even been tried yet, and you've already convicted him, James."

She had to give the widow credit for spirit, Prissy thought, appreciating the woman's attempt to defend Sam. If only Sam had this much spirit left to defend himself.

Now if she could just avoid the step that creaked, she could ascend the stairs and get into her room without her father ever knowing she'd sneaked out and gone to see Sam against his express orders.

However, Houston, who'd been dozing on her bed when she'd left, scampered pell-mell down the stairs, yapping happily to see her.

The door to her father's study was thrown open.

"Prissy! I thought you were upstairs," her father said, then looked at her more closely. "Where have you been, young lady?"

"At Sarah's," she began. It was the truth, she told herself. She *had* just come from Sarah's, for she had been too upset by Sam's refusal to see her and his dispirited manner to go straight home. Sarah had done her best to console her friend, but once Prissy stopped crying, she'd realized all the tea and sugar cookies Sarah could serve wouldn't change anything.

Prissy suddenly decided there was no reason to lie to her father. She was a grown woman, and the man she loved was in trouble. She'd done what she had to do.

She lifted her head and faced him. "But before that I went to see Sam, Papa. You needn't worry," she added, when his eyes narrowed at her. "Nick told me to leave, and even if he hadn't, Sam wouldn't speak to me."

Her father studied her a moment. "Very well, then. I-I'm sorry you're so upset, Pris." He opened his arms to her, and with Mariah looking on, she went into his embrace and wept all the tears she had left.

* * *

Tolliver had finally ceased taunting him and subsided into a snoring slumber, but Sam couldn't sleep. He couldn't banish the vision of Prissy stumbling with tear-blinded eyes out of the jail, shrugging off any attempt by Nick to comfort her.

She can learn to love again, he told himself. There were bachelors coming into town all the time, thanks to the efforts of the Spinsters' Club. The mistake of loving him need not haunt her for a lifetime. He loved her enough to make a clean break of it so she could start over.

Thunder rumbled in the distance, promising rain before morning. That might delay the Houston bank president's arrival, which only meant more time to spend in this miserable cell before he was convicted and sent off to prison for the crime he hadn't committed as well as the one he had.

"Do you mind taking the first watch?" Sam heard Nick ask Luis.

"No, Señor Brookfield. Good night."

Luis didn't call the Englishman "Sheriff," Sam noted, though he was unfailingly respectful.

Nick favored Sam with a last frosty glare before stalking between the cells to the living quarters and shutting the door. Sam figured he had to be missing his wife and resenting Sam for making it necessary for him to take on the sheriff's job again.

"Do you need a blanket, Sheriff?" Luis asked Sam. "Or a glass of water, or water to wash with? And there is chocolate cake left that Señora Walker brought if you want some."

"Thanks, but I don't need anything, Luis."

"We will find a way out of this *problema,* you'll see," Luis assured him.

Sam wished he had Luis's faith. Nothing would ever make him worthy of Prissy again or bring back the town's respect. He pretended to sleep, so Luis would stop trying to cheer him. Soon Luis's eyes grew heavy and he nodded off in his chair.

At first Sam thought he heard an animal rustling about outside. The window that Tolliver coveted faced the narrow alley between the jail and the mercantile, and cats frequently hunted there at night.

Then he heard the whisper. "Hssst! Bishop, you awake?"

Sam had to stand on his bed to look out the narrow window, and as he did so, the cot creaked so loudly he turned to see if the sound had awakened the deputy. But Luis only stirred and shifted his position before settling into sleep again. He really ought to warn the youth about falling asleep on the job, Sam thought, even if he wasn't the sheriff any more.

"Who's there?" he called softly, and then a figure separated itself from the shadows.

"I come from th' boss." The man's hat was pulled low over his head, but even so, Sam thought he recognized the scarred jaw of one of the Alliance henchmen, one who had ridden with Tolliver before Tolliver had been arrested.

"Which boss?"

"Raney. He says if you change yer testimony when th' trial begins again, and say you saw Waters give Tolliver that watch—"

"Why would Waters have done that?" Sam interrupted, disdain in his voice. "It was engraved with his name."

"Mebbe he owed him money or somethin', how should I know?" the other man snarled. "Anyway, he says he kin get that bank president that's comin' to say you ain't guilty a' what yore accused of."

"Are you saying the bank president's part of the plot?" Sam demanded, furious at the idea that a bank official could be bought off in these circumstances.

"Sssh! Keep yer voice down!" the man hissed. "I ain't sayin' that, I'm sayin' Mr. Raney could make the whole thing jes' go away—mebbe he'd give the money back or somethin'."

It might keep him out of prison, but even if Raney paid off the missing amount, the damage had been done. Sam's reputation lay in ruins and Mayor Gilmore had forbidden him any further relationship with his daughter. Once Prissy thought about it hard enough, she wouldn't want anything to do with him, either, for he would have no job, no way to provide for her. He couldn't afford to buy the humble house on Travis Street, let alone fix it up.

"Tell Raney to go to blazes!" he whispered to the shadow by his window.

"That yer final answer, Bishop? You'll be sorry."

"Bishop, who are you talking to?" said a voice behind him, startling Sam so completely that he nearly fell off the cot.

Sam turned to see Nick standing in the passageway between the two cells that led to his quarters. His blond hair was rumpled, as if he'd just gotten out of bed, but there was nothing sleepy about the suspicious gleam in his eyes.

Luis had awakened, too, and looked sheepish.

Sam looked back out, but of course the Alliance man

had disappeared. Thunder cracked again, and then the heavens opened and rain descended in a solid sheet that would erase any trace the man had been there—if his boots had even left any impression in the dry, hard ground.

"Raney sent one of his men to try to bribe me," Sam said, raising his voice over the rain drumming on the tin roof. "He said if I'd say I knew Waters had given Tolliver that watch, he'd make the swindling accusation go away."

Nick snorted. "A likely story."

"Why else would I be standing on the cot?"

Tolliver woke then, his ugly face twisted with irritation. "Cain't a man git some sleep around here? Whatever you two're shoutin' about, cain't it wait till morning?"

"It certainly can," Nick snapped. "And since Bishop's claiming a midnight visitor, you can sleep in the cell with the window. Luis, help me switch the prisoners."

"I get the window?" Tolliver crowed. "About time!"

Sam scowled, for the sheets on Tolliver's bed were sure to be as malodorous as he was. Probably vermin-ridden, too. "Make him take his sheets with him," he said, and pulled his own off the cot.

Within minutes the two men had switched cells and remade their beds, and Tolliver was snoring in his new cell with the window. Sam didn't want any more late-night visitors anyway, so the new arrangement suited him just fine.

He closed his eyes and forced himself to sleep.

The bolt of lightning just before dawn struck inside the jail, so loud it had Sam half falling out of the narrow cot. Only it wasn't lightning, Sam realized as he saw the haze of gunsmoke and smelled the acrid stench of burnt gunpowder. He leaped to his feet, about to demand to know why Nick or Luis was shooting, only to see Nick take hold of the bars of the other cell, stare into it, then dash out the door into the rain. A second later, Luis stumbled out of the bedroom, still wiping the sleep from his eyes.

"What happened, Sheriff?" Luis asked.

But Sam could only point into the other cell, where Leroy Tolliver lay dead on his cot of a gunshot wound to his chest.

"Someone must have shot him through the window."

"Dios mio," breathed Luis, staring.

"That bullet was meant for me." Whoever had offered the bribe earlier had come back to kill him, since Sam had refused it. He couldn't have known the prisoners had switched cells.

Nick returned a few minutes later, panting and wet, his pants mud-splattered. "I lost him, whoever he was. But he left the bucket he stood on—how he managed to put that in place, stand on it and take aim, all without my seeing him…"

His voice trailed off and his gaze dipped to the newspaper lying on the floor. Sam guessed the Englishman was wondering if he'd dozed off, too, just for a moment.

Now they wouldn't need two trials, for Tolliver had been their only murder suspect. There was only Sam left to stand trial for Raney's trumped-up swindling charge.

Which would do nothing to rid the town of the problem of the Alliance.

Had the Lord saved his life, just to allow him to be sent to prison and lose Prissy, not to mention his short-lived good name?

* * *

Prissy learned of Tolliver's assassination over breakfast when a haggard Nick Brookfield came to notify her father.

After he blurted out the news, Prissy bolted out of her chair. "Sam could have been killed! Is he all right?" she cried. "He—he wasn't wounded? Please, tell me the truth, Nick!"

"He's all right, Prissy," Nick said. "No, he wasn't wounded. Luis is boarding up the window even as we speak." He turned back to her father. "I'm sorry I wasn't able to catch the b—the blighter, sir," he amended, after a glance at the Prissy. "I ran out of the office as soon as I realized what had happened, but he had too big of a head start and I lost him in the rain. I heard someone take off on a fast horse at the other end of Travis Street, but of course the rain wiped out his trail."

Prissy threw down her napkin and dashed to the door as she called over her shoulder, "I'm going to make sure Sam's all right! Disinherit me if you want, Papa, but I have to be sure!" She ran down the hall, threw open the door, and pelted down the steps.

"Wait, Prissy, I'm coming with you!"

Prissy skidded to a halt and turned, astonished to see Mariah throwing on her shawl as she sprinted down the steps after her, moving with amazing speed for a lady of her mature years.

"You don't have to do this," Prissy assured her, touched by the woman's caring and the anxious expression in her eyes. "It won't change anything—Sam will probably refuse to see me again even if Nick doesn't catch up and keep us from going in—and there's no need for Papa to be angry at both of us. I just have to see Sam with my own eyes to be sure he's all right."

"I want to go with you, dear. You shouldn't be alone if…if Sam refuses to see you," said Mariah. "You've had so much to contend with for a young lady. And if your father's angry at both of us, well…" She snapped her fingers. "He'll just have to be angry with both of us, or get over it. When I left, Nick was calming him down, telling him to let you at least see Sam. Your Papa's just worried about you, Prissy dear. He wants the best for you."

Impulsively, Prissy hugged her. "Thank you," she said, meaning it.

By tacit agreement, they hastened off toward the jail. As they reached it, Prissy spotted Luis Menendez pacing around outside, rifle in hand.

"Luis, has—has something else happened? Is Sam all right?"

"Nothing else, *señorita,*" he assured her. "Señor Brookfield only asked me to guard him from out here, in case that *malvado* Raney and his *hombres* try again. Doctor Walker is on guard inside. It is good you have come."

"Will he see me?" she asked, her heart in her throat. She couldn't bear it if he turned his back on her as he had yesterday.

Luis shrugged. "I don't know, *señorita,* but he *needs* to see you, whether he admits it or not."

She entered, with Mariah right behind her, to find Nolan Walker sitting in the sheriff's chair, another rifle lying at the ready on his lap.

"Hello, Nolan. I—I have to see Sam," she said.

"I figured you'd be here. Sarah said you'd come, once you learned about Tolliver."

Her gaze flew past the Yankee doctor to where Sam stood behind the bars of his cell, staring at her.

"I'm all right, Prissy," he said. "Luis has boarded up the window, as you can see. Raney won't try anything again. He doesn't need to, now that Tolliver's dead."

She stared at the empty cot in the next cell, where a board nailed over the high, narrow window shut out most of the light and air. Then her gaze flew back to Sam.

"I'm all right," he said again, as if she hadn't heard him before. "You can go home now, Prissy. There's no use in you being here. You need to start over, forget me." His eyes drank her in, though, like a dying man drinks his last cup of water.

Before she knew what she was doing, she'd joined him at the bars and taken hold of his hands. "I'm not leaving until you tell me why you've given up, why you're not willing to stand up for yourself, Sam Bishop!"

He smiled sadly at her. "It's no use, can't you see that? I didn't take the money from that bank. Yet Raney managed to plant those double eagles in my mattress, and that judge isn't going to believe I'm innocent. I did take that ring, but only after Raney had practically sliced open my face with it when I called him a cheater...never mind, Prissy. I'll be convicted, and I don't want you in the courtroom when it happens, do you understand?"

"No, I don't understand," she retorted. "You have to try, Sam!" She struggled against the fear and panic that threatened to swamp her.

Someone came into the jail then, and Prissy heard Nolan uttering a greeting, but she paid no attention. She had to convince Sam to fight before he insisted she leave. "I'll be there, and I'll tell that judge what a good man you are, how you raised your sisters and didn't let your family be broken up and parceled out to others…"

He squeezed her hands before letting them go. "That's not going to be enough to convince a judge that I'm innocent now, sweetheart."

"No, but what this man has to say might," said a voice behind her.

Prissy turned to see Reverend Chadwick, his gnarled old hand resting on the shoulder of Delbert Perry.

Chapter Twenty-Two

Mr. Gregory Timkin, president of the First National Bank of Houston, arrived in a hired carriage late the next day, accompanied by his head teller, Marcus Howell. The two were immediately escorted by a very smug-looking Kendall Raney to Gilmore House, where the judge was once again dining. Prissy, who'd answered the door, was gently waved aside by her father.

"These gentlemen can come in, but you're not welcome here, Raney," Prissy's father said, intercepting Raney on his doorstep. "You can go back to whatever rock you crawled out from under."

Still hovering in the hall, Prissy heard Raney chuckle. "That's fine, *Mayor*," he said with a voice that dripped with mock humility. "I understand completely. I'm sure I'll see you in court."

Her father ignored him and gestured for the other men to enter. "Mr. Timkin, Mr. Howell, you are welcome, of course. Judge Everson will be glad to know you've arrived. You're just in time to have supper with us, gentlemen."

Both men's clothes were rumpled and travel-stained. Over Flora's excellent roast beef, they recalled how they'd been drenched to the bone yesterday when the carriage became mired in a muddy creek bed. Then a wall of water had come roaring at them, and they'd been fortunate to escape with their lives. They'd been forced to take shelter at a nearby ranch until this morning.

Mr. Timkin said he'd be very glad if Sam Bishop's trial could proceed tomorrow, so he could regain the money Bishop had stolen and go on with the business of running his bank. And did Mayor Gilmore think he would be able to hire reliable men in Simpson Creek to guard him and the money on the way home?

Her father assured him all that could be arranged when the time came.

Prissy wanted to question the man herself, to know just why Timkin thought Sam had ever even entered his bank, let alone stole two thousand dollars, but like her father, she held her peace. Timkin didn't need to know she was engaged to marry the very man he was here to help convict. There would be time for all that tomorrow.

Judge Everson said starting Bishop's trial tomorrow suited him just fine, too, then suggested that to be ethical, they should not discuss the particulars of the case outside the courtroom.

The next morning, the saloon-turned-courtroom was even more packed than it had been previously, if that was possible. She got some odd looks as she carried Houston into the courtroom, but if anyone thought it odd that the mayor's daughter was bringing her dog into such crowded surroundings, they were too polite to say so. She'd already assured the judge she had a good reason.

The prosecutor started the morning by questioning the bank president.

"And just how did Mr. Bishop come to be employed by you, Mr. Timkin?"

"When I'm in need of a new employee, Kendall Raney, a long-time associate and friend, often suggests a likely prospect from among his acquaintances. Mr. Bishop must have been one of those."

"'Must have been one of those?'" Mr. Bryant echoed. "You don't recognize the accused man, Samuel Bishop?"

Gregory Timkin harrumphed importantly. "I have many employees, First National Bank being the largest in the Houston area—much larger than, say, the one in Simpson Creek." His voice, as he gazed over the assembled multitude in their closely packed seats, dripped with condescension. "I only became aware that a large sum was missing when Mr. Howell, the bank's head teller, informed me of it, and said that one of the employees had failed to show up that morning. I was told the employee's name was Samuel Bishop."

Howell, his head teller, was sworn in and confirmed the story. "That's the man," he said, pointing at Sam. "He came well recommended by Mr. Raney, but it was after he came that the money disappeared."

Howell must be the one in league with Raney, Prissy thought, seeing the way the narrow-faced man's gaze slid over Sam. If only she were a man, she thought, her fists clenching on her lap.

The prosecutor cleared his throat. "I have another question or two for you, Mr. Timkin," he said. "Consider yourself still under oath."

Timkin nodded, clearly somewhat surprised, and took the stand again.

"Would you say your associate Mr. Raney is a man with many business interests?" Gabe Bryant asked.

"I would, sir. That helped form the basis for our friendship, as we are both…men of varied interests, shall we say?"

"And were you aware that your business associate owned a gambling parlor in an unsavory part of Houston, known as The Painted Lady?"

Timkin shrugged. "As I said, Mr. Raney is a man of many interests and concerns," he said. "Hotels, restaurants, properties…he may have mentioned such a place, but I do not recall him mentioning it by name."

Prissy guessed Raney had never mentioned owning such a notorious business.

The prosecutor next called Sam to the stand. Sam testified that he had never been a bank employee at any bank, let alone the First National Bank of Houston.

"And how did you earn your living while you were in Houston, Mr. Bishop?"

Sam shot an apologetic glance in Prissy's direction. "I was a gambler, Your Honor."

The residents of Simpson Creek gasped and exchanged glances with each other.

"Were you good at it, Mr. Bishop?"

"Not particularly."

Prissy heard several chuckles.

"Please tell us what took place on your last night in Houston, Mr. Bishop."

Sam recited the events he'd told Prissy about only yesterday, events which brought her to the verge of tears again now—how he'd suspected Kendall Raney of cheating in his own establishment at the table where Sam was playing poker; how Sam had accused him, only to be set upon by

Raney's toughs who beat him within an inch of his life before Raney landed the final cheek-lacerating blow to his face and knocked him unconscious. He'd awakened trussed up like a Thanksgiving turkey as he was thrown to the floor in Raney's back room, and overheard Raney tell his ruffians he wanted them to return after supper and throw Bishop, along with the little dog that was caged in the room, into the bayou for the alligators.

"And what happened to you and the dog?" the judge asked, not waiting for the prosecutor. "I see that you weren't fed to the alligators, at least."

Again, there were chuckles.

Sam pointed to where Houston sat on Prissy's lap. "After I managed to untie myself and escape with the dog to Simpson Creek, I gave him to Miss Prissy Gilmore."

Several turned to smile at Prissy and Houston, and Houston obligingly wagged his tail as if he loved being the center of attention.

"You're accused of taking a vast sum of money, Mr. Raney," Bryant said. "You've already testified that you took no money from Mr. Timkin's bank, but did you take anything else from that room before you escaped?'

"Yes," Sam said and looked the judge in the eye. "I broke into Mr. Raney's safe and took back the money he'd cheated from me, and the ring he'd been wearing when he cut open my face," he added, pointing to the jagged white scar.

"Would this be the same ring?" Gabe Bryant inquired, holding up Raney's ring.

"It would."

"And have you ever been a lawman, Mr. Bishop?"

"No," Sam admitted.

"So you lied about the experience you claimed to have as a deputy in Tennessee and Louisiana."

"Yes. But I took the oath with every intention of serving Simpson Creek well, and I believe I've done so."

Bryant pulled a skeptical face. "And just how did you end up in Simpson Creek, Mr. Bishop?"

"I read an advertisement in an old newspaper about the Simpson Creek Society for the Promotion of Marriage, Your Honor. I decided I wanted to meet a nice lady and get married. So I came here."

Raney stood up at that point, much to everyone's surprise. "Your Honor, may I speak?"

Judge Everson's brows rose most of the way to his hairline, but he nodded.

"Your Honor, it all boils down to Bishop's word against that of an esteemed bank president and his chief employee, the word of an admitted liar and a thief. Who is more worthy of being believed?"

"I have another witness who might be able to help us on that issue," Gabe Bryant said, and gestured to the back of the room.

Prissy caught Sam's eye and gave him an encouraging smile.

Two men stood near one of the back rows of seats—Reverend Chadwick and Delbert Perry. As Sam watched, the old preacher put an encouraging hand on Perry's shoulder and whispered a few words in his ear, and then Perry walked toward the witness chair, head held high, as if he was clothed in an immaculate frock coat, trousers and shirt like Kendall Raney instead of the worn and much-repaired shirt, trousers and sack coat he wore.

Still sitting in the defendant's seat near the judge, Sam

gazed at Prissy, still unable to believe that she was standing by him through all this. The moment of truth had arrived—what Perry was about to say was their only hope of proving Sam innocent. If the judge didn't believe Perry, Sam thought, all was lost.

I am with you always.

This time Sam believed the truth of that.

Raney pointed at the weathered man about to take the oath. "Why is *he* testifying?" he called out, scorn lacing his voice. "Someone told me he's the town drunk—and he's going to be a *witness?* To what? The view inside a whiskey bottle?"

Hammond, sitting next to him, snickered behind his hand.

Judge Everson rapped on his gavel. "That's enough out of you, sir. Any more outbursts like that will result in your removal from my courtroom."

Raney looked pointedly around him at the rows of liquor bottles and glasses behind the bar and seemed about to argue, then shut his mouth.

Delbert Perry was sworn in, and Gabe Bryant stepped forward to question him.

"Mr. Perry, I'm going to start with the accusation Mr. Raney made. Can you tell us why you'd be a reliable witness? Isn't it true you've been known as the 'town drunk,' just as he said?"

Sam saw Perry's lips spread into a smile. "Yessir. I was exactly that, until the last time I shot up th' saloon the day Mr. Bishop became the new sheriff. I nearly kilt Mr. Brookfield accidentally, an' that's a pure fact. An' Mr. Bishop arrested me, and Mr. Brookfield talked to me that evenin' while I was soberin' up in my cell."

"He talked to you? About what?"

"About Jesus. He'd talked to me before 'bout Him, but this time…I dunno, it jes' *took* this time."

Bryant's brow furrowed. "Took? Explain what you mean, Mr. Perry."

Delbert Perry beamed. "He'd been tellin' me th' Lord wanted to forgive me a' my sins, 'cause He had better things for me t'do than stumble around drunk all the time. But I had to accept Him. This time I did, an' I ain't drinkin' no more."

Sam saw Perry look out over the sea of townspeople's faces until he spotted the man he was looking for. "I ain't been in th' saloon to drink since, have I, George?"

George Detwiler half stood and called back, "He's tellin' the truth. I pay him to help me clean up after the saloon closes at night, but he doesn't drink. Not even from leftover bottles."

Judge Everson rapped on his gavel again. "I'm going to allow that last remark, but anything further anyone has to say, you have to be sworn in."

Gabe Bryant cleared his throat. "So what do you spend your leisure time doing, now that you're not drinking, Mr. Perry?"

"When I'm not doin' odd jobs, like I do for George at closin' time, I'm gen'rally out walkin', talkin' to th' Lord. 'Specially at night, when I cain't sleep. That's when I'm most tempted t'slide inta my old ways, y'see."

Bryant nodded. "And do you encounter people when you're out walking?"

"Sometimes," Perry said. "Early in the evenin', before I'm at the saloon cleanin', but once in a while late at night."

"Do they speak to you, generally?"

"Folks I know do. Sometimes they just nod, friendly-like. But sometimes they don't even see me."

Sam darted another glance at Raney. He and his two partners looked distinctly uneasy now, and he saw Byrd begin to whisper to Pennington behind a cupped hand. Kendall Raney looked over his shoulder at the batwing doors.

"And on the evening of August fifteenth, did you happen to encounter some people talking, whose conversation you overheard?"

"Well, I wouldn't 'zactly say I encountered them. I was jes' sittin' on the stoop out back a' the saloon, watchin' the heat lightnin' flashin' in the sky and talkin' t' th' Lord like I told you, when these two fellows stopped to talk at the side of the saloon buildin' near me. They didn't see me sittin' there in th' dark, and they seemed like they had somethin' important to discuss, so I jes' held my peace."

"Who were they, and what was being said?"

"That feller there—" he pointed at Raney "—he was talkin' to another man, someone I hadn't seen before or since. He was rough-lookin'—a saddle tramp sort a' man."

"Your Honor, I object!" roared Raney, on his feet now, his face beet-red.

"You can't object, you're not a lawyer in this case!" roared back the judge. "Now, keep your mouth shut, or I'll have you gagged. Is that clear?"

Raney sat down. Sam thought he looked more and more like a trapped animal that wanted to flee but hadn't found a way yet. Trapped animals could be dangerous. Sam wished he had his pistol in its holster on his hip.

Bryant turned back to Perry. "As I was asking you, what were Mr. Raney and the other man speaking about?

"Mr. Raney, he said he and his partners, Mr. Pennington and Mr. Byrd, wanted this fella—he called him 'Jace'—t'go talk to Sheriff Bishop in th' jail, but quiet-like, after everyone else there was asleep. He was t' offer 'em a bribe—"

"A *bribe?*" Gabe Bryant repeated, turning to look at the court.

Everyone's gaze was riveted on Perry and the prosecutor, Sam thought, and none more so than Kendall Raney's. If Raney could have killed anyone with a look, he would have started with Delbert Perry.

"Yessir, a bribe. If Sheriff Bishop took the bribe, Raney would give the money back to th' bank president so he'd drop the charges against Bishop, but after that Sheriff Bishop was to go along with anythin' they said—he was to be their man, like the sheriff of Colorado Bend is, so the Alliance could take over Simpson Creek, too. From what this Jace was sayin', it was plain he was the one who planted the money and the ring in Sheriff Bishop's mattress while everyone was in here when the other trial was goin' on."

The buzz started then, only to die down when Everson pounded his gavel and shouted, "Order! Order in this court!"

"Was that the end of the conversation?" Bryant asked Perry.

Perry shook his head.

"Nossir. Mr. Raney said if Bishop refused t'go along with his offer, he was t'shoot Bishop through th' window. Shoot him dead."

Suddenly everyone was talking at once. Judge Everson pounded again on his gavel repeatedly, yelling "Order! Order!"

In the hubbub, Sam saw Pennington and Byrd try to slip unobtrusively out of their row and make their way to the door. They were ushered back to their seats by Luis Menendez, who had been standing sentinel at the door. Raney had stood, too, but Nick Brookfield, a hand resting on the butt of his pistol, stood in front of him and he sat back down.

Finally, quiet settled over the courtroom as everyone held their breath to hear the rest of what Delbert Perry would say.

"So you're very sure that Mr. Raney said his two partners, Mr. Pennington and Mr. Byrd—" he pointed at them "—were in on the plan?"

"Yessir."

"Then what happened?"

"Why, I followed them fellas till Mr. Raney turned in at th' hotel, an' then I followed that Jace till he got to th' jail."

"And he didn't see you?"

"Not then, no. I followed real quiet-like an' kept to th' shadows. Jace got to th' jail and he stood on a barrel and called Sheriff Bishop to th' window."

"You heard Samuel Bishop talking from inside the cell?"

"Yessir. I know his voice, 'cos he's the one who arrested me that last time I shot up th' saloon, remember? He coulda shot me dead, but he just shot the gun out of my hand. And then Mr. Brookfield talked to me about Jesus." Perry beamed at Sam, and then at Nick.

"Yes, you've told us about that day," Bryant said, struggling to hold back an amused smile. "So you heard Sam Bishop's voice—what did he say when Jace offered him the bribe?"

"He turned him down flat. He told Raney to 'go to blazes'! This Jace fella, he said he'd be sorry, but Sam Bishop didn't change his answer none."

"And did the man called Jace shoot him then, as he'd been ordered?"

"No, sir. I heard a commotion from inside, an' suddenly Mr. Bishop's face disappeared from the cell window, like maybe someone inside caught him talkin'. An' Jace hightailed it into the bushes down by the creek."

"Then what happened?"

"I stayed right there for a while, but then I figgered I'd better go up to the jail an' warn them what that fella was goin' to do. Only when I did, someone leaped up behind me and knocked me out, I guess." He rubbed the back of his head, and turned around. "I still got a lump there, Judge, kin ya see it?"

"I see it," Everson murmured. "Quite a bruise."

"And when did you come to, Mr. Perry?" Bryant asked.

"I woke when Reverend Chadwick went out for his early mornin' constitutional, and found me. I was all drenched from th' rain. I told him what happened, what I'd seen. An' he helped me go to th' jail, but they was all in an uproar 'cos Tolliver had just been shot a few minutes before through the cell window as he lay sleepin'."

"But I thought Bishop was the one with the cell window."

"He was when I'd heard him an' Jace talkin', but when the preacher an' me went back, we were told Sam Bishop and Tolliver had had their cells switched durin' th' night, after Nick caught Sam talkin' to Jace outside. They said that Jace got clean away—which is too bad, I say."

Everson then turned to Nick. "Sheriff Brookfield, I

believe I've heard enough to declare Sam Bishop innocent of the theft of the money from the First National Bank of Houston…"

Sam could hardly believe his ears.

A second chance. He was being given a second chance.

God, I have no idea what to say, how to thank You. But I promise, I won't let You down again.

Chapter Twenty-Three

Cheers erupted from all over the courtroom. Sam saw Prissy move shakily from her seat toward him, laughing and crying at once, when Everson began speaking again.

"Furthermore, Sheriff Brookfield, based on the evidence just presented, I am ordering you to arrest—"

Suddenly Raney lunged out of his chair and yanked Prissy against him, holding her in front of him like a shield. He turned and faced them all, his pistol held against her temple.

"Anyone comes close to me, she dies!"

Prissy turned her face toward Sam, her blue eyes large as dinner plates. Sam was already on his feet, his eyes scanning the courtroom, looking for a way to save her, fighting off the desperation that clutched at his heart.

Nick had been standing near Raney, but he was taken by surprise and he didn't dare fire, for he couldn't shoot Raney without risking hitting Prissy, too. Luis, at the door, had the same problem—if he shot Raney in the back, there was a risk the bullet would hit Prissy.

Everyone froze—everyone except Raney, who was inching toward the door, pulling Prissy with him, his eyes on Nick and Luis.

Help me, Lord, Sam prayed. *Help me get Prissy out of this.*

Suddenly, out of the corner of his eye, Sam saw Nick turn and face him. Sam took his gaze from Prissy's desperate eyes and read Nick's intent as clearly as if the Englishman had spoken to him.

Nick tossed him the pistol and Sam caught it. Before Raney could adjust to the change in direction of the threat, Sam took aim and fired. It was a shot only a man who'd grown up shooting squirrels out of the trees could have been sure of making.

Raney's arms flew up, and then he went down without a cry.

In the uproar that followed, Sam reached Prissy, holding her against him to shield her from the sight of Raney's still body, while Nick arrested Pennington and Byrd on suspicion of conspiring to murder William Waters and Sam Bishop, and on suspicion of being part of the conspiracy to defraud the First National Bank of Houston.

Sam saw Nolan kneel by the sprawled corpse of Kendall Raney, feel for a pulse and shake his head when he found none. He motioned for Mr. Dixon, the undertaker, and together they carried the body out through the batwing door.

Everson was banging on his gavel once more.

"This trial is not over!" he roared. "Everyone sit down!"

Obediently, if a little confused, the people of Simpson Creek did as they were bid. But Sam knew what was coming. He hardly cared—Prissy was safe and he could see her love for him in her eyes, plain as day. Nothing else mattered.

"Sam Bishop, come back up here. There's still the matter of the theft of an expensive ruby ring, which you admitted you stole from the late Mr. Raney."

Sam let go of Prissy. When he heard her utter a cry of protest, he whispered, "It's all right, sweetheart, it's all right." He went to stand in front of the judge.

Everson banged the gavel again. "Mr. Bishop, you admit you stole the ring."

"Yes, I did, Your Honor."

"After meeting Kendall Raney—" the judge glanced toward the door through which Raney had been carried "—it's the judgment of this court that he probably didn't come by such a ring honestly, either. But theft is theft, and you're guilty of that, Sam Bishop."

Sam felt a lump in his throat, but he swallowed and nodded. The truth was the truth, and it would set him free in the most important way, even if he had to serve time for foolishly taking a ring he should have left where he found it.

"Yes, sir."

Judge Everson banged his gavel a final time. "I am finding you guilty of the theft of the ruby ring, Sam Bishop." He raised a bony hand when cries of protest erupted. "But I am *suspending* the sentence, providing you continue to serve this town in the same exemplary fashion you have in the past as sheriff. Is that an acceptable solution to you, Mayor Gilmore?"

In a haze of disbelieving joy, Sam saw Prissy's father smile at him before nodding at the judge.

"Sam Bishop, I am further ordering you to sell the ring,

with the profit to go toward rebuilding the Simpson Creek Church. Is that solution acceptable to everyone?"

A roar of approval gave the judge his answer.

"Consider yourself still bound by the oath you took to serve and protect this town, Sheriff Sam Bishop," the judge said. "You may go."

Sam turned to Prissy, his arm around her waist, her head leaning against him, and walked unimpeded out into the sunlight, a free man once more.

"Everything is just perfect," Prissy said with a blissful sigh, leaning back in Sam's arms on the porch swing when they were at last alone that evening. A sense of peace overwhelmed her with a quiet joy.

A five-pointed star once again adorned Sam's shirt, proclaiming him the sheriff of Simpson Creek. Both of them had been swept into an impromptu celebration by the townspeople after the judge had rendered his verdict, with everyone wanting to clap Sam on the back and assure him that they'd known all along he was innocent of any bank swindling and that he'd continue to be the best sheriff Simpson Creek had ever had. That was followed by a feast at Gilmore House with her father, Mariah Fairchild, Nick and Milly, Sarah and Nolan, Reverend Chadwick and Mrs. Detwiler.

Prissy had asked Flora to take a share of the feast down to the jail, where Luis and Teague were guarding the jail's new prisoners, Garth Pennington, Francis Byrd and one Jace Marcum, whom Prissy had identified earlier when he'd been brash enough to ride right past the saloon just as they were leaving the celebration. Pennington and Byrd were indignant about having to share a cell, but neither wanted to share a cell with Marcum.

"There goes another pair of them," Sam said, indicating a couple of scruffy-looking men riding by Gilmore House and heading onto the road that led southeast out of Simpson Creek.

"Like rats off a sinking ship," Prissy commented. They'd seen others riding by when they'd left the party at the saloon—all Alliance men leaving town because their bosses were dead or in jail.

They might never be able to prove Tolliver had actually killed William Waters. So far, Nick had said, Pennington, Byrd and Marcum were still trying to deny everything. But it was likely at least one of them would turn on the others if it meant he could avoid a rope.

"The bank president says he's going to try and contact anyone who was pressured to sell their properties to see if they wanted to return," Sam said.

"That's good," Prissy said with a happy sigh. "I hope they'll all come back."

Sam nodded, then took a deep breath as he turned to face her. "Prissy, I'm going to make a promise to you right now—I'm never again going to keep any secrets from you, sweetheart. I'd told you I'd lied to your father and Nick about why I came to Simpson Creek, but the more I fell in love with you, the more awful I felt about the bigger things I was keeping from you—the truth of what kind of man I'd been—a gambler, a thief..."

She searched his face and saw only honesty there, with no shadow darkening his eyes. "I knew there was something wrong, something you weren't telling me," she admitted.

"I've never had the love of a good woman before, Prissy, a woman who believes in me, even though she knows the worst about me. I never knew before that God loved me, though I can't imagine why. I surely didn't deserve it."

"That's the best part," she told him with a smile. "There's nothing we can do to deserve it—any of us."

"After all that's happened, I've become a better man, thanks to you and the Lord—the kind of man I want to be all the days of my life. I love you, Prissy, and I always will."

"Oh, Sam—I love you, too!" she cried, and then he had pulled her closer, and was kissing her, and she knew her whole life had been leading up to this very moment. She hadn't known her heart could contain such joy, such peace—or that kissing Sam Bishop would be better than she could have ever imagined it could be.

"There's still the problem of where we're going to be married," Sam reminded her a few minutes later. "You haven't changed your mind and decided to wait until the new church is built, have you?"

"Of course not," she said, and kissed him to show she was just as eager to be his wife as he was to be her husband.

"I know the perfect place," they said simultaneously.

Epilogue

And so it was, on a crisp clear day in October, a wedding took place under the gnarled limbs and rustling leaves of the ancient Wedding Tree, where couples from Indian times on through the early settlement period had made their vows. As Sam Bishop and Prissy Gilmore promised to love and cherish one another forever, each felt that a grand cathedral with stained-glass windows could have provided no more glorious setting for their marriage.

There had never been a more beautiful bride wearing a more beautiful dress. Milly Matthews Brookfield had outdone herself with this bridal gown, everyone said so, but only Prissy could have worn the confection of white *mousseline de soie* over white taffeta with such style.

Everyone in town was there—including Houston, of course. As the happy couple stood in front of Reverend Chadwick, Prissy's attendants stood to her left—Sarah Walker, Milly Brookfield and Hannah Kennedy, while Sam was attended by Nick Brookfield, Dr. Nolan Walker and Luis Menendez.

On one side of the front row, Prissy's father beamed with Mariah Fairchild at his side, along with Flora and

Antonio. Right behind them sat the rest of the Spinsters' Club, some with new beaux of their own, all smiling, some weeping happy tears. On the groom's side, the first three rows held three families who had traveled quite a ways to be there—Sam's sisters Etta, Lida and Livy, and their husbands and children.

The rest of Simpson Creek occupied every remaining seat—Mrs. Detwiler, her son George, and all their family, Mrs. Patterson the mercantile owner, Mr. Jewett the telegrapher, Andy Calhoun the livery owner, and of course, Delbert Perry—just to name a few.

The celebration at Gilmore House which followed was the talk of the town for at least a decade. There was enough food there to feed all of San Saba County, and possibly a good portion of Lampasas County, as well. And no one had ever known a bride who had a cake with four layers— vanilla, chocolate, strawberry *and* another one of chocolate, so everyone could have their favorite flavor.

"Priscilla Gilmore Bishop is an original—everyone says so," Prissy and Sam overheard Mrs. Detwiler telling Reverend Chadwick just before the dancing began.

Sam gave her hand a squeeze as they rose for the bridal dance. "Please don't ever change, Mrs. Bishop," he told her. "I think I quite like being married to an original."

She grinned back up at him, loving the sound of his name attached to her. "I don't think I could even if I would, Mr. Bishop." They led off the waltz together, dancing in perfect harmony, until it was time for her father to come to the floor and dance with Mariah Fairchild. Seeing his happy face, she could not imagine why she had minded the widow's coming to town so much. Love, *real* love, gave the heart extra room, she thought, so that no one, such as her mother, was squeezed out when the heart made room for someone new.

And so it was that when it came for the bride to toss her bouquet, Prissy smiled and very deliberately threw it to Mariah Fairchild.

* * * * *

Dear Reader,

Thank you so much for choosing *The Sheriff's Sweetheart*, the third book in my Brides of Simpson Creek series. I hope you enjoyed Prissy's story—she's truly a "girly" girl who would have been a "shop till you drop" girl if she'd been born in this time, but she has a tender heart for spiritual things, too. I have to admit I love "rascals" like Sam— they give an author an excellent chance to show how the power of God can transform a man into a hero.

I had already written the first books in the series when I actually got to visit San Saba County, the locale of the series, and the actual tributary of the San Saba River, Simpson Creek. During our time there, my husband and I got to visit the legendary Wedding Tree depicted in this book, a huge, venerable live oak whose spreading branches cover the narrow dusty road where it is situated. It's well worth a visit, if you're ever in the hill country of Texas, and it really did serve as a wedding place for Indians and early settlers. I could think of no better place for my hero and heroine to be married.

I love hearing from readers. You can contact me via my website at www.lauriekingery.com to hear about my upcoming books from Steeple Hill Love Inspired Historicals or through Facebook.

Blessings,
Laurie Kingery

QUESTIONS FOR DISCUSSION

1. Prissy Gilmore is a very fashion-conscious girl for her time and place. Do you think a girl who takes pleasure in fine clothing can be a woman of God? Why or why not?

2. What do you think of Sam's motives for taking the ruby ring belonging to Kendall Raney? How does this act snowball for Sam?

3. What do you think of Prissy's reaction toward her father's romance with Mariah Fairchild?

4. How do you think Sam's upbringing impacts his character?

5. How are Reverend Chadwick and the church a unifying force in Simpson Creek?

6. Is Prissy wrong to pressure Caroline Wallace not to give up on the idea of getting married and having children of her own some day?

7. How does Sam's childhood result in his initial lack of faith?

8. What meaning does the verse I've chosen as the novel's epigraph, Joshua 24:15—"Choose you this day whom you will serve…but as for me and my house, we will serve the Lord"—have for Sam?

9. What are Sam's values in the beginning of this story, and how do they change?

10. How does Prissy's character grow during this story?

11. Have you ever met someone to date through a match-making service like the Spinsters' Club? How did that work out?

12. Have you ever met anyone like Delbert Perry? Do you think such a transformation is possible?

13. How would you feel if your church building were suddenly unavailable to you? How much of the church experience is the building, and how much is the people?

14. Prissy Gilmore is not talented in sewing as Milly Brookfield is, or as skillful in baking as Sarah Walker. What is her chief talent?

15. Who should be the next heroine in the Simpson Creek series? What type of hero does she need?

INSPIRATIONAL

Inspirational romances to warm your heart & soul.

Love Inspired. HISTORICAL

TITLES AVAILABLE NEXT MONTH

Available May 10, 2011

KLONDIKE MEDICINE WOMAN
Alaskan Brides
Linda Ford

HANNAH'S JOURNEY
Amish Brides of Celery Fields
Anna Schmidt

ROCKY MOUNTAIN PROPOSAL
Pamela Nissen

THE UNEXPECTED BRIDE
Debra Ullrick

REQUEST YOUR FREE BOOKS!

2 FREE INSPIRATIONAL NOVELS
PLUS 2
FREE
MYSTERY GIFTS

Love Inspired.
HISTORICAL
INSPIRATIONAL HISTORICAL ROMANCE

YES! Please send me 2 FREE Love Inspired® Historical novels and my 2 FREE mystery gifts (gifts are worth about $10). After receiving them, if I don't wish to receive any more books, I can return the shipping statement marked "cancel". If I don't cancel, I will receive 4 brand-new novels every month and be billed just $4.24 per book in the U.S. or $4.74 per book in Canada. That's a saving of at least 23% off the cover price. It's quite a bargain! Shipping and handling is just 50¢ per book in the U.S. and 75¢ per book in Canada.* I understand that accepting the 2 free books and gifts places me under no obligation to buy anything. I can always return a shipment and cancel at any time. Even if I never buy another book, the two free books and gifts are mine to keep forever.

102/302 IDN FDCH

Name _____ (PLEASE PRINT) _____

Address _____ Apt. # _____

City _____ State/Prov. _____ Zip/Postal Code _____

Signature (if under 18, a parent or guardian must sign) _____

Mail to the Reader Service:
IN U.S.A.: P.O. Box 1867, Buffalo, NY 14240-1867
IN CANADA: P.O. Box 609, Fort Erie, Ontario L2A 5X3
Not valid for current subscribers to Love Inspired Historical books.

Want to try two free books from another series?
Call 1-800-873-8635 or visit www.ReaderService.com.

* Terms and prices subject to change without notice. Prices do not include applicable taxes. Sales tax applicable in N.Y. Canadian residents will be charged applicable taxes. Offer not valid in Quebec. This offer is limited to one order per household. All orders subject to credit approval. Credit or debit balances in a customer's account(s) may be offset by any other outstanding balance owed by or to the customer. Please allow 4 to 6 weeks for delivery. Offer available while quantities last.

Your Privacy—The Reader Service is committed to protecting your privacy. Our Privacy Policy is available online at www.ReaderService.com or upon request from the Reader Service.

We make a portion of our mailing list available to reputable third parties that offer products we believe may interest you. If you prefer that we not exchange your name with third parties, or if you wish to clarify or modify your communication preferences, please visit us at www.ReaderService.com/consumerschoice or write to us at Reader Service Preference Service, P.O. Box 9062, Buffalo, NY 14269. Include your complete name and address.

LIH11

*Amish widow Hannah Goodloe's son has run away,
and to find him, she needs help—which circus owner
Levi Harmon can provide. If Hannah can convince him.
Read on for a sneak preview of HANNAH'S JOURNEY
by Anna Schmidt, the first book in the*
AMISH BRIDES OF CELERY FIELDS *series.*

"I HAVE REASON TO BELIEVE that my son is on your train,"
Hannah said. "I have come here to ask that you stop tha[t]
train until Caleb can be found."

"Mrs. Goodloe, I am sympathetic to your situation, bu[t]
surely you can understand that I cannot disrupt an entire
schedule because you think your son…"

"He is on that train, sir," she repeated. She produced
a lined piece of paper from the pocket of her apron and
handed it to him. In a large childish script, the note read:

*Ma, Don't worry. I'm fine and I know this is all a par[t]
of God's plan the way you always said. I'll write once I
get settled and I'll send you half my wages by way of general
delivery. Please don't cry, okay? It's all going to be all
right. Love, Caleb*

"There's not one word here that indicates…"

"He plans to send me part of his wages, Mr. Harmon.
That means he plans to get a job. When we were on the
circus grounds yesterday, I took note of a posted advertisement
for a stable worker. My son has been around horses
his entire life."

"And on that slimmest of evidence, you have assumed that
your son is on the circus train that left town last night?"

She nodded. She waited.

"Mrs. Goodloe, please be reasonable. I have a business
to run, several hundred employees who depend upon me,

ot to mention the hundreds of customers waiting along the way because they have purchased tickets for a performance onight or tomorrow or the following day."

She said nothing but kept her eyes focused squarely on im.

"I am leaving at seven this evening for my home and ummer headquarters in Wisconsin. Tomorrow, I will meet p with the circus train and make the remainder of the journey with them. If your boy is on that train, I will find him."

"Thank you," she said. "You are a good man, Mr. Harmon."

"There's one thing more, Mrs. Goodloe."

Anything, her eyes exclaimed.

"I expect you to come with me."

Don't miss HANNAH'S JOURNEY by Anna Schmidt, available May 2011 from Love Inspired Historical.

Love Inspired **HISTORICAL**

Save $1.00 when you purchase
2 or more Love Inspired® Historical books.

SAVE
$1.00 when you purchase 2 or more Love Inspired® Historical books.

52609783

5 65373 00076 2   (8100)0 11736

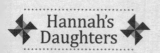

Praise for Elmer Kelton's
The Pumpkin Rollers

"Elmer Kelton does not write 'Westerns.' He writes fine novels set in the West—like *The Pumpkin Rollers*. Here a reader meets flesh-and-blood people of an earlier time, in a story that will grab and hold you from the first to the last page."
—Dee Brown, author of the *New York Times* bestseller
Bury my Heart at Wounded Knee

"A marvelous romantic western that will hold a reader's attention to the very end. Kelton is a wonderful storyteller who has won six Spur Awards. This book must surely climb to the top of his award-winning list."
—*Oklahoman* (Oklahoma City, OK)

"A big, brawling saga with enough action, character, suspense, history, rage, passion and wisdom to please anybody who likes their bestsellers bold and relentless. This is his finest."
—E. J. Gorman, *Mystery Scene*

"A coming-of-age tale, western style, and veteran genre-master Kelton handles the theme well. The key characters are all carefully and believably rendered. . . . Fine reading."
—*Booklist*

"Flavored with the believable characters and historical authenticity that characterize Kelton's work. . . . An especially compelling story."
—*Express-News Morning Edition* (San Antonio, TX)

"Elmer Kelton, winner of six Spur awards, has done it again with his latest novel . . . a vivid and accurate depiction of how the West came of age during the exciting times of our nation's expanse."
—*American Cowboy*

"A marvelous coming-of-age novel that will captivate readers from any walk of life. . . . No one writes better than Elmer Kelton, who is probably America's foremost novelist, and certainly one of this nation's treasures."
—Richard S. Wheeler, award-winning author of
Goldfield and *Cashbox*

Forge Books by Elmer Kelton

The Pumpkin Rollers
Cloudy in the West

ELMER KELTON

BUFFALO WAGONS

A TOM DOHERTY ASSOCIATES BOOK
NEW YORK

This is a work of fiction. All the characters and events portrayed in this book are either products of the author's imagination or are used fictitiously.

BUFFALO WAGONS

Copyright © 1956 by Elmer Kelton

Cover art by Thomas Moran, David David Gallery, Philadelphia/Superstock

A Forge Book
Published by Tom Doherty Associates, Inc.
175 Fifth Avenue
New York, NY 10010

Forge® is a registered trademark of Tom Doherty Associates, Inc.

ISBN: 0-812-55120-6

First Forge edition: November 1997

Printed in the United States of America

0 9 8 7 6 5 4 3 2 1

1

THE BUFFALO were gone.

Gage Jameson turned in his saddle atop a hill where the grass cured and curled an autumn brown. Squinting his blue eyes in the glare of the prairie sun, he frowned at the company hide train lumbering along far behind him, the six-yoke ox teams hardly straining at the double wagons.

Three months out, supplies about gone, and not enough hides to build a Sioux lodge.

Grimness touched Jameson's bearded, sun-darkened face as he stepped down from the big bay hunting horse and felt the drying grass crunch beneath his heavy boots. He was a man in his mid-thirties whose gray-touched hair and long growth of wiry black beard made him look far older. His wide-brimmed, grease-stained hat was pulled low to shade his eyes.

Last year, down in that valley yonder, his Sharps Big

Fifty rifle had felled sixty-two buffalo in one stand, so many that the Miles and Posey skinners had had to return the second day to finish taking the hides.

Now, with the first autumn weeks of 1873 slipping by, it had been ten days since he had sighted that last shaggy old bull. He had lifted his rifle for the kill, then had lowered it and ridden away, leaving the aged beast to graze alone on the short buffalo grass where once they had grazed in numbers so large that no man could count them.

What was one hide? One hide, when long stinking ricks of them piled up at Dodge City, awaiting shipment on the Santa Fe. No man could guess at the number. But this Jameson knew: the great Arkansas River herd was gone, like the Republican herd before it. Next spring the melting snows would bare carcasses by the hundreds of thousands scattered all over these Kansas plains.

A graveyard, it would be. A vast graveyard of gleaming white bones.

A blur of movement on another hill caused Jameson to jerk around, his hide-tough hand tightening instinctively on the sixteen-pound Sharps he carried.

He eased then, recognizing the sorrel horse Nathan Messick rode. Messick was his chief skinner and hide handler, and now and again he helped Jameson search out the buffalo. Rail-thin and gangling, Messick stood like a telegraph pole in his stirrups, waving his hat in long grand sweeps.

He's found buffalo, Jameson thought, a stir of excitement in him. There had been a time when it took a big herd to excite him. Of late, it was a great satisfaction to find fifteen or twenty head. He remounted and crossed the open, brushless valley in a long trot, the brown grass rustling underfoot. In places it reached to the bay horse's knees.

Climbing the hill, he found Messick still sitting there gravely waiting for him, his narrow shoulders slumped. An emptiness settled in Jameson as he read Messick's solemn eyes. "I thought you'd found buffalo."

Messick grunted. "Not exactly. I just wanted you to come look."

Messick reined his horse around and moved off the slope, his long shanks raised a little to heel the sorrel's ribs. Jameson trailed him, content in his weariness to move at a casual pace. Still young enough as years went, he no longer possessed the drive he used to have. Youth was slipping away from him, he knew. The frontier took it out of a man. The frontier and the war.

"There it is," Messick said somberly.

Scattered over several hundred yards of ground lay the bloated carcasses of some twenty skinned buffalo, now so rank that Jameson's horse snorted and shied away. Someone had shot them from running horses like a bunch of sport-crazy excursionists, instead of picking them off slow and easy from a quiet stand the way any sensible hide hunter would do.

"Tenderfeet," Jameson said harshly. "Even ruined half the hides, getting them off."

It had always bothered him, the awesome waste that attended the work of even the best hide hunters. Now he was galled at this senseless destruction which came at a time when the buffalo were getting to be so precious few.

"Hunters like that," Messick said slowly, "there ought to be a law against them. Spoil it for them that *does* know how."

Jameson shook his head. "Blame the money panic. They're hungry back East—no jobs, no food. And the railroad letting its construction crews go. They're swarming out here like flies. Anybody who can get his hands on a gun and a horse wants to hunt buffalo."

He saw something move, out by the most distant carcasses. His eyes cut questioningly to Messick's, and Messick said, "Buffalo cow. They shot her but let her get away."

"Why didn't you put her out of her misery?"

"I'll help you find them, and I'll skin them afterwards. But I ain't shootin' no buffalo."

Jameson rode to her. The gaunt cow moved painfully, dragging a shattered hind leg. Her bag was swollen and fevered with spoiled milk. One of those big bloated calves must have been hers. She was slowly dying on her feet, waiting for the gray wolves to come and drag her down.

Jameson stepped from the saddle and lifted the Big Fifty. Its octagonal barrel was thick and heavy and hard to hold true, but at this range it couldn't miss. The deep roar rolled back to him in the chill air. He ejected the hot cartridge case, let it lie on the ground a moment to cool, then shoved it back into his coat pocket to reload later. His nose pinched at the sharp smell of gunpowder.

"Tenderfeet," he said again, angrily.

He well remembered the awe which had held him spellbound years ago, when he had sighted his first herd of buffalo. He had been only a kid then, before the war. The buffalo had been one rippling blanket of black and brown, moving slowly across the land before him, the front of the herd lost in the dust of the northern horizon, the end of it still far out of sight to the south. The rumble of their tread, the rattle of dewclaws, had gone on and on for more than a day.

And he remembered how old Shad Blankenship had snorted at him in '68, when Jameson had asked how long it might take to kill out the buffalo.

"By Judas Priest, young'un, there'll always be buffalo. Ten thousand hunters and the U.S. Cavalry couldn't get more than the natural increase, one year to the next. Kill all the buffalo? Boy, you're talkin' out of your head.''

Now here it was—one old bull, one crippled cow, for ten days' ride. And these bloated, wasted carcasses.

Suddenly Jameson was weary of it, weary of the endless, hopeless hunt, weary of stench and sweat and caked dirt and disappointment, weary of scratching at the lice it seemed a man could never get rid of while he hunted the buffalo.

He drew the straight-edged ripping knife from his belt and knelt beside the cow, starting to slit the hide up the belly while fat ticks crawled for cover in the thick dirty hair.

"We'll salvage this one, at least," he said, his voice brittle. "Then we're going. I've had me a bellyful."

"Where to, Gage?"

"Back to Dodge City. The Arkansas herd is finished."

Dodge City, said the sign at the new frame depot. But everybody here just called it Dodge, for it was hard to use the word "city" and not smile doing it.

Dodge wasn't much to look at, a raw-looking, raw-smelling town of lumber shacks and dugouts and soddies and dirty tents, and a row of one-story frame business houses fronting each side of the shiny new railroad tracks. On down the way yonder extended sod corrals and a long row of hide stacks that you could smell almost as far as you could see, when the weather was a little warm and the wind from the wrong direction.

Something else was growing now: great piles of white buffalo bones, waiting to be shipped East for fertilizer and bone china and Lord knew what else.

Last year the railroad construction gangs had found Dodge already a bustling little village, huddled up on the north bank of the Arkansas River, halfway between Missouri and Santa Fe. It had started out as a whisky camp for the soldiers at Fort Dodge, five miles to the east. Then the buffalo hunters had located there, and for a while they called it Buffalo City. By the time the railroad came, there were by actual count one general store, three dance halls and six saloons.

But to a buffalo hunter coming in after three months out on the prairie, the town was as pretty as a new bride. Didn't matter whether the lumber was painted or not, long as the ladies were. Nobody complained if dirt trickled down from sod roofs and got matted in a man's hair or fell into his collar and went gritty there. At least there *were* roofs.

Who was going to be bothered if the bar was nothing more than a raw buffalo hide stretched across a framework of poles? Who would holler if the whisky was maybe pure alcohol with a little coffee coloring, or even that tobacco- and pepper-treated contraband stuff that some of the guttier ones slipped off and traded to the Indians? It tasted as good as French wine if you'd been out on the buffalo range for months. And by the time you started getting critical, you ought to be dragging it back to the prairie anyhow.

Two miles out, Jameson's crew came upon an old man in tattered clothes and dry-split leather shoes pitching buffalo bones into a wire-patched wagon that threatened to fall down and die right there. A layer of white dust clung to him from these chalky bones that still had a peculiar stench of death even after the months of bleaching in the sun.

This, the bone picking, was the last grim harvest.

Some of the wagon crew hadn't smiled, hadn't spoken a civil word in three weeks, for they were being paid by the hide, and the hides were mighty few. Now, as Dodge finally showed up ahead of them, a yell burst from dry throats. A fair sight she was.

Jameson grinned, though it came near to cracking his wind-dried lips. He wasn't a hard-drinking man, but like the others he found pleasure in the thought of bellying up to one of those flint-hide bars. The change, if nothing else.

Nathan Messick rode up beside him and pointed. Worry was in his eyes. It always was.

"Ever see so many outfits camped? Scattered to kingdom come, all over the edge of town and up and down the river."

"Poor hunting, Nathan. Out of supplies, sick of hunting and not finding anything. Maybe getting a little worried about the Indians."

"They could be out picking bones. There's a million of them."

Jameson shrugged. "Pride, I reckon. *I* wouldn't want to do it. Would you?"

"Nope, I reckon not."

Rough-looking men lounged in scattered camps, hunkering over fires for lack of anything better to occupy their time. They had gathered here in town, waiting, not knowing what they were waiting for, not knowing what else to do. As the Miles and Posey wagons drew close, the men would walk out and gaze curiously at the hides Jameson was bringing in.

Ahead of him Gage saw a familiar figure standing in a camp, and he smiled broadly. The old man's back was turned to him, but he would recognize Shad Blankenship if he found his hide in a tanyard.

Shad was an old-time mountain man. He had drifted up the Missouri and dodged Sioux and Blackfeet way back in the days of the beaver trade. And although white men often skinned him, no Indian had ever laid a hand on Shad's thick growth of rust-red hair.

"Nathan," Jameson said, "take them on to the Miles and Posey yards. I'll be along directly, after I chew the fat with Shad a little."

Shirt sleeves rolled up halfway to the elbow and sweat soaking his old hickory shirt, the old hunter had put a wagon jack under the axle of one of his three hide wagons and was taking the wheel off to tar the hub. At the call of his name he turned quickly, his blackened hand raised in greeting, his red-bearded old face broken with a grin.

"Hya-a-a there, young'un." As far as Shad was concerned, Gage Jameson was a young'un and always would be. Shad had picked him up as a half-starved runaway kid back there twenty years ago, nursemaided him along, wiped his nose for him, and made a frontiersman out of him.

Shad's big shaggy black dog came trotting out, growling deep in its throat, Blackfoot-mean, until it caught Jameson's scent. The growl stopped. It wagged its tail in recognition.

Jameson stepped down out of the saddle and patted the dog's head. "Hi there, Ripper. You catching enough rabbits to keep that old musk hog fed?"

Blankenship walked out, grinning. "I don't need no dog to feed me, young'un. I'm still a better hunter than you'll ever be, and don't you forget it."

He shoved his big hand forward, then drew it back quickly.

"Forgot about that tar. Wouldn't want to muss up a hide skinner's clean hands." There was a shade of irony in the way he said that. He wiped the hands on his trousers, already so black that a little extra wouldn't be noticed.

"Them your wagons going yonder?" he asked, then nodded his own answer. His grin was gone. Jameson could see that Shad hadn't done much grinning lately, either.

"You done as well as any of them, I reckon. A heap sight better than *I* done."

Looking closer now, Jameson could see worry clouded deep in the pale blue eyes. It was the same discouragement he'd seen in all the faces that had come out to watch his wagons pass.

Shad Blankenship motioned apologetically to the wagon he was working on: "Them wheels don't really need any tar. It's oozing out all over. But hell, what else is there for a man to do? He'd go crazy sittin' here waitin' for the buffalo to come back."

Jameson frowned. "You really think they'll come back, Shad?"

The old man shrugged gloomily and turned back to the wagon. He started to lift the wheel into place again. Jameson got hold of it with him and fitted it onto the hub. Shad faced him then, and his eyes held a hopelessness.

"They ain't, Gage, they ain't. They're gone, and we'll never see things again the way they was. Wish sometimes I'd died back yonder while things was the way they used to be. Wish I'd never seen the way the country's been ruined."

Jameson put his hand gently on the hunter's thin shoulder. "Come on into town directly and I'll buy you a drink. We'll talk about old times."

Shad's eyes were bleak and pinched in the corners.

"Ain't the town she used to be, Gage. New bunch has taken over. There's every kind of riffraff in there now, just waitin' to see if you got any money on you. There's some will cut your guts out with a dull knife or strangle you with a leather cord. And if the cutthroats don't get it, them crooked gamblers will.''

Jameson thought he knew what the trouble was. No matter how many months old Shad had worked for it, or what he'd had to go through, when he got his big chapped hands on a roll of money he was drawn to the poker tables like a fly to a freshly skinned buffalo. Likely as not they'd taken him the first night he hit town. Lucky he hadn't lost his wagons, to boot.

Shad shook a crooked finger at Jameson. It had been broken in some trading-post brawl long since forgotten.

''You tell them men of yours they better watch out for theirselves. Quick as they get paid off, there'll be a dozen wolves around to pick their bones.''

''I'll tell them.''

He had long wondered why an old frontiersman like Shad, wily and sure as a fox out on the prairie, should forever be so improvident when he came to town. He had made a couple or three fortunes in his time, and they had all gone the same way. He would never accumulate anything of value and hang onto it if he lived to be a hundred and six.

Shad frowned darkly. ''I been thinkin,' Gage. Thinkin' about going East to Missouri and taking up farming.''

Jameson blinked in surprise. Shad added quickly, ''I growed up on a farm in Tennessee, don't you know that? Had me a right smart reputation. Wasn't no young'un there could plow a straighter furrow or get more work out of a pair of mules. But the place just naturally got a little too small for me and my Paw both. So when I decided I couldn't whup him, I took my old squirrel gun and lit out.''

Jameson smiled and shook his head. ''You'll never do it, Shad. Maybe there was a time you could've gone back, but you'll never do it now.''

"You don't think so?" Old Shad narrowed his eyes and poked his finger at Gage. "I get the chance, young'un, I'll show you. You just wait."

Jameson caught up to his hide wagons just before they reached the Miles and Posey yards. The partners leased from the Santa Fe a long stretch of ground adjacent to the tracks, where the hides could be loaded directly onto the cars with a minimum of extra handling.

The hide stacks Jameson had seen here the last time were greatly diminished, but the smell of them was about as strong as ever. He watched some of the yard crew toss hides onto a press and squeeze them down into a tight bale to be shipped. Down at the lower end a huge rick of buffalo bones was steadily growing. Miles and Posey was branching out.

C. T. Posey stood in front of the unpainted frame office, chewing a dead cigar and frowning thoughtfully at a short load of hides in a sagging old wagon.

Jameson reined up and waited, grinning. That was Posey, all right. He handled them by the tens of thousands, but he could still enjoy haggling with a hunter over fifty or sixty common cowhides.

Trying not to be obvious about it, the man on the wagon was showing Posey the hides with the hair side up. And seeing right through him, Posey was turning them over to the flesh side, one by one, so he could tell how many bullet holes, peg holes and knife slashes were in them.

Posey saw Jameson and nodded a greeting, then went back to his trade. He studied a moment, wrote a figure on a piece of paper, then showed it to the hunter. The man shook his head determinedly. Posey shrugged and started toward the office. The hunter ruefully called him back. Posey nodded and did some figures on the paper. Then he wrote out a check and handed it to the hunter.

The hunter, grinning now, climbed on his wagon, flipped the reins and headed for the end of the hide stack where some of the yard crew would unload him.

It was an old stunt of Posey's to beat the price down as far as it would go, then give the seller a few extra dollars on the check to bring it up to some nice round figure. Always left the man smiling, outtraded or not. He'd be back someday with another load.

Posey strode up and shook Jameson's hand, a genuine gladness in what could be the deadest poker face in town when necessary.

"Mighty pleased to see you, Gage."

"You may not be when you look at my wagons."

Posey stood back and surveyed Jameson's incoming hide train, his hands shoved deep in his pockets. He chewed heavily on the unlighted cigar, a nervous twitch pinching one side of his face. He was dressed in tailor-made clothes of good fabric but was undisturbed about the drying mud caked on his shoes and his trouser cuffs. He was a slight, balding Yankee trader, a pleasant man to work for as long as you played it straight. Cheat him and you'd better never come back.

Posey shifted the cigar to the other side of his mouth. "Can't complain, the way some of the others have come in. Stump Johnson hardly had a wagonload."

"How about the hide prices?"

"A little better. Should get better yet. Prospect of a scarcity."

Jameson looked at the men sitting on the wagons, men bearded and dirty, with a trailweariness in their eyes.

"As long as prices are up, could you give the boys a little bonus? They haven't made much this trip."

Posey came about as near smiling as he ever would. "Maybe I can see my way clear." As the wagons pulled up and halted he spoke loudly, "You boys pile off of there and go over to the Dutchman's. Tell him I said give you a good feed. The yard crew can take care of the wagons.''

The men jumped down laughing, exulting at the feel of Dodge's half-muddy ground beneath their feet.

"How about you, Gage?" Posey asked.

Jameson shrugged. "Not hungry. I'll go later."

Ever since he had arrived he had noticed a tall, well-dressed man of about his own age standing at the door of the shack, watching him, watching the wagons. Now Posey motioned to the man. "Come here, Ransom. Want you to meet somebody."

The man stepped forward, a smile lifting the ends of his trimmed mustache. "You don't have to tell me. He's Gage Jameson. I've heard plenty already. My name's King, Jameson. Ransom King."

He stood an inch or two taller than Jameson. He wore black trousers and a white shirt with a string tie. His flat-brimmed hat with its rounded crown was as clean as a man could expect to find in a place like Dodge. Jameson wouldn't exactly call him a dandy, like Hickok or Cody, but he was well above the average cut. More than that, he looked like he might be man enough to wear the clothes and get away with it.

"Glad to know you, King. Seems to me I've heard the name around. Hide hunter, aren't you?"

King smiled. "That's right. Been hoping for a good while that we'd cross trails somewhere."

He turned then to Posey. "I can see you're going to be busy a while, C. T., so I'll work on up the street and come back later. You sure you're not ready to meet my price on those hides?"

"Not yet," Posey answered with good humor. "You're just trying to make a killing on one deal so you can retire."

"Now, C. T.," King responded with a laugh, "that's not fair. You know I'm a man of simple tastes and a small ambition. All I want is to get rich."

He started to move away, a spark of laughter still dancing in his eyes. "See you later, C. T., and you'd just as well make up your mind to pay me my price. You're going to do it sooner or later anyway, so why not now?"

He reached for Jameson's hand again. "Glad to've met you, Jameson. Perhaps we can get better acquainted over a bottle of good whisky, if you come down to Wash's saloon."

"Maybe later," Jameson said. As King walked away, Jameson looked to Posey with a question in his eyes. Posey answered it.

"Good hunter, that King. He's had luck right along, even with the buffalo playing out. And when it comes to selling, he's as independent as a hog on ice. I'll spar around with him a little, but in the end I'll have to give him what he's asking. I know it, and so does he."

Jameson tested the name on his tongue. "Ransom King. Sounds like something out of a book."

Posey shrugged. "May be where he got it. Lots of people around here aren't using the names their mothers gave them." He turned and walked into his little frame office, Jameson following him. "That King," Posey said, shaking his head. "They lost the pattern after they made him."

He dug into a desk and brought out a record book. Blowing the dust off it, he asked, "Want to watch the yard crew count off the hides?"

"Won't be necessary." Jameson pulled a tally book out of his pocket. "Got the figures here for every wagon."

Posey picked it up and riffled the pages. "And they'll

be correct, too, right down to the last kip." Humor was in his eyes.

While Posey pulled open a door at the bottom of his heavy rolltop desk and brought out a bottle and two glasses, Jameson looked around the office. It was strictly a working man's setup, not meant for entertaining royalty. Papers were piled high and seemingly without care on top of the desk and the heavy iron safe in the corner. But Jameson would bet his Big Fifty, reloading outfit and all, that Posey knew where to find anything he needed. Not a single picture on the bare wall, but there was a solitary little calendar, notes scribbled in careful hand around many of the dates. Three Indian-tanned buffalo robes lay rolled up along one wall.

There was a faint aroma of tobacco and whisky, but it was overpowered by the strong smell of heavy grease and buffalo hides.

Once Jameson had asked Posey if the stink ever bothered him.

"Sometimes," came the bland comment, "when the prices start dropping."

Posey poured two shot glasses full. Jameson took his down in one long, appreciative swallow, his face squinching up at the burn of the whisky. It was good bourbon. Posey had it shipped to him all the way from Kentucky.

He eased out a long breath and nodded in approval. "First one I've had in months."

"Didn't you take some along for medicinal purposes?"

"We turned that wagon over the third week out. Broke every bottle but one. We *did* have to save that one for medicinal purposes."

He turned serious. "How does it look, C. T.?"

Posey shook his head. "Not good, Gage, not good. She's cutting mighty thin. You saw how many hunters are camped around town here. They've scoured the whole Arkansas. By spring there won't be enough hides left to sweat a pair of mules. Indians are restless, too. Cheyennes killed one of Stump Johnson's men.

"Trouble is, there's nowhere to go from here. The army's turning hunters back from the northern territory because of the Medicine Lodge treaty. And south—well, you know what's to the south."

Jameson squeezed the whisky glass. "The Cimarron. And below that, the Canadian. And buffalo, C. T. ... there's bound to be a world of buffalo down there."

"And a world of Comanches."

Jameson looked directly into Posey's eyes. "Comanches or not, I want to go."

Posey straightened, taken aback. "Knowing you, I shouldn't be surprised. But I can't afford to send any Miles and Posey wagons down there. Not till I know we've got a better than even chance of bringing the men back alive and the wagons full of hides. Right now, I don't think we have that chance."

Jameson stood up and looked out the open door toward the hide wagons with their light load. "We haven't got much choice, have we? It's go south or pick bones. And C. T., I'm no bone picker."

Posey shrugged. "You're right, Gage. We both know it. But the question is, when? The time's not right, not yet."

"And when will the time be right? When somebody goes down there and proves it can be done. What's going to happen when somebody comes back from Texas with a string of wagons piled high with hides? I'll tell you. It won't matter if the whole outfit has arrows sticking out of it like the quills on a porcupine—men'll run all over each other trying to get down there. Price of wagons and teams will shoot up. You'll be offering two dollars a day—maybe three—trying to get skinners and teamsters.

"I want to be that first man."

Posey only stared at him. "I'd like to do it, Gage. I'd like to let you go. But Jason Miles is half of this partnership, and he'd hit the ceiling. Me, I'm the flighty type. I'll shoot the works on a scheme that looks halfway good. Jason is so hidebound he wouldn't invest a nickel if he couldn't see a dime lying in front of him. So we balance each other off. I keep Jason prodded along, and he keeps my feet on the ground. Right now, no amount of persuasion would move Jason Miles."

Jameson's eyes grew keen. He pointed his chin toward the big safe in the corner. "That money the company's been holding for me—got it at hand? Got it where I could get it if I wanted it right quick?"

Posey's face tightened in worry. "Yes, but what's going on in that Indian mind of yours?"

"Just this, C. T.: if Miles and Posey doesn't want to send me, I'll go on my own. There's buffalo down there in Texas. I'm going to get them!"

2

JAMESON STOOD at the door, watching the yard crew take up reins and holler at the heavy-muscled ox teams as they moved the hide wagons down to unload them at the end of the stacks. He noted that the crew was no longer so large as it used to be.

"The frontier's fading fast," he said. "So's the hide game. Man's got to make himself a stake now—get into something that'll last—or pretty soon there won't be much chance left. I'm thirty-five already. Forty's looking at me from around the corner. How many more years have I got to make myself a start, C. T.? I've got to do it soon or I'll be going around in circles like old Shad Blankenship.

"Shad doesn't know anything but the frontier. He can see it getting away from him, and he's scared. What's going to be left for him when it's gone? He's been out here since they dug the Arkansas River, and what's he got to show for it? What's he ever *going* to have? Nothing."

He squatted down in the doorway, in the manner of a man in camp, and leaned against the doorjamb. "I've saved money since I've been working for Miles and Posey, but it won't be enough. And I can't add much to it hanging around up here where the buffalo are all gone.

"So I'll take what money I've got and buy wagons with it, and supplies. I'll hire me a tough crew and go down where the buffalo are. Sure, I know it's risky. But what that ever amounted to anything wasn't a gamble?"

Posey studied him long and hard. He leaned down and filled Jameson's glass again, then his own.

"You're right, Gage. You generally are. But what kind of outfit could you put together with the money you've got, and still buy supplies? Five or six wagons at the outside. How many men could you hire, even if you found some willing to go? Not enough to put up much defense. The Comanches could swallow up a little outfit in five minutes. You need a big one."

Posey had a way of looking at a man and into him.

"There's more to it than just the money, Gage. What else is it?"

Fingering the glass, staring out at the sweating yard crew, Jameson was a minute in answering.

"You didn't see this country before the hide hunters got thick, C. T. But I did. I came out here with a freighting outfit when I was just a kid. There was nothing but a few army posts along the immigrant trails. Stray off a few miles and you were in land only a handful of white men had ever seen. Every kind of wild game you could imagine. And the plains themselves, reaching on and on as far as a man could see, just the way it must have been when God finished it.

"It wasn't all littered up with buffalo bones, or houses,

or railroads, or busted-down wagons. It wasn't spotted with rotting corpses.

"And the buffalo . . . I've seen them in herds so big that in the rutting season you could hear the bulls fighting from miles away. I've seen a big herd on winter mornings with the steam hanging low over them like a cloud of smoke. Once a man sees those things, they're never really out of his mind again. He never forgets. He doesn't know what they mean to him till they're gone. Then he keeps looking, hoping maybe he'll find it somewhere else.

"Maybe that's a big part of it, C. T. Maybe down there I'll find it again the way it used to be. And even if I don't, I won't be satisfied till I've gone and looked."

Posey had chewed his cigar down to half size. "And what if you *do* find it? It'll be spoiled again in a little while. You'll help spoil it yourself."

Jameson said ruefully, "Funny, isn't it? We thought it would stay like that forever. Seemed like the country was so big that nothing we did would matter. But we spoiled it. Now I'm ready to go along and watch it happen all over, just to get to see it once again the way it used to be."

Posey sat awhile, frowning, that nervous twitch in his face as he studied his hands and chewed his cigar. He was deep in thought. Finally he spoke. "Look, Gage, I've got money of my own, money Jason Miles hasn't got any claim on. You go on and buy whatever you need. Make it big enough so you can defend yourself. I'll back you just as far as you need to go."

Jameson stood there like someone had clubbed him. "C. T., I . . . I don't hardly know what to say."

"You don't have to say anything. Just come back."

Jameson rubbed his smooth-shaven chin and looked at himself in the barber's cracked mirror. He had to grin at the whiteness of his face where whiskers had shielded his skin from sun and wind since he had taken the wagons out months ago. On the rough floor at his feet lay a thick mat of hair that the barber had whacked off. The short hair felt unnatural now, freshly washed out with strong soap.

The barber said, "Better watch yourself a day or two till you get used to it, or you'll catch cold. You're like a fresh-sheared sheep."

Behind a partition stood a big wooden washtub, more than half full of cold water. Two buckets bubbled and steamed atop a big cast-iron heater. The barber slowly poured their contents into the tub, then stirred until the water was evenly warm.

Over the back of a wooden chair Jameson draped a suit of clean new clothes he had bought down the street. Undressing, he threw the dirty clothes into a corner, far from the clean ones. He settled into the warm water for a long, comfortable soak, lighting a black cigar and leaning back relaxed, wondering if a man could ever get all the buffalo smell off.

A barber sees about as many people as anybody in town except maybe a bartender. Jameson called to him beyond the partition.

"Heard anybody quote prices on wagons and teams lately?"

The barber was sweeping the hair into a dusty pile to throw it out the back door. "If you got any to sell, you're hubbin' it, mister. There's plenty for sale and mighty few buyers."

"I was thinking I might buy a few wagons and a good string of mules if the price was right."

The barber stopped sweeping and looked around the partition. "Better not say that too loud. They'll run over you."

Jameson picked up the rough brown bar of soap and began to rub it briskly over his wet arms and shoulders. "You might spread the word that I'm in the market. Name's Gage Jameson. With Miles and Posey."

Bath finished, he strode far down to the edge of town, where an aging Negro woman lived in a rude shack close to the riverbank. She did washing and ironing while her husband helped hustle teams at the Miles and Posey yards. Under his arm Jameson carried a sackful of dirty clothes, on his shoulder his bedroll.

He found Callie out back of the shack, shoving firewood into the flames under a huge smoke-blackened pot full of boiling water, a big red neckerchief tied over her hair.

Seeing him, she dropped the wood and began to shake excitedly, grinning broadly as if he had come back from the dead. "Mister Gage, Mister Gage. I declare I thought them Injuns had got you."

"Callie, I was so dirty they were afraid to touch me."

He dropped the sack on the ground, along with the bedroll. "Brought some clothes and some bedding. Wish you'd give every bit of it a good slow boiling, right down to the last pair of socks."

She shook her head. "I'll do it, but boilin' is almighty hard on clothes. These buffalo hunters do beat all, the way they want their stuff boiled."

He grinned. "Callie, I've seen men bet a hundred dollars on which one could reach in his pocket and come up with a louse first. That's why we boil our clothes."

He looked at the poor frame shack she lived in, and pity moved him. Once he had asked the old woman about it, and she had told him of the good cabin she and Rufe had shared in Georgia, before freedom. Then she had added with a fierce pride, "I wouldn't trade back, Mister Gage. This one, it ain't much. But it's all ours."

He dug into his new coat and brought up a paper-wrapped package. "Got something here for you. Traded it off of old Limping Wolf's Sioux when we came across them a while back."

Excitedly she tore the paper off and found a pair of fancy leather moccasins with a fine job of beadwork. Her eyes widened, and her white teeth gleamed proudly. Then she sobered.

"Mister Gage, you shouldn't of. With all the pretty girls there is in town, you could've found you a good one to give them to."

Gage said evenly, "There are pretty ones, but there aren't many good ones. That's why I got the moccasins for you."

Later he walked through the open door of a frame dance hall, pausing to let his eyes accustom themselves to the dimmer light indoors. A chubby barman gave him a crooked-toothed grin and lifted a big hand in greeting.

"Jameson. Gage Jameson!" He held a bottle high, beckoning with his chin. "It's on me, Gage."

Shaking hands, Jameson looked out over the room. Not much business yet. Some of his own crew sat at a big table, drinking and playing cards. They nodded at him.

"How's business, Wash?" Jameson asked while the man poured each of them a drink.

Wash had been a buffalo hunter too, but he had early decided there must be some easier way to make a living. And he hadn't been able to think of anything with so steady and sure a trade as the whisky business. Once he had tried to talk Jameson into going in partnership with him. But Jameson hadn't been able to picture himself as a saloon keeper. Sure, he was looking for something that would beat buffalo hunting. But this wasn't it.

"Business is getting slow, Gage," Wash complained. "Hide trade is falling off fast. Should've set up in Wichita or Ellsworth, I reckon. Cattle drives from Texas really pour the silver into those towns. They tell me a cowboy ain't got no bottom to him when it comes to putting away drinking liquor. But I don't suppose Dodge City will ever get any of that cattle trade. We come too late.''

Jameson finished his friendly drink with Wash, then angled across the room to where the lanky skinner Messick sat at a corner table, laboriously scrawling a letter. Jameson pulled out a chair and sat down facing him.

Painfully Messick said, ''Writin' to my sister. Got to tell her about George Hobart.''

Jameson nodded. ''That's what I figured.''

The memory of it brought an angry twist to his face— the sight of three men lying dead in the remains of a hide camp, wagons and stock gone, their bodies ripped by gunfire, slashed by knives.

''How much are you going to tell her?''

''Just that her husband is dead, and we found him there. What else can I say? I can't tell her what they did to him—the way they scalped him and . . .''

Messick broke off, long face purpling.

''Worst job of butchery I ever saw,'' Jameson said. ''No old warrior would've taken any pride in it. Young bucks, maybe. Likely got ahold of some firewater.''

Messick's eyes narrowed with rekindled anger. ''And maybe it wasn't Indians at all. Maybe it was hide thieves, coverin' up. Wagons was gone, you know.''

Jameson shrugged. Messick had spent a lot of time among Indians, and he liked them. ''It was probably Indians, all right. They're stirred up over the buffalo killing. But we'll never know.''

He stood up again, digging into his pocket. He brought out forty dollars and looked at it a moment. He'd spend it here anyway. Might as well see it go where it was needed.

He pitched the money onto the table. "Put this in with the letter. Tell her we found it in his pocket."

Jameson started to walk back to where the rest of the Miles and Posey crew sat. Just then a man shoved through the door, slammed it shut behind him and hollered in high good humor. "Whisky for everybody, Wash!"

It was Ransom King. He stood there chewing on a black cigar that must have been a foot long. His teeth gleamed happily beneath his trimmed mustache. "Sold my hides," he announced loudly for everyone to hear. "Got my own price, and it was a honey. Go on up, boys, don't be bashful. And don't let Wash give you the cheap stuff."

King moved to the bar, leaned over it, and reached way down, bringing up a bottle. He had known just where it would be. He looked at it quizzically, seeing that half of it was gone.

"Hey, Jameson," he called, "come on over and have one with me. Told you I'd get my price out of Posey."

Jameson grinned. It had been a long time since he'd met anyone like Ransom King. King caught his elbow and gave him a gentle shove toward a chair. "Sit down, my friend, and let's drink a toast to salesmanship."

Seated, Jameson noted that the bottle in King's hand held good whisky, if the label didn't lie. It wasn't the stuff Wash commonly served over the bar. It struck Jameson that King was the kind who would know what was the best and make sure he got it.

King poured them each a drink and lifted his glass. "Here's to the buffalo."

Jameson downed his with care, for another free drink or two would leave him walking on air, unused to it as he was. King took his with one swallow, cleared his throat and poured a second one. Jameson put his hand over his own glass, declining another.

King walked to a set of wooden stairs that started in a back corner and disappeared into the high ceiling.

"Hey, Rose," he shouted, "come on down here."

He came back without yelling again. Jameson smiled. "Sure she heard you?"

"She heard me," King replied confidently. "She listens for me."

He scratched a match across the seat of his good pants and held the flame to the end of the twisted cigar until the tobacco began to glow. He puffed big clouds of strong smoke, getting the cigar going, squinting his eyes against the smoke's bite.

"Yes sir," he said, "with those hide stacks dwindling down, old C. T. isn't in any position to haggle over a good batch of hides. He's got to pay for them. You ought to have heard him holler."

The thought of it struck King funny. He threw his head back and laughed. At first Jameson thought he might have emptied a bottle or two before he had ever come in here. Then he decided this was just the way King acted when he was feeling good.

He wondered how King might act if he felt bad. Even with the laughter there was a steel-keen look to King's square face. No doubt those sparkling eyes could as easily turn to flint.

A woman came down the stairs, trying to be graceful but lacking the ability. Dark-haired, young, she wore a golden gown cut low in front with two thin straps up over her wide, soft shoulders. The dress fit tightly against her ample upper body and down over her trim hips.

"See there?" King winked. "Told you she heard me."

He pushed to his feet and strode across to take her by the arm. "Come on over, Rose, and meet a real buffalo hunter. Rose Tremaine, this is Gage Jameson. They say he's even better than me."

Rose smiled at Jameson. He nodded and spoke to her. He remembered having seen her here before. And not with King.

"Sold those hides, sweetie," King said, pinching her chin so hard that it was white a moment, then red. "We'll celebrate a little tonight, you and me."

King walked over to the scuffed piano. The cigar sticking up at a jaunty angle, he picked out a rowdy dance hall tune with one finger. "Give us a little music, Rose," he said.

By this time everybody was watching Rose, and Jameson could see in her brown eyes how she gloried in this admiration. She seated herself at the piano and began to play and sing the tune King had started. King stood awhile with his elbow on the piano, watching her like a hungry cat watching a mouse. Finally he walked back to the table where Jameson sat.

"Quite a gal, that one," King said.

Jameson nodded. She did look mighty good to a man who had been three months out on the buffalo range.

"You ought to get acquainted with her, Jameson," King said.

"Looks to me like you've already got the deed."

King shrugged. "Women are all right for a while, for a little diversion. Can't seem to get along without them. But you get tired of one after so long. I've been hoping someone would come along and take Rose off my hands. Man needs a change in diet occasionally."

Jameson smiled, thinking he might be tempted if he didn't have so much of more importance on his mind.

King poured himself a third drink. As quickly as it had come, the laughter went out of his face and he turned serious.

"Barber told me you're in the market for wagons and teams."

"That's right."

"I've done some thinking about it. The way I see it, you must be planning to go south."

Jameson looked at him in surprise. King explained, "You're a man of considerable reputation as a hunter, Jameson. You wouldn't waste money on wagons to hunt in this country. The army's not letting anybody up into that northern territory. So you *must* be going south."

Jameson studied King's changeable face, wondering what the man was aiming at.

"There's buffalo down there, Jameson," King said with enthusiasm. "Big herds that can load a man's wagons with flint hides in a hurry. I've seen a few of them, just enough to set my blood to racing and the seat of my pants to itching. I took four wagons south of the Arkansas last spring. But you could fairly smell Indian in the air. Half my men panicked and deserted me. I had to turn back before we had skinned out a wagonload.

"A man could make himself a small fortune down there, Jameson, a first-rate hunter with plenty of guts and more than common judgment. They tell me you're that kind of man."

Jameson took the compliment without reply, knowing King was working up to something.

"Main thing," King said, "would be to take enough men and wagons that an outfit could defend itself. The Comanches aren't foolish. They fight when they think they can win. When they don't think they can, they don't try."

He drank half the whisky out of his glass and pointed his finger at Jameson. "Now it happens I know a man who has a string of wagons and all the teams you'll need. He'll sell them cheap. Tell you what, you make the rounds and price the wagons and mules that you find. Whatever kind of deal you're offered, my man'll do better, I guarantee you."

Jameson eyed him levelly. "Where's your profit, King? You're not doing this for nothing."

King broke into a high, loud laugh. "They were right about you, Jameson, you're a perceptive man. All right, I have a motive of my own. I wanted to get on your warm side so you'd let me take my own wagons with you into Texas. I wasn't going to make that proposition until I'd built you up for it. But there it is."

Jameson rubbed his chin thoughtfully, then slowly shook his head. "This is going to be my own expedition, King. I don't want to have to consult anybody or worry what anybody else thinks. I'm my own boss. You can't be that way when there's another outfit with you. I've seen too many hunters go off together, then fall out. No real leader, everybody a free agent. A little friction starts and you're done for."

"There won't be any conflict. You'll be the wagon master. What you say goes, any time."

Jameson shook his head. "I'm sorry, King."

Ransom King studied Jameson, his eyes unreadable. Presently he shrugged. "No harm done, and no hard feelings. What I said about those wagons still stands. Come around to my camp when you've priced the others. My man'll make you a better deal."

Jameson smiled a little. "No motive this time?"

King laughed. "He owes me money, and I want to get paid." He looked at Rose, and he looked at the stairs. "See you tomorrow, Jameson?"

Jameson nodded, beginning to like this tall, brash man. "Tomorrow."

* * *

Old Shad Blankenship was pacing impatiently about his camp when Jameson rode up into the firelight.

"About decided you wasn't comin' after all," he said half peevishly, raking the fire restlessly with a stick. "Been dark an hour. Thought you'd found you some redheaded filly and plumb forgot about that bottle you were going to bring me."

"Now, Shad," Jameson grinned, "do you think a filly could make me forget the man who taught me how to shoot a buffalo gun and talk sign language and cure out a green hide?"

A flicker of humor showed behind Shad's deep scowl as he grabbed the bottle from Jameson's hand and began to worry the cork out of it.

"If she couldn't, you're a sight older than I think you are. When I was a few years younger a filly could make me forget my own name. Way it is, the whisky's all that's left for me. That and the cards."

There wasn't a great deal of the whisky left, either, by the time Shad finally laid the bottle aside, wiping his hand on his ancient, deep-stained old buckskin jacket from which most of the fringe was long since gone. Shad frowned at Jameson as the glow began to work upward in him.

"Now what's this foolishness I hear about you wantin' to buy wagons and mules?"

"Where did you hear it?"

"Man, it spread over town like the cholera through an Injun camp. Been a dozen men here to ask me about you. Have you plumb lost your head?"

"I hope not."

"What good is wagons when the buffalo is gone?"

"There's buffalo to the south, Shad."

Blankenship snorted and uncorked the bottle again. "Jason Miles would jump ten feet and fall over dead."

"He's not in on it. Just C. T. Posey and me."

Shad stared hard at Jameson until he was sure the younger man wasn't joshing him. "Then you *have* lost your head."

"Shad, sooner or later somebody's going to go down there. It had just as well be me."

Blankenship narrowed his eyes, and he slowly shook his head. "Come spring, your scalp'll be dried and hanging from some heathen Comanche's lodgepole, that's for sure. But don't listen to me. Go on down there and get yourself knocked over."

He held the bottle out to arm's length, trying to read the label. "Just let me get my paws on some of your money first. You want to buy wagons? All right, I'll sell you mine."

Jameson looked sharply at him. "Sell me yours? What would you ever do, Shad? You've been a hide man so long you'd starve to death trying to make an honest living."

"The hide business is goin' to the devil, and I ain't makin' the trip with it. I'm heading back to the settlements and take up farming, like I told you."

"It wouldn't last a month. You'd be back out here skinning buffalo if you had to walk the whole way barefooted."

Shad Blankenship flared, the whisky beginning to get him. "A man crazy enough to do what you're figuring on ain't in no shape to be givin' advice. Just buy my wagons. Three of them, and the teams—the whole works, tools, camp gear, lock, stock and barrel—for a thousand dollars. And cheap at the price."

Studying the old man, Jameson wished Shad hadn't said it. The outfit was worth far more than he was asking for it.

"Shad, that's the whisky talking. Let's let it wait till morning."

"If you don't buy it, I'll sell it to somebody else."

Jameson finally shrugged. "All right, if that's the way it's got to be, you've just sold out. What say I give you a hundred of it here and send the rest on ahead?"

Blankenship shook his head, angering. The hint was plain enough—he couldn't take care of the money.

"I'll take it all right now, right here, thankee."

"Shad, you won't get out of town with a dime of it."

Blankenship arose quickly, his fists knotting. "By Judas Priest, you listen to me, young'un! I was a grown man trapping beaver and dodging the Blackfeet before your Maw and Paw ever even thought of you. Don't you think I got sense enough to know what I'm about? You just pay me, that's all you got to do."

Unwillingly Jameson said, "All right, Shad, however you want it."

He knew what would happen as soon as Shad got his hands on the cash. He had seen it too many times.

"Look, Shad, keep your wagons. Come with me to Texas. We'll split the take according to what each man puts in."

It was exactly the deal he had turned down for Ransom King. But he knew Shad Blankenship. Shad would be worth three of most men, if he ever got out of Dodge.

But Shad's feelings were hurt. "I ain't gonna take orders from you, young'un, just because you got the most wagons. No, sir, you just take me to town and pay me off, right now. I'm goin' to Missouri."

Jameson spent most of the next day riding through the camps scattered up and down the river, looking at wagons and mules. He found many men eager to sell. The prices they quoted him were low compared to what they had been last spring.

He could have gotten oxen even cheaper, but winter was coming on. Mules would be better for the long haul where feed had to be carried. And mules were faster in a pinch. Trouble with mules, the Indians liked them too. Nothing appealed to an Indian's horse-stealing tendencies more than the thought of a fat mule's hind leg smoking over an open fire.

Late in the day, before angling toward Ransom King's camp, Jameson stopped to see Shad Blankenship. One look at Shad's pain-twisted face, his sick and stricken eyes, told him the whole story.

"I been a first-class fool, Gage," the old man lamented, running his gnarled fingers miserably through his rusty mat of long hair. "You had me pegged right enough. I got drunk and fell into a poker game. Them highbinders melted my roll like a snowbank in August. I ain't goin' to Missouri. I ain't even got the cash to get out of Dodge."

There was no use saying I told you so, even if Jameson had been of a mind to. He laid a hand on Shad's shoulder and sat down beside him on the dirty old buffalo robe the hunter had spread out inside his grimy tent. He looked at Shad with sorrow in his eyes, and a disturbing thought took hold of him:

A few more years the way I'm going and I'll be just like him.

That was why he *had* to go down and find that Texas herd, had to make him a stake now while there was still time.

"How about going south with me, Shad?"

"I'd be in your way. I ain't got sense enough to get in out of the rain."

"Shad, you're still the best hide man in the business,

barring none. I'll be needing your advice down there.''

"You're just feeling sorry for me. You got no call to.''

"That's not it. I need those sharp eyes of yours. There's few hunters can bring down as many buffalo as you can and smoke up as few cartridges doing it. You didn't lose your rifle in that poker game, did you?''

"No.''

"Then oil it up. You'll be using it.''

3

RANSOM KING shifted to one side in the saddle. "Yonder's his camp," he said. "Looks like a hog sty, but he's got the goods to sell."

The wagons were scattered around in no particular order, some of the harness done up on the wheels, some of it thrown carelessly out on the ground. Cooking utensils lay about, unwashed, some of them caked up with dried-out food. The whole place had an unpleasant odor to it that wrinkled Jameson's nose.

Jameson counted the wagons to himself, raising and dropping his hand. Six doubles and a single. They were of several kinds and of various sizes, as if they had been picked up a few at a time. Most were good Studebaker wagons or their equals. A few wouldn't do for a bone hauler.

A bulky man walked out slowly, carrying himself with

a deliberate ease that tried to say he wasn't afraid of anybody in the world.

But Jameson's keen eye told him this bearded man was only a weak imitation, a bluff, hollow inside.

"Gage Jameson, Adam Budge," King said by way of introduction.

Budge shook hands but stared belligerently with black eyes, as if this transaction wasn't going to be to his liking. His hands were grimy, his black beard dirty and greasy. Half the buttons were gone from his salt-crusted shirt.

The man stood awkwardly a minute before he broke his silence. "King says you want to buy wagons. I got them to sell."

Jameson nodded. "Tell you right now, I've had some cheap prices quoted to me today."

Budge glanced questioningly at King. King said, "Whatever they are, Budge'll beat them. You want to look over the outfit?"

Jameson walked among the wagons, carefully checking under them and over them. Finally he said, "Three would have to come out. I'll take the others, if the price is right. Now how about the mules?"

"Down on the riverbank," Budge said. "Got a man herding them."

An unkempt stock tender sat on the ground, holding an old horse that stood hip-shot. He had the mules bunched loosely on the grass not far from water.

Jameson rode slowly into them, looking for harness sores, making the mules move around so he could tell if any of them limped. He found a cripple or two that way and eased them out of the bunch. He cut back a couple of old and unthrifty mules that might have a hard time getting through the winter, and on a long haul at that. He looked for well-built animals with long legs placed sol-

idly under their bodies like the legs under a table. He
looked for flat backs, good head, good ear, good foot and
bone. He cut back two or three narrow-bodied mules with
legs too close together that indicated a lack of stamina.
He always remembered what Shad had told him once
about picking mules.

"You see one that's got forelegs comin' out of the
same hole like a rabbit's, you leave him alone. One knee
says to the other, 'You let me by this time and I'll let
you by the next.' "

A wild-eyed mule wheeled as Jameson came to him.
He lashed out with a hind foot and narrowly missed
Jameson's leg. Quickly Jameson cut him out, too. He
didn't want any fractious mule getting a whole team in
a jackpot and tearing up a pair of wagons, especially
wagons loaded with flint hides that might fetch two dollars or more apiece.

Back in camp, Ransom King sought out cups from a
wooden box in a wagon bed and poured coffee. Jameson
looked dubiously at his cup, which had a thin scum of
grease on it. His eyes caught King's and he knew King
had the same thought. But Jameson had been around hide
camps so much that it took a lot to make him sick. For
courtesy's sake he sipped the bitter black coffee without
comment.

Budge scowled over his own coffee. "All right," he
said sharply, "what'll you give?"

Jameson leaned forward, setting the cup down. "Well,
I've had good wagons offered to me as cheap as three
hundred dollars a pair, and mules at fifty a head. I know
that's mighty little, but some of these boys are desperate."

Jameson felt a pleasant tremor of excitement, the tingle
that always came to him when he was trying to make a
close trade. He was that much like Posey. This was

cheaper than he had ever hoped for. Used to be that a good new wagon and a well-matched team could run a man an easy thousand dollars.

Budge chewed his whiskered lip, showing a set of yellow teeth streaked brown from tobacco. "Last spring they was worth a sight more."

Jameson shrugged, keeping his face bland. "I can buy them from somebody else."

King said, "Budge will sell them to you."

Budge nodded his shaggy head, the reluctant words dragging from him like pulled teeth. "Yeah, yeah, I reckon so."

Jameson said, "Four thousand even for the ten wagons and that string of mules, minus the ones I cut out. All right?"

Budge sloshed his coffee around, trying to get the sugar up off the bottom of the cup. He drank, then wiped a filthy sleeve across his mouth. "Yeah, I reckon that'll have to do."

Jameson relaxed slowly, letting out a long breath. For weeks on the prairie he'd thought about taking his own expedition south if Miles and Posey didn't go for the idea. He hadn't let himself hope for anywhere near this many wagons.

"When do you want to be paid?" Jameson asked.

Budge said, "I want to square up a few accounts"— he flicked a half-resentful glance at King—"and catch the first train East. I'd be obliged if you paid me tonight."

"How about coming to the Miles and Posey office with me?"

Budge shook his head. "Can't. I got to go see a man who'll take them cut-back mules and extra wagons off my hands. He'll rob me, but leastways I can get the money tonight and catch that train."

He scratched his black chin. "You know where the Queen of the Arkansas Saloon is?"

Jameson nodded. It was a rat hole of a place, a half dugout on the wrong side of the tracks. Cheap whisky, low-stakes poker.

Budge said, "The man I got to see owns the place. Why don't you meet me there?"

Jameson wasn't sure it suited him, carrying four thousand dollars in cash. It would be well dark before he got back. But he had seen hide buyers moving around freely all over Dodge in the past, their pockets stuffed with greenbacks. If anybody ever molested them, he hadn't heard about it.

"All right," he said, dismissing the thought. He looked at King. "Ready to go?"

Riding away, King smiled. "You got you a great buy back there."

"I know it. Just one thing worries me. Budge isn't the type. A skinner or a teamster, maybe, but not a man to own and boss a string of wagons."

King shrugged. "Maybe he's found that out. That's why he's selling."

"What kind of a squeeze have you got on him, King?"

"I just told him I was tired of waiting, and if he didn't pay me I'd peel the hide off of him, an inch at a time. He looks rough, Jameson, but he's as scary as a squawking old hen."

Jameson caught C. T. Posey just as he was closing his office, and got the four thousand dollars in cash out of the big safe. He shoved it into the deep pocket of his coat. Then he strapped his six-shooter on over the coat, just in case.

It wasn't far to the saloon, so he unsaddled his horse and turned him loose in the company yard. Then he walked over the tracks and down on the other side.

None of Dodge City looked very polished or respectable, but here was the seamiest part of it, raw frame saloons and dance halls, others built of nothing more than sod, a few even dug into the ground, only the top half reaching above ground level. He heard fiddle music and rough laughter. Yonder he saw a woman standing watching him, the yellow flicker of lamplight behind her outlining her in a doorway. She spoke to him, but he didn't catch the words and didn't want to.

A lantern hung on either side of the door at the Queen of the Arkansas, yellow flame licking at the wick. The nearly flat sod roof was only waist-high to Jameson, most of the building being dug into the ground. He thought idly what would happen to this place if a sudden cloudburst should send water cascading down the street. It would fill up like a jug.

A match suddenly flared, and a man's face glowed as he touched the flame to a cigarette. "You Jameson?"

"Yes."

"Then go on inside. Budge is waitin' for you."

Vaguely disturbed, Jameson hesitated a moment, looking through the ground-level windows and seeing light inside. Carefully then, he moved down the warped wooden steps to the sunken doorway.

The wall-trapped reek of smoke and whisky and unwashed bodies slapped him in the face. It reminded him of a wolf den he had crawled into once. This was like it, more den than house.

The light was dim, for the owner was stingy with his lanterns. But Jameson easily spotted Adam Budge's bulk. He sat at a table with another man, his broad back turned to the door. His shirt was soaked with sweat. The man at the table looked up at Jameson. He was a cheap gambler, Jameson remembered, who went by the name of Frenchy. Dirty, unkempt, he was not in the class with the gamblers who stayed around the bigger places.

Budge licked his lips, and his voice had a high pitch to it. "Jameson, c-c-come on over."

Jameson hesitated, with a sudden quickening of alarm. Budge is scared half to death, he thought. His hand moved down toward the six-shooter.

"Hold it, friend!" The words were short-clipped. Jameson glanced quickly at the bar. The tender held a shotgun, aimed straight at him.

"Go shut the door, Mick," said Frenchy. The man behind Jameson shoved the door shut and took the bartender's shotgun. "Now come on over," Frenchy said to Jameson. Jameson slowly stepped forward, looking into the muzzle of Frenchy's derringer, knowing the shotgun was at his back. He felt his six-shooter being jerked from the holster.

Budge's chin was trembling. So were his hands, placed judiciously on the table where all could see them.

"Now," said Frenchy, rising to his feet, "where is it?"

"Where is what?" Jameson bluffed, knowing it was a waste of time.

"The money. You got it. Budge has told us all about it."

Budge's voice shrilled desperately, "Jameson, they're fixin' to kill us!"

Jameson said, "Somebody's steered you wrong. There isn't any money."

In the back of his mind was a wild hope that when they reached for him to search him, he might grab a gun.

So suddenly he didn't see it, a leather whip or something lashed at his face. A cry swelled in his throat, and he bent over, his hands clawing at the fire which seared his cheeks.

"Don't stall me around," Frenchy gritted. "Where's that money?"

Jameson made no reply, clenching his teeth against the burn. The lash struck again, across the back of his neck.

"Search him."

Rough hands jerked him around. Through pain-reddened eyes Jameson saw that the man behind him had set the shotgun down, just out of his reach. Hands dug into his coat pockets.

"Here it is, Frenchy. Holy smoke, look at them greenbacks!"

For a second then, while they feverishly eyed the money, Jameson thought he might have a chance. He reached for the shotgun. But someone was ready. A gun barrel slanted across his skull, sent him sprawling on the packed dirt floor amid cigarette butts and dried tobacco juice. He lay half conscious, brain hammering with pain.

"Supposed to be four thousand there," someone said. "Count it."

They ran through it and satisfied themselves.

The bartender said, "What're we gonna do with them two? Can't have them runnin' loose. Give me the word, Frenchy, and I'll shoot them both."

"No," replied Frenchy, more concerned over the money than over the men. "Too much noise. Knife's just as good and a heap quieter."

A cry of terror from Adam Budge helped bring Jameson groping back to consciousness. "Don't do it," Budge quaked. "I won't tell nobody, Frenchy, I swear it. You can keep the money, only don't do it."

Budge arose shaking, letting his chair fall back across Jameson's legs. He began to dodge away from the man with the knife. He kept crying, "No, Frenchy, no!" He pushed the table out, trying to keep it between them.

Without moving, Jameson sought the shotgun with his

eyes. It still stood where it had been, propped against the sod wall. A slim chance, but the only one he had.

The door burst open. Two men stood there, guns in their hands. In the split second before the guns roared, Jameson recognized Ransom King and saw a wild fever in the man's eyes that was like a look into hell. Jameson grabbed for the shotgun, got it, and rolled over onto his back.

He saw the bartender drop the knife and spin away from the force of the first two bullets, then fall, limp as a sack of grain. Frenchy whirled toward the door, bringing up the derringer. Jameson swung the shotgun around and squeezed the trigger, the roar of it swelling like a dynamite blast in the tiny room. The impact slammed Frenchy against the wall. He fell forward then and lay crumpled, his fingers convulsively digging into the packed earth.

The third man cowered back, raising his hands.

Beside King stood a heavy-bodied man with ragged beard, wolf-gray eyes shining in savage pleasure. He turned his six-gun to the third man and shot him where he stood, triggering two more bullets into his body after he fell.

"That's enough, Trencher." King spoke sharply.

"I reckon it is," the man called Trencher replied calmly. "He's dead." His eyes glittered, his wide mouth lifting a little at the corners. Standing there in the heavy, circling cloud of gun smoke, he flexed his gun hand nervously, eyes flicking back and forth among the fallen men, as if hoping one of them might move a little.

But they never would again.

Jameson pushed up weakly, leaning against the dirt wall and rubbing the back of his head where the gun barrel had struck him.

Budge was on his knees along the same wall, his face

chalk-white, his body shaking so Jameson could actually hear his teeth clicking. Budge tried to talk, but all that would come from his throat was a hollow squeak.

Ransom King stepped behind the bar and picked up a bottle. He blew dust from a glass and poured it half full. He handed it across to Jameson. "Here. You need this."

Jameson downed most of it and braced himself against its fiery jolt.

King lifted the bottle to his lips and took a long pull. Face suddenly flushed and twisted, he spat it out across the bar. "Wow!" he exclaimed. "Man who'd sell stuff like that doesn't deserve to live anyhow."

He walked out from behind the bar and handed the bottle to the trembling Budge.

"Buck up, Budge, and drink this. We got some money to count."

The whole thing had happened in the span of a few seconds. Now that it was over, reaction set in. Jameson's hands began to quiver, a little like Budge's. He pulled up a chair and sat down to let the spell pass, drinking a little more of the poor whisky in an effort to settle himself. He grinned sheepishly. "Some time to get scared, now that it's over."

King shrugged. "Man who doesn't get scared once in a while is the rankest kind of a fool."

"You were just in time," Jameson said. "How did you know?"

King grinned then, the tension gone. "I didn't. It was just luck. Budge there isn't exactly a paragon of virtue. I got to thinking how easy it would be for him to take the money, quick as you paid him, and skip out on our little debt. The more I thought about it, the more worried I got. So I came over here to keep him honest. Just happened to peep in that window yonder first, and saw what the deal was."

Jameson sat there, letting the strength come back to him as he watched the big man Trencher filling his deep coat pockets with bottles from behind the bar.

Finally he said, "King, after this, if there's ever anything you want, just let me know."

King smiled. "Well now, as a matter of fact, there is. I still want to take my wagons to Texas with you."

Jameson looked down at the dead men sprawled out on the dirt floor.

"After this, how could I say no?"

4

SHARP COLD clung to the early-morning air. Gage Jameson looked at the stars and shivered. He fastened the top button of his woolen coat, wondering why it always took so long to shake the chill when a man was fresh out of bed.

He ate breakfast at the Dutchman's. He had arranged for the Dutchman to feed his men so they could get started without the delay that came from cooking and washing all the camp utensils. Besides, it was likely to be the last town meal they would get for a long time.

"My bunch all been in?" he asked, sipping his hot coffee and chewing on a thick slice of sugar-cured buffalo ham.

The stout old cook shrugged. "*Ach,* and more. You say please to feed fifteen men. It is already more than thirty that have come. I think you got a bunch of bums say they with you and they not."

Jameson frowned, until the humor of it touched him. He ought to have known the word would get around. Finishing up, he gave the old man twenty dollars.

"That cover it?"

The cook nodded vigorously, rubbing his stubby fingers over the paper money as if it had been silk. "*Ja, ja,* and you come again soon *wieder.*"

Soberly Jameson said, "I hope so."

He walked briskly on down to the yards, the coffee and the hot meal making him warmer now. He could hear the restless stir of men and mules, the rattle of trace chains and the popping of leather as teams were pulled into place and hitched to the wagons. Men laughed and cursed and hollered one to another. Mules balked. Mules squealed and kicked. He heard the quick gust of breath from one as another's hind feet slammed into its stomach. A man yelled, and leather slapped hard across a mule's rump.

Jameson caught his horse and threw his heavy saddle across its back. He rubbed his hand over the saddle, liking the feel of it. It was one he had just bought, one somebody had picked up from a Texas trail hand in a cow town down the tracks. High cantle, high horn to tie a rope to. It was sturdily built, and Jameson thought it would be like riding a rocking chair after the light saddles he had been used to.

He looked up into the sky and picked out the Dipper, then the North Star. It wasn't easy to find now, for daylight was rapidly washing it out. He turned his back on the star and looked ahead in the direction to which the wagon tongues were pointed.

South. South across the deadline. South toward Texas.

Nervousness began to ripple in him now that the time was upon him. It always did when he set off for someplace he'd never been. He began itching to be on the move.

He would be glad to get away from Dodge again, away

from its evil-smelling saloons, its gambling dens, the shady men who hung around them—not hunters, not men who toiled with leather-tough hands, but leeches who stole from other men what they had earned with their sweat, and sometimes with their blood.

Yet he could remember the eagerness with which he had gone into Dodge, an eagerness that seemed to grow a little more each trip. A taste for the whisky, a desire to play a little poker, an urge to look at the girls.

It wasn't what he really wanted, yet it was here, unbidden, and it was growing, a general aimlessness that eventually would put him in the same shape as old Shad Blankenship. There was no hope for Shad. He was too old to change.

Jameson wondered if soon there might no longer be hope for himself. Dodge was a reminder to him that time was going on, that he didn't have long left to find something permanent, something he could anchor to and hold solid.

He swung into the saddle and walked his bay horse down the line of wagons, seeing that the mules were harnessed up. He checked the trail wagons in each pair, making sure their short tongues were firmly bolted to the coupling poles of the lead wagons. His horse stepped gingerly, the bite of nippy air bringing out a touch of bronc that still slept within him.

Up at the head of the line he came to the chuck wagon, its hoops standing like barren ribs, the cover rolled up in the bed of the wagon with the heavy load of cooking gear and supplies, flour and sugar, baking powder, dried apples—and most of all, plenty of coffee.

Shad Blankenship stood leaning relaxed against his own saddled horse and eyeing Jameson quizzically. He trimmed a thick shaving off a plug of Lorillard tobacco and shoved it into his mouth. His breath already had a sweetish tobacco smell, and a trickle of brown worked into the rusty beard.

"What do you think of the layout, Shad?"

Shad never had been one to mince words. "I think that if a marshal was to come snooping around, about two-thirds of this crew you hired would drown theirselves tryin' to get across that river. What jailhouse door did you prize open?"

"I wanted them tough. They won't stampede back to town the first time we run into an Indian with the paint on."

Shad shrugged, still not liking it.

"Well, there's one of them ain't goin'. He got in a little argument last night and didn't have a sharp enough knife. Other feller just naturally gutted him. Shows what kind of an outfit *we* got."

Jameson swore under his breath. One man lost and they hadn't even started yet.

Shad said, "We'll have to watch them like hawks or first thing you know some of them are liable to run off with our stock."

Jameson was still troubled about the man they were short. "I figured you and me are strong enough to handle them."

Put that way, there wasn't much Shad could do except sourly nod assent. "I reckon."

Despite the early hour, despite the chill which still penetrated the men's light coats, a good-sized crowd of onlookers gathered. This expedition had aroused a lot of comment. Most people agreed it was foolhardy. Jameson would be so busy fighting Indians he couldn't hunt buffalo.

He'd had poor luck finding men who would hire on. He didn't try to get any of the Miles and Posey men, for he felt that would be unfair to the company. Besides,

C. T. Posey wanted to send them out for one last attempt up against the edge of the northern treaty territory. Jameson had managed to get three men who had worked for Miles and Posey a little in the past. They weren't what he wanted, but they were all he could get.

Then Ransom King came to his rescue and rounded up a crew for him.

"These are good men that'll take you down there and bring you back," King had said. Then he had reflected a moment and added, "Maybe 'good' isn't just the right word. 'Tough' is more like it."

Now Jameson pointed his chin toward the crowd of onlookers who stood around and watched. "They'll do a lot of thinking, Shad, sitting around here doing nothing. Then they'll get the fever. There'll be other outfits down there by winter, unless I miss my guess."

Shad observed, "It'll be a good thing we was the first."

Jameson gave him a dig in the ribs. "That's what I've been trying to tell you all along."

C. T. Posey came striding up, chewing rapidly on his cigar. If anything, he was more nervous than Jameson.

"Look at me," he said, holding out his hand. "Quivering like a whipped pup and not even going."

He rubbed the palms of his hands on his trousers. "Everything looks good, Gage. You won't have to worry about the military. Won't be a patrol across your route in two days."

Jameson glanced at Shad Blankenship, grinning. It never ceased to amaze him how Posey could know what was going on at Fort Dodge. The army was supposed to keep hunters from working south of the Arkansas. But it was a careless hunter who couldn't slip past the soldiers. It was as if a tacit agreement existed between the hide outfits and the officers at the fort.

He remembered what Colonel Dodge had said when J. Wright Mooar asked him about heading south. "Boys, if I were hunting buffalo, I would go where the buffalo are."

It was almost universally agreed among the plains army officers that destruction of the buffalo was the quickest way to peace. The reservation looked good to a hungry Indian.

Ransom King rode up to them mounted on a fine big sorrel with three stocking feet. Jameson hadn't seen the horse before and stopped to admire its good lines, the deep heart girth, the strong legs that could carry a man all day and not give out.

King nodded at Jameson, then said to C. T. Posey, "What did you think of those hides, C. T.?"

Posey replied, "I thought they were plenty expensive."

King threw back his head and laughed. Presently he said to Jameson, "My wagons are ready, any time yours are." His gaze swept down Jameson's line of wagons and to the extra horses and mules bunched at the lower end.

Jameson said, "We're about ready, I think. I've already lost a man, and the wagons haven't turned a wheel."

King nodded. "Heard about it from some of my crew. Fool got in a fight over a poker game. Just a five-dollar bet, that's all it was."

Jameson started walking down the line of wagons, leading his horse and making a last check of each wagon as he passed it. The wagons contained primers and gunpowder and lead, corn and salt and everything else it would take for a long hunt on the prairie. Jameson reasoned that as the hides stacked up, the supplies would diminish and make room for them.

"Mighty little to die for, five dollars," he mused to King, who rode slowly beside him.

"Lots of people die over money," King replied lightly. "What else *is* worth dying for, when you boil it down? But if I ever do it, it won't be over any measly five dollars."

Jameson frowned. That was a mighty narrow way of looking at life, the way he saw it. Or death, either.

A woman pushed through the crowd and stopped in front of it, holding her long gray coat tight at the throat, not caring that her slender ankles showed amid a swirl of petticoats.

"There's Rose," Jameson said, "wanting to tell you good-bye."

King nodded, resignation in his face. "I'm glad I'm getting to do it. I'm bored to death with her."

Jameson smiled. "If I had to die, that's the way I'd want to do it, bored to death by someone as good-looking as that."

King shrugged. "Well, I gave you the chance. You didn't take her."

He started to pull away, toward Rose. He turned back to say, "I've thrown my extra animals in with yours, and my wagons will drop in behind when yours lead out. See you later, down the trail."

He moved his horse out and swung down beside Rose.

Jameson rode back to the head of the line. A lean, long-legged man strode toward him in the dawn, wearing faded old army clothes, carrying a rifle in his hand and a heavy roll of bedding over his shoulder. It was the skinner, Messick. Dropping the roll in the street, Messick leaned the rifle against it and raised his hand in greeting.

"Mornin', Gage."

"Morning, Nathan."

Messick glanced over Jameson's wagons, where everything seemed to be ready to travel. "I want to go with you."

Jameson said, "I didn't aim to steal anybody from Miles and Posey."

"You ain't stealin' me. I just quit. I've worked with you so long, Gage, there ain't anybody else I can get along with."

Jameson smiled, glad to have him. Messick never was one to add any cheer, but with a man like him in charge of the hides there wouldn't be any spoiled goods. "Hop up on a wagon, then. We're fixing to roll."

Messick pitched his bedding up onto the chuck wagon, shoved his rifle under the seat, and climbed up beside the little cook. The cook nodded at him, clenching the whipstock in one hand, the lines and the coils of his rawhide whip in the other. Two thin men, one short, one uncommonly tall.

Shad Blankenship rode up to Jameson, rocked back in the saddle and spat a stream of tobacco juice at a lanky gray dog which nosed around a wagon wheel. Then Shad's big black dog charged up and put the intruder to flight, trotting back with a grand air of self-importance.

Shad waved his hand at the line of wagons. "All set, Gage."

C. T. Posey was there, too. He held out his hand, and Jameson bent down to take it.

"I envy you in a way, Gage," the hide buyer said. "I never saw this country the way it used to be. I'd like to see it, just once in my lifetime. But I'm smart enough to know my limitations, and you have none. Best of luck to you."

"Thanks, C. T."

Then Jameson pulled away and looked back at his long string of wagons, the stamping mules, the impatient men.

"All right, Shad. Let's take them to Texas."

5

ANGLING SOUTHWESTWARD, he didn't try to push the wagons hard the first day. With untried mules, untried wagons and untried men, it was better to take it easy and watch. By the time he reached Crooked Creek late in the afternoon, he had seen half a dozen mules and at least a couple of men he probably should have left in Dodge.

Too late now to do much about it. He had other mules he could put into the teams. But he was stuck with the men.

Shad Blankenship rode up to him and pointed to the creek. "Pretty good camping spot over here. Want to pull up the wagons?"

"Not till we get across. I get nervous on the wrong side of a creek or river. Spent too many days watching them flood and wishing I'd gotten across them when I could have."

Shad argued, "This one ain't fixin' to get out of banks. Ain't a cloud in sight."

"Call it a policy. We're crossing it anyhow."

Normally it was an easy crossing. It would have been this time, except for the nigh leader on the chuck wagon. He had been kicking and fighting all day. When the cold water splashed around his legs, he came in two.

The pots and pans, buckled on the chuck box, set up a clatter as the wagon began to jerk. The cook cracked a whip over the mule's ears and swore in language such as Jameson had seldom heard before, a careless mixture of the most profane of both English and Spanish. Jameson grinned, wondering how a man so small could have so powerful a voice.

The mule kept pitching and kicking, getting his forelegs over the neck of the animal beside him and stirring the whole team into a frenzy. They whipped the wagon back and forth at the water's edge until it began to rock.

The thin, bewhiskered cook began looking for a way to get off, but it was too risky. The moment he jumped, the well-loaded wagon might tip over on him.

Jameson spurred back across the stream. Plunging in next to the mules, he grabbed the reins up close and wrapped them around his saddle horn, pulling the nigh leader's head hard against his leg. He half dragged the reluctant animal across the stream. By the time he got him out on dry ground the mule had stopped fighting. But it was rolling its eyes and dancing about in the traces.

Breathing hard, Jameson said, "He needs to be worked till his belly drags—work the foolishness out of him."

The cook was still talking to himself. "Needs a good dose of hickory limb right between the ears, that's what he needs. I thought for sure I was fixin' to get me a bath in that cold water."

Jameson began to see humor in it then. He couldn't help but think that a bath wouldn't have hurt the young cook much. But he had found that some of the best hide-camp cooks never washed anything but their hands. That much Jameson demanded.

He had tried this cook's handiwork in Dodge before he hired him. Now, in the first night camp, he knew he hadn't made a mistake. The cook was a short, thin Texan named Pruitt—"Reb" Pruitt they called him, because he had been in the army of the Confederacy. He was thirty or thereabouts, with a deep browned skin and an irresponsible growth of whiskers that made him look much older. He had come up the trail to Abilene with a couple of thousand Longhorn steers and a salty bunch of Texas cowhands. The way Jameson heard it, he had been in some sort of scrape down there and couldn't afford to return to Texas—not the settled parts, anyway. So he'd been cooking for the hide outfits.

Homesick, he had seized upon the chance to see his native state again, even though it would be only the buffalo plains, a couple of hundred miles from any settlement—or any law.

After Jameson had dropped his tin plate and cup into a washtub with the rest, he called the men together. Old Shad Blankenship stood beside him as he counted them. Ransom King and his small crew stood in the background, listening.

The little Texas cook rattled the tinware as he washed it in the tub, and he grumbled constantly to himself. But he was listening, too.

"I've called you together in a bunch," Jameson said, "because there's a thing or two that needs saying. I want them said right at the start, so no man can claim he didn't hear them.

"There aren't any tenderfeet in this outfit. I chose you

on purpose because you all knew something about the hide business. There's not a man among you who hasn't fought Indians, so I don't think the sight of a feather or the smell of gunpowder is going to run you off. But if you think it might, I want you to say so right now.

"It's one thing to loaf around Dodge and talk brave. It's another to belly down in the grass a thousand miles from home and try to get some Indian before he puts an arrow through you. Anybody who wants to turn back can do it right now, and no hard feelings. But after today, there won't be any turning back. Not for me and not for you. We're going down into Comanche country, and we're not coming back till every wagon is loaded with hides.

"Now then, is there anybody that wants to leave?"

The cook had stopped rattling the tinware. Jameson stared hard at the silent faces, one by one. Not a man moved. He hadn't thought they would.

The utensils began to clatter again.

"The next thing," Jameson went on, "is the Indians. Now we're not going down there to fight. We're going down there after buffalo hides, and that's all. We'll go a long way to get out of a fight if we have to. A battle is too costly, even when you win it. You always lose men and you always lose stock. Wagons aren't any good to us without the men to load and handle them or the stock to pull them.

"We're bound to run into Indians. But there won't be any shooting unless it has to be done. If they act friendly, we'll treat them accordingly. If they're hostile, we'll try to keep out of their way. We'll fight only as a last resort.

"So I don't want any itchy trigger fingers around here. If any man gets us in trouble needlessly . . . I'll shoot him."

He paused a moment, studying the faces as that soaked

in. He wasn't sure exactly why, but he cast a glance at King's man Trencher.

"The last thing," Jameson said, "is about the hides. They're mine. I'm paying you well for skinning and stretching and for handling the mules. But every so often somebody gets a notion he can make more by stealing hides and stashing them away for himself.

"Well, it won't work here. I know that most of you aren't wearing any halo. But I don't care what you've done in the past as long as you shoot straight with me.

"In the first place, there'll be no way for a thief to come back and get the hides. In the second place, I'll be keeping a good tally of the buffalo killed and the hides we stack up. If I ever catch any man trying to steal from me, he'll wish the Comanches had him."

The cook had stopped washing the utensils and sat staring at Jameson, the wash water dripping from his fingers. Only when Jameson turned away did he go back to his job. And he had stopped grumbling to himself.

Jameson walked out to where his bed lay on the ground, still rolled up. He sat down wearily.

A heavy silence hung over the camp awhile, an uneasy silence as the men weighed what he had said. He could feel the resentment from some of them. It had been strong talk. But it had needed saying.

Finally he heard the riffle of cards and someone saying, "Who's game for a little poker?"

Jameson leaned back against his bedroll. He had brought a few tents, but they wouldn't be used while the weather was still good. He enjoyed sitting in the open, watching the stars brighten against the darkening sky.

Shad Blankenship stuffed his stinking old pipe with tobacco and lighted it with a burning stick from the Texan's dying cook fire. He flopped down beside Jameson and puffed silently on the pipe. Shad chewed tobacco all day, but at supper he always spat out his quid. He customarily lighted up a pipeful of tobacco and smoked it out before crawling into his blankets.

Shad took an awl from his pocket. With it he carefully began to worry a diagonal hole through the end of a big lead rifle bullet. Jameson watched him with curiosity as the old man finished one and blew the lead shavings out of it, wiping it slick on the leg of his trousers. Shad put that one in his pocket and started on another.

"What's that for?" Jameson asked him finally.

Shad held the second one up and eyed it critically. "That there is a squaller."

"Squaller? Never heard of it."

"Man told me about them last spring. Says they work pretty good."

"What're they for?"

"Maybe I'll show you sometime, before we get off of this trip."

Jameson knew there was no use prodding him. Shad would tell him in his own good time, if he wanted to. Or he might not do it at all, for he could be as contrary as an old bear.

Shad fixed up four or five bullets with the holes in them, then put away the awl. Presently he glanced at Jameson, puffing the pipe.

"Some of them Sunday-school boys didn't much like it, you puttin' it to them so blunt. But I reckon you'd just as well square off with them right at the first. You ain't exactly got a camp meeting here, and they ain't no deacons."

"It's a hard life, Shad, and it takes hard men. Think I can handle them?"

Blankenship drew deeply on his pipe. "You *got* to."

* * *

They had breakfast over with and the mules all hitched
to the wagons by daybreak. All of them, that is, except
the nigh leader on the chuck wagon, the same knot-head
that had come so near to turning the wagon over in the
creek. With a lightning-quick flick of his hind foot he
dealt the cook a glancing blow to the left leg that sent
him spinning.

So angry he couldn't even cuss, the cook tried to get
up, fell, tried to reach the mule with a whip, couldn't,
and finally grabbed up a handy rock and heaved it at him.
It missed.

Jameson ran to the man. He knelt down and carefully
felt of the leg.

"Doesn't seem to be broken. Need somebody to drive
for you?"

Pruitt got his voice back and exercised it well, showing
a wide range of vocabulary. Then he said, "All I need is
the loan of your buffalo gun and one cartridge."

Jameson wanted to smile, but he didn't. Seldom had
he seen such magnificent anger.

"I'll take that mule out of the traces and throw him
back with the loose bunch," Jameson offered.

The cook considered that, then slowly shook his head.
"No, leave him where he's at. I'll get a right smart of
pleasure popping his rump with a whip every time he
wiggles an ear."

Two teamsters finished harnessing the cook's team for
him while Jameson helped him up into the wagon seat.
Pruitt rubbed his leg tenderly.

"Come noon," he said, "it'll be blacker than the ace
of spades."

He picked up his heavy rawhide whip with a certain
fondness and fixed a baleful eye on the mule. "Ready,
anytime."

They moved out without further incident, and things

went well enough until past noon. About two o'clock Shad Blankenship motioned Jameson up to the lead and pointed toward a rise in the prairie. Jameson squinted. It was a long way off, and at first he thought it was a couple of antelope, watching the wagons in their great curiosity.

But Shad Blankenship had the eagle-keen eye of a man who'd been dodging Indians for forty years.

"Cheyenne," Shad said. "They been watching us quite a spell."

"Hunting party?"

The old man grunted and shrugged his shoulders. "More than likely. But then an Injun will hunt for a good many things besides game, you give him half a chance."

Jameson looked back at the wagons, not liking the way they were straggling out. He didn't think anybody else had seen the Indians yet. He reached down for the reassuring feel of the saddle gun under his leg. He had left the heavy Fifty in one of the wagons.

"I'll ride out and have a look," he said. "You better get those wagons pulled up close together. Have them ready to circle in a hurry."

Shad moved to comply, then pulled up short and pointed back to the rise. "You don't need to ride out. They're comin' to us."

Suddenly the two Indians had multiplied to twenty-five or thirty, moving down toward the wagons. Not fast— just an easy walk—easy and determined the way only an Indian could be.

"Powwow, looks like," Jameson said. "But pull those wagons into a circle, just the same."

By now others had seen the Indians, and the word passed back down the line like fire crackling through the cured dry grass. Gun barrels glinted as the men on the wagons prepared themselves. The stock tender quickly shoved the spare horses and mules in close. At Shad's signal the wagons began pulling into a circle, the stock inside.

King spurred his horse into a lope. Flanked by his hulking man Trencher, he pulled to a stop beside Jameson.

"War party?" he asked. Jameson saw no excitement about the man, nor a trace of fear. King was as cold as the waters of the Arkansas in January.

"Hunting party, I imagine. But it could turn into a war party if they like the odds. We can't let them come into camp."

He noticed the way Trencher deliberately drew his saddle gun from its sweat-caked scabbard. No need to check the load. It would always be loaded. Trencher's eyes were hard, eyes that enjoyed looking down the barrel of a rifle at an Indian. Or maybe at anybody.

Jameson said, "Go easy on that rifle."

A sudden defiance flashed into Trencher's gray eyes, as if to say: I'm King's man, not yours.

Jameson spoke evenly. "What I said last night goes for you, too."

King reached across and touched Trencher's arm. "He's the wagon master. Listen to him."

Trencher nodded resentfully. He wasn't a man who liked to be ordered around. Jameson had an idea he would as soon tell King where to head in as he would anybody else. And King more than likely would knock him flat on his back.

The Indians stopped a couple of hundred yards from the wagons. The leader made some show of handing his weapons over to the braves beside him so the white men would know he was coming in unarmed.

He was Cheyenne, all right, a warrior of some years, obviously a leader of standing. He rode in slowly, proud, arrogant, dark eyes touching each man briefly, then somehow picking Jameson as the leader. He was looking at Jameson as he reined up twenty feet short and swung his arm in an arc, pointing northward. He did it twice, and there was no mistaking what he meant by it.

You're over the line, he was saying in effect. You're on forbidden ground. Go north, to your own treaty lands.

Jameson shook his head negatively and pointed south. He swept his hand toward the wagons and again pointed south.

Even at the distance, he could see anger flare in the old warrior's black eyes. The Cheyenne pointed at his own chest, then northward, and said something.

Jameson looked at Shad, puzzled. "He's trying to talk English."

The Indian tried it again. *"So-ja. So-ja."*

Shad spoke. "He said 'soldier.' He's trying to say he's fixin' to fetch the soldiers."

Trencher lifted his rifle. "He ain't bringing no soldiers."

Jameson's pistol leaped into his hand.

"Trencher!" He let the man hear the deadly click of the hammer.

Trencher lowered the rifle. His eyes seared Jameson, and there was murder in them. Then he roughly jerked his horse around and spurred back toward the King wagons.

King said, "Trencher's got a head like a rock."

Without patience, Jameson replied, "You remember the agreement. Either he takes orders from me or he leaves the outfit."

"I'll talk to him, and he'll take orders. I'll need him, later on."

The Indian had sat solemnly watching it all. His eyes had widened when Trencher brought up the rifle, and his hands had lifted on the rawhide reins tied to the lower lip of his paint horse. But he had made no move to run.

To Shad Blankenship, Jameson said, "You speak Cheyenne, and I'm poor at it. Tell him we want to treat with him. Tell him there's no need for the soldiers."

It took Shad four times as many words to get it into Cheyenne, and he made much use of his hands, Indian style. The Indian replied, talking for at least a minute. It took Shad only seconds to put it into English.

"He says we're south of the treaty line in Cheyenne hunting grounds. Says the buffalo is scarce enough without us makin' an extra swath through them. Says get, and get fast."

"Tell him we've got gifts for him. Tell him we're passing through his land without killing any buffalo. Tell him we're going across the Cimarron to the Staked Plains, into the Comanche country."

Shad translated that, and Jameson thought he could almost see a smile on the old Indian's face. The Cheyenne talked for two minutes.

Jameson eased a little. "I thought he might be happier if we promised him gifts."

A spark of laughter came into Shad's pale eyes. "It ain't the gifts made him grin. It's that we're goin' into the Comanche country. Says this is one bunch of buffalo hunters he won't have to worry about again."

Jameson winced. The man who said Indians had no sense of humor didn't know much about Indians. But occasionally their jokes got a little too close to where a man lived.

King guffawed. His sense of humor was as bad as an Indian's, Jameson thought sourly.

"Go get him some tobacco, Shad," Jameson said, "and a little sugar."

Blankenship brought these things and handed them to the Cheyenne. The old warrior received them with dignity. He began talking again. In a moment Shad turned back to Jameson.

"Says this ain't much. Says the white men killed most of the buffalo, and his braves' bellies are empty. Says ain't we got somethin' for his men?"

Impatience stirred in Jameson. They hadn't killed any buffalo yet. How could they furnish meat for all these Indians?

He heard a stamping of hoofs and the squeal of fighting mules. He looked back toward the wagons, straightening as an idea hit him.

"Tell him yes, we've got something for him. Just wait a little."

Quickly Jameson rode to the chuck wagon.

"Pruitt, hand me a piece of rope." He signaled a couple of men to come to him. "Help me unharness this mule, then go get another one out of the loose bunch to take his place."

Reb Pruitt came close to smiling as Jameson put a loop around the cantankerous nigh leader's neck and pulled the harness off.

Jameson led the mule back and handed the rope to the chief. The old Indian made no effort to hide his delight at this tasty gift. His smile didn't even break when the mule stretched its neck, teeth gleaming, and tried to bite a chunk out of the paint horse.

The Cheyenne wished them a good trip over the Cimarron, then led his unwilling prize away.

Jameson signaled the wagons to move out again. And as the chuck wagon came by, a new mule in harness, the little Texas cook said:

"Jameson, I reckon you're a fair to middlin' kind of a Yankee after all."

* * *

The Cimarron!

For years Jameson had heard of it. Now he was seeing it for the first time as it quartered its way slowly down across the plains.

It wasn't much to look at here, the banks sandy, almost flat. Dried salt glistened on the ground far beyond the present bounds of the river, showing where it overflowed during its occasional sudden floods. The river itself was two hundred yards wide, maybe closer to three.

"Looks shallow enough to wade," he said as Shad Blankenship pulled his horse up beside him and looked down at the reddish water which moved sluggishly through the sand.

"Don't fool yourself," Shad said. "There's a heap sight more to this river than meets the eye. She's quicksand, all the way."

Jameson knew. He'd heard a lot about this river. Its deep bed was filled with sand. Through it moved a treacherous undercurrent which dragged down the unwary. He had seen other quicksand streams filled with the rotting corpses of buffalo which had been bogged down and had died there, helpless. Men said this one was the worst of all.

"We'd better hunt us a crossing," Jameson said.

While the wagons waited, he and Shad moved up the river. A few hundred yards away they found an old, well-beaten buffalo trail leading into the water. He looked up at Shad.

"You seldom go wrong, following the buffalo trails."

"Maybe," Shad said. "But there ain't no crossing safe forever. The sand moves around."

Jameson spurred into the water. Within fifteen feet of the bank he could feel the drag of the quicksand on his horse's feet. The bay felt it, too. He moved quickly, nervously, not letting his feet stay in one place long enough to get caught. Jameson rode him all the way across, Shad following.

Gaining the far bank, Jameson reined up to let his horse breathe.

"Not too bad," he said. "We need to pack it some."

On the other side again, they signaled the wagons up to the crossing. Then they went for the extra mules and horses.

"We'll put them back and forth across, six or eight times," Jameson said. "Pack the bottom down so the wagons can get over easier."

By the time the horses and mules had splashed across the muddy river for the last time, the bottom was as solid as Jameson could ever hope for it to be. They unhitched the doubled wagons and took them across one at a time. The chuck wagon was the first to go.

Reb Pruitt popped his whip at the team. The mules hit the water, splashing mud over the Texan as he cursed them on. Only once did the wagon slow down. The whip popped and sang, Pruitt standing up in the bed of the wagon, his lusty voice reaching clearly across the river. In moments the wagon had gained the far bank and pulled up, the dirty water trailing back to the river in deep ruts the iron rims had left. Pruitt pulled up far out of the way and proceeded to make camp.

The next wagon rolled in, and the next, and the next. When half of them were over, the mules were brought back and hitched to the trail wagons.

When all had finished the crossing, Jameson sat his horse on the bank and looked back at the angry boil of red mud which bled slowly down the river from the line where the wagons had gone over.

Shad Blankenship swung down beside him and stretched his weary legs. "Life's full of river crossings of one kind and another, seems like. We've put a tough one behind us, Gage.''

Jameson nodded and faced back around. He looked south across the great reach of open, rolling plains. From here on, they would have little to go by. There were no maps, no descriptions other than the vaguest kinds.

Ahead of them now lay the Llano Estacado, the Staked Plains, the great unknown land. Anglos had probed at the edges of this great mystery, but few had penetrated deeply into it. None were known ever to have gone completely across.

Far, far to the south lay the settlements of Texas. To the east strung the great dusty cattle trails over which millions of Longhorns were being trekked northward to the shining new ribbons of steel. To the west huddled the ancient adobe villages of New Mexico.

Yet here in the center was this vast tableland of buffalo grass, stretching on and on, dreaded because it was unknown. Unknown because none had yet had the heart it took to try it. Even the army had left it alone. Most of the maps still left it blank.

A few went so far as to say why. A few said the word that really explained: *Comanche!*

Gage Jameson looked southward into the edge of this great land and felt a chilling awe come over him. He knew he was going where few white men had ever gone. He might see land no white man's eyes had ever seen.

Never before in his life had he felt so alone, had he felt this tingle that moved up his spine as he looked southward into the forbidden land. He had crossed the Cimarron. Somehow he knew that something had changed. Nothing would ever be quite the same again.

6

SOUTH OF the Cimarron, then across the narrow neutral strip. And one day Jameson knew they must be in Texas.

Already he had begun to see a difference. Here the grass did not grow tall and rank as it had in Kansas. He had heard tell of this great turf of short grass stretching down across the Texas plains like a huge rolling carpet. Hardly more than boot-top high, the dry leaves curling like thin wood shavings—buffalo and mesquite grass, with a strength unmatched by the taller feed to the north. And it had a little longer to go before winter too, because this was farther south.

He stepped out of the saddle and poked with the toe of his heavy boot at the cured brown grass. He kneeled and felt of it and looked up keenly at Shad Blankenship.

"Been a good while since it rained, you can tell that. And the summer has been plenty hot down here, I'd bet my boots. But look how much green this stuff still carries at the base.''

Shad nodded. ''Sure, she's a real buffalo country, Gage. That's why they like to drift south come fall. Grass down here stays strong through the winter—don't dry up and go weak like broomstraw. You mark me, young'un, there's gonna be buffalo enough down here for everybody.''

So they moved on south, the iron wheel rims leaving the dry grass broken and crushed to the ground, the trails stretching out behind like endless ribbons. Gage Jameson rode far out in the lead, topping every rise, his eyes searching eagerly for the distant black dots that meant buffalo grazing out across the plains.

But he didn't see them. Always there were buffalo chips, some not long dry. In places great concentrations of the shaggy beasts had grazed the grass down almost to the ground. Everywhere there were the deep corduroy buffalo trails, often dozens of them running parallel, only feet apart.

But now the buffalo had gone.

Three days the wagons lumbered slowly along, the crews breaking camp late and setting up again early in the afternoons, while Gage Jameson, Shad Blankenship and Ransom King scattered out to scour the prairie, to search up and down every creek and header they could find. Each evening the riders followed the wheel tracks into camp and dismounted stiffly from tired horses, their faces telling the other men without need for words. There weren't any buffalo.

Firewood was scarce on these long stretches of grass, even up and down some of the little creeks. Reb Pruitt began using wood only to kindle his fires, then kept them going with dried buffalo chips.

''Some deal,'' the Texan laughed, raking the fire and

adding the fuel that was a staple of the plains. "We come after buffalo hides and all we find is buffalo chips."

But if it was a joke to Pruitt, some weren't taking it that way.

Jameson could feel the restlessness among the crew even before the complaints began. The first he heard was from a man named Tully, one of the three old Miles and Posey men he had been able to hire. It wasn't meant for his ears, but he heard it anyway, from the off side of a wagon.

"The boys was beginnin' to say he was jinxed that last trip out. Maybe they was right. He never found much buffalo then. He ain't findin' any now. There's plenty of sign—we've all seen it. But where's the buffalo?"

Jameson made no reply—didn't even let the men know he had heard. Out in camp this way, they always tended to gripe when things weren't running to suit them. A man had to expect it.

But the fact that they were talking began to rowel him. He rode harder, looked a little farther each time he went out.

Then one day, along with the buffalo sign, he found something else. Horse sign, and a lot fresher. Unshod horses, a couple of them with ragged hoofs badly in need of a trimming. He followed them a way, coming at length to a creek lined with hackberries. There the men had dismounted to drink and water their mounts. The footprints remained plain in the mud. No heels. No straightedged leather soles. These had been flat-bottomed moccasins, the toes tending inward.

Comanches.

In camp he told Shad Blankenship. Shad just nodded his rusty head.

"Seen it yesterday. Found an antelope they'd put an arrow in and took the guts and a hindquarter from."

"Why didn't you tell me?"

"No use getting the camp all stirred up. Anyhow, you knowed there was gonna be Injuns before you ever started." A flicker of humor showed in Shad Blankenship's sharp old eyes. "I thought we was huntin' buffalo."

Impatience prodded Jameson. Shad's idea of a joke would be a scalp-hungry Indian catching a bald man.

"I want to know about the Indians, anyway, in case they decide to start hunting *us*," Jameson retorted.

It was a hunter's paradise, if the hunter had anything besides buffalo on his mind. Every day Jameson spotted antelope grazing in scattered bunches. At sight of him their heads would bob up, and off they would go in a flash of broad white tails. They would run awhile, then stop upon a rise and look back at him, standing in single file like a string of Indians, poised to run again if he angled their way.

Then there were the lobo wolves, bigger than most dogs, ranging far out from water, preying on jackrabbits and prairie hens and anything else that didn't get out of their way, watching all the while for buffalo or other large animals that might be lamed or mired or somehow at a disadvantage. Their slashing fangs could bring down a full-grown buffalo, with their superb teamwork and just a little luck.

Along the creeks Jameson saw quail, mink, skunk and raccoon, and on one timbered stream, beaver.

It seemed to him that he had never in his life seen anything quite like it. Here in the brown weeks before the onset of winter, these high Texas plains seemed to be reaching their peak. The grass was cured. The game was fat and sleek, putting on hair for the cold times not far distant. The prairie and its teeming life drowsed under an autumn sun that had lost the sullen scorch of summer but still possessed a gentle and loving warmth.

A wonderful country, Jameson thought.

But where were the buffalo?

Taking care of the livestock was the biggest problem he had, for here on the Llano Estacado lived the best natural horse thieves ever born. With so many horses and mules, hobbling and sidelining every one of them at night would be a monumental task. Instead, he circled the wagons, putting the horses and mules inside the circle for protection against the rare skill of the Comanche.

A sudden low growl almost at his ear snapped Gage Jameson out of a sound sleep in the middle of the night. He sat up straight, shoving back his blankets and grabbing at the six-shooter under his pillow. A gentle hand touched his shoulder.

"Quiet," Shad Blankenship whispered. "The old dog says there's somethin' out yonder that don't belong."

Blankenship's shaggy black mongrel, almost invisible in the pale moonlight, growled in deep-grained hatred.

Jameson held his breath, listening.

All he could hear was the gentle night breeze with its autumn chill, searching restlessly among the wagons. That, and the dry rumble deep in the throat of the big black dog.

Shad Blankenship sat rigid, listening, too. But Jameson knew Shad couldn't hear anything. Age had sharpened his eyes, but his hearing wasn't what it used to be.

The dog suddenly stiffened, hackles rising. Jameson sank to the ground, looking in the same direction, trying to see some movement against the sky. He waited a long moment, hardly breathing. Then he caught it—the form of a man crouched low, stepping slowly, carefully, almost straight at the wagon under which Jameson lay. He saw the slant of a feather.

Indian. Jameson wondered how many more there were.

The dog's growl went louder. The Indian stopped suddenly, hearing it.

There was not enough light for good aim. Jameson drew back the hammer, aimed by instinct, and squeezed the trigger.

With the sudden crash of the gun, mules and horses jumped, hoofs clumping excitedly on the thick turf of grass. Men burst out of their blankets, yelling. Other guns sounded, the racket echoing off into the night as men fired at shadows and at the wind whispering through the grass.

After a time all went silent again. Men settled down to watchful waiting. Some few even crawled back into blankets and went to sleep again. But most were awake for good, talking nervously in low voices if they talked at all.

Shad Blankenship was as calm as a stock pond on a still day. He stretched out on his blanket, unworried. "I reckon they got as big a scare as we did. They won't be nosing around any more tonight."

"Wonder how many there were?" Jameson mused. "I only saw the one."

"Ain't any tellin'. Maybe just a lone buck wantin' to steal him a horse and make a good showing back in camp. Or maybe a whole passel of them hoping to catch us asleep and leave us afoot. What difference does it make now?"

"Lucky thing that dog of yours smelled them coming."

Blankenship snorted. "Luck, is it? You didn't think I kept that shaggy old monster around for his looks, did you? Wasn't for him, they'd have laid me out in the grass a long time ago."

Jameson grinned, the tension leaving him. "Well, from

now on I don't care if he looks like Lucifer, just so he keeps on hating Indians.''

Best they could make out next morning was that four, maybe five Indians had attempted the raid on the stock. Spots of red in the dry grass proved that Jameson had at least winged a would-be horse thief.

Ransom King came out to look over the sign.

"From now on," Jameson told him, "we'll keep two men on guard at all times, in one-hour shifts. With the stock inside the circle, and that black dog around, we shouldn't have any trouble."

King frowned. "Maybe all the trouble won't be from the Indians."

Jameson looked sharply at him. "What's that supposed to mean?"

"There's a lot of loose talk drifting around the camp. They're saying, some of them, that you're not ever going to find any buffalo. They're saying they don't mind Indian risk when they're skinning hides and making money. But they're not getting any hides."

With a nettle of anger Jameson said, "What do *you* think, King?"

King smiled quickly. "If I didn't believe in you, I wouldn't have joined you with my wagons."

Sometime that night someone shook Jameson's shoulder. He sat up quickly, reaching for the pistol, thinking the Indians were back. But it was a hide handler named Ludlow, a silent, morose, black-bearded man who never mixed with the others, always stayed to himself.

"I think some of the boys has shucked the harness, Jameson," he said. "Tully is gone. I don't know how many of the others."

Jameson stood up angrily, throwing aside the blankets.

"Tully had guard duty just before me," Ludlow said.

"He was supposed to wake me up when it come time to relieve him. He never did."

"There was another man on guard. Where is he?"

"One of Tully's buddies. He's gone, too."

Jameson stomped out into the wagon circle. "Everybody up!"

As the men gathered in the darkness he mentally counted them off. Three gone. Tully and the other two old Miles and Posey hands.

It was too dark to check the livestock, but Jameson knew within reason that they had taken a horse apiece. Saddles too, and he had few of those. He saw his own bay hunting horse standing nearby and felt relief that they hadn't gotten him.

The rest of the men knew now what had happened. He could not tell by their faces whether they were considering trying the same.

Shad Blankenship watched Jameson closely as the anger played in his face. "Nothin' you can do about it now, Gage. They're gone.

Jameson said in a brittle voice, "We're *going* to do something. If we don't, some of the rest may pull the same stunt."

He crawled back between his blankets, but he didn't sleep any more. At the first paling of the night sky he was up and punched Shad awake.

"Roll out, Shad. I may need those eyes of yours."

The cook got up, too. Yawning and scratching and talking incessantly, Pruitt soon had coffee boiling for them, and a bait of antelope meat was ready by the time the two saddled their horses. Jameson impatiently wolfed his down, swung into the saddle and spurred out.

Shad, a slow eater, caught up to him after a while. Jameson was moving into a long-reaching trot, sometimes in a lope, his grim eyes following horse tracks in he grass. The thick turf kept the hoofs from cutting into he ground much, but the brittle grass, broken underfoot, made a trail a man could read.

All morning they rode, slowing down to save the horses when it became clear that they weren't going to make a fast catch. Sometime past noon Jameson began to regret his haste in eating breakfast. Hunger commenced to tug at him. The long ride over the unchanging prairie had drained the anger from him, leaving only a stolid determination. He would catch those men if he had to ride all the way back to the Cimarron.

Presently Shad reached back into his saddlebags and brought out a little bundle done up in oilskin. "Cold biscuits and meat," he said. "Good thing I come. You'd have starved flat to death."

Jameson grinned then, relaxing from the grimness that had held him.

They stopped at a little stream and watered and rested the horses. Impatience prickled Jameson, but judgment told him to wait. Though he could push himself till he dropped, he couldn't ever afford to overpush the horses. He sat and drummed his nervous fingers on his boots, while Shad Blankenship lay so relaxed that Jameson couldn't tell whether he was napping or not.

Presently they were on the go again, pushing as hard as they dared. Along late in the afternoon, Jameson reined up and squinted at something far ahead.

"What does that look like to you, Shad?"

Shad stared, his eyes narrowed against the sun, the reddish brows knitted up close. "It's them. They're restin' by that creek yonder."

Jameson waited a moment before he moved out, looking for a way to ride in close without being seen. He reined the bay around, riding back the way they had come until he passed down under a rise and well out of sight.

Then he angled westward, crossing the creek and coming up in cover of underbrush.

Near the quarry, the two men reined in to study the situation closer.

"Asleep, I think," Shad whispered. "All three of them. Must've rode half the night and all day. Horse about give out, I reckon, and the men, too. If we was Comanches we could get us three juicy new scalps."

"Not looking for scalps, Shad. I just aim to get them horses back."

Dismounting, they tied their own horses. Saddle gun in hand, they eased forward. The creek was shallow, the water not reaching quite to the tops of Jameson's black boots as they waded across. The leather was so heavily greased that little of it would seep through.

The two were within twenty yards of the sleeping men when one of the horses suddenly raised its head and whinnied. Tully jerked erect, blinking and feeling desperately for the rifle that lay beside him.

"Don't touch it," Jameson said evenly. "Just stand up there and leave it alone. The rest of you the same."

The other two were awake now. One glared at the other. "Thought you was gonna keep watch."

"Shut up," Tully barked impatiently at them. Then to Jameson he said sullenly, "All right, so you caught up with us. Now I guess you're taking us back."

"No," Jameson said, "I don't want you back. I don't want to have to watch you all the time we're out."

"Then what did you trail us for?"

"Those horses. They're mine."

The runaways stiffened. Tully licked his dry lips. His voice lifted. "Look, Jameson, this is the middle of Comanche country. You wouldn't set a man afoot out here would you?"

"You'll have your guns. And you're halfway to the

Cimarron already. Walk all night and hide all day. You can be in Dodge in a couple of weeks if you get high behind.''

Tully's eyes were frightened. He looked down at his rifle on the ground, then up at Jameson, but he didn't dare make the try.

''Pick up their guns, Shad,'' Jameson said. ''We'll carry them with us a ways, then drop them off.''

The men looked around them at these endless plains which reached on into infinity. They were awesome enough to a man on horseback, but they were terrifying to a man afoot. Jameson could see dread settle over the runaways like a black shroud.

A hollowness was in Tully's voice. His eyes pleaded. ''Jameson, this is the worst thing you could do to a man.''

''Not quite,'' Jameson replied flatly, without pity. ''Hanging's rougher. That's what horse thieves generally get.''

He waited until Shad brought up their horses. Mounting, he started to push the three runaways' mounts southward again. Then he stopped just long enough to untie canteens and sacks of supplies from behind two saddles and let them drop to the ground. He gave them this gesture of mercy, and this one only.

After they had ridden awhile, pushing the three horses in front of them, Jameson dropped the guns to the ground and looked back. The three men trailed them at a walk, a far piece behind. They wouldn't get to the rifles in time to use them.

Shad Blankenship grinned. ''I been worried all day what you was gonna do when you caught up to them. I was afraid this morning you was fixin' to shoot all three.''

"This morning," Jameson said flatly, "I was mad enough to."

It was well past midnight by the stars when Jameson's instinct led him to the camp, and he saw the red glow of campfire coals, kept barely alive by the succession of guards. They turned the horses loose. Then, before he did anything else, Jameson walked around the camp, grimly counting the men rolled up in their blankets.

Ransom King sat at the remains of the campfire, drinking black coffee which Pruitt kept on the coals all night for the guards. He didn't get up as Jameson and Shad approached wearily. He sat there, watching.

Jameson poured himself a cup of coffee, and Shad followed suit. Jameson sat on his heels, his eyes touching Ransom King. King silently studied him awhile before he brought out the question. The way he said it, it wasn't really a question at all.

"You fetched back the horses but no men."

"They won't be coming back."

King's eyebrows arched, and in the firelight his gaze dropped to Jameson's gun.

Jameson said, "I didn't shoot them. But by the time they walk all the way back to Dodge, they may wish I had."

King poured the dregs of coffee out into the grass, pushed to his feet and stood there, some dark humor seeming to stir him.

"You've got a soft streak in you, Jameson. *I'd* have shot them."

He walked off into the darkness, toward his wagon.

Shad Blankenship watched him disappear, then commented, "He would have, too. He's got it in his eyes."

Jameson nodded. He remembered the fury in King's eyes that night the man had rescued him in the Dodge saloon. He knew King could catch afire as easily as he could break into wild laughter.

Jameson finished his coffee, letting it drive out the chill the night air had settled upon him. Then he crawled into his own blankets. But he didn't sleep. He lay awake, listening, watching.

Sometime up in the morning Shad Blankenship's snoring broke off. He lay quiet a little, then raised up on one elbow.

"You ain't ever been asleep, have you?" he said, frowning.

Jameson shook his head. Weariness was stone-heavy on him, but worry was heavier.

There was a little of admiration in the old man's voice, and admiration didn't come lightly to Shad Blankenship. "Then sleep. Nobody is fixin' to slip away this far up in the mornin'. Anyhow, I'll watch. It don't take much sleep for an old man."

Jameson hadn't expected the men to like the way he had set the runaways afoot. He wasn't much surprised, then, when at breakfast he felt the hostile eyes of some of the crew upon him. They didn't say anything. They didn't have to. But he could smell revolt in the air, just as he could smell a faint hint of winter in the dawn wind.

He ate in silence, counting those men he felt might side with him, and the count didn't come to much. Only two men were left with whom he had ever worked—Shad Blankenship and Messick.

Looking at Reb Pruitt, he mentally gave him a question mark. This small, thin man was a good cook, and Jameson had an idea he was a scrapper from way back yonder in spite of his flapping jaw. But Jameson was a Yankee, and so was the rest of the crew. He didn't think Pruitt was going to get worked up much over any kind of a fight between Yankees. More likely he would sit on his hands and grin as he watched it.

He glanced at the hide handler Ludlow, that brooding, heavy-bearded man who sat to himself now as he ate. He made friends with no man, and he never spoke except when it was necessary to the work.

Jameson shook his head. No, he didn't think Ludlow would help him, either. There would be no one except Shad Blankenship and Messick. And maybe Ransom King. Maybe. . . .

One thing certain, Jameson couldn't afford to get out of sight of the camp. It was his conviction that most of the crew—maybe all of it—would appropriate horses and mules and head north the minute he was gone over the hill.

"Shad," he said, "I've been trying to keep north, so we wouldn't have so far to go if we were forced to run for it. But now I'm pointing them south, across the Canadian. We'll find buffalo if we have to drive all the way to the Rio Grande."

Jameson allowed himself to ride as far ahead as he could without letting the wagons drop back out of his sight. They crossed over the sandy Canadian, fighting its treacherous undercurrent much as they had done at the Cimarron. Then they pushed on south, angling a little westward.

Long days came and went, and long nights in which Jameson slept little or not at all, trusting hardly anyone any more. Bone-weariness and the lack of sleep sank his eyes back deep beneath his brows, put an aching slump in his shoulders. But he kept on riding, kept on watching the men, kept on looking for buffalo.

In camp at evening the men gathered silently around a poker game that started as soon as supper was over and lasted far into the night. Almost invariably the winner was the man who promoted the game, a short, fat little skinner named Blair Farley, a man with a loud, quarrelsome voice and thick, stubby fingers which were amazingly efficient with a deck of cards. His greedy eyes seemed able to read a man's thoughts. Already his pocket was stuffed with IOU's against half the wages the men might expect to earn on this expedition—if they found buffalo.

This too was making the crew surly, knowing that much of their pay already was gone. It added to the charge of tension that slowly built up in the camp.

Sometimes even Shad Blankenship's eyes turned longingly to that poker game.

Then one day about noon Jameson heard a shout and blinked quickly at a movement atop a promontory half a mile southward. Shad Blankenship had ridden out on a scout. Now he came spurring his dun horse, the dust rising behind him.

One thought raced to Jameson's mind. Comanches. He reached down for his saddle gun and at the same time yelled to the men on the wagons.

"Look sharp. It may be trouble."

But it wasn't trouble. Shad eased up on the speed as he loped in. He drew rein and stopped the heaving horse just in front of Jameson. A wide grin cut across his dusty, red-bearded face.

"We've found them, Gage," he said excitedly, loudly enough for the men to hear him. "They're over that hill yonder and down the valley, a million of them. We've found the buffalo!"

7

THE WEARINESS seemed to lift from Jameson's wide shoulders and the burning tiredness from his blue eyes as he stepped stiffly off his horse atop the hill. He gazed down the creek with its scattering of big cottonwoods, its banks lined with smaller timber. His look moved on out across the level prairie where not a mesquite or sagebrush blocked the view. His pulse quickened.

There they were, the buffalo, scattered in small grazing bunches as uncountable as the stars in a crisp night sky, fly-specks out yonder as far as a man could see. They brought up bittersweet memories of old days on the Republican and the Arkansas, times that had vanished with the high-plains wind.

There were bunches of cows, many of them trailed by big stocky, glossy calves, blackish brown now after shedding the reddish hair of their first months. Some calves grazed alone, already weaned. In among the cows he could see young spike bulls, not old enough yet to challenge the big bulls for mastery, not ready to take their place as sires. The older bulls grazed separately now, in little groups of three or four to as many as twenty. Breeding season was over.

Far out yonder amid the specks of black, Jameson saw a band of antelope, and a big gray timber wolf sneaking along looking for the crippled or sick, the buffalo warily eyeing him, an occasional bull tossing his head threateningly.

Jameson watched a pair of old bulls in a buffalo wallow, rolling in the dust, digging in with their horns and throwing dirt high over their backs with their massive heads, trying to drive away the buffalo gnats.

Presently the wagons came. Men walked to the top of the hill to gaze out upon the sight. The threat of rebellion had disappeared like a wisp of smoke.

No one shouted. No one jumped up and down. Men stared silently or swore softly to themselves. They stood there a long time as if they couldn't see enough of it, as if they had never seen buffalo before. Even the somber Ludlow, who had never shown any emotion except an everlasting contempt for his fellow man, softened and smiled a little, squatting on the grass and unconsciously whetting a skinning knife against the black leather tops of his high boots.

"You men just stay here and look awhile," Jameson said. "Shad and I are going to hunt a good place to make camp."

The creek flowed in a northerly direction, emptying into the Canadian somewhere above. The two men rode southward toward the head of it. Bands of buffalo grunted and scattered away from water. The animals would run off a way, then stop and turn to look back with their tiny weak eyes, water dripping from the long stringy beards that sometimes almost dragged the ground.

"Ain't got much fear for a man on horseback, have they?" Shad commented. "Ain't been choused much— maybe none at all."

Jameson nodded in satisfaction. "That's a hopeful sign. Means the Indians haven't been hunting around here."

Jameson picked a flat spot high up enough from the creek bed so that a sudden rise of floodwater wasn't likely to wash away the camp, yet close enough so that water-carrying would not become burdensome. A few big cottonwoods there would spread shade over the men working in camp during the heat of the autumn afternoons. Smaller timber would provide fuel for the fires and poles for the rough, semipermanent corrals that would take the place of the wagon circle in protecting the stock at night.

Jameson saw more buffalo grazing upwind along the creek.

"Shad," he said, "you go bring the wagons, I'll try to get us some fresh meat."

He slipped the saddle gun out of the scabbard, circled around downwind of the buffalo and came up behind them. When he was close enough, he let them see him. They started down the creek toward the camp site, shuffling along in a trot. He picked out a nice fat cow which either hadn't had a calf this year or had already weaned it so she could store up flesh to carry the next calf already conceived within her. He let her pass on through the camp site so there wouldn't be any lingering smell from the butchering.

When she was about right, he spurred in and fired at her from the saddle, aiming at her lungs. The second shot slowed her, and the third brought her to the ground. He stepped down from the horse, dropped the reins and

moved up. Taking care that she didn't thrash her head
and catch him on those sharp curved horns, he stepped
in with his thick-bladed ripping knife and cut her throat
to bleed her and lessen the risk of spoiling the meat.

Soon the wagons arrived. The crew began setting up
camp, unloading gear, emptying several wagons which
would be used to haul fresh green hides back to camp as
the kill got under way.

Messick and another skinner set to work on the cow
Jameson had killed. They slit through the jawbone first
and took out the tongue. They ripped the hide up the
belly and skinned out the legs past the knee. With their
curved skinning knives they began to lay the hide back
away from the flesh, working from the belly downward
toward the back bone on one side, then straining together
as they turned the heavy carcass over to skin out the
other. Normally they would hitch a pair of mules to peel
the hide off once they got it started. But this kill was for
meat, and the hide under the carcass would help to keep
it clean.

Jameson put the other men to work chopping posts and
poles for corrals and digging holes to set the posts in.

With a purpose before him now, something there that
he could see, he no longer felt his weariness. Having
something to work for gave him new wind and new will.
He walked back and forth through camp a hundred times,
making plans, directing work, pitching in where it wasn't
going fast enough. When it looked as if the corral job
was moving along satisfactorily, he walked out to the flat
area downwind of camp, the hide-drying and stretching
ground. It had to be cleared of tree limbs, dead stumps
and other obstructions.

By dark the fence posts were up. The poles hadn't been
laid between them, and there wasn't time now before
night. But long ropes tied to the posts made a handy

enough substitute for one night. Maybe tomorrow. . . .

He flopped down across his bedroll, savoring the good dry smell of burning wood and thinking he would rest awhile before supper.

When he awoke the sun was coming up red on the cloudless eastern horizon. Someone, Shad of course, had spread blankets over him to protect him from the night chill. He pushed them back and grinned sheepishly at the old man who sat cross-legged, studying him with amusement in the glow of dawn light.

"Thanks, Shad."

Shad made a "forget it" motion with his big old freckled hand. "You look a heap sight better this mornin'. Got them black satchels out from under your eyes for a change. Think you're ready to shoot some buffalo?"

"That's what we came for."

The hump steak from the fat buffalo cow, he thought, was the finest he'd ever sunk a tooth in.

Ransom King walked over and sat down beside him as he finished breakfast. King was already shaved. He wore clean clothes, although they were rumpled from the trip.

"I'm ready to do some shooting this morning, Jameson, if you are."

Jameson nodded. "We'd better pick our hunting grounds so we won't be shooting at each other. Shad and I will go south this morning. Why don't you work north, down the creek?" He looked at King's rifle and saw that it was a Sharps like his own.

"We'd better learn the sound of each other's guns," Jameson said. "Maybe it'll be important someday, if we hear guns that don't belong to us."

King said, "Good idea. I'll do my own shooting, as far as I can. If my skinners get to catching up with me too fast, Trencher can help me bring down a few."

They waited around camp, helping finish preparations, until Jameson's big pocket watch showed it to be nine o'clock. There was plenty to do.

"Let's get started, Shad," Jameson said finally. "They ought to have grazed by now."

With bellies full of the strong grass and the morning sun getting warm, the buffalo would settle down, stop moving around. Listless then, they were less likely to scare away at the roar of the big guns.

Jameson slipped on his coat with the deep pockets that held extra shells. He fastened the cartridge belt around his waist, every one of the thirty-two loops holding a loaded cartridge. Shad Blankenship did the same.

"Never have taken a good look at that gun of yours, Shad," Jameson said. Shad handed it to him. It was a Sharps Forty-five, a fourteen-pounder with a thick octagonal barrel that could stand the heat of a lot of firing. Jameson rubbed his hands over its smooth finish and read the two words imprinted deeply on the left-hand side of the breech, *Patented 1869.*

"Used to carry a Fifty, didn't you?"

Shad grunted. "Used to be young, too. But for a man of my age, this fourteen pounds turns to forty soon enough. I just got to get a mite closer sometimes, that's all."

The wagons followed them, drawn by four mules apiece. Two mules could do it, but a man never could tell what might be over that next hill in strange country. Four mules in a run could pull a heap faster than two.

In half an hour the two horsemen rode partway up an eminence, far enough so that they could easily see over it. A couple of hundred buffalo were scattered under the brow of the hill, some still grazing a little, most of them full and resting, already chewing cuds, lying with noses to the wind.

"Fair chance of a good stand down there for both of us," Jameson said, and the old man nodded.

Jameson didn't need to wet his finger and stick it up to get the drift of the breeze. It was out of the northwest and had been all morning. They rode back down from the point and eased a little farther south, so the breeze blew from the buffalo to them.

The skinners crawled out of the wagons and squatted in the grass, patiently sharpening their ripping and skinning knives on the steel that each man carried on his belt. One man drank water from a five-gallon keg that was wrapped in a piece of old woolen blanket, wet to keep it cool. Here the men would wait, out of the way, until the shooting was done.

Blair Farley was already shuffling his cards, trying to promote a time-passing game.

There was nothing to tie the horses to, but nothing was needed. They had been trained to stand where the reins were dropped. Jameson and Shad left them and walked directly up the side of the little hill. Pausing a moment at the top to look the situation over, they started down again on the other side, walking carefully, directly at the buffalo.

It was a peculiarity of the buffalo that he paid little attention to a man afoot, especially if the man walked straight at him. Jameson thought it was probably because the buffalo could detect little motion that way, his eyes being weak and sometimes half grown over with thick hair. Many times Jameson had walked up within rock-throwing distance of buffalo before they began to shy away. On horseback he could never have approached so close.

Two hundred yards from the buffalo, Shad said quietly, "About far enough. Too close the first time and they're sure liable to scatter."

Carefully, making as little motion as possible, Jameson sat down, taking off his cartridge belt and laying it on the dry grass before him where he could easily reach it. He removed the coat and laid it out where he could get to the extra cartridges in the pockets and keep the belt loops full. He laid down his canteen, which he might have to use to cool the barrel.

He looked at Shad, seated six feet from him so they wouldn't be in each other's way. His eyes asked, "Ready?" and Shad nodded.

There was usually a leader in any bunch. If this leader moved away, the others would follow him. Without him, the buffalo generally stood around in confusion. There never was any sure way to know which one the leader was. For that, a man had to depend on instinct.

A big cow was looking around suspiciously, her nose in the air, testing the breeze. Jameson eased down to a prone position, setting up the rest stick over which to lay the heavy barrel of the Big Fifty. He studied the breeze, thought he knew how much to allow for it. He shoved the cartridge into the breech, took long, deliberate aim, held his breath and squeezed the trigger.

The deep roar was enough to set a man's ears to ringing. The cow jerked violently and began backing up, slinging her head. He had missed the target, he knew. He had shattered her jaw. A few more seconds of this, throwing the blood around that way, and she would stampede the whole bunch.

At the heavy boom of the gun, the other buffalo shied. Those which had been lying down jumped up. But they didn't run. They stood in confusion, not knowing what was happening, not seeing any enemy.

Jameson aimed and fired again, correcting his windage. The puff of dust just behind the cow's shoulder was right where he had tried to hit her. She squatted back, hind legs going limp. She swung her head from side to side, then lay over heavily, kicked a time or two and sank slowly into death, her little black eyes staring into nothingness.

Shad Blankenship squeezed off a shot. Another buffalo staggered a step, then fell.

Jameson looked up and saw the white smoke of the gunpowder rising, drifting off into the gentle wind. On a still day a man could nearly suffocate himself in smoke with a Sharps. And no joke about it, he could deafen himself eventually, exposing his ears to the roar of the big guns year in and year out.

They settled down to shooting them, taking their time to keep from overheating the guns, yet wasting no time, either. Nearly every shot bagged a buffalo, although sometimes it took an extra bullet or two to dispatch one. Instead of running, the other buffalo would look on in bewilderment. After the first few shots, they stopped shying from the roar of the guns. A few even lay back down, losing interest in the strange noise and going back to chewing their cuds.

"Good thing we got a little breeze," Shad said quietly. "Keeps them from gettin' the blood smell."

At length an old cow began to move away, and it looked for a moment as if the rest of the bunch would follow, breaking up the stand. Jameson drew a bead, allowing more windage for the long shot because she was at least four hundred yards away. The first shot stopped her momentarily, sent her squatting. But she got up again and began to move once more, dragging a little.

Jameson thought the stand was lost. Then she stopped and turned sideways, looking back as if to find her hidden assailant. Shad's rifle roared at the broad target. The dust puff from the brown hair was just where it should have been. She went down and stayed down.

Jameson looked at the old man in admiration. "Did you ever miss a shot in your life?"

"Once. Didn't eat for four days, either."

After awhile, lying still in the sun, Jameson could feel sweat work from under his hat and trickle slowly down his dusty face. It burned his eyes. When he rubbed them he got gunpowder in them from his hands, and that made it worse. His shoulder ached from the recoil from the big rifle.

He could feel the intense heat from his heavy gun barrel and knew it needed to cool anyway. Opening the breechblock, he picked up the canteen and poured water down the muzzle, jerking his hand away from the scalding steam. When the barrel had cooled some, he pushed the corner of a greased patch into the eyelet of his wiping stick. He ran it into the barrel and worked it up and down to break loose the accumulation of burned powder.

He laid the rifle down to let it cool off. Already he could count some thirty buffalo lying dead or dying on the ground. Shad Blankenship was still shooting, waiting as long as two minutes sometimes between shots. He wasted precious little powder.

It had always been a puzzle to Jameson why the buffalo would stand and take this murderous fire instead of stampeding away. They nosed curiously at the fallen, and now and then a cow hooked at one of the dead. Each time one acted as if it had begun to get the scent of blood, Shad or Jameson brought it down.

For two hours the stand held up, the band of buffalo slowly diminishing. At last the surviving animals commenced to get the blood scent, and then they broke into a run.

"Want to follow them up, Gage?" Shad asked. "They'll settle down in a little while."

Jameson shook his head. "I reckon we've done enough killing for now."

He stood up and walked out among the fallen buffalo. He flinched at the sight of the dead, glassy eyes, the bloody mouths and noses that resulted from the lung shots. Here and there a buffalo still breathed, still kicked. Those Shad and Jameson saw, they finished with their pistols.

Flies already were buzzing around the dead, expecially those shot earliest, where the blood had crusted and turned black.

Shad Blankenship shook his head. "A bloody business, Gage. Man has to get himself a hard stomach to stay in it, and there's few that really enjoy it."

"I never have, Shad. In a way, it doesn't hardly seem right. God put them here, and I expect He had a good reason. Now we're killing them off as fast as we can skin them."

Shad shrugged. "It's a business. About the only one left any more. A man didn't do this, he'd just about starve to death. If we don't shoot them, somebody else will. It's gonna be done, regardless."

Jameson nodded. "It's *got* to be done. It's a bloody job, but I don't reckon it's any worse than killing cattle in a slaughterhouse, except for the waste. And there's not much we can do about the waste. It's too far to market for the meat.

"And as long as there's buffalo, there'll never be any settlement. They feed the Indian and keep him fighting. There's no room for the farmer where the buffalo graze. There's no room for the cowman, either. It's a question of which we're going to have, the buffalo or the settler. When you look at it that way, it's not much of a question, is it?"

They signaled the skinners, who brought up the wagons. Each skinner moved along, testing the sharp blade of his knife across the rump of a fallen cow. If she quivered in reflex, she wasn't quite dead and he moved on to another. If there was no movement, he set right in to skinning.

Shad and Jameson climbed to the top of the hill and sat down there to watch the operation, and to keep an eye out for Indians that might have been drawn by the gunfire.

Shad bit himself a fresh chew of tobacco.

"Funny thing, ain't it? We talk all the time about civilization, and how do we get it? By killin', that's how. I first come out here, it was the beaver. We trapped beaver so the high-toned boys back East could sport them a beaver hat.

"Of course we weren't lookin' ahead. All we bothered about was makin' money. But what was really happening, we was gettin' to know the country. We was opening it up for them that was to come later. When the beaver trade folded, some of us started scouting for immigrant trains and surveyors and one thing and another, and we was shootin' game to feed them. Then the hide trade started, and we commenced to killin' the buffalo.

"And all the time we was killin' the Injuns, too. Killin' so we could have civilization. Some way to get it. Like a marshal I seen once, come to settle down a wild town. Slams his pistol down on the bar and he says, 'We're gonna have peace around here if I have to kill every one of you to get it.' "

Shad shook his rusty head. "And what happens to us old hands then, when civilization does come? We don't fit in. We brung it, but they got no place for us. We wind up in jail, or beggin', or livin' off the county. I seen many of them old mountain men thataway, just drunk theirselves to death. They'd destroyed the only kind of life they could fit in."

Jameson put his hand on Shad's patched knee. "There'll always be a place for you, Shad, as long as I'm around."

Shad looked him straight in the eyes and said, "How do you know there'll even be a place for *you*, Gage?"

8

THE AUTUMN weeks drifted by, the skies of an evening taking on that deep horizon-line purple that meant winter was nearly here. The hair on the buffalo became thicker now. Before long there would be good robe hides that fetched an extra price.

The hunting was all a man could want. Always the drying area was covered with a patchwork of hides, sometimes stretching two hundred yards along the creek. Each day the wagons came in off the hunting grounds loaded with fresh hides green and heavy, sticky with blood and undried flesh. The handlers pitched them down and spread them out upon the ground, dusting them with poison to keep the bugs away. Then they would stretch them on the grass with the hair side down, securing them by pounding pegs down through tiny holes slit in the edge. Here the hides would stay for three or four days, sometimes five or six now that the autumn's daytime heat had largely waned. When well dried, they would be turned over, hair side up. Finally cured, these flint hides would be loaded upon one of the wagons and lashed down, their space on the drying ground given up to fresh hides just coming in.

"Doing mighty well," Jameson said to Shad Blankenship late one afternoon, watching the handlers peg out forty green hides from that day's shooting. "Never saw hunting grounds stand up any better."

"Me, neither," Shad agreed. "Only moved camp twice, and then just a little ways up the creek so we wouldn't have so far to hunt and pack hides. Wouldn't be surprised if we're in Dodge before Christmas."

"You getting ready to go back, Shad?"

Shad pondered a moment, then darkly shook his head. "No, to tell the truth, I ain't. You know what always happens to me when I get to town. This is where I belong at. Even if it *is* a messy job, and a man gits sick of the killin', sometimes I wish I never had to go back. Wish all this would never change."

He turned to Jameson, melancholy in his pale eyes. "What is it gets into a man, Gage? Even with all the blood and sweat and dirt, this is a heap sight better than being in town, drinkin' that swill they sell for whisky, chokin' to death on tobacco smoke while you're losing everything you own in a crooked poker game. What is it gets into a man and sends him runnin' back to town like an ox to the slaughter, ready to take his whippin' again? Why is it a man don't ever have no better sense?"

Jameson shrugged. He didn't have an answer to that. He needed one himself.

Every time he left town, he fully intended to stay out until it was absolutely necessary that he return, and then to stay only long enough to pick up new supplies. But good intentions weren't enough. Now, already, he was beginning to get that restless itch, to start picturing Dodge in glowing colors. He didn't want it to be that way. He wished he could change it. But there it was.

If only he had him something to tie to. . . .

Shad nudged him. "Yonder comes Ransom King and his wagon."

Jameson watched, nodding. "A good hunter, Shad. He's a crack shot. He can put a bullet in a buffalo about as handy as anybody I ever saw."

"Yeah, and seems to enjoy it, too. Ever watch him when he's got a stand? Shoots for all he's worth. Somethin' takes hold of him, and he loses that nice smile. Worries me sometimes he'll burn up his gun barrel. And when the buffalo run, he jumps on his horse and takes out after them. Strings them out sometimes for a mile or two. Like a kid on a picnic."

Jameson commented, "Gets a lot of buffalo."

"And makes the rest of them so wild you can't get in a mile of them on horseback."

King rode in beside his skinners' wagon and dismounted, a little stiff from the ride. He watched distastefully as they pitched the day's green hides onto the ground. A big drop of half-congealed blood splashed off onto the leg of his trousers.

"Dammit," he shouted in sudden anger, "watch what you're doing."

Quickly he slapped at the blood with his hands, trying to get it off. Then he rubbed his hands together, scowling darkly at the smear of drying blood on them.

Shad said quietly, "Some of the polish is comin' off now, and the brass is beginning to show."

Even in camp Ransom King managed to stand a head taller than anyone else in appearance. He was the only man who shaved every day without fail. Even Jameson didn't try to do that. Often Jameson and Shad threw in when the work was heavy, skinning hides or moving them around. But King always found someone else to handle the dirtier details, avoiding the stain that stamped other men with the brand of their trade.

Seeing Jameson and Blankenship, he moved toward them, leading his horse. He had his laughing days and his black days. This was a black one. There was no dash or fun about him. He still scowled. He wiped the dust and sweat from his face with a clean handkerchief.

"Damn this business anyway."

In a light voice, trying to ease King's dark mood, Jameson remarked, "I always thought you liked the hide business. The excitement and shooting . . . selling your hides and counting your money."

King shoved the handkerchief back into his pocket. His mouth twisted as he watched his men spreading out the hides. "The shooting, sure. I like the feel of a gun in my hand. Always did. Like the feel of power it gives you. But the rest of it. . . ."

His eyes narrowed, and he cursed under his breath. "My stomach turns over every time I get the grease and blood of them on me. And the smell, Jameson, it sticks to a man like death. Get so I hate the sight of the lousy monsters. I'll be glad when the last one is dead and rotted."

Jameson looked at him questioningly. "For a man who hates the business, you've done mighty well at it."

"The money, Jameson, the money. You'd be surprised what-all I can stand if there's enough money in it."

There hadn't been any trouble during these weeks, nothing a man could rightly call trouble. Once a handful of Indians had tried to work up to the corral in the dead of night and get off with some horses and mules. But Shad's old black dog stopped that, just as he had done before.

The only other trouble was King's man, Trencher.

He had been busy enough at first so that he wasn't much bother to anyone. But later, as camp routine got old, he started getting restless. He began sitting in on Blair Farley's poker games and losing steadily. His IOU's to Farley were mounting up. Trencher sulked around, his eyes narrowed and mean, looking for a chance to stumble over someone's feet.

One night Shad Blankenship was busy tarring a wagon hub and spat a stream of tobacco juice without much attention to where it went. Part of it splashed on Trencher's boots, already thoroughly stained by mud and blood and buffalo grease. Roughly Trencher grabbed the old man's thin shoulder and spun him around. He wrapped his fingers in Shad's short beard and jerked Shad's face up close to his own, so hard that tears came to Shad's eyes.

Jameson saw it from afar and came running. But he didn't need to. Shad raised his boot and stomped down hard on Trencher's instep. Then his knee came up sharply, and Trencher doubled over in agony. Shad slapped him across the face with the tarbrush, leaving a heavy black smear. He planted the sole of his boot firmly on Trencher's hip pocket and roughly sent him sprawling under the feet of a mule.

Startled, the mule began to jump and kick. Trencher scrambled away on hands and knees, haste making him look ridiculous.

Shad's black dog piled in on him to make it worse, his long teeth seeking blood. Shad called him off.

Men who had seen it started to laugh. But when Trencher stood up, scowling and dusting himself, his furious eyes stabbing at them through the smear of tar, they shut up. He turned back to Shad, crouching a little.

But Shad stood his ground, his big fist clenched around

a wrench. The dog was growling, black hair standing stiff.

"By Judas Priest," Shad said angrily, "I was gougin' eyes and bitin' ears before you was ever weaned. Next time you come at me, bucko, you better have you a doctor handy."

For a moment they glared at each other. Shad didn't give an inch. Presently Trencher turned and stalked away. From then on, he never came at Shad again. He often eyed him from a distance, a goading hatred in his heavy face. But he always gave Shad plenty of air.

"I reckon I handled that." Shad's words were clipped in lingering anger.

"I reckon you did," Jameson agreed worriedly. "But you better watch your back from now on. Trencher looks like he'd have the memory of a bull elephant."

Blair Farley had been watching, hands tucked into the waistband beneath his heavy paunch. Jameson motioned him aside and said sharply, "You caused this, you and those poker games of yours. Cause me any more trouble like this and I'll let you walk back to Dodge!"

"It ain't my fault if Trencher's got his dander up," Farley replied in a whiny voice that grated against a man's nerves.

"No? Well, I'll tell you something else that had better set you to thinking. You haven't got a friend left in camp, Farley. Most of them hate you because you've been winning their money. We're a long way from town. We ever get in a scrap with Indians, what's to keep somebody from potting you during the excitement? Then nobody would owe anything."

He saw fear strike in Farley's eyes. "You don't think somebody would?"

Jameson shrugged. "You know these men. What do you think?"

Farley walked away, visibly shaken by a thought that never had come to him before. Jameson heard someone ask him about a poker game, and Farley turned it down.

Later Jameson spoke to Ransom King about Trencher. King listened, frowning in thought. "I'll let him shoot a few buffalo," he said. "That's all he needs. Let him kill something and it drains that meanness out of him for awhile."

Jameson shook his head wonderingly. "I guess you know him. But you've got a mighty peculiar taste in helpers."

"I don't pretend to like him, Jameson. He's crude and he's mean. But I can handle him, and he's a good man for the job he does. As long as I make money, I can tolerate anything or anybody."

Came a time when the buffalo were thinning. The bunches were so small now that Jameson and Shad never got to hunt together any more. They separated, each taking a wagon and his own skinners, trying only to keep within the sound of each other's guns. There had been some Indian sign lately, and Jameson's eyes constantly searched the skyline.

Shad said, "Been the time of year the Comanches like to go south and raid the settlements. That's maybe why we ain't seen much of them. But they'll be back here for the winter."

One day after Jameson had killed enough buffalo for his skinners to have an afternoon's work, he sought out Shad Blankenship and found him already through, sitting on a rise watching his men.

"Let's go hunt a new camp site, Shad, one where there'll be more buffalo."

They set out up the creek. There were buffalo, all right, but badly scattered. They rode ten miles, maybe twelve, and finally reached the rocky head of the creek, where a strong stream of cold, clear water burst forth from a fissure in the rocks to form a year-round spring.

Up here were more buffalo. Jameson liked the idea of camping by the spring. It was a good place, with lots of hackberry, stunted elm, and most of all the big cottonwoods. In places the buffalo had rubbed the trunks almost slick getting rid of the spring-shed hair, with its itchy lice and ticks. Even after all these months, a tuft of shed hair still stuck, here and there.

Shad Blankenship was worried.

"Look at them buffalo," he said, "turn tail and run quick as they see us. They ain't been so wild back down the creek. These buffalo has been hunted, Gage. Hunted on horseback."

"Indians, you think?"

"What else? Maybe we better have us a look around."

They skirted the spring and eased southward. Presently Jameson pulled up short, tilting his head to listen. "Shad, did you hear something?"

Shad shook his head. "Gettin' so deaf I can't hear thunder."

Gage listened a little, finally stepping down and dropping the reins, standing free of the horse so not even the squeak of the saddle would keep him from hearing. The sound grew. It was like thunder. But it rolled steadily, without a break, gradually swelling louder. Soon Gage could feel the ground begin to tremble a little beneath his feet.

"Stampede," he said sharply. "Buffalo stampede!"

His heart quickened. He stepped back into the stirrup and swung up, automatically looking about him for a place of escape and seeing little but the rolling prairie, the stream, the spring—nothing that would stop a crushing tide of buffalo.

"We've got to make a run for it, Shad," he said. "Let's get over that rise yonder so we can see how they're heading. Maybe we can get out of the way before they get here."

They spurred up over the rise. Even before they reached the top Jameson could see the cloud of dust that rose into the plains sky. Then he saw the buffalo coming fast, directly toward them.

"Lord," Shad breathed, "must be ten thousand head."

They were fanned out over a half-mile front. Jameson's bay horse was fidgeting nervously, wanting to run. Jameson felt his own pulse pounding.

"That way, Shad," Jameson shouted, pointing. "Maybe we can get past the edge of the herd before they run us down."

He spurred then, spurred hard, and the bay horse answered with speed. His long legs reached out. Jameson knew this was the payoff for his having bought a horse of strong body and strong lungs. Behind him he could almost feel the breath of the buffalo on the back of his neck. It was the movement of air set in motion by the surging body of the stampeding herd. Beside him Shad was leaning over in the saddle, talking to his dun horse, urging him to more speed.

Jameson looked back once at this thundering black sea of buffalo that would pound horse and man to powder if ever they made a misstep, if ever they fell in the path of this living avalanche. He saw the bobbing black heads, the black eyes, the little streams of saliva that trailed from the mouths of the running animals. He could feel the fear that swept the buffalo, that kept them surging forward, and it became his own fear, swelling in his chest, choking off his breath.

Little by little the spurring riders worked toward the edge of the herd. Some of the leaders were even with

them now, running along beside them. Jameson looked
back often, gauging how much farther they had to go,
already feeling the power begin to play out in the big
bay horse beneath him. He kept urging the horse on.

And finally . . .

"We're clear, Shad!"

They pulled up then to let the herd roar past them. A
rush of wind and dust whipped their faces. The horses
danced fearfully, still strung high from the long, hard run.

In a little while the herd had gone on past. Down there
somewhere the buffalo would run themselves out, and
they would settle down to graze again, as peaceful as if
nothing had happened.

"Reckon what tetched them off?" Shad asked, trying
to rub the dust from his watering eyes.

"I've got a sneaking idea," Jameson replied. They
trotted their horses a little, easing them down to a walk,
cooling them gradually.

The sound of the stampede faded away and there was
nothing left to show for it but a wide swath of trampled
grass and a lingering of stifling dust that slowly drifted
out on the easy breeze.

Now Jameson began to hear something else.

"Shooting, Shad. And I thought I heard somebody
yell."

Shad's eyes narrowed. Presently he heard it, too.

"Coming from somewhere across that hill yonder,"
Jameson said.

Dismounting and leading their horses, the two men
cautiously worked up the hillside. They dropped the
horses' reins and crouched as they neared the top, keeping low to present as little silhouette as possible. Shad
Blankenship dropped to his belly.

"Look yonder, Gage. Ever see such a sight in your
life?"

Down there a large group of Comanche warriors, stripped to breechclouts and all mounted on good horses, had driven a group of buffalo into a mass. Now they circled them, the dozens of hoofs churning up a billowing cloud of dust to drift away with the wind. Most of the Indians loosed arrows into the herd as rapidly as they could restring their bows. Now and again, as a buffalo made a rush to get out of the surround, a warrior charged after him with a lance. Those few Indians who had rifles were using them principally on the animals which broke into a run.

Jameson was glad he had brought the binoculars out of his saddlebags. He raised them to his eyes and watched a lancer lope up behind a running buffalo, holding the lance across his body, the off end the highest, his knees tucked under a rope wound around the horse's body. When he had gained the position he wanted, he thrust downward with the lance, shoving it hard, then pulling it out again as the buffalo faltered. The lancer pierced the animal a second time, pushing in and holding the lance until the buffalo went down.

He saw a bowman ride in close and loose an arrow at a running bull. As the missile drove home, the buffalo turned sharply, heading into the horse, sending it rolling. The Indian scrambled to his feet, grabbing his fallen bow and what spilled arrows he could snatch off the ground. In desperation he sent arrow after arrow into the charging animal, so rapidly Jameson lost count. The buffalo went to its knees, still hooking at the Indian. The warrior walked back to his horse, carefully looked him over for injuries, then remounted and returned to the slaughter.

Not a single animal escaped the Comanches.

Now the fun was over and the work part began. Other Indians materialized out of a brushy draw to start the skinning, the butchering of the meat. Jameson watched, fascinated, the skilled hands of the red men.

These were the Comanches, savage, brutal. Yet truly they were children of the land, nomads, akin to nature and the creatures in a way the white man could never be, following the rains, following the grass, following the buffalo.

Shad nudged Jameson. "This ain't the girly show at no fancy dance hall, young'un. They find out we're up here, we're liable to put on a little show ourselves."

"I wonder where their camp is," Jameson mused, still watching through the binoculars.

"It don't matter to me. I ain't been invited and don't aim to go."

Jameson grinned at him. Shad wasn't scared. But he had the deep-grained caution that had kept his hair on through forty years of dodging Indians.

Jameson said, "I've got a notion to trail them, at least far enough to locate their camp. I'd rather find it now than stumble on it some day by accident."

The wrinkles deepened in Shad's ruddy face as he narrowed his eyes, looking down upon the Comanches. "Whatever you say. You're the wagon master. We better step soft, though. Me, I'm an old man, and I've lived out a full life. But you're still owin' the house."

The Indians brought up pack horses. Rolling the meat in the fresh hides, they loaded it onto the horses and headed out, leaving little but scattered patches of blackened blood to show where the slaughter had taken place.

"Don't waste much, do they, Shad?" Unlike the white man, Jameson thought.

Shad shook his head. "Winter coming on, they can't afford to."

It wasn't hard to follow the Indians. It wasn't as if the Comanches were trying to hide their trail. Up here, in the middle of their stronghold, they probably had no thought of any need to do so. Riding slowly, his eyes squinted, nervously searching out the skyline and every patch of brush as they rode along, Jameson could feel the flesh crawl up the back of his neck. His mouth was dry, and he constantly licked his lips. But he kept riding, and he kept watching.

"They ever see us," Shad Blankenship said softly, "she's gonna be the biggest horse race you ever saw."

Jameson nodded, his hand tight and sweaty on the reins, his knee pulling in for the welcome feel of the saddle gun under his leg. He had left the Fifty with the skinners, so he wouldn't have to handle its heavy bulk on the ride. Now he wished he had it.

"Most of those horses looked like good ones," he commented. "Mighty good for Indians."

Shad Blankenship reined up, intently studying something ahead, then nodding as he satisfied himself that it was nothing to be alarmed about. "Comanches are good horsemen. Besides, they probably stole most of these from the Texans. Every fall, before winter sets in, they raid the settlements. Generally strike in the full of the moon. Comanche moon, they call it down there.

"Steal horses, women, children, anything else that ain't nailed down. What they don't steal, they kill or burn up. Then they hit it off back up to this country and winter on these plains. Ain't nobody ever reached them up here. The only ones know the trail are the Comanchero traders out of New Mexico. They're strictly contraband. They come out and trade for the stock the Indians have stole. That's where the Comanches get the guns and powder and other white-man stuff you see them with nowadays."

Sticking with the brush, they followed the trail six or seven miles along the edge of a draw that led eventually to another creek, much like the one on which the hide hunters had been camping.

They caught the drift of wood smoke before they saw the village.

"Yonder it is," Shad whispered finally, "on that flat aside the creek."

Jameson slipped out of the saddle and lifted the binoculars from the saddlebag again. He could feel his hair stiffen as he looked down on the tall buffalo-hide lodges, forty or fifty of them, strung out up and down the creek. It seemed to be a new camp, for the grass was not trampled out yet. Smoke curled upward from the smoke flaps, which were opened downwind. Indians hurried up and down through camp like so many ants, cutting the fresh buffalo meat into strips for drying, spitting huge chunks of it to be roasted immediately. It was mostly a woman's job from here on. The warriors who had done the killing now lolled around in camp, some of them washing themselves in the cold water of the creek.

Dogs fought up and down the camp site, struggling over fallen scraps of meat. Some of the children threw rocks at them. One pair of scrapping dogs felled a squaw, causing her to drop a huge chunk of red meat in the sand. Grabbing a stick, she chased the tail-tucking dogs all the way down to the creek while loafing men made fun of her.

Elsewhere, other women were working on the fresh hides, pegging them out, scraping them religiously clean so they could be tanned later with a mixture of liver and brains. Watching, Jameson lost much of the tension that had drawn taut within him.

Suddenly he saw something that didn't belong, something that made him draw his breath in sharply and lower the binoculars, lifting them again as if he didn't believe it.

Then he handed them to Shad. "Take a look," he said,

his voice unsteady. "See if that's really a white woman there, scraping a hide."

Shad took the glasses, searching among the lodges. Then he stopped. His red-bearded jaw dropped. "By George, I do believe it is. There, I see a squaw kickin' at her. She's a captive, right enough."

His binoculars back, Jameson studied the woman. He couldn't tell much about her. She wore deerskin clothing, old and greasy, evidently the castoffs from some squaw. He couldn't make out her face or guess her age. He could tell only that she was slender, even thin, that her light-colored hair reached far down below her shoulders.

He saw a brave come up behind her, look around quickly, then grab her long hair. He jerked her head back and with his other hand made the sign of scalping her. Then he gave her a rough shove forward.

A curse came up under Jameson's breath. His hands gripped the glasses so hard that they hurt. He saw another Indian walk up angrily and berate the brave. This man, Jameson thought, was probably the chief of the band— at least a leader of higher rank than the warrior. Even so, the warrior paid him scant attention. He turned insolently and strode off, leaving the leader staring after him.

For a moment then, the leader studied the white woman, who had gone back to scraping the green hide. She didn't look at him. The chief turned and walked away in a dejected attitude.

Jameson lowered the glasses. "Shad, I don't know how we're going to do it. But we're going to get her out of there!"

9

"**Y**OU'RE CRAZY, Jameson. It's not worth the risk."

Ransom King paced angrily back and forth before the campfire, his eyes jabbing at Jameson. "Do you really think you could get that woman out of there?"

Jameson stood motionless, his questioning gaze drifting from King to the other men standing around in the edge of firelight. He was still half stunned with surprise. He had never expected this opposition from King. Now he wondered how many more felt as King did.

"We've got to try."

"You think the Comanches will just hand her over to you? Have you any idea how it could be done?"

"I've got a notion how we might do it."

"*Might* do it!" King's voice was heavy with sarcasm. "*Might*. Even by the tone of your voice you admit how slim the chance is. You're crazy, Jameson, you're about to jeopardize everything we've come down here for. Use a little judgment, man.''

A stir of anger worked at Gage Jameson. It colored his voice. "King, I thought you'd be the first one to say 'Let's go.' Now I don't know what to think. I know it's not cowardice.''

"Of course it's not cowardice. It's common horse-sense. I've got an investment here, a big investment, and a chance of a big return. So have you. Do you think I want to throw it away, and maybe die too, on a ten-to-one chance of rescuing some woman you saw through a pair of field glasses? How do we know who she is, or what she is? She may have been there so long she doesn't even *want* out. Ever think about that? For all we know, she might be some dance-hall floozie like Rose.''

"Even if she was," Jameson said, "I'd do it.''

"Then you're an even bigger fool.''

Stiffly they faced each other over the campfire. The men watched them silently, staying back in the edge of darkness. Jameson couldn't tell how the sentiment went.

"Listen, Jameson," King argued, "Blankenship says they probably took her on a raid in the Texas settlements. A Texan. They were almighty independent a few years ago. If those Rebels want her back, I say let them come up here and take her themselves. I spent four years fighting them. I wouldn't risk what I've got here for a freight-car load of them.''

"She's a white woman, King. You can talk all night, but you can't alter that.''

King rocked back and forth on his heels, chewing his lip, his eyebrows drawn down half over his eyes.

"A woman. Just because it's a woman we're supposed to give up everything and go. It always did make me tired, listening to high-flown talk about the sanctity of womanhood. They put women up on a pedestal like some brass god, when all the time that's all they are—just brass. I've known a lot of them, Jameson. Even married one once. They're just animals like the rest of us. No better and perhaps a lot worse."

Jameson attempted no answer to that. Even in his anger he could understand King. Only two things meant much to this brash hide hunter—excitement and money. Money most of all.

King made one last attempt. His voice was level now, persuasive instead of bludgeoning. "Look at the percentages, Jameson. Chances are heavy you won't even come out alive. But *if* you do, stop and consider. We've had good hunting here. There are still plenty of buffalo. Indians haven't bothered us to speak of. This new camp probably doesn't even know about us. We can move twenty or thirty miles and they never will know.

"But what happens if you raid that camp? Then we've got to move, fast and far. We may have to go so far to get out of their reach that we'll run out of buffalo. Those wagons are half empty yet. It would mean ruination, Jameson. Ruination."

But to Jameson there was no choice. There hadn't been one since the moment he had seen the woman in that Comanche camp.

He turned away from King, turned to the other men.

"I'm not telling any man he's got to go. There's no use lying to you, it's going to be dangerous. But I'm asking for volunteers."

The camp was silent and still, except for the cold night breeze moving through, flickering the campfire. Jameson searched the faces, red in its glow. Shad Blankenship stepped up beside him.

Reb Pruitt solemnly took off his sack apron, laid it on the chuck-box lid and walked to Jameson's side.

Then came the lank skinner Messick. But there it stopped. Vainly Jameson looked to the men for more help. They stood there, staring at the fire or at the ground or off into darkness, not meeting his eyes. And then he realized.

It was King. King had hired them for him. Even yet their allegiance was to King, not to Jameson. Disappointment settled within him.

Four against the Comanche camp.

A shadow raised up from out in the darkness somewhere. Ludlow, his beard black as the night, walked up, folding a knife blade against his leg. He shoved the knife into his pocket and tossed a whittling stick into the blaze. He gave the other men a lingering look of contempt and stood beside Reb Pruitt.

Five now. And five was all it was going to be.

Knowing that, Jameson said to them, "I won't hold you to it. You know five is mighty slim."

They didn't move.

Reb Pruitt said, "She's a Texas woman, Jameson. I'll go if I have to go by myself."

Jameson didn't say it, but the thought ran through his mind: No wonder it took us four years.

Then King restlessly dug his toe into the ground. "Oh, the devil," he said, "no use being so dramatic about it. We'll all go."

Looking around quickly in surprise, Jameson saw him nod.

"It's still a crazy fool idea," King said grudgingly, "and it'll probably get us all killed. But I knew all the time we'd have to go, if we couldn't discourage you. We can't afford to lose you, Jameson. This expedition would sink like a rock in the river."

Jameson smiled and shook King's hand. "Thanks, King. I knew you weren't afraid."

"Afraid? The only thing I'm afraid of is that someday I may get as stupid as you are. Call me when you're ready. I'm going to catch me some sleep."

For Jameson there was no rest. He put the men to breaking camp, loading the wagons. When they got back—*if* they got back—these wagons had to be ready to roll.

At last he lay down in his blankets, but sleep wasn't in him. He turned restlessly awhile before he gave it up. He looked wonderingly at Shad Blankenship, rolled up and snoring. Shad could sleep through a cannonade.

Jameson got to his feet and walked to the chuck wagon. He dipped water from a bucket and into the coffeepot. He poured a little fresh coffee among the old grounds and set it all on the coals, punching them up for extra heat.

He heard Reb Pruitt's voice behind him. "That's *my* job."

He turned and tried to smile. That wasn't in him, either. "Guess neither one of us can sleep."

They sat there watching the pot, wondering if it ever would come to a boil. He felt a deep need for talk, for something to take his mind off whatever was coming.

"What part of Texas are you from, Reb?"

"South Texas. The brush country."

"Fought in the war, did you?"

Pruitt nodded. "If you could call it fightin'. I got there late. Seemed like mostly all we could do was retreat and listen to the officers tell us we was just backin' up for a fresh run at the Yanks. We was always out of powder or lead or something to eat. Seemed like all we had left was guts, and they ain't worth much when your stomach's empty."

"It wasn't much fun for us either, Reb."

Pruitt poked restlessly at the fire. "I reckon not."

Sitting there watching Pruitt, Jameson felt a strong liking growing in him for this lean, hungry-looking little cowboy cook. There was more to the man than had earlier met his eye.

"It's none of my business," Jameson said, "and you can say so if you want to. But they tell me you got in trouble down there and can't go back. Something serious?"

Pruitt shrugged. "I shot a yellow-leg cavalry lieutenant with a sawed-off shotgun."

"Kill him?"

"No, I wasn't tryin' to. But where I hit him, it put him in the infantry for a good spell."

Only a pale rind of moon lighted their way as they moved along. But Jameson knew the direction. He kept his horse unerringly on it, moving at a jog trot across the silver tableland. Ransom King rode silently beside him, keeping his thoughts to himself.

Behind them came the men, all except a few they had left to guard the wagons and have them ready to move. Poker-playing Blair Farley had elected to stay, perhaps taking to heart what Jameson had said about someone shooting him during the thick of action to keep from having to pay a gambling debt.

There hadn't been enough saddles to go around, or horses, either. Several rode mules bareback. As they strung out of camp, Jameson counted fourteen men.

Angling across the flat prairie, they finally struck the other creek. Jameson reined up, studying it in the darkness. He looked at the Dipper, judging the amount of time he still had before daylight. The early-morning chill had him stiff, his back aching a little from the cramped way the cold had made him ride.

"Pass the word back," he whispered. "It's not far

now. Nobody talks. Nobody smokes. One wrong move and there'll never be another.''

He touched spurs lightly to the horse, easing him down into the bitter-cold creek and across. His heart quickened as he heard the other mounts splashing over behind him. Crisp air like this could carry sound a long way.

Up the other side, he kept riding, getting off some distance from the water. He remembered the line of timber and brush that had lain behind the village, indicating a draw that fed water into the creek in time of rain. This draw, he figured, would give them cover. He looked back again and saw the men bunched up close behind him, guns in their hands, ready.

Stars in the east had begun to pale when they moved their horses and mules up into the brush behind the village. Jameson caught the grease-smoke smell that always betrayed an Indian camp. The wind had stilled now in this pre-dawn darkness, but the chill was sharp enough to set a man to trembling.

He dismounted to let his horse blow, and the others followed his example. They walked the horses, leading them to cool them down gradually.

As the sky lightened, he could pick out the lodges one by one, their conical shapes rising up against the horizon, the poles above the smokeflaps showing clearer in approaching dawn. He was looking at the village from the opposite side now, and he no longer could be sure exactly where he had seen the white woman. He waited, and studied, and finally he thought he knew which lodge it would be. The question was, did she sleep there, or was it merely one where they made her work?

He could see no movement in the camp as yet. Part of it, at least, would be because of the buffalo the Indians had taken yesterday. They would have gorged themselves last night, eaten all they could stuff in, and then they would have fallen into a drugged sleep.

Scattered throughout the length of the village he saw horses hobbled or staked, twenty-five or thirty head. But most of the horses—a couple of hundred—were in a loosely held herd down past the lower end of camp, scattered over several acres of flat, grassy ground along the creek. Way out to one edge he saw an Indian horse herder sitting sleepily on the ground, holding the leather rein of a mount that stood droop-headed over him.

Jameson had had little experience with Comanches, but he knew within reason that an Indian on the war trail would never be far from his horse. Even sleeping, he would have the mount staked or tied close at hand. Stealing horses from a war party was well-nigh an impossibility, unless you were another Indian.

But now the Comanches were on their own ground, seemingly inviolate here on their impregnable Llano Estacado, easing down to the long monotony of winter life. And like white soldiers when they thought they were safe, they had let down their guard.

"We've got to have that horse herd," Jameson whispered to Shad.

Shad chewed heavily on his tobacco, frowning, his pale eyes leisurely working from one end of the camp to the other, not missing a horse track or a buffalo bone.

"Then let's just take it," he said casually.

He pointed his red-bearded chin. "That second lodge from the end yonder—ain't it the one where we seen her?"

"Yep." Jameson felt more secure in his judgment now, for he had picked the same one.

"Reckon she's still there?" Shad asked.

Jameson shook his head. "I hope so. It's the best bet we've got."

"The minute they see what we're after, they'll kill her."

Jameson's hand was tight on the saddle gun. "I know it. So we've got to get her before they see what we're really up to."

He lifted his chin, studying the sky. Light enough now, he thought.

"Shad, I want you to take King and most of the men and run off that horse herd. Make a lot of noise. Push it straight across the creek, and be in a hurry. The Comanches will be boiling after you like a swarm of hornets."

Shad smiled a little at the anticipation of action. "And how do you figure on amusing yourself in the meantime?"

"I'll take Pruitt and Ludlow and Messick. While you draw the warriors off on that end, we'll get busy down here. Later on we'll meet you somewhere across the creek, on the way back to camp."

He paused, then added, "If we're lucky."

Shad and the other riders moved away slowly, keeping under cover of the brush. Jameson held his breath until his lungs ached, listening for a giveaway noise like a horse stumbling or snorting in this knife-sharp morning air. It seemed to him that the strike of hoofs was gunshot-loud, but he knew that was imagination. Any minute he expected the camp dogs to sound the alarm.

He worried most about those men riding bareback. An Indian could give you a whale of a fight bareback, but these were white men used to saddles. Some weren't used to riding at all. They would have a hard time just staying on, if the going got rough. Their guns wouldn't be much help.

For a time then, Shad's men were out of sight as the brush swallowed them up. There was not even the muffled sound of hoofs. Jameson turned to the remaining three men. "Better check your guns again. One miss-lick now and we're dead."

A dog began to bark, somewhere down toward the horse herd. Another dog picked it up, and another and another. In a few seconds the alarm had racketed back into camp, every dog there adding to it his own excited yelp. Holding his breath again, Jameson peered through the brush and saw the horse guard straighten, looking around.

He thought desperately, now's the time, Shad, if you're ever going to do it!

And Shad did it. A sudden rattle of guns exploded toward the horse herd. Snapping unexpectedly out of sleep, the horses jumped one way and the other in excitement. The riders thundered down on them, firing guns, and they stampeded.

For a moment it looked as if they would plunge straight into the Indian camp. But someone intercepted them, headed them off. Then they were running for the creek.

Jameson watched the horse guard raise his rifle. Half a dozen bullets ripped the Comanche apart.

Pandemonium struck the camp. Warriors burst out of the lodges, rifles and bows in hand. Some shouted in confusion. Some took wild shots at the raiders who swept away their horse herd. Those who had horses tied or hobbled nearby ran to them. Even some of these horses jerked free in panic and stampeded through the camp, galloping after the herd. While the warriors ran after the raiders in helpless fury, squaws and children hurried out of the lodges to see what was taking place.

Jameson lifted his binoculars and watched that second lodge. Then he saw her. She stepped through the flap and stood watching the dusty, pounding scene of wild confusion.

"There she is," Jameson said quietly to Pruitt, shoving the binoculars back into his saddlebag. "You ready to get that Texas woman out of there?"

Pruitt nodded gravely. They swung onto their horses. Jameson jabbed with his spurs. The mount burst forward in a lope, out of the brush, racing swiftly toward the woman. She was about two hundred yards away. Or was it two miles?

Rifle steady in his hand, Jameson spoke tensely under his breath and realized suddenly that he was praying. He kept spurring. He could hear the clatter of hoofs behind him and knew the other three were right with him.

They hadn't been spotted yet. Jameson couldn't see a warrior anywhere who might oppose them. They had all run toward the other end of camp. But a man couldn't dismiss those squaws. They could fight like so many wounded panthers if they needed to.

The captive white woman saw them. For the space of two or three seconds she stood numb, not believing. Then she broke into a run toward them.

Squaws saw them now. They waved their hands excitedly, most of them turning to flee, shooing the children before them. But one, with a knife in her hand, started running after the white woman. The woman saw her and tried to run faster. But the squaw was fleet-footed and gained rapidly. Jameson raised his rifle but realized he couldn't fire accurately at the speed he was riding. He might hit the wrong woman. His heart clutched in dismay. He knew he couldn't reach her before the squaw did.

Then, just as the squaw closed the gap and raised the knife, a gunshot roared behind Jameson. The squaw stumbled, rolled in the grass and lay still.

Reb Pruitt had slid his horse to a sudden halt, thrown his rifle to his shoulder and fired. It was a perfect shot.

Heart racing, Jameson pulled to a stop, kicked his left foot free and reached down for the woman. She put her foot in the empty stirrup. He gave her a quick boost up behind him. Then, as her arms clasped tightly about him, he spurred the horse again.

Arrows began to whisper past them as some of the closer warriors saw what was happening. Even a couple of squaws had bows and were stringing arrows, letting them fly at a speed Jameson would not have believed if he hadn't seen it. He kept spurring. They were out of effective range already. If an arrow struck them now it would be by sheer accident. A few rifles sounded behind them, and Jameson could hear the deadly sing of bullets.

Jameson took one quick glance over his shoulder. He could see the tense, shock-pale face of the woman—a young woman she was—and her long blonde hair streaming in the wind. He could see his three riders close behind him, not one appearing to have been hit. It had gone off so quickly that it had been over before the Indians could act by anything other than reflex.

Now Jameson put his horse into the creek, splashed across, and spurred out on the other side again. They broke through the tangle of brush, then were out on the open prairie, running free.

10

To his right Jameson could see the horse herd still running, necks outstretched, legs reaching to gather in the miles, the dust rising up from the dry grass. He reined that way, staying in a hard lope. He couldn't see behind him well, but he knew there was certain to be immediate pursuit on any horses the Indians had managed to keep in camp.

Through the patchy brush he could see Comanches on horseback, pushing across the creek in a splash of water that flashed a spangled reflection from the rising sun. He couldn't count them, didn't try.

"You all right?" he asked the woman behind him, speaking to her for the first time. Her answer, in a voice strained almost to breaking, was barely audible. "I think so."

He caught the wood-smoke smell of Indian and knew it was from her frayed old deerskin clothes. He could feel her body against him, trembling, but it might well have been because of the cold. She had no coat against the chill of the morning. Even the sleeves were gone from the old squaw dress she wore. They had splashed a lot of icy water moving across the creek.

He had caught only a fragmentary glimpse of her face, but now he could see her hands, clasped tightly to the front of his coat. They were young hands—red, raw and bruised—but they were strong hands, hands that knew work.

Shad Blankenship edged out from the horse herd and angled his mount toward them at a run. Relief washed over his rough old face as he saw the woman and noted that none of Jameson's group was hurt.

"We got company comin', young'un," he shouted against the wind and the hammering of hoofs.

Jameson looked back over his shoulder at the line of Indians. Fifteen or eighteen of them. They were making a gain, for the hide hunters were hard-pressed to keep the horse herd moving on.

He got another look at the woman, too. He saw deep blue eyes etched with pain, a face haggard from hardship and taut with the remnants of fear. A mouth with lips drawn in tight, a chin firm and strong, indicating the fortitude to face up to what might come.

Ahead Jameson saw a buffalo wallow, not deep but good enough for at least some protection. He pointed to it, and Shad saw, nodding. Shad waved his hat. The men with the horse herd began pulling toward him, letting the Indians' horses run on. Pushing hard, they converged on the buffalo wallow. The Comanches were coming in, making it a tight race.

Jameson slid to a stop in the wallow and let the woman swing to the ground. The place was a depression, possibly thirty or forty feet across, where the louse- and fly-ridden buffalo came to wallow in the dust for relief from the constant itching.

Jameson motioned the woman to lie down against the bank for protection. The other hide men rode in and jumped from their horses and mules. Urgent though the situation was, not a man failed to stop long enough to glance at the white woman. Even Ransom King.

"Hold onto those mounts," Jameson yelled. "This is no time to be set afoot."

Kneeling, lying prone, some of them standing, they waited. Bridle reins were tight in their hands or looped over their arms, the rifle barrels bristling at the edge of the buffalo wallow.

The Indians closed in, shrieking and yelling.

"Hold your fire till they get close," Jameson said loudly. "Then get the horses, that's the main thing. Don't let a horse get away."

He raised his saddle gun, lined the sights on the Indian in the lead. This man, he realized suddenly, was the chief he had watched through the glasses yesterday. He waited, his breath held until a slow fire kindled in his lungs. Then he squeezed the trigger. The rifles on either side of him roared. Some of the hunters' horses and mules broke loose in terror and plunged away.

He saw the chief jerk back, clutch desperately at the horse's mane, then tumble off to struggle out his last breath on the ground. Other men's bullets tore into the charging line. Horses stumbled and went down. Indians rolled in the grass. Some jumped to their feet, some lay cramped and still where they had landed. Men and horses screamed in pain. The murderous gunfire went on. Jameson fired again and again, each shot bringing down a horse.

In seconds every Indian horse was hit. The vicious fire had riddled the Comanche line like a scythe whispering through wet grass. Few of the Indians had had time to loose an arrow or fire a shot. Now many were dead or wounded, and the rest were afoot, their fallen horses thrashing.

The surviving ones tried to return fire, bellied down in the cover of grass or behind the fallen mounts. In the wallow a mule screamed and went down kicking.

But the hunters poured out a fearful hail of lead. They didn't have time to let themselves get pinned down here, Jameson knew, and he figured the others realized it, too. Given time, the Comanches would have reinforcements afoot from the camp.

Half the hunters had lost their mounts, either from their jerking away and running or from the Indians' fire.

One man lay on his face in the wallow. Jameson felt of him and shook his head. He had skinned his last buffalo.

"Mount up double," he ordered. "We've got to clear out of here."

He and Shad and a couple of others kept up fire while the rest mounted. Then they swung up, too, and they moved out in a run.

This time the woman was in the saddle and Jameson was behind, protecting her. The few remaining Comanches fired after them. Jameson heard a man cry out. Reb Pruitt drooped in the saddle, an arrow in his arm. Thinking the Texan might fall, Jameson pulled in beside him and caught him, holding him in the saddle.

"I'll make it," the little cook said through gritted teeth. "Nobody ever had to hold me on a horse yet."

They rode a mile. Then, knowing there could be no pursuit, Jameson reined in and stopped Pruitt's horse. He slipped off and helped the cook down. The woman swung to the ground.

"Bleedin' like a stuck hog," Pruitt breathed painfully, as if ashamed of himself for getting hit.

"Through the flesh part of the arm," Jameson said. "Arrowhead went through clean."

Shad Blankenship took one man to each mount and went after those horses and mules that had run away.

Jameson took out his knife and cut the arrowhead from the shaft as carefully as he could. It was a steel one, he noted in anger. Something from the Comanchero trade.

"Can you help me hold him?" he asked the woman. Tight-lipped but looking as if she knew what she was about, she put her arm around Pruitt's shoulder and held tight.

Jameson gripped the shaft and said, "This is going to hurt, Reb. Grit your teeth and cuss or say anything you want to."

Pruitt nodded, white-faced. "Just get on with it."

Jameson jerked. The shaft came out clean. Pruitt's head rocked back, his eyes shut, his jaw clamped hard. Slowly he expelled his breath and opened his eyes. They were moist with pain. But he managed a semblance of a grin at Jameson, and at the woman.

"Wasn't so bad. First time I've had a woman's arms around me in I don't . . . know . . . when."

He slumped back, unconscious.

"Shock," Jameson said. "We'd better stop the bleeding."

With her help he pulled off Pruitt's coat and rolled up the sleeve. The other men crowded around to watch. Blood flowed slowly, sticky and warm. Jameson searched his hip pocket for a handkerchief. He frowned at it. Not clean, but the best he had. He bound it tightly around Pruitt's arm. The cook was beginning to stir again. The woman held his head, keeping him as still as possible.

"That'll hold it," Jameson said at last. "We can do better when we get him to camp."

He really looked at the woman for the first time now, admiration warm in him at the calm way she had helped him with Pruitt.

"You've got a steady nerve," he said.

"The Comanches taught me that," she replied.

It was hard to guess at her age. She might have been anywhere between twenty and thirty. Captivity had ground harsh lines into what must have been a pretty face, or close to it. The fear was gone from her eyes now, but a lingering of pain was still there. Her lips were dry and cracked from the sun and wind. Her long blonde hair was wind-tangled but freshly washed, and it appeared to have been combed out not too long ago. The thought came to Jameson that it was lucky she hadn't been killed way back yonder instead of being kept captive. Many an Indian would give his right arm to own a scalp like that one, to keep it brushed down so it would glisten in the firelight at night as he bragged to other warriors about the many scalps hanging from the point end of his lance.

She was shivering again. The morning air was still cold. Jameson took off his coat and held it out to her. "Here. Put this on."

She took it hesitantly. "What about you?"

"I've got a heap to do. Being busy will keep me warm."

The coat was twice too big for her, but he could see the relief in her eyes at the warmth of it.

"We don't even know your name yet," he said.

"Westerman. Celia Westerman. And yours?"

"Gage Jameson. Where did the Comanches capture you?"

"Down on the San Saba, in September."

September. Two months and more. She had been through it, all right.

"A great many women would have died before now," he said.

She nodded gravely. "That might have been the easiest way," she replied.

Shad Blankenship and some of the others had brought back the runaway mounts and had rounded up the Indian horse herd again. Jameson looked it over. He picked a few of the best-looking to replace the animals that had been killed in the buffalo wallow.

"Brands on most of them," Shad observed. "Been stole, almost every hoof in there."

Ransom King's eyes glowed as he looked at them. "How many would you say there are, Blankenship?"

"Two hundred, a few more or less."

"They'll fetch a price in Dodge," King commented enthusiastically, the dollars shining in his eyes.

Gage Jameson frowned and checked his saddle gun. "We're not taking them to Dodge. We're shooting them."

He thought King was going to burst, the way anger made his neck veins stand out. "You're crazy, Jameson! Think what they'd be worth in Dodge!"

Jameson said flatly, "We've got no right to sell them. They're stolen horses."

"What owner is ever going to get a chance to claim them? They were lost when the Comanches got their hands on them. It's salvage now, Jameson, same as a sea captain salvaging a wreck."

"I don't know anything about salvage laws. But I know these are stolen horses. We've got no right to sell them."

King's voice went almost shrill in anger. Here was money, easy money, untainted by blood and grease and the smell of dead buffalo. And it was slipping from his grasp.

"Then what right have you to shoot them?"

"Just this: afoot a Comanche isn't much. Let him get on horseback and you're in trouble. They'd steal these horses back from us, King. We've got all we can do to keep them from taking what stock we already have. Take this many more and we'd likely lose them all, our own stuff, too. Then we'd be in it for sure. As long as these horses are alive, they're a millstone around our necks."

King declared, "I don't care what you say, Jameson. If you're going to shoot them, I'll claim them. They're mine."

Short of patience, Jameson flared. "Take them, then. Take your wagons, too. Cut out for Dodge the quickest way you can."

That stopped King. He stood stiffly, hands clenched in fury. But he was whipped and he knew it. His wagons were not yet half full of hides. He had come after hides, not horses. Alone with his small crew of men, he wouldn't stand a chance of getting to Dodge with those horses. They would be stampeded before he could travel thirty miles, perhaps his own stock with them.

He shrugged, anger still splotched red in his face. But he was helpless to alter the situation. He forced a smile that wouldn't stay.

"Shoot them, then. You're the wagon master."

He started to walk away, then stopped to look at Celia Westerman. His narrowed eyes swept over her, head to foot. A lingering of malice was in his voice. "What about *her*, Jameson? Now that you've got her, what'll you do with her? She's a little like the horses, isn't she? A millstone around your neck?

Jameson glanced at Celia Westerman, then quickly looked away as he saw a sudden tightening in her face.

King had hit him squarely. He had been so busy trying to free her that he had given no thought to what he would do afterward. The hide camp was no place for a woman. Yet what could he do about her?

Hating the horse-killing job and now confronted with another problem, he spoke to Shad a little curtly, and instantly regretted it. "What're we standing here for? Let's get this job done and move out."

With his saddle gun and a pocketful of extra cartridges, he walked out toward the horses. He flinched, his stomach coiling in revulsion at what he had to do. Then he raised the rifle.

11

JAMESON WAS glad to be on the move again, to get away from this place with its gagging stench of gunpowder and blood, the screams of the dying horses still in his ears. Someday men would come upon this gaunt stretch of bleaching bones and wonder what great massacre had occurred there.

Celia Westerman rode beside him, knowing what put the bleakness in his face. "There's no point in worrying yourself about it."

He nodded grimly. "I know. But I've never had a job I hated so much. A man gets a feeling for horses, depending on them the way I have. Shooting them is almost like shooting people."

She was silent awhile, studying him as the group rode westward, driving the few animals they had chosen to keep.

"I don't know how to start saying thank you. I don't know any words half strong enough."

He eased a little then. It had been many weeks since he had heard woman-talk. He liked the way she spoke, slowly, deliberately, not quite a drawl like Reb Pruitt's, but slow anyway.

He said, "I know what you mean. I've been in the same kind of fix myself."

"But why did you do it? You didn't even know who I was. It was a terrific risk to take for a stranger."

"You were a woman, a white woman. That's why we did it."

"That seems mighty little reason, looking back on it."

Jameson said, "Several times in my life I've been in a tough spot, something I couldn't get out of by myself. Somebody always came along. Most often it was a stranger, somebody I never saw before or ever saw again. Seems like we go through life owing gratitude to strangers. The only way we can ever repay them is to help some other stranger. It all evens up, in the long pull."

Then he said, "To your family, I suppose it'll be as if you'd come back from the dead. Married?"

She shook her head. "Not married."

"Father? Mother?"

"I still have my father and a couple of brothers. I lost one in the war."

She studied him gravely. "I haven't figured out yet what you men are. You're not Rangers. You're not Comancheros. What are you?"

"Buffalo hunters. We're down from Kansas."

"From Kansas." He caught the disappointment before she managed to cover it up, and he knew what she was thinking. She had hoped they were Texans, that they could take her home.

"We'll find a way to get you home," he promised.

Some of the pain went out of her deep blue eyes, and a brightness came to them, shining warmly. "Home." She spoke the word softly, caressing it.

He watched her, and Ransom King's words came back to him. A millstone around his neck. He felt a nudge of anger at King for saying it, yet he realized that in a sense it was true. He had Celia Westerman now. But what could he do with her?

The circled wagons looked deserted. Gage Jameson reined up to study them, for caution was second nature to him. He motioned Celia Westerman to hand him the saddle gun from the scabbard beneath her leg. She did, and he signaled her to pull back. The other riders approached warily too, rifles ready.

Then there was movement at the wagons. The men who had been left on guard stepped out into sight, holding guns. They stared curiously at Celia Westerman.

"We couldn't tell at first." Fat Blair Farley spoke with nervousness. "You might of been Injuns."

The stock was all inside the circle. Camp was broken. The wagons were loaded. The only thing still to be done was to catch up the mules and hitch them to the wagons. But Jameson looked at the men around and saw the fatigue heavy in their faces from the long night ride, the hard action, the strain and the fear. Hunger gnawed at him, and he knew it must be the same with the others.

"We could do with a strong meal before we get moving," he said. He looked at Reb Pruitt, stretched out now in the shade of the chuck wagon. Reb hadn't lost much blood. Most of what ailed him was shock. Two or three days, he'd be doing a one-handed cooking job and talking his head off. Right now, he wasn't in much shape to talk or to help.

"Shad," Jameson said, "you're a good hand with a

coffeepot and a Dutch oven. Let's see what we can fix to eat.''

Celia Westerman had been kneeling beside Pruitt. Now she stood up and came to the chuck box. "Here," she said, "I'll help."

Jameson said dubiously, "You've been through a lot. Don't you think you ought to rest?"

She shook her head. "No, I can't afford to sit still right now. If I ever did . . ." She held out her raw hands for him to see. They trembled a little. "I might go to pieces. I've got to keep busy till I can steady down."

Jameson nodded. "I guess so. But cooking for a bunch like this isn't exactly a woman's job."

"I grew up on a cattle ranch. Lots of times I've cooked for a big crew. Just help me find what I need."

Jameson built up the fire again while Shad Blankenship put fresh coffee in the pot.

"Ignorant hide skinners," Shad grumbled, "they throwed out the old grounds. Can't make good drinkin' coffee without the old grounds."

Jameson climbed into the wagon and cut fresh hump meat. Watching Celia Westerman handle the Dutch ovens and the big pots, he knew she hadn't been bluffing. She had done all this before.

Presently the coffee was boiling and fresh meat was frying deep in bubbling grease inside a lidless Dutch oven over the fire. Reb Pruitt always kept biscuit dough made up for days ahead. Celia Westerman broke the dough into biscuit-sized wads and put it in ovens, setting them on live coals. Jameson heaped more coals on the lids when she finished.

There wasn't much to do now but wait. Jameson sat on his heels close by the chuck wagon and watched Celia Westerman. Occasionally his eyes drifted to the eastern horizon, but no anxiety was in them. Having left these

Comanches afoot, he had no fear of immediate pursuit. Still, he knew it was high time to clear out of this part of the country. They wouldn't be afoot forever.

Something was worrying Celia Westerman. She carried it a long while, then looked at Jameson. "I keep thinking about that man who died back there in the buffalo wallow. He died for me, Mr. Jameson."

"It was a risk we all took. We all knew it before we started."

"But *he* died, and I was saved. I can't help thinking about it. What was his name?"

"Andregg. Milt Andregg."

"Milt Andregg." She tried the name. "What kind of man was he?"

Jameson shrugged. "A good buffalo skinner. Beyond that, I don't know much." He knew a little, but it was pointless to bring it up. The man was dead now. The manner of his death compensated for whatever he might have been or done before.

"Did he have a family?"

"None that I knew of."

"I hate to think of him lying back there unburied. You know what the Indians will do."

"You couldn't help that. None of us could."

"No, I guess not. But someday I'm going to put up a marker for him, in a Christian cemetery. It'll tell his name, and what he did. Then he'll always be remembered. As long as a man is remembered, he's not really dead, is he? I mean, as long as he lives in somebody's mind . . ."

"I don't know. I've never thought about that kind of thing very much."

She lowered her head. "I have, lately. I've had lots of time to."

Jameson could see a little of the pain come back into her eyes as she remembered.

"You want to talk about it?" he asked. "Maybe it would help."

She nodded. "Maybe." Her face seemed to grow older as she thought back on it, and the harsh memories crowded into her mind. She hesitated a little, then she started to tell it.

"Times haven't been easy, these last few years in Texas. The carpetbag government took our ranch away from us. I'd been to school, so I got a job teaching. It was a small log building at the edge of town. Hadn't been any Comanche trouble there in a long time. We never even thought about it anymore. One afternoon a storm came up just as I was letting out school. Most of the kids ran for it. But there were a little boy and girl—brother and sister—who had to ride five miles home. It wasn't more than a good thunderhead. I figured an hour or so and it would be over. So I told them to stay.

"They came in the rain, the Comanches did. They were in the schoolhouse before we saw them. We didn't even have a gun there. One of them, his name was Kills His Enemies, took a liking to my hair. He had a hatchet in his hand and was about to kill me when the leader came in. I found out later his name was Buffalo Finder. He looked me over, and he made Kills His Enemies turn me loose. Later, Buffalo Finder told me he'd wanted me for a wife. They took us out and put us on horses.

"They had made quite a foray. It was a big raiding party, no squaws or children along. They had perhaps four hundred horses that they had stolen from the ranches. They knew white men were after them, so they pushed hard.

"Some of them spoke a little Spanish, and so could I. It was rough on all of us, but especially on that poor little boy. He was sickly. He couldn't keep up. The first day in the rain was too much for him. He got sicker and sicker and was holding back the bunch. They wouldn't even let me help him.

"Kills His Enemies kept beating him with a mesquite limb. The third day, two of the warriors took the boy out in plain sight of us and pitched him into the air. And when he came down, Kills His Enemies was waiting with his lance. . . ."

Celia Westerman closed her eyes. A tear squeezed out and found its way down her cheek.

"He's a devil," she said, her voice tight, a deep hatred rising in her face. "A devil out of hell.

"Somewhere up on the cap rock we joined the squaws and children they had left behind. Then we came on up here to the high plains to a deep canyon, bigger than anything I've ever seen. A creek runs down the middle of it, and in places the walls go straight up for hundreds of feet. We camped there a little while. Mexican traders— Comancheros—came in and traded for about half of the stolen horses.

"One of them tried to trade for me. He said he wanted to return me to my own people, but that wasn't it at all. I could see it in his eyes. He offered a lot of trade goods, but Buffalo Finder wouldn't give me up. Then after him came an older man, named Felix Alvarez, and he was a kind one. He took pity on us, the girl and me. He said he had lost a daughter about my age. He traded for the girl. She's on her way home by now. He offered everything he had to get me free. But the chief still wanted me for wife. And Kills His Enemies still hoped to get my hair. The old man stayed until he knew it was getting dangerous for him. And when he left, there were tears in his eyes.

"The day they left, I stole a knife. I walked down to

the creek, and I tried to kill myself. But I couldn't do it, Mr. Jameson. I was either too strong or too weak, I don't know which. Life is hard to turn loose of, even when there's little left in it. I tried to hope Felix Alvarez might still find a way to rescue me. But I guess I knew he couldn't. It would have been suicide to try, and the little girl would have died, too.

"The chief started trying to get me to consent to be his wife. He didn't have to do it that way. He could have forced me. But he wanted it to be of my own will, I guess. I held off, hoping. And all the time, I knew I would die if I didn't. He had other wives. The number-one wife was jealous. If anyone tells you a Comanche woman can't make life miserable for her husband, he just doesn't know.

"And Kills His Enemies was working on him, too, trying to trade for me. A few days ago we moved here to set up a permanent winter camp. I knew the time was getting short. Either I had to submit to Buffalo Finder or let my hair hang from Kills His Enemies' lance."

Celia Westerman looked darkly at the ground.

"I've always been taught that death is better than dishonor. But it's easier to say it than it is to face the decision and die. I should be ashamed to admit it, but it's the way it was. I had just about made up my mind when you came. I didn't want to die.

"You killed Buffalo Finder this morning. I saw him fall. Kills His Enemies will take over now. He won't stay afoot long. He'll get horses and he'll be after you if you're anywhere on these plains. That's the way he is. He's not human."

Jameson looked into the cook fire a long time, admiring her strength, trying to make up his mind. "How far would it be to a Texas settlement?"

She shook her head. "I don't know. Perhaps a couple

of hundred miles. If you're thinking about trying to take me, don't. No white man has ever done it, so far as I know. Only the Indians know the way.''

"Couldn't you find the trail back, the way you came?''

"We made it too fast, and we made a lot of it at night. You have to know the waterholes. A quarter-mile miss on some of them and you're lost. I couldn't be sure I could find them again.''

Grimly Jameson said, "Then the only way out is Kansas. We can take you to Dodge. You catch a train to one of the trail towns, and then you can get one of the Texas cow outfits to carry you home with them when they go back.''

She looked over the wagons, and her shrewd blue eyes quickly sized up the situation. "It's a long way to Kansas, too. And those wagons aren't more than half loaded with hides. If you take me now, you'll hurt yourself, won't you?''

He would ruin himself, he knew. But he wouldn't tell her that. "We've got to get you home.''

She shook her head again. "Not at that price, Mr. Jameson. It's been a long time. I can wait a little longer.''

"A hide camp is no place for a woman.''

He looked around at the men. As he had expected, most of them were staring at Celia Westerman. A woman in a hide camp could cause as much trouble as a woman at sea, if luck took that kind of a turn.

"I know what you're thinking,'' she said. "But there won't be any trouble. I won't let there be any trouble.''

Judgment told him to say no. But he couldn't keep from looking at his hide wagons, only half loaded.

"You sure you want it this way?'' he asked her, wanting her to say yes but afraid that decision would not be the right one.

"You'll hardly even know I'm here,'' she told him.

Then she stood up and walked to the fire, to lift the lids off the ovens of brown bread and to take up the buffalo steaks.

A crinkle came to the corners of Jameson's eyes. There she was wrong. Never for a minute would he forget she was here.

12

FIVE DAYS they angled westward, working generally up the Canadian, and a little to the south of it. They crossed several creeks and streams of varying sizes. Along most of them Jameson found ample sign of buffalo. The land took on a sandier texture as the wagons moved westward. There was more bunch grass in places. But mostly it was still the short, thick turf of buffalo and mesquite grass, strong feed that kept his horses and mules fat on a minimum ration of corn.

Five days, and he thought they had gone far enough.

Reb Pruitt was cooking again now, with help. He remained pale, his left arm tightly bound. But his feet were as active as ever, and his mouth, too.

Because of Pruitt's bad arm, Jameson had suggested getting one of the other men to drive the chuck wagon for him.

"I can do it," Celia Westerman offered. "I've handled

wagons almost ever since I was big enough to climb up on one by myself.''

So Reb Pruitt rode beside Celia Westerman on the chuck wagon seat, his eyes taking on the glow of a pet dog's. He would have thrown the coffeepot at anyone who had offered to take over Celia Westerman's driving job.

"Handles that wagon better than I could," Pruitt told Jameson in admiration, watching her pull it into place. "I always could make a hand with a bronc, but I never was no great shakes with a team. That there's a woman, Jameson.''

The little cook frowned. "Just one thing worries me, and that's them squaw clothes. They ain't fitten for a white woman. We got to do somethin'.''

Jameson agreed but didn't know what they could do about it. "I don't know what she could make a dress out of. All we've got is a wagon sheet, and that wouldn't be of much account.''

Pruitt reached into the chuck wagon bed and fetched down a canvas bag. "I got some extra clothes with me. Little as I am, it might be some of my stuff would fit her.''

Jameson smiled. "I don't know that a shirt and pants would be much more proper than what she's wearing now.''

"At least they didn't come from no heathen.'' Pruitt gave second thought to that and grinned a little. "No heathen *Comanche,* anyway.''

Celia Westerman's presence in camp was making some difference. Reb Pruitt wasn't the only one who had taken up shaving almost every day. Even old Shad took to washing the tobacco out of his beard and combing his rusty hair regularly until one day he studied himself awhile in the cracked mirror he used, then pulled a gray hair out of his head and scowled. He grunted something about a chuckle-headed old fool and lapsed back into his accustomed habits.

The new hunting grounds were as good as those they had been forced to vacate, far to the east. Jameson was still bringing down twenty to thirty buffalo at a stand, most days. One time, when there were enough in one bunch for him and Shad to shoot together, they brought down fifty-three head without having to move more than three hundred yards.

November was well along, and he expected a howling blizzard to come streaking down across the plains almost any day. When it finally came, it wasn't so bad. Only one day was it so cold that they had to stay in camp, and there were only a few flurries of dry snow that never even settled on the ground, blowing about like so much powder. Soon the weather was warm and the hunting was good again. Even better than before.

In spite of this, Jameson found himself getting restless, wanting to go somewhere else, do something else, though he didn't know what it was.

He sat at a distance, watching the skinners work through the buffalo he had shot. First, with their straight-bladed ripping knives they would rip down the belly, starting at the throat and working all the way back to the tail. Then they circled the legs below the knee, slitting down to the belly. They cut the hide up to the ears, leaving the thick mat of curly black hair that grew on the huge head.

Taking their curved skinning knives, they then began to slice beneath the hide until the neck and legs were skinned free and the hide had been worked at least halfway down from belly to backbone. They used pritch sticks with a nail in one end to prop the carcass, feet up, so they could work down the tallowy sides.

This much done by knife, they rolled up a big flap of hide at the neck and tied it to a rope, with a pair of mules hitched on at the rump end of the buffalo. They shouted and flipped the reins, forcing the mules to peel the hide backward off the carcass.

Shad Blankenship rode up and dismounted, stretching himself, then squatting down beside Jameson. "What's the matter, Gage? You got a nervous look."

"It's just those skinners. Seems to me they're getting almighty slow lately."

Blankenship watched them a little. "Ain't nothin' slow about that. It's just you. You got the itch to get back to camp, and it ain't for supper, either. That Texas girl has got you goin' in circles, young'un, the same way she has Reb Pruitt."

Jameson felt the color rise in his face. Shad was striking mighty close to home.

Jameson had felt it coming on for several days. He would look at himself in Shad's mirror and snort the way Shad had. Thirty-five years old, already getting a fair sprinkling of gray in his hair. What was he doing, thinking about Celia Westerman?

But he liked to watch her, liked to listen to that gentle, slow way she had of talking.

As the days went by, the harsh lines in her face began to fade. She seemed to get younger. She moved with a new buoyancy, her captivity drifting into the past like a nightmare after the awakening. Occasionally now she even sang a little as she worked around the wagon, helping Pruitt cook as he had never cooked before.

She still wasn't really pretty, if a man wanted to look at her with a critical eye. But she had a way of making a man think she was.

To Shad Blankenship, Jameson said, "I was worried

about her. I was afraid she might bring trouble in camp. It looks like I was wrong."

Shad said dryly, "We ain't in Dodge yet. They're all watching her, don't ever think they ain't. And Ransom King—you take a look at his eyes sometime when he's got them on her. That feller has more on his mind than buffalo hides, I'm tellin' you."

The days went by, and the hides piled up. Dried hides had to be taken off the ground to make room for green ones coming in. Jameson watched with satisfaction as the handlers pitched these flint hides onto a wagon. After awhile it was loaded, lashed down securely with thick strings cut from a green hide.

Another load finished.

"We haven't got far to go now, Shad," he said. "We've got to move camp in a day or two. I think we'd just as well work over the Canadian, start drifting north a little."

Shad nodded without enthusiasm. Jameson could see what was working on him. Shad didn't relish going back to the settlements. It would be the same old story with him, soon as he got there. He knew it, and he was fighting it.

Jameson had something to worry about, too. Usually, with the prospect of an early return to town and the pay-off, a hide crew got a new spring in its step, got to feeling jolly. But not this one. A tension was building, something hard to trace, hard to put his finger on. More than once he had to step in and stop a fight.

Even Reb Pruitt commented on it.

"Maybe it's the Indians," the cook volunteered. "You don't see any, but the air's got an Indian smell to it, someway. They're around. You can feel it."

To make it worse, Blair Farley had gotten brave and gone back to playing poker. And he was winning. A majority of the men in camp had fallen victim to his skillful fingers to one degree or another. Some already had lost more than they could hope to earn out of the whole expedition. Trencher was one of these. He stalked around the camp like an angry bull, brooding over his losses. Everyone stayed out of his way.

One morning in the first flush of dawn Jameson sat up straight in his tent. He had heard someone shout. He listened a moment and heard it again. Pulling on his boots, he hurried out. He saw several men moving toward the edge of camp.

Someone was calling, "Get Jameson!"

He quickened his step, and the men moved aside for him.

On the ground, a hundred feet past the stock corral, a fat man lay sprawled in his own blood. It was Blair Farley.

A skinner named Darcy Crosson stood by the body, excitement flushing his face. "Injuns," he said breathlessly. "Blair didn't come wake me for guard duty like he was supposed to. I found him thisaway."

Jameson knelt beside the dead man. Farley had been killed with a knife, a cruel ripping job that had laid his stomach open. And he had been scalped. It was rough, crude work that made Jameson's belly tighten, just looking at it.

"Bloody Comanches," somebody breathed in anger.

"Maybe," Jameson said. "And maybe it wasn't Comanches at all."

The men looked sharply at him. He said, "There's hardly a man here who didn't owe him money, lots of money. Now nobody owes him anything."

He could see the idea strike them like a hot iron. They looked furtively at one another, each wondering if the man standing next to him had been the one who had wielded the knife.

Shad Blankenship came up. Jameson asked him, "He always kept those IOU's in his pocket, didn't he?"

Shad nodded. Jameson knelt and went through Blair Farley's pockets one at a time. They were empty, all of them.

He left all the pockets turned wrong side out, letting the men see them, letting them answer the question for themselves.

Someone went for a shovel, and someone else brought out a tarpaulin to cover the body. No one seemed to mourn Farley. Lately he hadn't had a friend in camp.

Shad Blankenship stood with eyes narrowed, watching Trencher lean idly against a wagon.

"Gage," he said, "you got any ideas?"

Jameson nodded. "One or two."

Blankenship's lips drew thin. "I reckon they're the same as mine."

One morning Celia Westerman walked out of her tent and moved toward Jameson.

"Do you know what tomorrow is, Gage?"

He shook his head. "Thursday, I think. Or maybe Friday. I haven't been keeping much track."

"It's Thursday. Thanksgiving. I wish we could have something special to fix for the men tomorrow. They've been brooding a lot the past few days. Maybe a good Thanksgiving meal would cheer them up."

Jameson brightened a little. How many Thanksgivings had he gone through and not even given them a thought?

"You might have something there. Yesterday I flushed a bunch of wild turkeys in a chinaberry thicket up the creek."

Next morning he dug out a shotgun that he had shoved

away among the gear in one of the wagons. Filling his pockets with shotgun shells, he motioned Shad Blankenship to him.

"Shad, how about you doing the buffalo shooting this morning?"

Shad looked him up and down, eyes dwelling on the shotgun.

"I'm going to get a few turkeys for Celia," he explained. "She thinks they might go over good with the crew for Thanksgiving."

Shad's eyes took on a glow of humor. "Now you're gettin' some sense. I only wish that when I'd been younger there'd been somebody for me to shoot turkeys for."

Jameson saddled his bay, sliding the saddle gun into the scabbard. The shotgun was all right for turkeys, but that saddle gun would always be handy in case something else showed up over the hill.

Celia Westerman walked out to the corral, wearing one of Pruitt's coats buttoned up to the neck against the winter wind. "Could you use some help? I'd like to go."

He hesitated, liking the thought of her company but a little skeptical just the same. "Always a chance of Indians."

"You'd be there, Gage," she smiled. "I really would like to go. I'd like to get out of camp a little while, just for a change."

He relented, knowing how monotonous it had been for her. "I can get another shotgun, if you want it."

"All right. I used to be a fairly decent shot."

He wasn't surprised. He had quit being surprised at the things Celia Westerman could do.

They rode out together, past Ransom King's wagons and hide grounds.

King stood and stared at them as they went by. He

nodded at Jameson. Then he tipped his hat to Celia, and his eyes followed her. There was a trace of hunger in them. Time King was getting back to Rose Tremaine, Jameson thought.

Celia looked behind her once, but she didn't speak until they were well away from camp.

"I'm not sure I like your friend King," she said.

"King's all right," Jameson replied. "He just takes a little getting used to. He's up on a cloud one day and deep in darkness the next. He's wild, he's brash, and maybe a little selfish. But I guess it's selfishness that has made people stick with this country. Nobody would put up with it all, unless he thought he could get something out of it."

Celia frowned. "I know this—that if it had been up to him, I never would have been rescued from that Indian camp."

That blabbermouth Pruitt, Jameson thought with sudden impatience. "Who told you a thing like that?"

"Nobody. I just know it, that's all. I know that if it hadn't been for you, Gage, I'd still be there. Or I'd be dead. I'll always be in your debt."

Jameson found himself pulling closer to her, wanting to touch her but not doing it.

"You don't owe me anything, Celia. It's me that owes you. You don't know what it's been worth, having you in camp. In a way I'm going to hate to see you go home."

She nodded, and her blue eyes met his. "I know. In a way I'm going to hate to go. Sometimes I find myself wishing I could stay here. This is a good country, Gage. It'll be a good country to live in, someday."

They looked at each other until Jameson felt a warmth rising in his face, and a strong compulsion to reach across and pull her to him, to kiss her with all the hunger that was in him.

Suddenly he brought himself out of it, self-anger rising in him. Damn it, this isn't some dance-hall girl like King's Rose. What am I thinking of?

He rode silently awhile, trying to put his mind on other things. But she was too close to him.

"You said you aren't married," he said. "Are you promised to anybody?"

She looked at the ground, her eyes absently following her shadow. "Not exactly. There's a man there—we grew up together. We've talked about it some."

Jameson drew up within himself. Well, he thought, that puts an end to it. Now maybe you can get your mind back on the buffalo.

13

REB PRUITT put water on to boil as soon as he saw them coming, turkeys flung across their saddles. Jameson had no desire to get into the work of cleaning the birds. But he stood and watched as Pruitt and the girl did it. The Texas cook handled the job with ease. Jameson finally asked him:

"How did you ever come to be a camp cook, anyway?"

Pruitt looked up, laughter in his eyes. "Well now, I used to have to ride a lot of rank broncs, back there on that ranch where I worked. One day they fetched me one I couldn't ride, and they had to leave me at the wagon to heal up. I got to watching that fat, lazy cook. Come to find out he was makin' fifteen dollars a month more than I was, and he didn't have no saddle rubbing a callus on his rump, either. So right then I knowed I'd missed my callin'."

Shad came in and unsaddled. He'd had a good stand. Now he sat down, back to a wagon wheel, gun kit in hand. He stripped down his big buffalo rifle, swabbing its barrel clean and wiping a thin trace of oil on it before putting it back together.

Jameson brought the empty cartridge cases he had been soaking in vinegar to get all the burned powder out. Now he set the cases up on end and poured black Dupont powder out of a can into a bowl. He started filling the shells with powder, stopping half an inch from the top. He tamped it down with the rammer, put the wad in, and spilled a little more powder atop the wad. He wrapped a piece of paper around the base of the bullet, then forced it into the shell, clamping it down tight.

"Get your turkeys?" Shad asked.

Jameson nodded.

Shad said, "Great country for game, ain't it? Man wouldn't never starve here, if he had powder and lead, and a little salt. He could live fine, the way we done a long time ago."

That far-off look was in Shad's eyes. He was back into times long past, savoring some elusive fragment of fond memory. "It's like the rest of the country used to be before they come and ruined it." He considered that and added, "Before *we* ruined it."

"I know what you mean, Shad," Jameson replied. "It's been that way with me. I get a feeling about this country, a feeling that maybe this is what I've been looking for all my life. You ever look out across it at sundown, Shad? Sundown's the time to look at a place, if you want to see the beauty in it. I get a feeling I don't ever want to leave. I want to stay here, and I want the country to stay just like it is."

Shad grunted, some bitter taste coming in his mouth. He spat and rubbed a greasy sleeve across his red beard.

"But it won't. Three, four years, the buffalo'll all be gone, the way they was from the Republican and the Arkansas. What would there be to stay for? How would you make a livin'?"

"I don't know for sure, Shad. I've thought about cattle. I guess Reb Pruitt put it in my head, always talking about the Texas cow business. This would be a fine cow country, Shad, as good for cattle as it is for buffalo."

"You'd have to get the Comanches off first, and they might not see it just your way."

"When the buffalo are gone, Shad, there won't be any more trouble with the Comanches."

Shad nodded. "But you've never had any experience with cattle, other than maybe popping a whip over a bull team. Takes more than bulls to run a cow ranch, I expect."

Jameson smiled. "A man can learn. *We* could learn, Shad, you and me together. The frontier is going. This would give us something we could both tie to."

Shad Blankenship's wrinkled old face held the beginning of a smile, and his pale eyes were looking far off again, far back into memory. Then, slowly, the smile faded. The memory was gone. The present was here again with its jarring reality. The present, and the future.

"Won't work for me, Gage. I'm too old to change over. The only hope I got is that when my time comes I can die out here someplace and be buried where I can listen to the wind blow and the wolves howl, instead of in town where all I can hear is a piano clinkin' and somebody bellyachin' about the price of beans."

He pointed his finger at Jameson, jabbed it at him.

"But *you* can make the change, Gage. Make it before it's too late. Get you those cows, and grab onto some of this land. And get you a wife, young'un. I never had one, and that's where I made a mistake. Life gets pointless for a man when he ain't got a home, ain't got a woman of his own. One of them dance-hall gals is all right for a young man still sowing his oats. But comes a day he needs to settle. You've come to that day, Gage. You watch or you'll pass it up, and then it's too late. You need a good woman, like that Celia Westerman. If I was you, I wouldn't let her get away.''

Shad was right, Jameson admitted to himself. He wanted Celia Westerman. He needed her. But it seemed she already had gotten away, even before he met her.

The whole crew was waiting when at last the turkey was done. The sun was going down. The stock had been fed, and all the work had been finished. Nothing was left but to sit down and enjoy the Thanksgiving meal.

The anticipation of it was having the effect Jameson had hoped. The tension had eased.

Even the burly Trencher showed a semblance of a smile as he roughly shouldered his way into the line, digging a fork into one of the turkeys and knifing off a huge section of it.

But something went wrong. The first man to fill his plate shoved a big bite of turkey into his mouth and started to chew, grinning. The grin suddenly left him. His mouth twisted. He spat it all out, choking. Seeing that, another man judiciously tested a small piece of the turkey on the tip of his tongue. His face stretched awry in dismay.

Not seeing them, Trencher bit off a big chunk. He spat turkey for six feet, coughing. He looked up then, a flash of rage in his eyes. He flung the plate to the ground and stalked toward Reb Pruitt.

''You miserable, dried-up Johnny Reb, you're tryin' to poison us all!''

Pruitt stared at him, uncomprehending, until Trencher made a grab. He stepped aside quickly. But Trencher kept coming. He pinned Pruitt to the chuck wagon, swung his big fist and knocked the cook to his knees. He grabbed the little Texan by the shoulder and jerked him erect again. He slammed him against the wheel.

Jameson took long strides across to the wagon. He grabbed Trencher's arm and held it. "Stop it, Trencher!"

Trencher struggled with him, trying to free himself. "I'll kill the little whelp!" he grunted.

Finally, seeing he couldn't pull free, he whirled on Jameson.

"All right, Jameson," he breathed, "I been wantin' to do this for a long time." His eyes glowed with a wild fever of rage. He rushed at Jameson, his arms reaching forward from his heavy body. Jameson did not try to dodge. Instead, he lowered his head and drove straight into Trencher's hard belly. He made Trencher overreach, while his own fists pounded into Trencher's ribs. The big man grunted at the shock, and he reeled a step or two sideways. Jameson kept pushing, pressing this initial advantage, driving at Trencher's belly and ribs.

But the surprise lasted only a moment; then Trencher had his wits back. He plowed in now, his rage driving him on. He was apparently oblivious to the worst punishment Jameson was able to give him. He fought only to win, his heavy feet grinding down on Jameson's toes, his knee trying at Jameson's groin, his fingers grasping and twisting Jameson's ears. Pain rocketed through Jameson, pain and desperation. He knew Trencher would kill him if he could.

Somehow he managed to bring up his knee, hard and quick. His heavy boot smashed against Trencher's shin, taking the hide as it drove downward. Jameson saw an opening and arched a fist into Trencher's ear. The big man cried out and turned away from him. Jameson's fist slammed into Trencher's kidney, once, then again.

Trencher doubled over. Jameson jerked Trencher's head up and hit him hard in the throat. Trencher fell heavily to the ground and lay there gasping.

Jameson took a couple of steps backward, heaving for breath. The chuck wagon was behind him. He moved to it and leaned on it for support, his chest rising and falling rapidly as the breath came back to him. He wiped a dusty coat sleeve across his forehead, and it came away wet.

For a moment his eyes were off Trencher. He didn't see where Trencher got the gun. Suddenly there it was, in the man's trembling hands, and Trencher was standing spread-legged, grinning with his lips while his eyes crackled with hatred.

"Now, Jameson," Trencher breathed heavily, and the barrel tilted upward.

Jameson could only stand there, his back to the chuck wagon, staring helplessly at the six-shooter. His mouth went dry. All he could think was, Where did he get that gun?

He sensed a sudden movement beside him. Trencher jerked aside, but not in time. A heavy iron pot hook from Pruitt's chuck box slammed into the man's head. Trencher fell heavily, the gun dropping from his fingers. Before he could grab it, someone else had it. Messick, the skinner. Jameson looked around and saw Pruitt still bent forward, the way he had been when he let the pot hook fly away, singing.

"Thanks, Reb," Jameson whispered.

As suddenly as it had begun, it was over. Ransom King helped Trencher to his knees. "I'm sorry about this, Gage," he said. "Trencher has a bottle hidden away somewhere, and he's been working on it. I'll get him sobered up. It won't happen again."

Jameson tried to speak, but his throat was leather-dry, and no sound came out. He watched narrow-eyed as King and one of Jameson's own men helped Trencher stagger away.

Angrily Trencher jerked free of the men who were holding him. He turned half around, his hate-filled eyes on Jameson.

"I'll get you, Jameson. Your time is about run out. I'll get you and don't you forget it!"

King took hold of the man and roughly yanked him away. "You're drunk, Trencher. Come on."

Celia Westerman hurried to Jameson. Her fingers anxiously explored the cuts and bruises on his face. "I'll take care of those," she said.

He waved his hand. "Never mind. I'm all right."

But she went anyway to the chuck box, hunting for antiseptic. The rest of the crew melted away, chewing on bread, sipping coffee, but leaving the turkey alone. Pruitt stared at it, puzzled.

"I can't figure it out. I know it wasn't nothin' we done. But that meat's so bitter it makes you sick."

It struck Jameson then, as Celia painted his wounds with iodoform. The chinaberries. He hadn't thought of it before. The turkeys had been feeding on chinaberries. That had tainted the meat.

"Dandy Thanksgivin'," Pruitt said disconsolately. "Nothing much here to be thankful about."

Jameson slowly shook his head. "One thing, Reb. We can be thankful we've got those wagons about loaded. I think it's high time we headed for Dodge."

14

Rainin' way yonder," Shad Blankenship said, watching the heavy clouds scurry across the morning sky. "It would rain here too, if a man was to look at them clouds a little cross-eyed."

Jameson could smell the promise of rain in the sharp wind searching across the prairie. Riding beside Shad, holding the Big Fifty in his lap, he frowned at the skies. "Maybe. Been hoping it would hold off a little. Three or four more days and we'd have all the hides we can pack."

"We got plenty now," Shad said. "She starts in to rainin', we better settle for what we got and move out."

Shad spat, and his big black dog jumped aside. Shad let his pale eyes lift to the horizon. "Something else too, and that's that Injun, Kills His Enemies. I'd just as soon not have to mess with him. But there's Injuns around, Gage. I can feel them in the back of my neck."

When Jameson smiled, Shad said quickly, "Don't laugh. Dodge them as many years as I have and you get so you don't have to see them anymore. You can smell them, like a hound dog."

Jameson looked back toward the two wagons that trailed them, slackening his pace when he saw that they were getting some distance behind. Like Shad, he was getting that uneasy feeling, wondering each day if it might not be smarter to pack up and string the wagons north than to ride out for another day's bag of green hides.

They didn't have to ride far to find buffalo, for a big herd had drifted in along the creek where they were camped. The animals grazed in scattered bunches up and down it for miles. They were almost black now with the thick coat of winter hair that made them look bigger than they had a few weeks ago. These winter hides would bring more money. With that heavy hair they could be turned into robes instead of being cut up for leather.

It was this that had kept Jameson here, the robe hides and the ease of the kill. Had the buffalo been hard to find, he would have started north a week ago.

"Well, Shad," Jameson said, "let's split up and get this over with as soon as we—"

He broke off, for Shad had stiffened. Jameson turned quickly and saw what Shad saw—Indians.

Ten warriors swept down the crest of a hill toward them, whooping and yelling as they came. Ten warriors against two men, with the wagons still behind.

"We can't get back to the wagons, Shad!" Jameson exclaimed. "They'll cut us off."

Desperately he began to look for a hillock, a buffalo wallow, anything for cover. But there was nothing.

Shad stepped out of the saddle and dropped prone to the ground. He began to dig in his pocket. "Good a time

as any to see if that man was right about these squallers,"
he said. He was as casual as if he were about to try a
new gun on the buffalo.

Jameson had almost forgotten about those bullets Shad
had bored the holes in. Now, dropping down beside Shad
and ramming one of his own cartridges into the breech,
he remembered.

Shad raised the rifle and fired. The bullet screamed as
it sped through the air, the bored hole catching the wind.
Shad put another one in and fired again.

"Squall like a banshee, don't they?" Shad said.

The Indians hauled up short, and Shad put a third one
over their heads.

"I only got two left," Shad complained. "If they don't
work, I'm gonna have to tell that feller he's an awful
liar."

He fired the fourth one. Now the Indians began to pull
back, gesturing excitedly. Shad balefully eyed the last
bullet, then slipped it into the breech. It was even louder
than the rest, one of the weirdest sounds Jameson had
ever heard. It made the hair stand on his neck.

It did the job. The Indians wheeled their horses and
took out across the hill again. Jameson lowered his own
rifle, still unfired.

Shad grinned and spat tobacco juice out across the
grass. "Superstitious lot, Injuns are. Come up against
them with somethin' they ain't seen or heard before, and
they don't hardly know how to take it. Come to think of
it, somebody shot one of them things at me, I wouldn't
know how to take it, either."

They stood up, catching their horses.

Jameson looked at the hill over which the Indians had
come and gone. And he made a decision.

"I think we've got all the hides we'd better try for.
We're heading north, Shad, while we still can."

Swinging back into the saddle, Shad nodded in agreement. "Now, young'un, you're talkin' sense."

They rode quickly back to the two wagons, not knowing if the Indians had been frightened enough to keep away, or if they might come back over that hill at any minute.

The men at the wagons had pulled up together and jumped to the ground, rifles ready. They still stood there as Jameson and Shad rode up.

The tall, thin skinner Messick solemnly shook his head. "We thought sure you was goners, both of you. And we wasn't even sure about us." His eyes went to Shad. "What in the name of heaven was that you shot at them? Not even a Comanche can make a sound worse than that."

Shad explained the squallers. "Worked this time. But they'll probably figure it out. Next time they won't be so easy fooled."

Jameson said, "Turn the wagons around and head for camp. There won't be a next time if we can help it."

They had not ridden three minutes before they heard other gunfire, farther away. Ransom King's. You could always tell by the sound of the guns who was doing the shooting. No two of these buffalo rifles made quite the same report.

Suddenly Jameson straightened, his ear turned toward the sound. The first tremor of alarm moved through him. There were more guns than there ought to be, and the firing was getting faster. That wasn't the way you shot buffalo. Jameson glanced at the other men and saw that they were listening, too.

"They've hit King," Jameson said. "Let's roll."

Messick and the other driver flipped their reins. The mules lunged forward, jerking roughly against the traces, bouncing the wagons. Jameson spurred into a lope and took the lead. Shad Blankenship fell in just behind him. Jameson leaned forward in the saddle, listening to the crackle of guns.

He looked back and saw the wagons trailing behind him, moving as fast as they could without bouncing the wheels off.

A mile. A mile and a half. The shooting was close now. They topped out over a ridge and there the battle was, below them. King and Trencher and two skinners were barricaded behind an upturned wagon. Around them lay four dead mules and King's sorrel horse.

A dose of our own medicine, Jameson thought.

Around and around the men fifteen or eighteen Comanches circled, whooping, yelling, letting arrows fly into the flimsy barricade. Three or four Indians and as many horses lay fallen on the prairie. And inside the barricade Jameson saw a man lying still, on his stomach.

He signaled the wagons to pull up, for he saw no practical way to get them down off the steep ridge in time to be any help.

"We'll do a better job shooting from up here anyway," he said to Shad. The skinners piled out and came running, bringing their rifles. Jameson signaled one man to hold the horses and mules, the rest to spread out in a line. He bellied down in the grass, put up the rest stick for his Sharps and drew a bead. The first shot sent an Indian horse plunging into a somersault. Beside Jameson, the other men opened fire. Two more horses went down, and Indians fell.

The Comanches hauled up in surprise. While they stood there, trying to locate the source of fire, well-aimed bullets cut down two more. One Indian made a signal, and the others followed him, leaving the battleground in a run. Jameson sighted down the barrel, held his breath and squeezed. The Indian who had signaled pitched to the ground. The others kept riding.

The hide men on the ridge continued rapid fire, and the men behind the barricade were doing the same. Another horse fell. The rider jumped up limping. Two Comanches turned back, leaning down and drumming heels into their horses' sides. Riding on either side of him, they picked him up and carried him off between them, holding him that way until they thought they were out of bullet range.

Presently Jameson stood up, pulling the rest stick out of the ground, wiping the dirt off it onto his pants leg.

"Looks like it's over, Shad."

"Maybe. And maybe it's just started."

A drop of water struck Jameson's hat brim. He looked up, and another hit him on the cheek. His gaze went to the horizon. He saw that it had faded out into a gray pall of rain.

"Fixin' to get wet," he said. "Let's see what we can do down there."

Without going back for their horses, Jameson and Shad walked down the ridge toward King's upturned wagon. Messick followed behind them, using his rifle to help his balance as his long legs hurriedly worked down the steep slope.

One of King's skinners walked shakily out to meet them, his face gray as an ashbank, hands trembling. "Man alive, but you fellers came just in time. They had us, I'll tell you, they had us."

King stood beside the upturned wagon, rifle in his hand, the sprinkle of rain striking its hot barrel and turning to steam.

"You saved our hash, Jameson," he said levelly.

Jameson shook his head. "That evens us up. You saved mine once, in Dodge."

But Trencher glared angrily, his hatred for Jameson still burning in his eyes. "We was doin' all right," he said sullenly. "We'd have whipped them off without you." He turned sharply and trudged out to look across the field of battle.

Jameson knelt beside the man who lay facedown in the grass. One of King's crew. He touched him, then stood up. The man was dead.

Jameson looked at King. "There'll be more dead if we don't haul out of here. I think I've got all the hides I need. How about you?"

King looked up at the horizon over which the Indians had poured down upon him. "I'm satisfied. Those boys will be back, and I'd just as soon not be here."

The lean Messick was walking around over the battle scene. At length he paused to look down on three Indians who lay still within twenty feet of each other.

Trencher strode that way, taking a skinning knife from his belt.

"I'm gonna count coup this time," he said brutally.

He knelt by the first Indian, cut a crude circle around the top of the head with the sharp knife and roughly took off the scalp. He moved to the second. But this one wasn't dead. When the half-conscious Indian cried out at the fiery touch of the blade, Trencher jerked back as if he had touched something hot. Then he lifted the knife and plunged it into the Indian's throat. He grinned savagely as he brought it up and stabbed down again.

A moment later Trencher was wiping the knife in the grass and dangling three gory specimens of crude butchery, the grin cutting across his broad, bewhiskered face like a knife gash itself.

Messick stood watching him, his back stiff, some of the color drained from his cheeks. When Trencher had gone, Messick glanced toward Jameson and beckoned him with his sharp chin.

"What does that remind you of, Gage?"

"Blair Farley?"

Messick nodded and said tightly, "Yeah, and even farther back than that. Remember George Hobart, and those two men we found dead with him that last trip out for Miles and Posey?"

Jameson knelt and looked closer at the scalped Indians, remembering how it had been with the white men, wondering if possibly . . .

"Nathan, it couldn't have been . . ."

"But it could. The thought struck me when I saw Blair Farley, but I didn't believe it then. Now I do."

Jameson protested, "He works for Ransom King. How could he have killed Hobart?"

"He doesn't work for King all the time. They tell me sometimes he goes out for himself, when King doesn't need him. Who knows what he does when he's out that way? He's no hunter, Jameson. Man hunter, maybe, but not a buffalo hunter."

"We'd have to be sure."

"That knife he had—I caught a quick look at it. I'd swear it was George Hobart's. George made his own knives, and there never was anybody else ever made one just the same as his."

A chill passed through Jameson. He had to concede that Messick might be right. There was a brutality, a killer instinct about Trencher. Jameson had seen it often enough to know. He'd even been pitted against it.

"We'd still have to have proof before we could do anything."

Messick's eyes were narrowed in cold fury. "I'll get you the proof. I'll get my hands on that knife someway.

And if it's George's . . . I'll put it in Trencher's throat, the way I'd do a buffalo.''

Jameson closed his eyes, remembering last year when he had helped run down three hide thieves who had murdered a hunter and stolen the hides he had worked months to get. They had gone so far as to scalp the victim, trying to shift the blame onto Indians. But another hunter had stumbled upon the scene and run for help.

Jameson would never forget how they had hanged the thieves one at a time, out on the treeless prairie. They had used the upended tongue of the stolen wagon. The last two had watched ashen-faced and trembling as the first one had choked and slowly died.

And later, when it was all over, somebody had scalped all three of them.

Messick said, ''I'll get that knife. Then we'll see what we do.''

The rain was falling steadily as they hurriedly broke camp. They took up the half-green hides from the drying grounds and loaded them on the last empty wagons that had been used to haul each day's bag in from the killing grounds. At the first sign of rain Reb Pruitt had stretched a wagon sheet over the hoops of the chuck wagon to keep the remaining supplies and bedding dry. Then he had stretched a tarpaulin out overhead to give the men a place to stand out of the rain while they wolfed down a quick meal.

Gage Jameson stood on the creek bank, watching the angry swirl of mud-brown water. The creek was rising steadily. A couple of hours more and it would be out of banks from the rain which had already fallen farther upstream.

Shad Blankenship pointed his rusty chin toward the

chuck wagon. "You better grab you somethin' to eat so we can drag it out of here."

Jameson shook his head. "In a minute. Just looking at that creek, Shad. Think we could put the wagons over it right now?"

Shad frowned, watching the brown water rush past. "Maybe, maybe not. Another hour or so and nothin' will get over it."

"That's what I was thinking. If we could get across it now, it would give us a lot of protection from the Comanches, at least till it went down. And we could get a long way by then, if we kept traveling."

Shad rubbed his chin. "It'd sure be some gamble. We might lose every wagon we got."

"No telling what we'll lose if we have to fight those Comanches. We'll try it with one wagon—*I'll* try it. If it works, fine. If it doesn't . . ."

He let it drop there. He turned and hurried back to camp. He sought out the wagon with the smallest load of hides on it and called a pair of teamsters.

"Let's hook a team to this wagon, quick."

He disconnected the trail wagon while they caught up the mules and put the harness on them. This would be the way, one wagon at a time, then come back for the trail wagons. Seeing what he was about to try, the other men gathered to watch anxiously. They all knew what this meant—a chance to avoid a battle.

Jameson shed his coat, his boots and his hat in case he had to swim. He started to climb up to the wagon seat. Celia Westerman caught his arm. Her blue eyes were big with fear.

She said, "Gage, I . . ." Her lips went tight, and she choked off the words. "Gage, be careful."

He squeezed her hand, then crossed two of her fingers.

"Keep them that way," he said. He climbed to the seat and flipped the reins.

"Hya-a-a-a-a!"

The mules jerked against the traces and the wagon lurched forward, the iron rims slipping in the slick mud. Jameson swung the mules around, straightening the wagon before it reached the levelest part of the creek bank. The mules seemed to sense the danger. They began to falter. He took the long whip and lashed far out with it, popping it over the ears of the leaders, yelling as he went.

The leaders plunged into the water. Jameson kept the whip talking, kept the other mules pulling hard. The foamy water lapped up against the wheels of the wagon as they splashed down off the creek bank.

"Hya-a-a-a-a! Keep on moving there! *Hya-a-a-a-a!"*

The mules angled with the powerful current. For a moment Jameson's hopes soared high. It looked as if they would make it to the far bank without a hitch.

Then the full force of the water hit the flat side of the wagon. He felt a sickening lurch. He saw panic sweep through the swimming mules. He found himself wishing they were horses. Mules almost always were the most sensible in a tight situation, but in the water horses had them bested.

The wagon began to tilt, top-heavy with its load of hides. The mules were fighting, plunging up and down. One went under water, came up, then went down again.

He's lost, Jameson thought fearfully. Let him get his ears full of water and he's lost.

He felt the wagon begin to heave over beneath him. He jumped from the seat into the brown foam, his hands tightly clutching the lines. Over the heavy roar he heard the splash as the wagon went over on its side, then over again, the wheels up out of the water. He heard the snap of the tongue.

The wagon was doomed now, and the mules threshed in terror. Another was out of sight, adding its dead weight to drag the rest down. Jameson managed to grab the bridle of one fighting mule and hold while he drew the knife from his belt. He cut at the harness, trying to free the mules from the wagon.

But the heavy pull of the current wrested the harness from his hands, and somehow he lost the knife. He felt himself being pulled away from the wagon, away from the mules.

All was lost now, he knew, hopelessness sweeping through him. The mules, the wagon, the hides—all of it. All he could do now was try to save himself.

He swam desperately, managing to keep his head above water as the raging current carried him on. He fought to return to the bank. He was working nearer. But his mouth was full of the muddy water. He choked, swallowing some of it. His arms were afire with pain, heavy as anvils.

He realized suddenly that he was drowning, that he would never make it to the bank. Swallowing water, his arms giving out, he was done.

But he kept fighting, trying for the bank.

Then he saw someone out there on horseback, rope in hand. The horseman rode into the water, as far as he could without being swept into the current. Going down, Jameson saw the rope swinging. He fought to the surface again, and he felt the rope settle and jerk tight about his shoulders. Instinctively he grabbed it. He felt it burn cruelly into his flesh as he hit the end of it. Then the rope began to pull him against the current. He swung slowly but surely toward the bank. He felt the slick mud underfoot and tried to help himself ashore. But no more strength was left in him.

The rope dragged him onto the bank, out of the water. He stayed there on hands and knees, coughing up muddy water, nausea sending the world reeling about his head. He was conscious of the clean rain beating down on him.

Reb Pruitt jumped from Jameson's bay horse, dropping his end of the rope. He rushed to Jameson's side. He took off his coat and threw it over Jameson's wet shoulders.

"Go on now," he said gently, "bend over there, keep coughin' that water up. You'll be as sick as a horse if you don't."

Jameson kept coughing. Gradually the world stopped spinning and he could see. "How far . . . how far?"

Pruitt shrugged. "Quarter mile, maybe. That's a mighty fast current."

Jameson caught Pruitt's hand. "Thanks, Reb."

The little Texan grinned, recoiling the wet rope. "You're a pretty decent kind of a Yankee, Jameson, and I figure we better hang onto any of that kind we can get. There ain't many."

Men came running afoot, the quarter mile down from camp. Men, and a woman. Celia Westerman rushed to Jameson. Breathless, seeing he was all right, she threw herself into his arms.

Jameson held her tightly, his cheek against hers.

The rest of them were staring, and he didn't care. He held her a long time.

"Celia," he said at last, "we've got to go. It didn't work. All we can do now is travel, and travel fast."

15

MOVING THE wagons out, Jameson tried to ride his horse. But the muddy water he had swallowed made him lean over and heave until at last he was too weak and head-spinning sick to stay in the saddle. So he moved to the seat of the chuck wagon, beside Celia Westerman, and let the cowboy cook ride the horse.

He had changed to dry clothes. Now the cold, steady rain had soaked even those, and he hunched up in a miserable knot, a raw chill penetrating him to the bone.

He looked back often to the long line of heavy-laden hide wagons strung out behind. Their wide rims cut through the brown cured grass and squeezed dirty water up into deep muddy ruts that ribboned out in their wake.

A blind Indian could have followed them, he thought darkly.

Celia Westerman touched his arm. "Look, Gage, yonder."

He glanced up where she pointed. His eyes still burned from the muddy water, but he could see the eight or ten horsemen far off there in the rain, hunched under blankets, watching the wagons.

"We can't get away from them," Celia said. "They'll follow us until they're ready. And then they'll come."

They kept rolling all the rest of the day and well into darkness. Shad Blankenship and Reb Pruitt rode in front, feeling out the low places for soft spots that might bog down the wagons. The rain was letting up some, for which Jameson was thankful. Much more of it and the ground would become so boggy the wagons couldn't move.

Jameson looked often to the right, and usually he saw the Indians there, following along patiently out of range.

Men in the other wagons were watching them, too. Someone said angrily, "Why don't they come on and get it over with?"

"They're just waitin'," came the answer in Nathan Messick's even voice. "Injuns don't like the rain. They'll come down in their own due time."

When they didn't come before dark, Jameson felt some relief. At least they weren't likely to strike before daylight.

Reb Pruitt came up, and Jameson called him. "Let me have the horse awhile, Reb."

Celia Westerman caught Jameson's hand. "Gage, are you sure you can ride?"

"I feel a lot better now. Anyway, this shouldn't take long."

With Shad Blankenship, he rode along the creek bank, looking for a likely spot for camp, a spot that would help them present a good defense. The rain had stopped, but the creek was still running high.

"You ain't thinkin' about tryin' to cross her again, are you, Gage?" Shad asked worriedly.

Jameson shook his head. "No, thanks. I already had my bath."

He found what he wanted, a place where the creek bank had caved back far enough from the water itself so that the stock could all be herded down there out of reach of the Comanches.

"Reb," he said as he rode back to the chuck wagon, "I've found a good place where we can line the wagons up in a row right on the edge of the bank. We'll put the horses and mules down below. That'll give us the water at our backs so they can't circle us. Follow me."

The cave-off was perhaps a hundred yards long and the sharp bank about five feet high, a kind of pocket against the creek. Carefully they pulled the wagons up within feet of the edge, angling the tongues outward so the front of one wagon was almost touching the tail gate of the next. As the teams were unharnessed they were turned loose below the bank.

Working in darkness, the men cut timber and threw up a barrier at each end to keep the stock inside. Reb Pruitt built his fire below the bank with wood he had kept dry all day under the wagon sheet. Shivering with cold, their clothes thoroughly soaked, the men filed by to fill their cups with hot coffee, then went back to work. They shoveled wet earth high under the beds of the wagons as protection against bullets and arrows.

Only when the work was finished did they stop to eat. The hot coffee and the buffalo meat brought strength back to Jameson. His head was clear, and he was no longer sick at his stomach. He could almost forget the soggy clothing sticking to his skin, the cold that stiffened him and turned his lips blue.

Ransom King walked over and sat on his heels beside

Jameson and Celia Westerman. "What now, Gage?"

"Nothing, just wait. I don't believe we could find a better place to make a stand. No more running. We'll wait here for them."

King looked worriedly back toward the water, which still roared in the darkness. "What if that creek rises some more?"

Jameson's lips drew tight. "Then our bread just turns back to dough."

Waiting, Jameson reloaded all the empty cartridges he had. Celia Westerman sat beside him, brooding. "Gage," she said finally, "it's all my fault. If it hadn't been for me, you wouldn't be in this."

Gage shook his head. "It's not your fault. You weren't captured by your own choice. You didn't know we were going to try to free you until we'd done it. There wasn't a thing you could have done or changed. Besides, we'd likely have run up against them sooner or later anyway. We knew when we came down here we'd have a fight getting out. So now we have it."

"What do you think of our chances?"

He shrugged. "We've got a good defensive position here. We've got buffalo rifles that can shoot farther and straighter than anything these Comanches have ever seen. We've got powder and lead, and plenty of food and water. Whatever happens, they'll have a run for their money."

The glow from the faraway campfire barely lighted her face. She was looking at Jameson, her eyes soft. Presently she touched his hand.

"Gage," she said, "do you have a girl waiting for you somewhere?"

"No," he replied. "There's never been one."

She leaned to him a little. She said, "I told you once that there was a man back home. . . . I thought there was,

Gage. But I know now that there never was enough between us.''

She tilted her head upward. "Gage, whatever happens, I want you to know . . . I love you."

His arms went around her. He pulled her to him, and their lips met in the darkness.

Daybreak, and every man was up, peering anxiously out over the earthwork defense they had piled up beneath the wagons.

"Nothin' there," Shad Blankenship said. "Maybe they want us to sweat."

"Maybe they think we're going to move again," Jameson commented. "They want to catch us strung out in the open. But we'll fool them on that. We wait right here."

Reb Pruitt called out, "Grub's ready. Come and get it!"

The men filed by, and Jameson watched their faces, wondering how well they were going to hold up. In most of the faces he saw a tenseness, but if there was real fear, he failed to detect it.

Suddenly he became aware that someone was missing. Nathan Messick!

He climbed up on the bank and looked over the camp. "Anybody seen Messick?" he called.

Nobody replied. Most began looking around for him. Reb Pruitt had the loudest voice. He called again and again. But Messick was gone.

"Them Comanches," Pruitt muttered angrily. "They must of snuck up here in the night."

Puzzled, Jameson glanced at Trencher. He noticed that Trencher's knife was gone from the scabbard on the man's belt. And he remembered what Messick had said:

"I'll get you the proof. I'll get my hands on that knife

someway. And if it's George's, I'll put it in Trencher's throat, the way I'd do a buffalo.''

It hadn't been Comanches, Jameson knew. Messick *had* gotten hold of that knife, sometime during the night. But something had gone wrong.

Jameson looked down at the flooded creek, still rolling and foaming. He knew where Nathan Messick was. He choked back the fury that welled up inside him.

When this is over, he promised himself, I'll get you, Trencher. I don't know how, but I'll get you.

After breakfast they sat and waited, an hour, two hours, three. Jameson watched the clouds lose their heavy gray. Slowly they thinned, the glare of sunlight showing in weak spots. By mid-morning there were definite breaks in them. The rain was over. The sun would be out soon, and the mud would begin to dry. The wagons could move faster.

"Here they come!" Shad Blankenship called.

Men scrambled for their places beneath the wagons. Most lay prone on their blankets to keep out of the mud. They had their ammunition lying beside them, ready.

Jameson looked up and caught his breath. The Indians came in a body, riding at a lope. The solid group spread out fanwise, and suddenly the Indians began to yell.

Jameson was held by the deadly magnificence of the sight. Never had he seen its equal, and he knew it was something he was likely never to see again. Shrieking and yelping, the Comanches came rushing across the rain-soaked ground, waving their bows and lances and guns, their heavy bull-neck shields. The bodies of Indians and horses alike were splashed with red and yellow. War bonnets streamed in the wind. The barbarically painted bodies glinted with metal ornaments and charms. In horses' manes and tails there fluttered bright red cloth, plaited to stay.

Jameson felt the hair lift at the back of his neck.

"Get down, Celia," he said. "Stay down."

She shook her head. "I'll help you reload."

"All right, then. But keep low." Then he yelled for the men, "If they get too close, shoot for the horses. Don't let a horse come through."

He flopped down on his blanket then. He rested the barrel of the rifle across a wagon spoke.

The Indians were bearing down on them, two hundred yards away.

"Trying to ride over us the first time," he said. He drew a bead on one of the nearest Indians and fired. The Indian spun half around and fell off the horse, blown open by the heavy bullet of the Big Fifty. Other rifles roared. Indians tumbled. Horses sprawled, other horses stumbling over them and crashing down.

The buffalo hunters kept up a rapid fire, lacing the Comanche line. Behind them, under the bank, their own horses and mules milled excitedly. When some of the Comanches appeared to be breaking through, the rifle muzzles tipped downward, and the horses rolled. Two Indians who fell near the wagons jumped to their feet and came running, only to be torn apart by bullets before they reached the breastworks. Others turned and fled afoot, some falling under fire, some managing to swing up behind other Indians who had not lost their horses.

The first attack was broken. The Comanches retreated in a ragged line, leaving the plain dotted with fallen horses. Some of these animals threshed and screamed in pain until merciful bullets sought them out.

The Comanches tried to pick up as many of their dead and wounded as they could before they rode away. Jameson counted ten warriors carried off. He could still see six or eight lying in the grass, too close to the wagons for the Indians to recover them.

One fallen Indian raised up on his elbow and began dragging himself away. A rifle cracked, and he fell face-down in the mud. Jameson saw Trencher lower his rifle to reload it, grinning.

The Indians rallied far out yonder on the prairie, milling around, arguing. They would be a little while.

Jameson pushed to his feet and slowly made the rounds to see how the crew had fared.

"Any dead?" he called.

There was no answer to that, and relief lifted a heavy weight from his broad shoulders. "Any wounded?"

From two places came an answer. One of King's skinners held a rag to his shoulder, stopping the flow of blood from a flesh wound. Face a shade pale, the man said, "I've had mosquitoes do worse."

He found the other man kneeling over, pants pulled down, while Reb Pruitt grinned and poured antiseptic into a cloth, daubing it on an angry red streak across a tender part of the man's anatomy.

Reb said, "You Yanks taught me a long time ago that you had to keep more than your head down."

Jameson asked, "Think you'll be ready to fight again when they come back?"

The skinner nodded darkly. "Just as long as I don't have to sit down."

Jameson walked to Ransom King's place. "How's it going over here?"

King looked up and grinned at him. "Just send us more Indians."

Trencher lay beside King on a spread-out blanket. He wouldn't look up at Jameson, just kept scowling out over the muddy mound in front of him. Jameson looked down at the empty knife scabbard at the big man's belt. The anger came back to him.

But he had to bide his time now. They needed every

man they had, even Trencher. It might be that the Comanches would get Trencher and Jameson wouldn't have to.

Jameson returned to his own place and found Celia waiting there, rifles loaded and extra cartridges laid out neatly. He touched her hand.

"I still wish you'd get down below the bank," he said.

She shook her head. "I'll stay by you."

He stood beside the wagon and watched the Indians milling far off in the distance. The group began to move forward again.

"Get ready," Jameson called. "They're coming back."

The tactic this time was the same as before. The Comanches fanned out and came riding in a lope again, shrieking and yelling, their line ragged but unwavering. Brown bodies glistened in the sun, war paint shining. Feathers streamed.

This time Jameson did not wait for them to get near. Lying down, he again rested the rifle barrel over the wagon spoke and took careful aim. At four hundred yards his bullet brought a horse down. The other men began to fire. Long before the Indians were near enough to use arrows or their own guns, the hunters' fire had cut another ghastly swath through their lines.

The Comanche attack this time was halfhearted. Two hundred yards from the wagons the Indians began hauling back before the deadly fire of the hunters' long-range guns. Gathering their dead and wounded again, once more they fled the field.

Jameson had been holding his breath until his lungs ached, cold sweat breaking out all over him. Now he stood up again to breathe heavily. Celia Westerman stood with him, leaning her head wearily against his shoulder. Black gunpowder streaked her cheek.

"Think perhaps they're leaving?" she asked him.

He shook his head. "I doubt it. They'll probably try again."

Once more he made the rounds to check casualties. He was pleasantly surprised that there hadn't been any this time. The Comanches had never gotten close enough.

Shad Blankenship took a fresh chew of tobacco and patted his black dog. "They probably don't know what to make of these big buffalo guns. The way you picked that Indian off awhile ago was enough to set them to thinkin'. Turn them back one more time like that and I'd bet we've seen the last of them."

Jameson was grim. "I hope so."

He went back to Celia and sat down beside her. Her presence strengthened him. He poured water down the Big Fifty to cool the barrel and carefully swabbed it out to remove the burned powder.

"Pretty rough," he said to her presently. "Still think you like this country?"

She picked up the ramrod and used it on his saddle gun. Firmly she said, "It won't always be this way. A few years from now people will be moving onto these plains to stay, to ranch and to farm. There won't be any buffalo or any Comanches."

"What about *you*, Celia? Would you come back here, with *me?*"

Her eyes lifted to him and warmed. "I would, Gage."

"I've thought about it a good many times," he said. "A few more hunts and I'll have enough money saved back to go into whatever kind of business I want to. I've thought that as soon as this country opens up, I could bring cattle here. Shad Blankenship with me, and maybe Reb Pruitt, too. Reb knows the cattle business. And after what's happened this trip, I'd want Reb with me wherever I went."

He took Celia's hands and held them. "I've spent a lot of time thinking about the place I'd build. Lately it seems like you're always there with me."

She leaned to him, her head against his chest. "I *will* be there, Gage."

Shad Blankenship yelled, "Get set, boys. They're comin' back."

The Indians began to move toward the wagons, slower now, cautiously. Just outside effective rifle range they broke into three groups. One rode north, one south. The other waited.

Shad Blankenship squinted. "What're they up to now?"

Alarm began to tingle in Jameson. "I'm afraid I know. We've got two weak points, Shad, the ends of the line. They're going to outflank us on both sides."

The worry settled deeply into Shad's pale eyes. "And the other bunch will hit us in the middle, just like they been doin'."

"We've got to pull some of the men out of the middle and use them to strengthen the ends," Jameson decided quickly. He walked down the line, singling out men to move.

"Ammunition is no problem right now," Jameson told them loudly. "So use all you need. Start shooting as soon as you see a target. Thin them out as much as you can before they get here. There'll be more than enough of them left to go around."

He found himself sweating, and he rubbed his hand across his face. It left the acrid taste of burned powder from the rifle-cleaning job. Then he thought of something else.

He dug out four cans of gunpowder from below the bank, where he had placed them to keep stray bullets from striking them. Two he handed to Reb Pruitt. "Run those out there a couple of hundred feet and drop them. When the Indians get on top of them, put a bullet in them, blow them up.''

Jameson hurried to the other end of the line with the remaining two. He climbed over the bank and ran out into the grass, a can of gunpowder under each arm. He dropped them off thirty feet apart and ran for the wagons. The shrill cries of the Indians came up behind him. He picked up speed, plunging down the steep bank almost on top of the hide handler, Ludlow.

''When they get on those cans of powder, be good and sure you shoot straight,'' he yelled.

He sprinted back to his own position and dropped down on the blanket, grabbing up the Big Fifty. He started to open the breech.

''It's loaded,'' Celia said.

The men along the line had already begun to fire. Jameson drew down on the Indians coming into the center of the line and squeezed the trigger. A horse went down, but the Indian line never faltered.

''They're coming on in this time, I think,'' he told Celia. ''They're going to get us or give up.''

The flanking Indians were the closest. They moved in a run, shouting, firing what guns they had even before they were within range. Jameson counted thirty or more coming in on the left flank. As many more came on the right.

Choking gun smoke rose over the buffalo hunters, hovering like a dark gray cloud. Horses and Indians went down, but there were more to take their places.

Jameson felt his heartbeat quicken. The flank charges were going to overrun the defenses. There were too many of the Indians to stop. They were three hundred yards away now, two hundred. Now arrows began dropping in behind the wagons. Hunters feverishly worked their breechblocks, keeping their rifles blazing.

On Pruitt's side the Comanches were nearly upon the wagons. Suddenly one of the powder cans went up in a fierce blast, hurling half a dozen Indians to the ground, sending their horses rolling in a cloud of smoke. Other horses near the blast began to jump and pitch, squealing in panic. The second can exploded. For a moment then, that charge was broken. Bucking horses threw their riders and raced away. Indians left afoot made a run for the wagons, but they were easy marks for the rifles. Those still on horseback gathered themselves for another rush.

One Indian slammed his horse into a wagon, jumped onto the stack of hides and dropped down upon a skinner, knife blade flashing. Reb Pruitt swung his rifle barrel up against the Indian and shot him point-blank through the lungs.

Then the Comanches were coming in on the other flank. Heavy rifle fire had thinned them, but many still were mounted. Someone fired too soon at the first of the powder cans. Its blast set a couple of Indian horses to pitching in terror, but it did little to slow the charge. The Indians came streaming in.

Ludlow pushed to his feet to fire at the second can. It went up almost in the middle of a tight group of Indians.

But a handful of Comanches came on. They sent their horses running headlong at the timber barricade. Two came leaping over. Rifle fire caught one horse in mid-leap and he came down dead, falling on his rider and pinning him helpless against the ground. Ludlow lifted his rifle as the second Comanche came over. The Indian's lance caught him, spun him around. He fell, the lance driven through his body. The Indian whirled, raising his bow and whipping an arrow out of the quiver at his back. Bullets cut him down, even as someone grabbed up Ludlow's fallen rifle and brained the trapped Indian with the butt of it.

Jameson was still firing at the Indians who charged headlong into the middle of the wagon line. They were close now, what was left of them, making a last desperate attempt to overrun the hide men. Bullets ripped into the beds of the wagons, buried themselves in the hides: They puffed up dust and mud from the earthen breastworks. Behind him Jameson twice heard men cry out and knew that this time the casualties were running high.

Heart in his throat, he saw that the Indians were going to overrun the line. He fired so rapidly the gun barrel was red-hot in his hands.

"Get down!" he shouted desperately at Celia. "They're coming in!"

A Comanche tried to jump his horse between two wagons. The animal wedged. Jameson whirled and shot the Indian off the struggling mount's back.

Another Indian came over a load of hides and dropped to his feet behind the wagon. He fell upon a hide man with his knife and plunged it into the man's body. Ransom King brought the Indian down. He swapped ends with his rifle and clubbed another Comanche crawling under a wagon.

Relieved of the pressure at the ends of the line, men came hurrying back to bolster up the middle. Withering fire began throwing the Indians back. Jameson raised up to fire a shot.

Suddenly a bullet struck him with the force of a sledge. He fell back, dropping his rifle, grabbing at his left shoulder. Celia was instantly at his side, desperately seeking the wound.

"Look out," Jameson cried. "Another one."

She whirled and grabbed up the rifle he had dropped. "It's Kills His Enemies," she breathed. She raised the heavy barrel, propped it against a wagon bed. The painted Comanche came streaking in, his war bonnet strung out in the wind behind him. He saw her and raised his lance, screaming.

The rifle belched fire. Kills His Enemies fell back, a gaping hole in the streak of red paint that crossed his chest. He rolled over in the muddy grass and lay still. Then only the war bonnet moved, the feathers still fluttering in the wind.

The gunfire slowed and finally dwindled to silence.

Celia Westerman knelt over Jameson and began to work his coat off his left shoulder. "They're gone," she said gravely. "I don't think they'll be back, not after all this."

The retreating Indians were almost out of sight now. Behind them they left a bloody battlefield strewn with fallen horses and fallen men. There would be wailing in the lodges tonight, Jameson thought grimly.

Celia tore away Jameson's shirt. He grimaced, clenching his teeth to keep from crying out. "It went through," she said. She pulled her shirt-tail out of the trousers Pruitt had given her and tore off a large piece of it to stanch the bleeding.

Jameson lay back weakly, trying to hold himself firm, trying to keep the sky from starting to spin. His head ached unmercifully.

"What about the others? How many casualties?"

Shad Blankenship and Reb Pruitt came up in a moment. "We got three dead. One of them's Ludlow," Shad said. "Several wounded. They can all walk but one. He may not live. Arrows brought down six or eight mules we may have to shoot."

Jameson nodded weakly. "All right. Let's move, quick as we can."

They buried the three dead men a few yards from the

creek bank, carefully moving the sod back, then replacing it to hide the grave. Sitting down, Jameson read over them from the old Bible he always carried. He felt a deep touch of sorrow, especially at the loss of Ludlow. The brooding, dark-bearded hide handler had been one of the best, when the time came.

Celia bandaged Jameson's shoulder and bound it tightly. The crew harnessed the mules and hitched them to the wagons. In a while they had them strung out, ready.

Jameson tried to stand, but he could not. He leaned weakly against a wagon, Celia holding his arm. "All right, Shad, let's get them rolling."

Shad moved away. Ransom King stood there, and Trencher. It suddenly occurred to Jameson that almost everyone was there. Trencher held a shotgun in his hand. Jameson's shotgun. He was glaring at King.

"You gonna tell him, King, or do I have to?"

They had been arguing. King said, "It's not the time."

"For what?" Jameson demanded weakly. "Time for what?"

"Time to tell you you're stayin' here," Trencher declared. "We're takin' your wagons!"

16

JAMESON FELT his knees give way as the meaning soaked through his drumming brain. He held harder to the wagon.

"King," he said tightly, "I can't believe it."

In a rough voice Trencher said, "You can believe it, Jameson. We had it hatched out before we ever left Dodge. He was ready to call it off after you helped us out of that fight yesterday. But *I'm* not ready. And I'm not goin' to be."

King looked half defiant, half sour. "Sorry, Jameson. It looked like a good idea at the time. I didn't know I was really going to get to like you."

Jameson looked angrily down the line of hide wagons. "But you like money better."

King smiled wryly. "These hides, the wagons and mules, will fetch a fancy price. I'll be able to clear out of this country and never have to look at a stinking buffalo again.''

"The minute you set foot in Dodge they'll have you. They haven't forgotten these wagons.''

"We won't go to Dodge. There are places west of Dodge, like Granada, where they buy hides and mules and wagons. Then I'll fade away, Jameson. I won't be seen again.''

In the grinding of futile anger, Jameson's hand clenched the rim of a wagon wheel. Realization came to him. "You've been a hide thief all along, haven't you, King? I'll bet even these wagons you got for me were stolen. That's how you were in with Budge. That's why he didn't fit the part.''

He looked at the men. They were backing King now. He knew he had no one left but Shad Blankenship and Reb Pruitt. Pruitt wouldn't be any help. One of the men held a gun on him.

And Shad . . . where was Shad?

Celia was pleading with King. "You can't leave him here, wounded like this. He'll die.''

Trencher grinned viciously. "Who you think it was put that bullet in him? It wasn't no Injun. I just didn't make as good a shot as I aimed to.''

King glanced quickly at Trencher. "You didn't. . . .''
"I did.''

King's face darkened as he glared at Trencher. Then he turned back to Jameson. "I didn't plan on that. But it can't alter things now. We've got to leave you—you see that, can't you, Jameson?''

Fury welled in Jameson, fury that gave him a sudden strength. He stood clear of the wagon, swaying a little.

"I see you'd better kill me now, King, because if I *do* get out of this I'll hunt you down. I'll find you if it takes years. You can't go far enough to get away from me.''

Trencher leveled his shotgun. King struck it down.

Trencher said angrily, "You heard what he said."

King nodded with grimness. "But he *won't* find me, Trencher. We're leaving him alive, like we agreed."

Then Shad Blankenship's voice cracked like a whip. "Put them guns down, King!"

Shad stepped from behind a wagon, his big Sharps in his hand. Surprise in his face, then dismay, King dropped his gun. Trencher made a motion as if to lay the shotgun down. Suddenly the muzzle tilted upward and spat flame. Shad jerked back, slamming against the wagon. His rifle slipped from his fingers. He crumpled.

"Shad!" Jameson cried. He lurched toward the old man and fell to his knees beside him. "Shad!"

But Shad Blankenship had lived out his days. Now he was gone . . . gone the way of the other mountain men.

Jameson arose, fury ridging his paled face. He made a grab for Shad's rifle but never touched it. Something struck him across the back of the head. There was a burst of fire in his brain, and he pitched forward into darkness. . . .

"Gage!" Celia Westerman's voice broke in anguish. King grabbed her arm. She whirled back to fight him. In sharp impatience he brought up his fist and sent her sprawling.

"Blast you," he exclaimed, "I never wanted you here in the first place. I knew you'd get in the way when the time came. I've got a good mind to leave you here with him. But I won't."

He turned to one of the men behind him. "Pitch her in the wagon yonder."

Then he faced the other men, his fists knotted. "Anybody changed his mind and want to stay here?" No one moved. He glared at Reb Pruitt. "You weren't in on it,

Pruitt, but you can be. Which had you rather do, stay here with Jameson or go on with us?"

Pruitt looked at Jameson, lying unconscious across Shad Blankenship's body. Then he glanced at the wagon where Trencher and another man had carried Celia Westerman. He chewed his lip, studying hard.

"I reckon I'll go," he said.

Consciousness was slow in coming back to Gage Jameson. The wound had drawn him down even more than the blow on the head. He raised up on his good elbow and heard whimpering. A hairy body touched him. It was Shad Blankenship's old black dog.

"Easy, Ripper," Jameson said softly. "Easy."

He sat up, his head seeming to whirl around and around, throbbing unmercifully. He blinked until his sight cleared. The black dog nuzzled him and whimpered again.

Jameson turned painfully and looked down at Shad's slack body. He turned the old man over onto his back and stared into the wrinkled face until the tears welled hot and stinging into his eyes. Tenderly he picked the caked mud from the rusty beard and smoothed it out.

"Shad," he whispered, his throat so tight it felt as if a knife blade were cutting into it. "Shad, you shouldn't have tried it."

The black dog nuzzled Blankenship's face, whimpering. Jameson reached across and patted Ripper on the head. "Both of us, boy," he said. "Both of us."

He looked about him then. The wagons were gone. He had no way of knowing how long it had been. An hour anyway, perhaps two. He tried to push to his feet and fell back. The second time he made it. He stood there swaying until some strength returned to him.

The dead Indians and horses still lay where they had fallen in that last wild charge.

Jameson knew the Comanches wouldn't leave these dead out here to rot. They would be back for them. And if they found him here . . .

"They didn't leave us anything, did they, boy?" he said to the dog. "No gun, no food, nothing." His hand dropped to his belt. They had taken his pistol. And he had lost his knife in the flood.

"Lot of good it'd do me if I had one," he commented painfully. "I couldn't catch a turtle."

Even his hat had blown away, probably down into the creek. So had Shad's.

Shad. Jameson knelt beside the old man again. He couldn't just leave him here. He knew what vengeance Indians sometimes took on a dead body. Revulsion rose in him at the thought of leaving Shad here for that kind of treatment.

He couldn't bury him. He had nothing to dig with, even if he had the strength.

He listened to the roar of the creek. It was falling now, but it still carried a lot of force.

Jameson caught Shad's arm with his good hand and began to drag. He got him four or five feet the first time before he gave out and had to sit down to rest. The next time he got him to the edge of the cave-off. After resting again, he eased Shad's body down the steep bank and finally got it to the edge of the creek.

"It's a long way from a Christian burial, Shad," he said regretfully. "But it's better than the Comanches would do."

He took Shad's knife and stuck it in his own belt. He pulled Shad out into the creek, wading as far as he could hold up against the current. Then he gave the old man a hard push, out where the current would pick him up and carry him away.

Perhaps down there somewhere the creek would find Shad a grave in the deep sand. He remembered what Shad had said:

"The only hope I got is that when my time comes I can die out here, and be buried where I can listen to the wind blow and the wolves howl."

He watched Shad disappear, and a terrible loneliness swept over him. For more than half of his life, Shad Blankenship had been his teacher, his guide. He had been even more than that—a father.

Now he was gone.

Yet Jameson realized that Shad had outlived his time, that he had dreaded this new, unknown world that would come as the frontier faded. Maybe he would have wanted it this way. Maybe it was meant to be.

Jameson waded out of the creek and reached down to touch the shaggy black dog. "Come on, Ripper. It's you and me now."

He climbed up the creek bank, having to stop and sit awhile because of the shock of blinding pain. Setting out to follow the deep wagon ruts, he could feel the fever building in him. He ached until he was numb. His legs cried out for him to stop, to fall down and rest. But now he had a job to do, and he kept walking, his feet dragging heavily in the mud.

On the battlefield lay Indian guns and knives and lances, weapons he might have used. But the fever was numbing his brain now. All he could do was keep moving. All he could think of was to get Ransom King.

"Get some sense, King; take it easy," Trencher said irritably. "It's dark already, and you been drivin' these mules like the devil was after you. You'll kill them all if you ain't careful.''

Ransom King turned nervously in the saddle and looked toward the wagons. Because of darkness he could see only those closest behind him. Grudgingly he said, ''All right, then, let's make camp.''

''About time,'' Trencher grumbled, and turned back to bring up the rear wagons.

''Swing into a circle, Pruitt,'' King said sharply. ''You know how.''

Pruitt never nodded, never answered. But he swung the chuck wagon around in his accustomed manner. Without a word he dug a pit and began to build a fire.

''Damn you,'' King exploded, ''put that out!''

''We can't cook without a fire.''

''We'll eat it cold.''

Chilled, hungry, worn out after losing a night's sleep, going through the battle, then driving the wagons hard far into darkness, the men grumbled about not having a hot supper. Most of all they missed the coffee. But King would not relent.

They ate cold biscuits, as far as they went, and jerky. Then wearily the men began hauling down their bedrolls.

''Double guard tonight,'' King said.

Groaning, one of the skinners commented, ''Man, we need sleep. After today we ain't fixin' to have any more Injun trouble.''

King swung his fist and knocked the man to the ground. ''I said double guard. I'll shoot the next man who opens his mouth!''

Even after the guards were posted, King stood in the darkness at the edge of camp, peering intently out into the black, straining to hear.

Trencher came up behind him. ''Forget it, King. He won't be comin'.''

King turned quickly. "What do you mean?"

"I know what's eatin' you. Been eatin' you all day. You think Jameson will be after us. What you think he is, some kind of devil? He's dead by now. If that wound didn't kill him, the Injuns have. Now forget it."

King clenched his fists. "Maybe he's dead and maybe he isn't. If he isn't, he'll be after us."

Trencher grunted and looked back into camp, where Reb Pruitt was putting up a tent for Celia Westerman. "It ain't Jameson that worries me. It's them two."

He drew his knife and tested the cutting edge with his thick finger. "We ought to have left that woman with Jameson. We got to do somethin' about her before we get anywhere near the hide camps or they'll string us up. What do you say I walk her out into the dark a little ways, her and that cook both? It's got to be done, sooner or later."

King shook his head. "The men won't stand for killing her," he said. "We've got to figure something."

Disgustedly Trencher spat. "She's gettin' to you, that's what's the matter."

Sharply King responded, "You're getting too big for your britches, Trencher. I'm still the boss here, and don't forget it."

Trencher straightened, angrily holding his ground. "She's yours then, for now. Do what you want to. But before we get to the hide camps, we got to get rid of her."

17

THE SECOND day Jameson knew he was losing his mind. The sun hammered down from a cloudless sky, steam rose from the damp ground and wrapped the heat around him like some angry fiend. Long ago he had ceased to feel hunger, but the torture of thirst continued. His mouth was locked open, his lips dried and cracked, his tongue swollen and afire from the fever that burned in him. The little potholes of water had all dried out.

A maddening ache drummed in his bare head, and through his whole body. Soon now even his sight would be gone. He could see only the wavering image of the prairie ahead of him, dancing and shimmering, an endless reach of grass . . . grass . . . grass like the .pitch and roll of the boundless sea.

Long ago he had strayed away from the wagon ruts, away from the creek. He dragged his heavy boots, know- ing within reason that he was weaving aimlessly. He

knew that soon he would fall to his knees again as he
had done so many times already—that next time perhaps
he would be unable to rise and would lie here forever in
the short grass of the buffalo plains.

He had no idea now where he was going, little hope
any more of getting there. The grass looked soft and cool,
and he longed to lie down and give it up . . . lie down
and sleep and never waken again.

But a single stubborn thread of will remained, and he
kept going . . . going . . . going until his mind in its torture seemed to sink back into sleep, and only his legs
still moved.

At his side the black dog walked, stopping when Jameson stopped, licking Jameson's face when Jameson
fell. Staggering along on the brink of unconsciousness,
Jameson tried to force his mind to work. He knew the
dangers he faced. At any time now Indians might ride up
over the horizon. He wouldn't see them, he knew. Maybe
he wouldn't even feel it. Maybe it would be the merciful
thing.

Or if it wasn't Indians, it might be a blue norther, with
its frigid winds that could cut down even a strong man
caught out here in the open. This was early December,
and here on these high Texas plains the temperature
might plunge murderously fifty or sixty degrees.

Yet somehow he hardly cared. Only two thoughts kept
him moving—the need to find Celia Westerman, and his
hatred of Trencher and King.

Unable to see, he felt himself suddenly lurching down
an incline. His feet went out from under him. He pitched
forward on his face—into water.

Water. His fevered body cried out for water. His mouth
and throat were leather-dry.

But somehow within him a single sentry of alarm still
watched. Go easy, it told him. Go easy, for the first taste

of water may leave you unconscious. You may fall into it and drown, unable to help yourself.

He pulled back, cupping his good hand and lifting a few drops of water to his fever-parched lips, holding himself back by firm will. At the taste of the water he lapsed into darkness.

After awhile he came to again, now stronger than he had been. He felt the dog nuzzling him, licking his face. Once more Jameson cupped his hand and drank slowly, cautiously. He sat on the edge of the waterhole a long time then, feeling the strength slowly return. Cool water drove the fever back. His sight gradually cleared. In time he was able to regain his feet.

Thirst quenched, Ripper began to nose around in the grass for food. Presently he jumped a rabbit that had come up out of its burrow. He ran the rabbit down and brought it in his mouth, its stout hind legs still kicking.

Hunger had come back to Jameson as the fever had diminished. He took the rabbit from Ripper's jaws and slammed its head against the ground to complete the kill. He skinned and gutted the little animal awkwardly, having only one hand to work with. While Ripper worried the castoff parts, Jameson dug in his pockets and found dry matches. He felt of the grass. Away from the waterhole, the sun had dried it again so that it would burn. He found many buffalo chips there, but they were still wet from the rain and of no use as fuel.

He pulled up dry grass and twisted it as tightly as he could, setting some of it afire, feeding grass twists into the flame and holding the rabbit over them on the point of the knife.

Ravenously hungry, he was unable to hold himself back long. He began to tear the rabbit apart and wolf it down half cooked.

It wasn't enough, but it partially satisfied his hunger

and added to his growing strength. He lay down to rest awhile, knowing he had to get moving soon, had to find that wagon trail. It must be to the west of him, for he knew he had not crossed the creek. He could only have strayed eastward.

Sleep settled over him. Sometime much later he awakened, hearing Ripper growl. He pushed up quickly with his good arm, ice in the pit of his stomach. He knew without looking.

Indians.

Cautiously he pushed to his knees and peered out over the rim of the waterhole. Yonder, still hundreds of yards away, came a lone rider. But it might as well have been a thousand of them, for Jameson had no defense except the knife. And with his wounded shoulder, that would do him little good.

To his right was a little hummock. Keeping low, Jameson crawled behind it and lay still, the ripping knife gripped tightly in his hand, his heart thumping rapidly.

It was a single Comanche warrior, perhaps out scouting for buffalo. He carried a rifle instead of a bow, and a white man's leather cartridge belt instead of an arrow quiver. One feather was fastened in his straight black hair. There was no paint on his round, hard-boned face.

The Indian came straight for the waterhole, knowing where it was. He rode over the rim of it and dropped his leather reins, lifting his left leg over the horse's neck and slipping off to the ground to stretch. He went to his knees to drink of the water. Then his gaze touched the burned grass and scattering of rabbit bones. He turned suspiciously, eyes darting, rifle lifting in his hand.

Cornered, Jameson thought in despair. But he had one chance.

"Sic him, Ripper!" he shouted at the growling black dog. Ripper bounded over the hummock and dove straight at the Comanche's throat. Caught by surprise, the Indian went down under the hurtling weight of the big dog. Ferociously Ripper tore into him, fighting to reach the Indian's throat. Unable to straighten and fire the rifle, the Comanche desperately tried to club the dog with it.

Jameson moved in with the knife. He raised it quickly, and brought it down.

Later he patted the dog's black head. Ripper continued to grumble, hide still rippling with nervousness.

"Good boy," Jameson said quietly. "Now we've got a horse and a rifle. Now we can travel."

With his bad shoulder he had a hard time mounting bareback. Pain knifed through him, and once he thought he had broken the wound open. But finally he managed to get on the horse. His good right hand holding the rifle and the rawhide reins, he pulled the mount around and headed him west.

Ransom King tipped the bottle up and drank long and hard.

Resentment burned in him as he looked at the men scattered about in their blankets. Rebellion, that was it. The badly wounded Crosson had died late in the afternoon. The men had halted the wagons at dusk, ignoring King's orders to keep them moving. Silently they had buried Crosson, their eyes flashing anger at King for not stopping to ease the dying man's pain. They had built a fire, and Reb Pruitt had cooked them a hot supper. Now King had ordered another double guard and no one had paid him any attention. The men had dropped wearily into their blankets, worn out by the hard drive and loss of sleep. Even Trencher.

King walked to the edge of camp and gazed out into the darkness, wondering about Gage Jameson, wondering at the chill that came to him. Trencher was right. He *had* to be right. Jameson *was* dead. He couldn't have lived this long with that wounded shoulder, with no gun, no food.

Even if alive, he couldn't be following them. He would be holed up somewhere, hiding from Indians, nursing that shoulder and slowly starving to death.

Sure, it was foolish to worry about him. Better for King to spend his time planning how to spend the money he'd get for all these hides, and the stock and wagons. With any luck, he could find a way to avoid having to pay the rest of the crew their share. That, with the rest he had stashed away, would set him up big in Mexico, or in Central America. He could feel the gold in his fingers already. It gave him a warm glow just to think about it.

All his life he had dreamed of pulling off a coup like this one. Now here it was, safe in his fist.

He raised the bottle again and walked back into the wagon circle. Fools. They hadn't even pulled the wagons up tightly. There was a three-foot gap between the chuck wagon and the next vehicle where a mule could walk right out without scraping a rib.

"Pruitt," he said irritably, finding the cook still up, "plug that gap."

Pruitt made no sign of hearing him. King scowled. They'd have to do something about that cook, sure enough. He sat down against a wagon wheel and looked about camp. Under the wagons men slept exhausted, rolled up in their blankets. Not a man on guard, he'd bet.

Well, he'd stay on guard. He'd stay up all night if he had to. But they'd remember it later. They'd remember it when he got away with all the money.

His eyes drifted then to Celia Westerman's tent. The whisky was warm in his stomach, and he felt a light-headedness he hadn't allowed himself in a long time. His mind had dwelt on Celia Westerman a lot lately. He hadn't thought of much else but her, and Gage Jameson, and all those wagons loaded with hides.

It wasn't that she was so extra good-looking. In a big town a man wouldn't give her more than a second glance. She didn't have the blood-stirring beauty of a Rose Tremaine, for example. But she *was* a woman, an attractive woman, and she was here.

He sat and pulled on the bottle, staring at her tent. The hunger grew in him. There was no movement about the camp. He took a last drink, emptying the bottle, and let it drop to the ground. Then he pushed to his feet and walked carefully toward the tent. The whisky had really gotten to him now. He found himself weaving.

He ducked to push through the tent flap, finding to his annoyance that the strings were tied. They gave way. It was dark inside, but his eyes quickly adjusted themselves. He could see Celia Westerman lying in her blankets, awake, watching him.

He whispered, "I want to talk to you."

"Get out," she said. "I don't want to hear it."

"They're going to kill you," he said. "Trencher's afraid to leave you alive, to talk."

She made no answer, gave no sign she even cared. He could feel her hatred of him like an electric charge, even though he could not see her eyes.

He said, "Say the word and I'll get you out of it. We'll go off together, you and me. You'll live like you've never lived before."

She pushed the blankets aside and stood up. She was still wearing Reb Pruitt's clothes. "Get out, I told you!"

He grabbed her shoulders. "Listen to me. I want to save you. I'm in love with you, can't you see that? I want you."

She struck at his face. He grabbed her wrist and shook her violently.

"Stop it, Celia!"

She fought with him until she lost her footing. She fell backward, and he went down with her. The contact with her body set his pulse to racing. In the darkness, he found her lips and kissed her roughly, crushing her down.

Too late he saw her hand come up, the wrench in it.

She's been ready for this, he thought, helpless to move away. His brain seemed to explode with the impact. He went down on his elbows. He felt her move away from him, heard the wrench swing again. This time he tumbled forward into darkness.

Celia Westerman paused then, listening, wondering if the struggle had been heard.

She heard nothing. She picked up her coat and began to move toward the front of the tent on her hands and knees.

She stopped abruptly as the tent flap moved. She raised the wrench again, heart in her throat.

Reb Pruitt cautiously poked his head in. He held a six-gun, ready. He saw her poised there to strike him, and his eyes widened. His gaze dropped to Ransom King, lying unconscious.

"I ought to've known a Texas girl could handle herself all right," he whispered. "Now come on, and let's get out of here."

Gage Jameson saw the two horsemen as they came down over the rise far ahead of him. Heart quickening, he pulled the Indian pony back from the dried-out wagon ruts and eased down into a hackberry thicket on the creek bank.

"Come on, Ripper," he said to the dog. "Get down."

He slid down off the horse and checked the Comanche's old needle gun. It had been stolen out of some Texas home or off some luckless white man after a battle, he figured. The barrel was half plugged with powder, for Indians knew little about taking care of a gun. But it would still fire. Tensing, he went down on one knee and rested the rifle across the other, wondering how he was going to hold it steady with one good hand.

The two riders came into plainer view and he nervously licked his dry lips. Most of the fever had burned itself out, but a little still remained. He saw that one of the two was leading an extra horse.

Suddenly Jameson lowered the rifle and stood up, blinking unbelievingly. It couldn't be. But it was!

He walked out, leading the Indian pony, letting them see him. He saw Reb Pruitt swing a rifle up, then lower it in recognition.

Celia Westerman stepped down from her saddle and ran to meet him. He quickly moved toward her. He caught her with his good arm and crushed her to him, dropping his cheek down against the top of her head, her long blonde hair.

"Gage, Gage," she said softly, holding him as tightly as she could. He could feel the hot tears on her cheek as he brought his hand up to her chin.

Reb Pruitt stood there first on one foot, then the other. Finally he took the sack of grub down from Celia's saddle.

"May not be the best time to mention it," he commented dryly, "but if you're hungry . . ."

Jameson devoured food out of the sack while Reb and Celia told him what had happened, how they had gotten out of the camp with three saddled horses, some grub and several guns.

"I didn't have any hope of findin' you alive," Pruitt admitted. "I tried to talk her into heading north to find some hide outfit. But she wouldn't have it that way. So we come south, riding in the edge of the creek to keep them from tellin' which direction we went.''

Hunger satisfied, Jameson grimly looked at the guns Reb and Celia had brought. A pistol apiece. A rifle. And his shotgun.

It was the shotgun Trencher had used on Shad. Looking at it, Jameson clenched his fist.

"I'm going to get them," he said tightly. "I've *got* to get them—for Shad."

Reb said, "I don't aim to take up any for King, he don't deserve it. But it was Trencher who shot Shad. It wasn't King."

Jameson said through gritted teeth, ''When a man cuts loose a wolf, he's got to answer for whatever that wolf does.''

"What're you going to do?" Celia pressed anxiously.

"Going to trail after them. Going to cut the ground out from under King a little at a time. Going to make him sweat while I take everything away from him. And finally, when he's lost everything, I'm going to ride in there and get him. Get him for Shad Blankenship."

18

JAMESON AND Pruitt sat their horses on a small promontory and gazed down at the hide wagons, strung out like a long snake far below them.

"Still pushing hard," Jameson said. "Been like that every day, daylight to well after dark. Wonder he hasn't killed half the stock by now."

Reb Pruitt nodded. "And half the men, too. Stirred up as they were when we got out of there, I'm surprised they haven't run off and left him. Somethin' was eatin' at him pretty bad. I think maybe he sensed that you were following after him."

Jameson swung down from the saddle to rest awhile, never taking his eyes from the wagons. His left shoulder was stiff and sore, but the fever was several days gone now. He had lost much weight. Still, his strength had returned, for the most part.

His beard was a week or more long, black and wiry.

His clothes were crusted with mud and dirt. He was still bareheaded.

"Not over a couple of days' ride now to the Arkansas," he estimated. "They're going to be jumpy as cats down there, afraid you and Celia went after help and will be bringing a hanging party down on them."

"You think they might run if we was to prod them a little?"

Jameson shrugged. "I don't know. But we're fixing to find out."

At nightfall the three of them moved in toward Ransom King's camp. Working up close while Celia stayed back and held the horses, the two men watched the teamsters circle the wagons and drive the stock inside. Ransom King rode up and down the outside, shouting orders with a fury born of desperation.

"I'll bet he ain't caught much sleep since we been gone," Reb whispered. "Nor let anybody else get much, either."

They stayed out there until the camp quieted down. Then they moved up close to seek out the guards. Satisfied, they crept back out to Celia.

Jameson asked, "Reb, do you think you could move that chuck wagon a few feet, with that horse and your rope?"

Pruitt nodded. "I reckon. Wagon's not heavy loaded any more."

"Then you're going to open a hole in that wagon circle. And I'm going to run out all the horses and mules I can."

They remounted their horses. Celia walked up and pressed against Jameson's leg. "Don't take chances, Gage. Be careful."

"We won't crowd our luck too much," he promised.

Moving their horses in a walk, they worked carefully

up toward the wagons, the black dog trotting at their heels. They split, Jameson riding far around the circle and coming in toward a spot where he had seen no guard. On the other side, Pruitt was moving in at the chuck wagon.

Jameson halted near the wagons, looking for a hole where he might put the horse through, listening for Pruitt's rope to sing. But it was silent.

Suddenly he heard the creak of the chuck wagon as a horse lunged against a rope. He saw the wagon lurch, then wheel out, leaving a gap in the circle.

Six-gun in hand, Jameson fired into the air and yelled. Horses and mules within the enclosure began to mill and stomp. Then, seeing the opening, they broke out, running. Jameson kept shouting and firing until he saw men rushing toward him. He started to spur away.

Then he recognized the bulky man who came in the lead. He heard the man's roar, saw the gun in the man's hand.

Instead of running away, Jameson touched spurs to the horse and headed straight toward the man. It was Trencher. He saw the spurt of flame from Trencher's gun, felt the heat as the bullet cut by his ear. He brought his own six-shooter down level and squeezed the trigger. He saw Trencher stagger back, and he fired again.

That, he thought, is for Shad.

He pulled aside as the other men began firing at him. He leaned low and pushed the horse into a lope. He circled around and met Reb Pruitt riding away, driving a sizable string of horses and mules. The black dog was running too, barking at the animals' heels.

"We got maybe half of them," Reb shouted, "before they cut them off."

Half of them. Jameson felt a glow of triumph. That would hit King where it hurt the most.

"Let's keep them running," he said.

He half expected pursuit, but it didn't come. Next morning they moved in cautiously and found the train already pulled out. Six wagons loaded with hides sat there, deserted for lack of mules to pull them.

"This," Jameson said, "is what will kill King, having to leave these hides."

They found Trencher lying unburied, just where Jameson had left him. They had all hated Trencher.

All day they trailed along well behind King's wagon train, pushing with them the horses and mules they had captured last night. Along in mid-afternoon they came up over a rise and saw a pair of wagons sitting there. Two men had a wheel off the tongue wagon.

"King must be getting panicky," Jameson commented. "Went off and left them." He checked his six-shooter and looked across at Reb Pruitt. "Want to take them?"

Pruitt nodded.

Jameson said, "You stay back with the stock, Celia."

They moved into a lope. They were almost upon the wagons before the men saw them. One man made a run for a rifle propped up against a wagon wheel. Jameson fired a pop shot at him. Dust puffed under the man's feet. He stopped abruptly and raised his hands.

The other man stood limply, his face drained of color.

"Jameson," he breathed. "I told them it was you last night. You and that black devil of a dog. I told King and he knocked me down. He said it was Indians. Said he'd kill the man who mentioned your name again."

Reb Pruitt grinned through his scraggly growth of beard. "Panicky, Gage, like I told you."

Jameson nodded and frowned at the two men.

"What should we do with them, Reb, shoot them right here?"

The two began to tremble. One pleaded, "Look, Jameson, we didn't know how it was going to turn out. We didn't expect any killing. They said all they were going to do was set you afoot."

Jameson scowled at them. "We ought to shoot you, but we'll give you a chance. Start hiking. If you're ever seen in this country again, you'll hang."

Reb Pruitt unhitched the mules while Jameson watched the two walk eastward out across the prairie, no rifles, no bedding, just a canteen of water from under the wagon seat and the knives in their belts.

Jameson frowned. "It'll give King some more to think about when these two wagons don't come in tonight. Eight wagonloads he's already had to leave behind him. That's half of them, Reb."

They watched from afar as Ransom King made camp. There weren't enough wagons left now to circle. Instead, King left them strung out and tied the remaining animals on picket lines, the lines secured to the wagon wheels.

"Won't be anybody asleep down there tonight," Jameson guessed. "He'll keep them awake, watching the stock."

No fire was built in King's camp that night. For awhile Jameson considered working down there and trying to cut some of the picket lines. But he knew they would be closely watched. It wouldn't be worth the risk.

"We'll worry them a little, just the same," he said. Taking the needle gun, he fired a shot down toward the camp. He heard a burst of shouts and the squeals of animals, then a pounding of hoofs leading off away from camp.

"There went a picket line," Pruitt laughed.

Jameson lay down on the ground to rest awhile, his eyes on Celia Westerman. He felt a stirring of pride at the way she had taken all this, the help she had been.

Occasionally during the night he would get up and move around, looking off toward King's camp. At the back of his mind lurked a worry that the men might come out looking for him. But he doubted, really, that they would. They couldn't know for sure who was stalking them, or how many.

Reb Pruitt shook him awake at daylight. "Gage, there's somethin' goin' on down there."

Jameson arose, pausing to smile at the sight of Celia Westerman still lying asleep beneath a blanket that they had taken out of one of the hide wagons yesterday.

Reb pointed. "What do you make of it?"

The hide men were knotted up together in a group, facing one man. That man could only be Ransom King. Jameson wasn't sure, but he thought King held a rifle.

He watched King gesturing angrily. The men milled back and forth, and occasionally some of them used their hands in violent argument. King raised the rifle, leveling it at them.

Someone threw something at King and he stepped aside, off balance. Then the men were on him. Jameson thought he saw a flash, and he heard the delayed report of a gun. The melee ended. The men scattered, catching up horses and mules. They streamed out of camp, heading east, abandoning the wagons.

"They're gettin' away," Pruitt said anxiously.

Jameson shook his head. "Let them go. We wouldn't know what to do with them if we had them, and we know they'll never dare come back. The one we want is still down there."

Only one man remained. He was stretched out on the ground. Watching from afar, Jameson thought for awhile that they had killed him. But presently King stood groggily and staggered to a wagon. He held himself up against a wheel, letting his strength return.

"Want to go down and get him?" Pruitt asked.

"No, let's wait awhile. Let's see what he's going to do. I want to see if he sticks with his wagons or if he gives up and runs."

King wasn't running, yet. Jameson could only imagine the frustration in King's mind as he leaned against the wheel, looking helplessly at the hide wagons strung out there, each pair laden with a thousand dollars and more in flint hides. All this he had held in his grasp. Now it had slipped through his fingers.

It was still there, its very presence a mockery of his extravagant dreams, his well-developed plans.

The hides were there within his reach, but worthless to him now because he could not move them.

This was what Jameson had been waiting for, to let the ground slip away from under King's feet and leave him with nothing but the gray ashes, the dark knowledge of defeat.

"We better get him, Gage, before he runs."

"He won't run," Jameson told Pruitt, "not so long as he thinks he can salvage a little of it."

Four mules remained on one picket line. King harnessed them one by one and hitched them to a pair of wagons. He popped the whip, and the mules strained so that the muscles bulged on their chests and on their legs. The wagons moved, but slowly. The mules would wear out before they had gone a mile. It was too heavy a load.

King pulled them up and sat there, looking back dejectedly at the wagons he was leaving. Finally he climbed down and unhitched the trail wagon, leaving it there with the rest.

All he had now was the tongue wagon, with no more than three or four hundred hides. Only this, where once he had had fifteen wagons, every one loaded.

"Like the dregs at the bottom of the cup," Jameson thought aloud.

King cracked the whip again. The mules strained, and the wagon rolled out.

Jameson watched him awhile, then rose to his feet. "Let me have that shotgun, Reb. I think it's time now."

Celia Westerman pushed back the blanket and got to her feet. "Gage, what are you going to do?"

"I'm going to get Ransom King."

Dismayed, she looked at the shotgun. "With that?"

"It's what they used on Shad."

Celia caught his arm. "Gage, please let the law handle him. Take him alive. Take him in."

He looked at Pruitt. "Let me have a couple of extra shells."

Reluctantly Reb handed them to him. "You ought to listen to her, Gage."

Celia pleaded. "You're not a killer, Gage. Don't make yourself one by doing this. You'll have it with you as long as you live."

But Gage Jameson could still see Shad Blankenship's broken body the way they had left it there on the prairie. That Trencher had paid for it wasn't enough. There was still the man who had cut loose the wolf.

He leaned down and kissed Celia. "Wait for me," he said. "I'll be back."

He rode out, paralleling King's wagon.

Later he could see a brushy creek far ahead, cutting diagonally across his path. He knew King would have to move over it. That would be the time to get him, while he had his hands full in crossing the stream.

For Jameson's shoulder was still stiff. He had only one hand with which to handle the gun. He had to take all the advantage he could get.

He rode on in an easy lope, splashing into the creek, pushing across and reining up on the far side. The water had been deeper than he thought, two and a half or three feet. Staying in the brush, he watched impatiently for King's wagon.

And at last it came.

King angled his mules toward an open spot on the brushy bank. There was a two-foot drop-off into the water. King hauled the mules up to a slow walk, easing them out into the creek slowly so the wheels would take the drop without breaking spokes or coupling pole.

Watching him from the cover of brush, Jameson felt his heart pound.

It's time, he thought.

Shotgun ready, he pushed his horse into the water with a splash. King reined up suddenly, whip in his hand, the front wheels of the wagon just starting to slide down the drop.

He stared at Jameson openmouthed, his face blanching. "I guess I knew it was you all the time," he said in resignation.

Jameson gripped the shotgun. "You're going to die, King. Die the way Shad did."

King's voice lifted. "*I* didn't kill him, Gage. It was Trencher."

Jameson's voice crackled with fury.

"You planned the whole thing. You set it up. You got Shad killed just as much as if you had pulled the trigger."

Moving out into the creek, closer to King, he lifted the shotgun.

"Gage," King exclaimed, "I haven't got a gun. Honest to God, they took them away from me. They left me unarmed."

Jameson hesitated, wondering if King might be lying.

Somehow, he knew he wasn't. And he knew he couldn't shoot King down in cold blood.

Instead of feeling cheated, he felt a vague sense of relief.

"Then I'll take you in," he said at last, lowering the shotgun. "But you know what they'll do, King. They'll hang you!"

King sat motionless on the wagon seat, his eyes sick at the contemplation of such a death.

"That," he said in a strained voice, "is no way for a man to die."

Suddenly his arm moved. He lifted the whip.

Before Jameson could bring the shotgun up again, the searing whip wrapped around him. His horse reared and plunged in panic. Grabbing at the horn with his one good hand, Jameson accidently fired the shotgun into the air. The kick of it set him off balance. He tumbled from the saddle into the cold water.

In desperation King hauled his mules around, trying to turn. But the front wheels slipped in the mud, and the right hind wheel skidded from the drop-off. The wagon tilted. For a moment it stood balanced precariously on two wheels while Ransom King struggled to keep his seat.

He slipped off and fell into the muddy creek. An instant later the wagon tipped over and crashed down on its side in a huge splash of water. It lay there then in the brown stir of mud, the left rear wheel spinning.

King never came up.

Jameson waded hurriedly to the wagon. He couldn't see for the mud. He dropped down under the cold water, feeling around for King. He caught King's hand, felt the man threshing wildly, pinned beneath the load of hides.

Jameson braced himself and pulled hard with his one good hand. He felt the hides shift just a little, but not enough. He pulled desperately, feeling King's struggle growing weaker. He pulled until the world went black before his eyes. But his own strength had been drained by the wound in his shoulder.

He heard horses running. He saw Reb Pruitt and Celia galloping up to the creek.

"Reb," he called in desperation, "come help me! Come quick!"

By the time Reb got there, King was limp. With Reb's help Jameson pulled him out from under the heavy hides. They dragged him to the bank. But it was no use.

"Too late," Reb Pruitt said quietly.

Jameson knelt, breathing heavily. "If it hadn't been for this shoulder . . ."

Regret touched him then, and he said evenly, "There was a lot that was likable about him. If he'd been honest . . . What gets into a man like that, Reb? What is it that sets him wrong?"

Reb Pruitt shook his head, looking at the overturned wagon in the creek, then at the lifeless body of Ransom King.

"Who can say, Gage? Stolen hides, stolen wagon. Only one man to help him, and that man crippled because of what King himself had done. Strange, ain't it, the way a man's life catches up with him?"

Celia took Jameson's hand. "I'm glad *you* didn't have to do it, Gage."

He nodded solemnly. "So am I. I wanted to, but now I'm glad I didn't."

He looked northward then. "Somewhere up yonder, past the Arkansas, we ought to be able to find some buffalo hunters out of luck and looking for something to do. We'll bring them and get the stock and wagons."

Reb said, "You'll have King's wagons, too. I reckon you've earned them."

Jameson shook his head, thinking of Nathan Messick, and the sister who was left with no one to provide for her. "I don't want them," he said. "But I know where they'll do some good."

Looking southward again, he said, "Someday we'll go back to Texas together, Reb, you and Celia and me. And we'll stay there."

"That'll be a good day for all of us," Reb replied. Then he turned back to figure a way of getting the overturned wagon out of the creek.

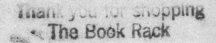

Westerns available from

Available by mail from